MW00423160

CHASING THE MONKEY KING

ISBN-10: 1540568326
ISBN-13: 978-1540568328

Printed in the United States of America

ACKNOWLEDGMENTS

Many, many thanks to Holly Pemberton, Philip Imber, Paige Rivas, Mickey Meece, Jamie Mingus, and Ellen Nason. This story would never have made it to print without their invaluable help.

NOTE TO THE AD/CVD COMMUNITY

The author took the liberty of reducing the specialized, verbose, and often mindboggling terminology of antidumping cases to a sort of layperson's language (*e.g.*, by referring to all manner of antidumping proceedings as "investigations" instead of "administrative reviews," "new shipper reviews," and so forth) so that readers wouldn't feel the need to look up definitions in the Enforcement and Compliance Antidumping Manual every five minutes. Sorry to anyone who was looking forward to seeing terms like "constructed export price offset," "difference in merchandise adjustment," and "final results of redetermination pursuant to remand" used in a work of fiction. Maybe next time.

For Holly and Haley

Chasing the Monkey King

ONE

Orin Thorvaldsson stood outside the sliding glass doors at the exit from Customs at Seattle-Tacoma International Airport, eagerly awaiting the arrival of his niece, Kristin, whose flight from Shanghai had just landed. Kristin was taking a vacation day on the journey back to her office in Washington, D.C. in order to visit family in the Puget Sound area. The plan was for Thorvaldsson to whisk her up to his home in the San Juan Islands for a big family dinner built around mountains of fresh Dungeness crab, dishes of melted butter, and local oysters on the half shell. He'd run her back down to the airport the following evening to catch the redeye back to D.C. It was August, and the San Juans were beautiful, the weather sunny and warm. Perfect for sailing or kayaking—two of Kristin's favorite things.

Thorvaldsson had no children of his own, and even though he had several nieces and nephews, Kristin was far and away his favorite—the closest thing he had to a daughter. They hadn't seen each other in nearly a year. And they had a lot to talk about.

At 6-foot-4, Thorvaldsson—a flaxen-haired, young-looking but late middle-aged Seattleite—had no trouble seeing over the crowd that had gathered in front of the sliding glass doors. He wore what he jokingly referred to as the Pacific Northwest business suit—a pale blue dress shirt with sleeves rolled up to the elbows, khaki pants, and a pair of thoroughly waterproofed brown oxfords. He held a welcome home treat in his hand—Kristin's favorite coffee drink, a hazelnut latte.

Yet for all the joy he felt in anticipating Kristin's imminent arrival, something didn't feel quite right. For one thing, she hadn't called to confirm that she would be on the flight. The lack of such a call wasn't, in and of itself, a huge cause for concern. But she hadn't emailed either. Nor had she text messaged upon landing as she usually did.

Disheveled and fatigued passengers from the Shanghai flight began emerging from the sliding glass doors, many of them being happily greeted by waiting friends or family. First they came in a trickle, then a steady flow, as they were processed by Immigration and Customs Enforcement officials and disgorged into the main terminal. For 15 minutes Thorvaldsson watched and waited as the doors slid open and shut, hoping to see Kristin's smiling face with its perpetually downturned, almost sad blue eyes, and the girlish blonde bob haircut she'd had since childhood. His niece. His little girl.

He pulled out his smartphone and double-checked for a missed call or text message. There were none. Then he logged into his email account. Nothing there either. A vague anxiety took hold of him as the flow of passengers began to thin. Two here, one there. A pause, then another three. The pauses grew longer. At last, an Arab looking man emerged with his shirttail hanging out and necktie untied and hanging around his neck, a thoroughly irritated expression on his face. The doors slid closed behind him. And that was it.

Thorvaldsson stood alone, waiting another 10 minutes, his shoulders sagging, staring at the closed doors, checking for messages again and again. He reasoned that Kristin had probably just missed the flight or had had to extend her trip in order to finish the job. Something like that, surely. She was still in China, but just fine. Perhaps she didn't have access to her email, was in an area without cell phone coverage, or her phone's battery had died. These were all perfectly plausible explanations.

But lurking in the back of his mind were several good and entirely legitimate reasons to worry—reasons he didn't dare allow himself to think about. Not yet. Still, as these reasons began their slow rise from the depths of his subconscious, Thorvaldsson found himself feeling empty and sad. His gut told him that something had gone terribly wrong. And if anything had gone wrong, he knew he'd have to seek help from an unconventional source.

TWO MONTHS LATER

TWO

No matter how many times Lars Severin had it, this particular recurring nightmare always felt real. Unlike other nightmares, in which he was often able to convince himself that he was just dreaming, this one always terrified him to the very end. And it always ended the exact same way.

He was in the small living room of a tiny Cape Cod cottage. An adorable 3-year-old girl with curly blonde locks stood staring up at him, looking confused and afraid. Gently, he held her soft and delicate little hand in his own.

"Where's your mom, Olive?"

"I don't know."

"You don't know?"

"No. She went away."

"Okay. Well, I need you to come along with me, okay?"

"Why aren't you wearing shoes?"

"Uh," Severin said, perplexed as he looked down to discover that his feet were bare. "I don't know. I guess I forgot to put them on."

"Where are we going?"

"Somewhere fun." *Somewhere safe*, he thought.

"I want my purple dress."

"We'll come back and get it later."

"I have to take Binkydoo."

"Who is Binkydoo?"

"My sleepy bear."

"Oh. Well, we can come get Binkydoo later too. He'll be okay."

"No. I need to take Binkydoo now."

"Run and get him, then."

"Her!"

"Run and get her. Hurry, Olive."

She ran off, presumably to find her bear. As he watched her go, his hand drifted down to his holster. *Oh, no.* It was empty. He had no gun. What the hell had he done with it? Where could it be?

A few minutes passed. Severin grew more anxious as he paced about, looking out the windows, watching the street. "Did you find Binkydoo, Olive?" he shouted up the narrow stairwell. Receiving no answer, he ascended the stairs and poked his head in her bedroom door. But she wasn't there. He searched, room to room, even checking the cabinets in the bathroom in case she was hiding in them.

His heart began to race. He had to get her out. He had no gun, and Olive's huge, violent, mentally ill father was due home at any moment. He ran back down the stairs, calling her name. But no answer came. Then he went to the door to the basement stairs, just off the tiny kitchen. Had she slipped downstairs without his noticing? He called down the dim stairwell. "Olive?" Again, no answer. He descended the bare plank stairs. The basement was dark. He felt around the wall at the bottom of the stairs but couldn't find the switch. "Olive?" he called again. The unfinished ceiling was low, with wires and ductwork running every which way, and Severin had to duck to keep from hitting his head on anything. The room smelled of fabric softener, perennial dampness, and mildew. The cold concrete floor was, for whatever reason, littered with loose nuts, bolts, and screws that bit into his bare feet with each step he took. Gutting out the pain, he stumbled about in the dark until he found a string pull to a ceiling light. Pulling it, illuminating the single, bare, underpowered bulb, he quickly scanned the basement to find it unoccupied. *Damn.* He had to get back upstairs quickly. But where were the stairs? He'd just come down them. Where had they gone? It was a small basement. How could he lose track of the stairs? He began pulling hangers and clothes off the long coatracks that surrounded him, pulling down stacks of dust covered cardboard boxes that seemed to close in, looking for the stairwell. But he couldn't find it.

Finally, in the far corner between two floor joists, seven feet off the ground, he spotted what looked like an open access hatch to the main floor. Daylight was shining down through it. He began sliding boxes over to the corner to build a structure he could climb to get out of the basement. It took a while, with his hastily constructed stacks of boxes repeatedly collapsing or falling over. But he was eventually able to scramble up to the open hatch and lift himself through. He was back in the tiny living room, his feet bleeding. Olive, her little brother, and their mother were now sitting side-by-side on the couch.

"Mrs. O'Ncil!" he half shouted at the mother. "We have to go. Your husband will be home any second. And I don't have my gun!" But Kate O'Neil didn't move. Neither did her two children. "We have to go," Severin said again. "Now!"

Suddenly, it occurred to Severin that none of them were blinking. Taking a closer look, he saw that their eyeballs were black. The sockets weren't empty. The eyeballs had simply turned solid black. Then one of them did move. It was Olive. She fell to the floor and rolled onto her back. There was a long, deep slash across her throat that gaped open. But there was no blood. In fact, the flesh around the wound was colorless. Her whole body was colorless. She was dead. So were her mother and brother.

As he stared down at the dead, colorless child, fear and horror of a magnitude he'd never known took hold of Severin's mind. He ran for the front door of the cottage, intending to call for an ambulance on the police radio in his car, already knowing his efforts were futile. He threw open the door, and a cold, howling wind blasted him from head to toe. Standing in the doorway, he found himself staring into an abyss of impenetrable darkness. The small front yard, the quiet street, his unmarked police car, the quaint neighborhood, all gone. No sky, no ground. Just total blackness. An infinite void. Oblivion.

He stood frozen on the threshold, afraid to go back into the house, afraid to step forward into the darkness.

*****

All at once, Severin realized he was awake. He was flat on his back in his uncomfortable motel bed, and his head hurt so much that he thought it better to keep his eyes shut. His heart was racing. Pounding. He could feel each beat pulsing in his neck. Could hear each beat drum in his ears. His fingertips felt cold. His mind raced through the more terrifying possibilities of what could be making his heart go crazy—of what could be wrong with his health. He had the distinct feeling that he might die. *Not this again.*

Perhaps the nightmare was causing these episodes. No. That didn't make sense. He'd been having the same nightmare for years and years, and it hadn't caused him any trouble aside from a lingering sense of anxiety and sadness that faded as the day wore on. Maybe he needed to cut back on his coffee intake. Or his tobacco chewing. Yes—less caffeine and nicotine.

Slowly, it occurred to him that his cell phone was ringing. It must have woken him. The shrill sound hurt his ears. Without lifting his aching head from the lumpy motel pillow, he forced one heavy eyelid open. Squinting, he turned and spotted his phone on the far corner of the nightstand, among half a dozen empty beer cans. Given that he would have to push himself up and stretch his arm over to retrieve it, and given his wretched condition, he decided it was too far away to bother with. He didn't foresee having any desire to sit up in bed for a good long while. Mercifully, the ringing stopped as the call finally went to voicemail.

The air in the poorly ventilated room was stiflingly humid. Steamy. The moisture in the air seemed to be drawing an unappealing mélange of aromas from the worn furniture and soiled carpet. There was also the harsh perfume of cheap motel shampoo drifting in from the bathroom. As Severin began to wonder where his bottle of ibuprofen was, and why the air smelled of shampoo and was so damned humid, he forced his other eye open and searched for the digital alarm clock on the nightstand. But before he found the clock, a smear of unfamiliar color caught his eye. It was lipstick on the rim of one of the empty beer cans. Lipstick of a shade favored by a generation considerably younger than his own. Bewildered, his gaze shifted to the alarm clock. It was well after 9 a.m. He had to get rolling.

Knocking over several empties, Severin grabbed an unopened can of beer from the night stand, hoping to find some modicum of relief by holding a cold can against his forehead. But the can was room temperature, of course, having sat there for hours. So he sat up, opened it, drank it down without pause, and reached for his cell phone. He had one voicemail from a number he didn't recognize. It had been left by whomever had called two minutes earlier. But there had also been a call an hour earlier, from his girlfriend, Janet. Janet, who insisted, rather irritatingly, that Severin pronounce her name in a pseudo-French fashion—like "Juh-nay." Janet, who, like all of them, wanted more from the relationship than he did. More permanence. More of what Severin thought of as undesirable emotional entanglement. Strangely, if his phone log was to be believed, Janet's call had been answered, and a conversation of 37 seconds had taken place. Despite the fact that he had no recollection of anything after roughly 11 p.m. last night, he was sure he'd have had enough clarity of mind to remember talking on the phone a mere hour ago.

A theory took shape in his mind. A young lipstick wearer Severin had absolutely no memory of had, after following him back to his room from wherever he'd been the night before, taken it upon herself to answer his phone when Janet had called just before 8. Then this mystery woman had taken a hot shower and bolted, leaving him to deal with the confusion and surely ugly aftermath.

Then something else occurred to him. He opened the drawer of his nightstand, grabbed his wallet, and opened it to discover that all his cash was gone. *Great.* Belching, feeling pathetic, he slid back down to the horizontal, let his head sink into the lumpy pillow, and closed his eyes. He was getting too old for this crap.

*****

After a quick shower, he put on his usual outfit—ancient Doc Martin boots, a pair of threadbare blue jeans, and a tartar-colored undershirt that had once been white. Because he was going to work, he added a collared flannel shirt to the shabby ensemble. Yet despite his unkempt appearance, he was a handsome man, standing 6-foot-2, with dark hair and a muscular frame that was relatively well defined even though he never, absolutely never, worked out.

He shoved his belongings in his old black duffel bag and stepped out his door into the nearly empty parking lot. It was a blustery, overcast day. Dust and bits of discarded paper were blowing across the cracked asphalt. His phone chimed as he walked toward the motel office. Looking down at it, he saw the expected text message from Janet telling him to go to hell.

He checked out of the motel and drove out of the small town of Clarkston, Washington—just across the Snake River from Idaho—to the organic farm co-op, a couple of miles to the north, that his employer had been hired to audit. There, feeling miserable, he sat down to finish the last few tasks of his investigative business records review.

Winding things up just before noon, he then drove more than 300 miles west—through the wheat fields of the rolling Palouse hills, through the lava fields and sagebrush of the high desert, over the Cascade Mountains, and down through the west slope rainforests—to his dumpy 1-bedroom apartment in Seattle, chewing an entire pouch of leaf tobacco and drinking two canned espressos *en route*.

*****

Severin pulled his old car to the curb half a block from his apartment, killed the engine, and took a deep breath. Only then did he finally bother to check the voicemail on his cell phone—from the post-9 a.m. call that had come from a number he didn't recognize. It had a Western Washington area code.

"Hey, you old jerk. I finally tracked you down. It's Greg Carlsen. A voice from your past, still living the dream up here in Anacortes. Give me a shout back. I have something to tell you about. I'll text you my cell, home, and office numbers. So give me call, alright?"

Severin wondered why on Earth Greg Carlsen, a former co-worker from his days on the Anacortes, Washington, police force, would call him out of the blue like this. They'd always been on good terms, but hadn't spoken in probably eight or nine years. Regardless, Severin was too tired to bother returning the call.

Making a quick stop at his mailbox in his ancient apartment building's musty entryway, he tucked four days' worth of mail under his arm before wearily trudging up the dimly lit stairwell to his third-floor apartment. There, he plopped down on his second-hand couch to polish off the rest of a bottle of Wild Turkey whiskey he'd brought home from Clarkston.

THREE

Severin's eyes popped open. It took him a moment to realize he was in bed at home. Again, his heart was pounding and racing. He took his pulse, discovering that it was over 130 beats per minute. His throat felt dry and tight. He tried to swallow, but found he couldn't. His fingers and toes felt cold.

He got up and, without turning on any lights, stumbled to the kitchen for a drink of water. Then he stood in the darkness at his living room window, gazing down at the light 3 a.m. traffic racing north or south on Interstate 5, taking a dozen deep breaths, waiting for his heart to calm down.

Initially, he'd felt ambivalent about Janet's abrupt exit from his life—even a bit relieved. He was, after all, something of a lone wolf. But now, alarmed by the worsening behavior of his heart, standing in darkness and watching vehicles pass by on the freeway, each of them rushing off to somewhere else, the weight of his solitude bore down on him. To his unhappy surprise, he ached with loneliness.

*****

The next day, Severin slept in until 10, then rose slowly. Looking out his bedroom window, he saw that it was raining. A slow, steady rain from low-lying clouds. He thought about finally calling a doctor about his episodes. But his medical insurance was crap, and he couldn't afford the co-pay. Plus, he hated going to the doctor.

Maybe the episodes would just go away. He'd been having them for several months now. But still, maybe they'd stop just as abruptly as they'd started. Perhaps if he changed his diet or drank less coffee. Perhaps if he started meditating, doing yoga, or drinking special calming teas. He'd always figured naturopathic and holistic approaches to illness were goofball nonsense, if not utterly fraudulent. But they were sounding better and better all the time.

He was tempted to get back on the internet for purposes of self-diagnosis. But the last time he made that mistake, he'd found that his symptoms could be attributed to anything from dehydration to ALS to brain cancer. So his attempt at figuring out what was wrong had only made it harder for him to sleep. Made him all the more anxious.

Donning a terrycloth robe, he made his way to his tiny kitchen, brewed a pot of extra strong coffee, and sat down at the kitchen table to go through mail. There was an overdue cable bill he tossed into the trash can without opening. But there was another overdue bill he couldn't ignore quite so easily—this one for his credit card. Scanning the statement, he noted a $450 charge from a bar in Bellingham and wondered whether it was fraudulent. He had indeed been in Bellingham on the specified date. But he had no recollection of the bar. Or did he? He vaguely remembered making a late night stop at a dumpy place with an uneven pool table down near the waterfront. But $450? What had he done, order a round of 20-year-old scotch for the whole bar? His balance was now at the card maximum of $10,000, not counting the past month's interest charge. He thought about applying for a new card with an introductory 0% rate on balance transfers. It would give him some breathing room.

He listened to voicemail on his land line as he poured himself another cup of coffee. Three prerecorded messages from politicians urged him to get out and vote for such-and-such or so-and-so in the upcoming election. Then there was another message from Greg Carlsen. "Hey, jackass. Trying your home phone now. You really should call me. Got something you should hear about. Check your text messages for my numbers. Call me. Really."

That sounded ominous. He gave a moment's thought to returning Carlsen's call, then sucked down his coffee and headed for the shower instead.

*****

An hour later, Severin stood in the office of his employer, an organic foods certifier called Agrisymbiosis. The company shared office space with two accountants in a neglected, drafty, and perpetually damp converted 1920s bungalow on Lower Queen Anne Hill, near old U.S. Highway 99.

"The mileage log and gas receipts are in the envelope," he said as he laid his investigative audit report on the desk of a slightly younger, unwashed man in a wrinkled flannel shirt who sat just inside the front door in what had once been the bungalow's living room. The man—whose official role was that of assistant to the firm's director, but who had also, with the director's apparent blessing, appointed himself the director's gatekeeper and first point of contact for contractors like Severin—was flipping through a men's fashion mail-order catalog. He had long blond hair that he'd obviously gone to a lot of trouble to make look as though he didn't care about it. A touch too perfectly unkempt.

"If you could just slip that into Amber's mailbox," the man said without bothering to look up at Severin.

"Is that a request, Channing?"

The man made brief eye contact, sneered, and gave a quick nod.

"I take it they didn't teach grammar or sentence structure where you went to school," Severin said, taking the report back and walking it over to the mailbox area. *You flip little Fabio-looking moron*, he might have added.

"Did you include an exhibit list this time, like Amber asked you to?"

"Of course, Channing." To keep himself in check, Severin visualized sending the man falling over backward in his chair with a solid palm heel strike to the underside of his chin. "You'll find a reference to it in the table of contents, under the title 'exhibit list.' Imagine that."

Severin had Channing pegged for a fraud. He did the 'friend of the earth' thing not because he was a believer, but because it got him dates. Because it gave him—a buffoon with a third-rate bachelor's degree from a third-rate university—a way to fool himself into thinking that he was of use to society. Severin was convinced that it was because of people like Channing that important environmental protection issues got so little traction among American conservatives. What conservative would ever pay heed to an abrasive, repulsive moron like him? Severin could just picture him taking the message to the street. *Hey, dude. You have to, like, sign my petition and, like, give money to save the whales. Or else you're, like, a jerk.*

Having delivered his report to the director's mailbox, Severin made to leave without saying goodbye, and was half way out the door before Channing blurted, "Amber has another assignment for you."

"Tell her to call me."

"No, you have to depart today."

"Where to?"

"Greenleaf Farm in Lewiston, Idaho. They're expecting you first thing tomorrow morning."

Severin turned and glared at him. "Are you kidding me? Lewiston? I was literally across the river from Lewiston yesterday. Why didn't you tell me that while I was out there so I wouldn't have to drive 11 unnecessary hours back and forth to Seattle while spending all your client's money on gasoline?"

"This week's assignments were determined at the strategy meeting this morning."

Severin stared at Channing, contemplating the nerve bundles and pressure points that, if struck, would inflict the greatest possible pain on the man.

"Email me the file," he said, heading out the door.

*****

Needing a walk in the fresh air, Severin made his way down through Belltown to the downtown Seattle waterfront where he ordered a large halibut and chips from Ivar's Fish Bar. It was cool out, but not cold, so he took a seat at one of the outdoor tables at the edge of the pier. Seagulls circled overhead, hoping diners would spill their cups of French fries. Severin could hear the low rumble of the massive diesel engines of one of the state's ferries as it offloaded cars at Colman Dock, a couple hundred feet to the south.

When he was half way through his meal, his phone rang again. Guessing it would be his boss, Amber, he licked his fingers and, without looking at the caller I.D., answered.

"Severin."

"Thanks for calling me back, jackass." It was Greg Carlsen.

"Oh, hey Greg, I just, uh—"

"Oh, hey Greg, I just, uh, nothing."

"No, Greg, really. I just got in from Clarkston. Catching up on voicemail, snail mail, email. All that good stuff. What's up? How are you doing?"

"Like you care. You don't even send me a Christmas card."

"I don't send anyone Christmas cards. I'm a man."

"I send people Christmas cards."

"I rest my case. So what's up?"

"I'll catch you up on all the very interesting details of my life over the thank-you beers you're going to buy me when this is all said and done. The reason I hunted you down is that I have a possible under-the-table sort of job for you. Probably a big payday for a fairly limited time commitment."

"Under the table? The hell does that mean? I'm not going to bodyguard a drug dealer."

"Would I do that to you?"

"No comment."

"Lars, this is a cherry gig. Easy money. Real money."

"I appreciate that you thought of me, Greg. But I kind of have a full plate right now."

"Arthur told me you're doing some kind of low-paying contract inspector thing?"

"I'm delighted to hear that my friends are talking about my low income. And Art's description is an oversimplification. But yeah, that's basically what I'm doing."

"Lars, man, you definitely need to hear me out then."

"Fine. What's the deal?"

"I don't have all the details. But you remember my Uncle Pete who lives on Lopez Island?"

"No."

"The guy who burned the hell out of his hand with fireworks at that 4th of July party we went to down near Shelter Bay."

"Oh, yeah. I remember him."

"Long story short, he plays bridge with this multimillionaire guy who also lives on Lopez. Orin Thorvaldsson."

"Orin Thorvaldsson? Never heard of him. Is he a Viking?"

"Apparently his niece is a U.S. government employee who up and disappeared while on assignment in some rural part of China. Nobody knows what happened to her. The State Department did some minimal investigation, threw out a few theories, and called it a day."

"What were the theories?"

"Again, I don't know the details. But in a nutshell, they think she and her colleague are dead. Murdered. That's where you come in. The State Department report was inconclusive and light on facts. The family wants answers."

"Hold on, Greg. It's been years since I investigated anything criminal, let alone a homicide. Plus, China? How is that going to work?"

"You speak the language."

"I speak just enough Korean to survive a consular cocktail party."

"Korean's pretty close to Chinese, isn't it?"

"No, moron. It isn't close. And which of the 50 million dialects of Chinese are you even talking about?"

"Well, you have experience working overseas, right?"

"In Korea. And that was a Customs thing. I haven't touched a homicide since I worked in Anacortes with your silly ass, what, eight years ago? And then, of course, there's that sticky little jurisdiction thing. You think I'm going to be able to prance around in China investigating a murder? You're cracked."

"I don't think this Thorvaldsson guy is expecting that you could act like a full-blown murder police over there. I think he has in mind more of a simple fact-finding mission."

"A simple fact-finding mission. In a country where I don't speak the language, where my pasty, 6-foot-2 self is going to be as conspicuous as all get out, and where I might not even be legally able to drive a car."

"They're talking about a big payday. I mean like tens of thousands, for a couple weeks of work. Probably just interviewing people."

"Greg, listen. It isn't the perfect setup, but I'm gainfully employed. I have a shred of stability in my life for the first time in I don't know how long. I can't drop everything for this wild goose chase sounding thing. Thanks for thinking of me. But I'm sorry. This isn't for me."

They chatted for another minute or two, making halfhearted promises to meet for beers and catch up at some point. Then, as Severin finished up his fish and shoved his plate into an overstuffed garbage can on the sidewalk, he watched a small white BMW whip into a disabled parking space. A disabled parking placard hung from its rearview mirror. A perfectly able-bodied woman emerged and ran through the main entrance to Pier 54, probably for a coffee. As he strode by, he tried the car door. It was unlocked. He reached in, grabbed the disabled parking placard, and tossed it in the next garbage can he came to as he strode along the waterfront walkway.

FOUR

That afternoon—the sky darkened by overcast—Severin repacked his duffel bag with several pairs of socks and underwear that he hadn't had time to wash since his return a day earlier. He put on the last clean shirt he had. It was an ancient red and brown flannel—a grunge music scene relic from the days, decades earlier, when he followed a half dozen soon-to-be world-famous bands from the Off Ramp, to the Crocodile Café, to the OK Hotel, to every other hole-in-the-wall Seattle venue where they once played. He microwaved and choked down a frozen bean burrito, bought a new pouch of leaf chew tobacco at a corner market near his place, and set off, tired and irritated, for Lewiston, Idaho.

Nearing the high desert east of the Cascade Mountains, he stopped to refuel at a dusty gas station in the town of Vantage, on the right bank of the wide Columbia River. A cold wind was howling down the Columbia River Gorge, so he jumped back into his car as the tank was filling, knocking his chew spit cup over onto the passenger seat as he did so. *Oh, crap.* With the cold wind blowing under his shirt and up his back, he searched the pump island for a paper towel dispenser, and, unsuccessful, went in to beg napkins from the clerk. A few minutes later, the brown chew spit wiped up to reveal a large new stain on the fabric of his car seat, Severin, with excessive force, turned the key in the ignition. The starter went through several cycles, making an anemic sound, but the engine wouldn't engage. Had he left the lights on? Even if he had, it couldn't have been more than five or six minutes since he turned the car off—not long enough to drain a half-decent battery. He turned the key back to off, checked that his headlights were off, waited a moment, and tried again. This time the starter was slower. The engine still wouldn't start. Two tries later, and the starter refused to budge.

Perfect.

He thought about buying a battery from the service station. But they'd charge him through the nose. His credit card was maxed out anyway, and his ATM card was linked to a bank account that wouldn't have more than $30 in it until his next payday at the end of the week. He could use the company gas card. But they wouldn't look kindly upon that, even if he was on assignment for them. They were beyond anal about extra expenses. No, he'd just get someone to give him a jump.

It took Severin the better part of half an hour before he could find someone who had jumper cables and was actually willing to help him out. By then he was freezing. Shivering. He thanked his rescuers, got in his car, and headed back toward eastbound Interstate 90. However, just short of the ramp, he pulled over and sat for a moment with the engine running, still shivering though his heater was on full blast. He was beat. But it was still another three hours to Lewiston. He packed a fresh wad of chew into his cheek and stared straight out the windshield.

What was he going to do—find somebody to jump start his car every morning in Lewiston so that he could go to work from his motel? Call Channing, admit to the bastard that his personal financial situation was pitiful, and then grovel to be allowed to purchase a new car battery with the company gas card? And to think he'd told Greg Carlsen that he finally had a shred of stability back in his life. Pathetic.

He squeezed the steering wheel with both hands until they grew tired. Then, popping a CD into his stereo—the one high-quality component of his car—he took several minutes to close his eyes, breath meditatively, and listen to his cherished Seattle symphony rendition of the second movement from Sonata Pathétique–Beethoven's Piano Sonata No. 8 in C minor, Opus number 13. The piece nearly always helped him calm down—helped him regain focus. The music carried his mind away to a happier time. A memory of a warm and sunny day. A sandy 4th of July beach of his childhood, just he and his parents sharing hot dogs and lemonade by the water's edge. A sailboat passing 100 yards offshore. The smell of salt on the gentle Puget Sound sea breeze. Everyone smiling. Everyone happy and healthy.

The sonata ended. Severin took one more deep breath, turned his car around, and headed for the ramp to westbound Interstate 90. It was two hours back to Seattle, and another hour and a half or so to the San Juan Islands ferry terminal in Anacortes. That would give him plenty of time to get back in touch with Carlsen and get the contact information for Orin Thorvalddson, the mysterious multimillionaire of Lopez Island. He'd call Thorvalddson for directions once he was west of the mountains.

FIVE

That afternoon, rain began to fall from a darkening sky as Severin made his way through Anacortes on his sojourn to the ferry terminal servicing the San Juan Islands route. His windshield started to steam up despite his dying defogger being on maximum power, and he had to wipe it with his sleeve in order to see. Just after passing a small shipyard on the right-hand side of the highway, he made a conscious effort to not look to his left, where a little neighborhood of well-kept houses climbed a gentle slope toward Cranberry Lake. If he'd allowed himself to look, he might have caught a glimpse of a small, old, white Cape Cod-style cottage that to most people would appear unremarkable. But to Severin, it would always be remembered as the place where he first peered into the abyss. His life had been forever split into two distinct periods divided by the day he last set foot in that house. No other point in time held the same defining, terrible meaning for him. Not even the day his parents were killed.

*****

The ferry ride to Lopez Island was unusually rough—especially once the vessel rounded Shannon Point and entered Rosario Strait, one of the main commercial shipping routes between Vancouver, British Columbia, and the open Pacific. A hard rain continued to fall from a layer of low, dark overcast. The clouds couldn't have been more than a few hundred feet above the cold, choppy, white-capped salt water. Some of the clouds trailed tendrils of mist that reached all the way down to the surface, as if tethering the sky to the earth.

The cavernous vessel rocked this way and that as Severin squinted through the thick weather in an attempt to make out the San Juan Islands through the forward observation windows. Headwinds pushed the rainwater sideways across the glass, distorting the view. But before long, Severin was able to just make out the dark, shadowy hills of Decatur Island a few degrees to port of their heading, with Blakely Island a few degrees to starboard. Once they passed between those two islands, he'd be able to see Lopez.

*****

Though he'd managed to start his car in order to board the ferry at the Anacortes terminal, Severin couldn't repeat the trick when it came time to disembark on Lopez Island. A deckhand tried to get him moving with a portable jump starter. But corrosion on Severin's battery terminals made it difficult for the deckhand to get an efficient contact with his clamps, and he quickly gave up despite Severin's insistence that he'd had no trouble jumping it earlier in the day. Another crewmember pushed his car off the ferry with a squat, yellow service vehicle they had onboard.

They left him in a paved turnoff just off the dock. And there, with a heavy rain pattering on the roof of his car, he sat, watching the other ferry traffic disembark and disappear up and over the heavily forested hill separating the ferry terminal from the rest of the island. Before long, a handful of waiting cars boarded, the gates closed, and the ferry steamed away for Shaw, Orcas, and San Juan Islands, disappearing around the misty, rocky point to the west, leaving him alone.

Seeing no alternative, he rang, for the second time that day, the number for Orin Thorvaldsson. As before, the phone was answered not by Thorvaldsson, but by one of his mellow-voiced and exceedingly polite employees. Severin explained his situation, and half an hour later, three men in two different green Land Rovers gave him a good look as they passed by, circled around, and pulled to the curb behind him. They stayed in their cars for a minute, appearing to focus on their smart-phones, leaving Severin to wonder whether he should initiate contact. Their delay got him wondering. Were they ordinary employees or security goons? If the latter, what was Thorvaldsson mixed up in that he felt he needed a security team on an idyllic, pastoral island like Lopez? Did he consider himself a target because of his wealth, or because of something else? And why the delay? Were they checking his license plate against some sort of quasi-legal private sector database? Making sure he was who he said he was?

At last, they emerged from their cars with a strangely precise simultaneity, and Severin studied them in his rearview mirror as they approached. They were dressed in jeans and matching baggy raincoats that made it impossible to see whether they were wearing holsters. As Severin rolled down his window, a trickle of cold water poured in, wetting his thigh.

"Mr. Severin?" asked a tall, broad-shouldered blond man with a high, tight haircut and a neck and chin like an old-school linebacker.

"That's me."

"It's a pleasure to meet you. I'm Paul. We spoke on the phone. I'll give you a ride down to Hughes Bay while my colleagues get your car jump-started. When they do, they'll follow us to the house."

"Okay."

Severin got out of his car and was headed for the passenger door of Paul's Land Rover when Paul stepped in front of him. After apologizing and asking for permission in his kindly voice, and as one of his associates held a large umbrella over Severin's head, Paul ran a metal detecting magnetometer wand up and down the length of Severin's body.

"I don't even own a gun anymore," Severin said.

"Thanks for your patience. Again, I apologize, but it's an unfortunate necessity for us."

"No worries. The world's full of creeps."

Before long, they were speeding south, through the forests and falling maple leaves, alongside golden pastures dotted with sheep, cows, and horses, past a small village on a quiet harbor, and at last down a lonely dead-end road to a set of impressive wood and iron gates. Paul entered a long key code, the gates swung open, and they made their way down a driveway that had to be a quarter-mile long, to a circle drive in front of a Pacific Northwest contemporary style mansion fronted with enormous rhododendrons and flanked by Japanese maples in vivid fall colors. Reds, oranges, yellows. The house was sided in cedar shakes. The window frames were a bright white. And the steep roof, which was a charcoal gray metal, angled upward, away from the driveway. The far side of the house must have been three stories high, with its windows facing picturesque, quiet little Hughes Bay.

As they parked and got out, a tall, late middle-aged blond man, presumably Thorvaldsson, stood under a huge umbrella, just in front of a wisteria arbor that framed the front entryway.

"Mr. Severin?"

"Call me Lars."

"I'm Orin. Thanks for coming. Let's get you somewhere dry."

Thorvaldsson walked him through the massive wooden front door, down a corridor lined with hanging, expensive looking Chilkat blankets. The blankets bore woven representations of ancient Salish, Tlingit, Haida, and Tsimshian spirits like the raven, bear, and orca. Severin's jaw nearly dropped as they emerged into an enormous great room where a large fire roared in a river-rock fireplace. The room had heavy timbers crossing the high cantilevered ceiling, walls with elaborate cedar trim work, and pedestal-mounted shadow boxes holding tribal artwork. One side of the room was a wall of floor-to-ceiling windows that Severin guessed were 18 feet high. They framed an incredible view spanning the entirety of Hughes Bay, in the middle of which a lone sailboat sat at anchor in the mist. There couldn't have been more than three or four other houses on the bay's rocky, forested shores. It looked like a postcard. Below the windows, a long, sloping yard lined with yellowing Yoshino cherry trees ran down to the water's edge where a floating dock extended out into the bay. In the foreground, just below the windows from which Severin was examining the surroundings, was a vacant helicopter pad complete with airport-grade perimeter lights and a windsock.

The house was immaculate, perfectly decorated, perfectly furnished. Everything in its proper place. Everything matched to the dominating dark browns and grays. To Severin, the overall effect was cold, despite the roaring fire. As he made his way through the room, his eyes were drawn to the one source of vivid color—a large wooden bowl of flawless, photo-quality fruit that sat in the middle of a dark barn-wood table. Grapes, bananas, pears, oranges, apples. He had to suppress a grin as it occurred to him that if he reached for an apple, it wouldn't have come as a surprise if he set off some sort of burglar alarm.

"Can I interest you in a glass of wine?" Thorvaldsson asked. "A bourbon maybe?"

"Bourbon would be great."

"How do you like it?"

"With one ice cube, if it isn't a bother."

"No bother at all," Thorvaldsson said as he took a seat in a brown leather wingback by the fire, nodding to a young Asian woman—apparently another employee—who'd materialized in the doorframe to an adjoining corridor. She wore a black button-down shirt and black pants that made her look like a catering employee. "I'll have the same. A double?"

"You speak my language," Severin said as the silent woman disappeared back down the corridor. His gaze drifted from the towering stone fireplace and chimney, up to the timbered ceiling, then back over to the wall of windows. "This is quite a house."

"Thank you. It was designed by the architectural firm of Christiansen & Lund, Copenhagen."

"Denmark? I would have guessed it was a northwest designer. It fits right in."

"I find that there are notable similarities between the architectural styles of the Pacific Northwest and Scandinavia. But then, given that so many Scandinavians settled here—at least in the Puget Sound area—I suppose that makes a certain amount of sense." He gazed into the fire. "How was your journey? Paul said that you began east of the mountains. That's quite a trek."

"I'm used to it. I drive a lot for my work. And speaking of work, if you don't mind my asking, what does a person do to be able to afford custom

Danish architecture on such a grand scale?" Severin asked, looking all about. "Are you one of those Microsoft millionaires I envy with such heartache?"

"You haven't heard of us? Thorvaldsson Trading?"

"Should I have?"

"Not necessarily. At least not in your line of work. But we're in the business section of *The Seattle Times* a lot. We're an import-export house. No particular focus. Wherever we see an exploitable margin in an unfulfilled market, we jump on the product. We contract with manufacturers, then set up our own exporters, importers, and distributors. Pacific Rim, mostly. A little bit of business with Latin America. Sometimes Europe. My siblings are co-directors. The whole thing was handed down to us by our late father. And really, his own father, who emigrated from Oslo in 1923 with little more than the clothes on his back, got *him* started."

"A family business."

Thorvaldsson nodded. "For better or for worse."

"And you run your business from here?"

"No. I usually only use this place on weekends. I have an office in Seattle, in the Columbia Center. My main residence is in Broadmoor." He slapped his hands on the leather arms of his chair as if readying to make an announcement. "I'll cut to the chase. I don't know how much Pete Carlsen's nephew, uh . . . ."

"Greg."

"Yes. I don't know how much Greg told you. But in short, our family has had to endure this nightmare—the disappearance of our Kristin—without enough information to reach any sort of closure. Oh—here is our bourbon," he said as the woman reappeared with a heavy silver tray bearing a crystal decanter, ice bucket, and two crystal tumblers. Without a word, she set it on the coffee table, placed a single ice cube in each glass, and poured. "This is a 23-year-old Pappy Van Winkle," Thorvaldsson said. "Supposed to be all the rage in bourbon circles at the moment. Harder than hell to get hold of. And I'll let you judge whether it's worth the $1,700 I paid a bourbon scalper for the one bottle."

Only the insecure insist on telling you the price of what they're serving, Severin thought as he took a good sip and sat back on the large couch opposite Thorvaldsson. "It's good." *But I wouldn't have paid more than $40 for it.* "Thank you."

"So, as I was saying, we're looking for information. My niece, my sister's daughter, Kristin Powell, was working for the U.S. Department of Commerce as a type of international trade dispute investigator. She was based at the agency headquarters in Washington, D.C. But her assignment took her and her partner to a remote, rural area of China, where they were conducting a sort of on-site audit and investigation of a Chinese company called Yinzhen Sorghum Processing Company Limited, or YSP for short—a processor and exporter of sweet sorghum syrup."

"Of what?"

"That's what I said. Sweet sorghum syrup. Apparently it's something they pour over biscuits in the South. I've heard it described as being like a cross between molasses and honey. Something half way between each. Anyway, by all accounts, Kristin and her partner wound up their investigation of YSP and were on their way back to Shanghai to catch a flight back to the United States. They never made it. Specifically, if I can even call it that, they disappeared somewhere between their worksite and Shanghai. The U.S. State Department conducted a pathetically brief investigation, took two months to produce an inconclusive report, and called it good. That's where we stand. But that isn't good enough. Not by a damned mile. We deserve better."

"Look, Mr. Thor—"

"Orin, please."

"Orin. There are a few things that need to be right out in the open before we have any further discussion on this. The first thing is my background. I don't know how much you—"

"I know enough. It doesn't concern me. In fact, I think you're a perfect fit for what we're looking for."

Severin stared at the man for a moment, wondering what the hell *that* meant, then shrugged his shoulders. "Fair enough. The second thing is that, because this involves an overseas incident involving an employee of the U.S. government, this is the sacred province of the State Department, and I doubt very much—"

"You mean the same State Department that apparently can't process a simple passport application in less than 90 days anymore? You mean the same State Department that produced this travesty of an investigative report?" he said, drawing a document from a leather folder on the coffee table and handing it to Severin.

The man liked to cut you off mid-sentence, Severin observed. He was probably the type who measured minutes by dollars.

"And," Severin continued, ignoring the interruption while thumbing through the very thin report, "I doubt very much that I'd be able to gather any more information than the State Department investigators did. I'm sure they did all they could."

"You're sure? Take a look at that thing. Does it strike you as at all thin? Does it strike you as mere window dressing? Does it strike you, perhaps, as the product of people who didn't want the real answers?"

Severin had to admit, the report was unusually thin. In his own experience, reports of even the most minor of investigations typically had at least twice as many references to witness interviews. Family, friends, co-workers, eye-witnesses, suspects. This report referenced barely a handful—

most of them residents of China. The conclusion section offered nothing but conjecture. It seemed reasonably likely, according to the State Department, that Kristin Powell and her male co-worker were abducted after attempting to obtain transport from the main airport of the Chinese port city of Qingdao, Shandong Province, to the Qingdao Shangri-la Hotel, downtown. Then, the report theorized, they were robbed, killed, and disposed of. The last interviewed person to see them alive—an American attorney who represented YSP in the investigation, and who had been traveling with them—said he and YSP's van driver left Kristin and her colleague curbside at the Qingdao airport with a slim chance of catching the last flight to Shanghai that evening. According to the attorney, if they missed the flight, they intended to grab a taxi to the hotel. The next day, in a suburb of Qingdao, someone used the pair's U.S. government travel credit cards to purchase gasoline, and later the same day attempted, unsuccessfully, to use the cards to purchase various items of consumer electronics and furniture. Chinese customs had no record of Kristin Powell or her colleague ever leaving the country, and there was no record of them boarding a flight to Shanghai.

"We refuse to accept the State Department's half-baked conclusion," Thorvaldsson said, a hint of desperation in his voice. "They have no proof."

Meaning they didn't find a body, Severin thought.

Aside from the brevity and seeming insufficiency of the report, there were several things that immediately jumped out at Severin as unusual or warranting further inquiry. First, the report was heavily redacted—sometimes with entire sentences blacked out. Second, the table of contents made reference to a classified annex that was left off of the public version of the report provided to Thorvaldsson. Yet the case revolved, ostensibly, around some sort of widely-known and entirely public international trade dispute. Why would the government feel compelled redact or otherwise exclude so much information? In Severin's experience, this usually only happened with documents concerning matters of national security—or espionage.

Additionally, one of the last people to see Kristin alive was her husband, Wesley. Like Kristin, Wesley was an investigator with the U.S. Department of Commerce and was scheduled to be in China the week after Kristin was there, at a job site in a different province. However, the report noted that he arrived early, met up with Kristin at her hotel in Yinzhen just after her work concluded, and then rode with the team part of the way to the airport before asking to be let out of the team's van, alone, on the side of a rural road. From there, he allegedly found his way to his own job site hundreds of kilometers away. The report didn't even address why he got out of the van.

"I see your point," Severin said. "This doesn't seem very thorough."

"They didn't even send American investigators to this Qingdao place," he said, pronouncing it *Kingdow*.

"In Chinese, the letter *q* is pronounced like *ch*," Severin said. "Ching-dow, not King-dow. Regardless, it's a serious possibility that what's in this report is really all that could be found, barring a miracle or detectives with ESP. In any case, I'm not at all confident that I could learn any more than this. The case presents a number of daunting obstacles to say the least."

"You don't speak Chinese. You don't have jurisdiction. You can't compel anybody to talk to you. I know all of this. It's already factored into the equation. Regardless, you might be able to find a lot of what you need on this side of the Pacific."

"Maybe, maybe not."

"Actually, YSP's exclusive U.S. importer, Sun Ocean Trade, is located in Seattle. Might be a good place to start. Plus, most of the people you'll probably want to interview live in Washington, D.C., which I understand you're already quite familiar with."

"I lived there for three years when I worked for Customs. Still."

"Still what? Do you mean *why you*? You have investigative experience. You have experience working overseas. Presumably, you have some familiarity with Pacific Rim international trade processes and practices, which at least in theory could prove relevant here."

"But no experience with respect to trade in Chinese sweet sorghum."

"Hey, I'd grab an interpreter and go search for answers myself, except that the Chinese won't grant me an entry visa."

Severin's eyebrows rose. "They've declared you *persona non grata*?"

"It's total nonsense, all over a dispute I had with a corrupt Chinese customs official. Crook tried to shake me down to the tune of almost half a million dollars. I won't bore you with the details. Nothing for you to worry about anyhow."

Severin considered pressing for further information on the matter, but decided to let it go. Still, his face betrayed his skepticism with the whole proposal.

"Look, Lars. The official channels have failed us, so we're going off the books."

And you have no one else to turn to, Severin thought. The man was rich, but probably not so obscenely rich that he'd be willing to burn the hundreds of thousands of dollars it could take to hire one of the big multinational investigative firms unless it was absolutely necessary. And given the inherent sensitivity of a case involving the disappearance and possible murder of agents of the U.S. government, those firms might not want to touch the case anyway, for fear of upsetting any of their special relationships with the various faces of Chinese government. For fear of losing their precious access. Plus, their bread and butter was simple things like background checks and inquiries stemming from due diligence investigations—not homicides or missing persons cases. Those were entirely different animals.

"I can't send one of my own people," Thorvaldsson said. "I can't send anyone with connections to our company. It's too sensitive a situation. Plus, Pete Carlsen's nephew says you had a reputation for being exceptionally clever and resourceful when you were on the Anacortes police force. A natural detective. The best he's ever seen in his 17 years as a cop."

"That was a thousand years ago."

"Regardless, assuming your reputation is deserved, would a large enough paycheck entice you to overcome these obstacles?"

"The money is a separate matter. But your expectations—"

"Lars, please. We're not expecting you to go over there and pull a Sherlock Holmes, where every conceivable loose end is tied up in a couple of perfect paragraphs. But there's more information out there. You know there is. It may not be much. But we want it, just the same. Maybe Kristin is still alive. But if she isn't," he said before pausing to swallow, "then we want to know what happened, who did it, and why. We want closure."

"Closure is an elusive thing, Orin. It's your money. But if I were in your—"

"We also owe it to Kristin."

"Owe?"

"We—I let this happen. It's my fault."

"No. You didn't let it happen. That feeling comes from something a detective friend of mine used to call guilt egotism. Whatever happened to Kristin wasn't your fault."

Thorvaldsson took a drink, his face betraying his sadness and rage. "I don't mean that in a direct sense, of course. But the totality of circumstances, the chain of life events that put her in that position, out on a limb." He stood and walked over to the window with his bourbon. He swirled it in his glass as he stared out, seemingly toward the gray horizon beyond the mouth of the bay. "Kristin was bulimic," he said at last.

"I'm not sure I follow you."

"Well, can you imagine what it would be like to be a child, to grow up, in a family of driven overachievers like mine? Think of it. A little girl." He shook his head. "Ludicrous expectations. Overbearing control. Subtle, insidious judgment and implied criticism. It all but ensures you reach adulthood with hardly a shred of self-esteem. With a bottomless hole in your heart that your whole life becomes a futile drive to fill." He turned to face Severin. "It's what made her want to get far, far away from us. It's what made her susceptible to the lure of an insecure possessive sycophant like her husband. Susceptible to the sappy emotional bait that a controlling, jealous, psychologically abusive worm like him is nearly always skilled in spoon-feeding to the women in his life. Dubious and entirely self-serving gestures and declarations of love. Exactly what an emotionally starved girl like Kristin will be drawn to like an addict to the needle—will be all too willing to delude herself into believing is wholesome and genuine." He finished his bourbon. "And all her life, Lars. All her life I saw it happening. But I still let it happen."

Severin took a moment to digest what Thorvaldsson was saying, thinking the man was something of a dime-store psychologist. "I take it you don't like her husband."

"I know little of Wesley. What I do know, I don't like. My gut tells me to recommend you take a close look at him."

"Spouses usually start off near the top of my list."

"I'm asking for two to three weeks of your time. I'll cover all of your expenses. *All* of them. And I insist that you stay in top hotels and treat yourself well when it comes to food and incidentals. Besides reimbursing you for expenses, I'll pay you $10,000 up front. If you succeed in getting us a considerably better idea of what happened, I'll add a $40,000 bonus."

"$50,000?"

"What else am I going to spend it on? Look around you, Lars." He smiled a sad smile. "That's the joke, see?"

"I don't understand."

"Everything that we gave up, thinking, all the while, that we were on target. That we were doing the right thing. That our relentless drive, our achievements, our successes would pay off in some profound and meaningful way in the long run. Everything we sacrificed with respect to relationships, friends, family. Time, happiness, love. For what? All this wealth. All the power and control that goes with it. But was it enough to protect my sweet niece? Will it be enough to save any of us in the end? No. So what good is it?" He shook his head again. "We're all hurtling toward the same inevitable, eternal darkness, Lars. All of us. And there isn't one damned thing any of us can do about it. That's the bitter lesson."

*****

Thorvaldsson's servant refilled their bourbons a second time as they sat discussing details and logistics.

"If I agree to do this, I'll need some help," Severin said. "I have a guy in mind."

"I'll cover his expenses too. You can share your fee however you see fit." Thorvaldsson's cell phone rang and he took it for a 20-second conversation. "Sorry about that. My people say that according to our friendly island mechanic, your car battery will no longer hold a charge. So they put in a new one for you and had your oil and sparkplugs changed."

"What do I owe you?"

"Don't be ridiculous. There's also an envelope in your car with cash for your time, fuel, and ferry tickets. If you take the job, we'll work out a reporting system for your expenses. In the meantime, can I have Paul run you back to the ferry terminal? I can tell my people to have your car waiting there for you. Then you don't have to drive for a bit."

"That would probably be a good idea."

"And we'd better get you out of here soon. The last ferry for Anacortes leaves in less than an hour."

*****

Severin stood on the car deck near the open bow of the ferry as it rumbled through the darkness, across Rosario Strait, back toward Anacortes. The cold headwind blew his hair straight back, while swells crashing against the hull sent fans of salt water shooting high into the air, raining a light spray down on him where he stood. It was cold, but the cold helped clear his head, as did the cup of strong, black coffee he'd purchased from a machine in the galley upstairs on the main passenger deck. It occurred to him that he was starving. A turkey pot pie from the Calico Cupboard Bakery in Anacortes—one of his old haunts—sounded good. But he didn't think it was open this late. He tried to forget his hunger by focusing on Thorvaldsson's proposal.

There was no doubt that it had an odd smell to it. Fifty thousand dollars for a quote-unquote better idea of what happened? Either Thorvaldsson and his family were nuts, or there was something else going on that they weren't telling him. Still, for the possibility of a $50,000 payday, Severin was willing to play along—at least for the time being.

*****

That night, reclining on his couch and finishing the half empty bottle of Pappy Van Winkle bourbon Thorvaldsson had sent him home with, Severin turned on his laptop. In a few minutes, he found Kristin Powell's pages on a handful of social media and networking websites. The first such site, designed for career networking, revealed that she was a fellow graduate of the University of Washington, with a double major in international studies and Russian. In photos on the more socially-oriented sites, she looked more or less as he expected her to look. Blonde. Sad eyes. A cowed expression. He poked around with a feeling that reminded him of touring the empty houses left behind by homicide victims. Most of the photos were of Kristin together with her husband, Wesley—his arm wrapped around her shoulders, as often as not, in a possessive sort of way. Wesley always seemed to bear the same chest-puffed pose and same pretend tough guy expression. It screamed insecurity.

Following an impulse, Severin followed a link to Wesley's own webpage on the same social media service. As expected, he found photos that Wesley had put there to convince the world of his greatness. Him on a mountain top. Him crossing the finish line of a half marathon. Him standing in front of a Mayan pyramid. Him shaking hands with the vice-president.

Severin went back to Kristin's social media webpage and scrolled through it. He studied her photos, her list of friends, and the comments people had left for her in order to ascertain who her closest acquaintances were. He wrote their names down on a note-pad, just below the names of the government officials and other interviewees mentioned in the State Department investigation report Thorvaldsson had given him. More people he might eventually want to speak with. Then he considered calling Thorvaldsson to accept the job, but held off. He'd call in the morning. It was late. And he didn't want to come across as desperate—even though he was.

SIX

The next afternoon, Severin was walking down an old alleyway of Seattle's International District, cold raindrops falling on his exposed head, the sky a dull, dark gray, the stink of half a dozen restaurant dumpsters hanging in the chilling, dank air. Multicolored neon lights glowed on overhanging signs with the names—in both English and Chinese characters—of various restaurants, tea houses, travel agencies, nail salons, and specialty shops. He was running down an address Thorvaldsson had given him—the address of what Thorvaldsson said was YSP's U.S. importer, Sun Ocean Trade. To ensure he wasn't setting off on a wild goose chase, that morning Severin ran an online search of Washington State Corporations Division records confirming that Sun Ocean Trade's current business address of record was indeed the same address Thorvaldsson had given him. Despite the chill of the large raindrops peppering his head, Severin was grateful that Sun Ocean Trade was, by happy chance, located in Seattle instead of one of the other major Pacific Coast port cities like Long Beach, Oakland, or some other faraway place.

He figured it couldn't hurt to go talk to the Sun Ocean Trade people, to see if they could give him any useful contact information. Perhaps phone numbers of company officials over in China who could tell him anything about the interactions of Kristin and her husband—and presumed widower—Wesley in the hours leading up to Kristin's disappearance.

He found the address—number 427. It was a tinted glass doorway that opened on a stairwell between two dim sum restaurants. Small placards on the narrow width of brick wall to the left of the door advertised, in English and Chinese, a Taiwanese apothecary, an accounting practice, and an acupuncture business that all apparently shared the address. Below the placards, a single, large, keyed mailbox. Severin opened the unlocked doorway, scanned the entry for motion sensors or other types of burglar alarm triggers, noted the brand and style of lock, and ascended the narrow, creaky wooden stairwell. The mouthwatering scent of ginger, frying onions, and soy sauce seeped through the risers from one or both of the dim sum restaurants on the main floor, below. Reaching the top of the stairs, Severin found himself at the end of a long, dimly lit hallway with six solid wood doors running down one side. A dozen flimsy, non-locking black plastic mailboxes were mounted on the wall to his right. Some had labels indicating the businesses to which they belonged—while some had clear plastic holders that were either empty or contained loose, easily removable business cards or pieces of paper with the names of individuals or businesses hand-written on them. None of the mailboxes were labeled with the name of YSP's importer, Sun Ocean Trade.

He made his way down the hallway, knocking on each door—three of which bore signs for the same three businesses advertised on the placards next to the front door, and three of which were unmarked. Whenever anyone answered a door, he asked whether they could tell him where the office for Sun Ocean Trade was, or where he could at least find somebody who worked for the importer. Nobody had ever heard of it. He then began asking who managed the mailboxes in the hallway, inserting or removing address labels and cards as businesses moved in and out. Each person he asked claimed to have no idea. But Severin thought it was more likely they did know, and, quite understandably, didn't want to give information to some stranger who might make trouble for somebody's cousin's unofficial, unlicensed post office box business. Nobody answered his knocks on the unmarked doors. What was behind them was anybody's guess. But he noted with interest that they were secured by nothing more than simple knob locks.

Mildly frustrated but, given his customs experience, hardly surprised at not being able to find any trace of what was supposed to be a legitimate and thriving import firm, Severin cheered himself up with an excellent and excessive dim sum lunch at the better looking of the two restaurants downstairs. Sweet and sour spareribs, pork dumplings, braised beef noodle soup, a steamed black sesame bun, a rice cake, and hot jasmine tea. After that, his belly uncomfortably full, he went home and took a two-hour nap.

*****

Just after 11 that night, in a move that was so out of character it made him laugh out loud, Severin was back in front of door number 427. He stood in shadow and sheltered from the pouring rain in the shallow recess of the entrance, pausing to look over his shoulder every few seconds as he patiently worked at the deadbolt lock with an old-fashioned set of picks he'd held onto from his detective days on the assumption he'd one day have to break into his own house after losing his keys while stumbling around drunk. The nonsensical shouts of a mentally ill or drugged out and presumably homeless man echoed through the streets.

Severin was out of practice, and it was incredibly tedious work. But 15 minutes and one hair-raising pass by a Seattle Police Department patrol car later, he had the deadbolt sprung. He stepped inside, closed the door silently behind him, and tiptoed up the stairwell by the dim glow of a nearby streetlight that shined through the tinted glass. At the top of the stairs, he switched on a tiny but amazingly bright key ring LED light to illuminate the floor of the dark hallway. First, he checked each of the black plastic mailboxes. Finding nothing of interest—certainly nothing to or from Sun Ocean Trade or the sorghum processor YSP—he strode to the first unmarked door. It was one of the three at which nobody had answered his knocks during his earlier visit. He popped the simple knob lock with a bent polycarbonate butter knife he'd brought along from a set of backpacker's flatware he'd dug out of one of his closets, stepped inside, and scanned the room with his LED. It appeared to be nothing more than a storage room for one of the first-floor dim sum restaurants—containing, among other things, plastic containers of spices, giant cans of cooking oil, burlap sacks of rice, crates of new water glasses, and a stack of surplus banquet chairs. The next door he opened revealed an empty room. There wasn't even a lightbulb in the lone socket. Finally, the third door opened on haphazard stacks of cardboard boxes. He opened one to find it full of documents—all of them in Chinese. He couldn't be sure, but his best guess was that they were invoices of some sort. Even the phone numbers were foreign. He had no way of knowing what type of transactions the documents might have recorded—whether for services, products, or anything else. Digging down through the box, he found it contained more of the same—as did all of the other boxes. With the idea that he'd find a translator, he used his smartphone to take photographs of documents that appeared to be representative of each box.

Annoyed that he hadn't found anything obviously useful, he took a deep breath, buttoned up his coat, and made his way back out into the cold, rainy night. If Sun Ocean Trading had ever really existed, and if they actually had an office at this address, they were long gone.

SEVEN

"Hey, Man Pretty," Severin said into his phone. "It's almost 10 a.m. You sound sleepy. Did I wake you?"

"Who—Lars?" Wallace Zhang said.

"How did you guess?"

"You're the only person who has ever called me Man Pretty," he said through a yawn.

"I'm sure other people think you're pretty, even if they don't say so." Severin paused, pondering where to begin. "So, anyway, do you still speak Chinese?"

"Do I still speak Chinese? Of course. What the f—"

"Listen, I have something I want to ask you about. Let me buy you a beer. You still live in Seattle, right? Or did you just keep your old cell phone number?"

"No, I still live in the Seattle area. Federal Way."

"Near your parents' old place?" Zhang was silent. "Wallace, tell me you didn't move back into your parents' basement."

"From a financial standpoint—"

"Oh, Wallace. Oh, wow."

"It's so nice to hear from you, Lars. So very, very nice."

"Busy this morning?"

"It's Tuesday."

"Busy?"

A pause. "No."

"Want to meet at our old U-District haunt?"

"Big Time Brewery? Does it still exist?"

"Opens at 11:30."

"Beer for breakfast?"

"Brunch."

"It's a little early, don't you think?"

"Oh, I'm sorry. I thought I was talking to Wallace Zhang."

"Lars—"

"*You* don't approve? That's actually funny."

"I don't hear from you in years and years, and now you want me to meet you for a beer breakfast. What's this about?"

"Long story. I'll explain when I see you. Suffice it to say there may be some serious money in it for you."

*****

Severin was already half way through his first beer when Wallace Zhang strode through the front door of the old brewpub, with its familiar high ceilings, dark wood-paneled walls, and antique bar, a block or so from the picturesque University of Washington campus. Severin and Zhang were dorm roommates during their freshman and sophomore years at UW. After that, they moved into studio apartments on opposite ends of the vast campus and drifted apart for no particular reasons aside from their having divergent class schedules and living in different corners of the University District. Zhang had been quite a football star at Decatur High School. An all-conference cornerback until an overmatched and pissed off wide receiver from a crosstown rival threw a chop block at his right thigh, blowing his knee out and fracturing his femur during a game midway through his senior season. He was tall, still muscular, in good shape for his age, and carried himself with the poise of a man who'd been through the gauntlet more than once and knew he could take it. He was overdressed, as always. His clothes perfectly pressed. His hair coated in heaven only knew what sort of shiny *en vogue* men's grooming product and sculpted to magazine photoshoot perfection. He was handsome enough for Severin to find it irritating. Severin thought Zhang could pass as a double for the actor Chow Yun-Fat from the films *Crouching Tiger, Hidden Dragon* and *The Replacement Killers.* When he spotted Severin, he grinned and shook his head. They shook hands, bumping chests in the manner of surfers or rugby teammates.

"So what the hell, Lars?"

"First things first. What will you have? Atlas Amber Ale, right?"

"Good memory."

Severin ordered his second as Zhang ordered his first.

"So the bartender tells me they're planning to tear down our old dorm," Severin said. "Probably because you and your digestive issues turned our room into a hazmat site. Cheaper to tear down than clean up."

"I didn't choose to be lactose intolerant."

"But you did choose to keep drinking chocolate milk."

"I like chocolate milk."

"So what has your pretty self been up to?" Severin asked.

"What have I been up to? You mean in the hundred or whatever years since you last called me?"

"Yeah. You're a doctor, right?"

Zhang yawned. "No, Lars. I'm not a doctor. Are you?"

"No. Married?"

"No. You?"

"Please."

"Girlfriend, at least?" Zhang asked.

"Sort of. Until a couple of days ago, I guess."

"Well, you know what my old friend Bill says," Zhang said through a yawn. "Most friendship is feigning, most loving mere folly."

"Oh, no."

In their time as roommates, after they'd dared each other to take the same class on Elizabethan literature in order to knock out dreaded liberal arts credit requirements, they would try to drive each other insane with quotes—usually bastardized—from the works of William Shakespeare.

"*Merchant of Venice*?" Severin asked.

"*As You Like It.*"

"Could we please not restart that?"

"Hard to say," Zhang said with a grin. "Especially since you insist on calling me Man Pretty."

"Point taken."

"So you're not a ladies' man then?" Zhang asked.

"No, sure I'm a ladies' man. Women love my self-defecating sense of humor."

"Good one. Shakespeare again?"

"The Capitol Steps," Severin said.

"The what?"

"D.C. comedy troupe. Never mind."

"So why only until a couple of days ago?" Zhang asked. "The girlfriend, I mean."

"I don't know. I always seem to end up sabotaging relationships some way or another."

"So, no med school? I know you had the grades. And you kicked ass on the MCAT, right? Didn't you get accepted anywhere?"

"Yeah. Couple of schools. UCLA. Georgetown."

"I thought you were going to be an orthopedic surgeon," Zhang said. "What happened?"

"I don't know. It's hard to explain." A pause. "Did you know my parents were killed just before we graduated?"

"No. Both of them? What happened?" Zhang asked.

"They decided to take an after-dinner walk along the tulip fields down the hill from their house."

"In LaConner?"

"Yes. Drunk washing machine repairman ran them down in his box truck. Didn't even realize he'd hit them. Drove home to his place in Stanwood. When they found him an hour later, he was watching a basketball game on ESPN and eating a bag of Doritos."

"I'm sorry, Lars. I had no idea."

"It was a long time ago. I didn't really advertise it. Plus, it was before social networking web sites and all that crap. Anyway, I guess I sort of went off the rails for a bit. Couldn't really motivate myself to do anything, let alone register for med school. Everything just all of a sudden seemed so petty, you know?" He took a hefty drink of his beer. "But what about you? You were going to med school too, weren't you?"

"I didn't even end up taking the MCAT," Zhang said.

"Why not?"

"I suppose the first crack in the road came when I was studying for a final exam in advanced biology and found that I just couldn't motivate myself to memorize the evolution of molecular structures in the Kreb Cycle."

"You know what?" Severin said, grinning. "I *still* have recurring final exam nightmares about not remembering how to draw the molecule for Acetyl-coenzyme-A."

"Then there was that time I threw up on my partner's arm in biology lab after getting motion sick from trying to count how many fruit flies had red or white eyes under a microscope while breathing formaldehyde vapors. But really, the final straw came during the summer after our junior year, when I interned at a family practice. The experience made me realize I'd never had any genuine interest in being a doctor. It also made me realize that I'd been following the med school track to please my parents. To meet their expectations. Maybe finally be deemed worthy of their approval and unconditional love."

"Damn, Wallace. I never knew you to have a shred of self-awareness. I don't even know who you are anymore." That got Zhang grinning. "Your parents were definitely of the emotionally unavailable taskmaster variety though, weren't they?"

"They were. They are. So I bugged out. Went to Alaska for a year. Worked on a factory trawler until I had enough money to buy a car. Came back down here and started DJing."

"You? A DJ? That's cool. And by cool, I mean something only a total tool would do."

"Took some computer programming classes. Started doing contract coding work. Supplemented my income for a little while dealing ecstasy at the rave parties I DJ'd. Sometimes weed. Nothing too crazy."

"You were a drug dealer?" Severin asked.

"Not a very serious one. It was just until the computer work started to pay."

"Do you use?"

"Smoke."

"A lot?"

"Whenever I can."

"That's not how I expected *you* to end up, of all people."

"Guess I kind of went off the rails too. So what's on your *curriculum vitae*?"

"Well, I was in law enforcement for a while," Severin said with a wide grin.

Zhang's eyebrows rose, his face betraying his shock. "You're joking. You're a cop?"

"Was. And not a very serious one," he said with a wink.

"Damn. That's not where I expected you to end up, either."

"Life is funny that way. After college, I was a patrolman up in Anacortes for about three years. Had a bit of a penchant for nailing drunk drivers."

"I can imagine."

"Was a detective for three years after that. The youngest detective ever on the force, actually. Then six years with U.S. Customs. Three as a special agent. Three as assistant customs attaché to the American embassy in Seoul, South Korea."

"What does customs attaché mean?"

"I was a sort of intelligence officer."

"What did you do?"

"All sorts of things."

"Like what?"

"Oh, you know. It's hard to explain without, uh—"

"Never mind."

"Since then, I've been doing investigations and audits for this outfit called Agrisymbiosis here in Seattle. It's what they call a third-party organic farm certifier."

"A what?"

"It's a company that farms pay to certify them as being in accordance with organic farming practices."

"What could you possibly need to investigate?"

"Mostly it's just checking their books to make sure they aren't secretly buying pesticides from Dow Chemical, genetically modified seed from Monsanto, or stuff like that. Looking for disguised or otherwise suspicious expenditures. They test the soil, too. But I'm not involved with that part of it."

"Why did you leave Customs? Especially an overseas posting? Isn't that a totally plum job?"

"Long story."

"Huh."

"Looks like neither of us are where we thought we'd be," Severin said. "But here we are."

"Do you ever hear from any of the guys from the dorm?" Zhang asked.

"I heard Tim Dawson is a millionaire investment banker or some such thing."

"That meathead?"

"I know. Crazy, right?"

"Jeff Tully is a heart surgeon," Zhang said. "Invented some sort of surgical tool that made him a fortune. Four kids. Hottie, totally cool wife who is a 767 pilot for UPS. They live in a Tudor style palace on Lake Washington, about five doors down from Bill Gates."

"Good for him." Severin looked reflective for a moment. "Do you ever wonder where you'd be if you'd just stayed the course? Not gone off the rails?"

"I don't know."

"We'd probably be rich orthopedic surgeons with big houses, wives, and kids. Big family Christmas gatherings. Vacations to Hawaii."

"Innumerable birthday parties at Chuck E. Cheese."

"Well, yes. But still."

"You sound a little sad," Zhang said.

"I'm not."

"So you're happy?"

"What a question."

"Really, though. Are you happy?"

"I'm too smart and well-informed to be happy."

"That's profound, Lars."

"I just wonder about how things could have been, if not for this, that, or the other thing, you know? I mean look at Dawson and Tully. We all lived on the same dorm floor. Ate the same food. Took a lot of the same classes. Probably wore the same brand of striped bikini briefs. It's just odd to consider that at one time we were all on more or less the same road."

"And then we took the one less traveled, and that made all the difference?"

"The difference being that you live in your parents' basement, Mr. Frost, while I'm edging ever closer to vagrancy."

"Comparison is the thief of joy," Zhang said.

"Shakespeare again?"

"Teddy Roosevelt."

"Remind me not to play against you in Trivial Pursuit."

*****

For the next 10 minutes—after learning that Zhang's anemic software design career left ample time for other things—Severin filled him in on the details of the Thorvaldsson case.

"Sounds like *The Girl with the Dragon Tattoo*," Zhang said.

"Sort of, I guess. Anyway, after a week or two of all-expenses-paid high adventure, if we can find enough information to make these people happy, they're going to cut me a check for $10,000," he lied, "which I'll split with you 50/50. Strictly under the table."

"Five thousand dollars tax free? And you want me to work with you because—what?—I speak Chinese?"

"And for your big brain and hacking skills."

"I'm not a hacker, Lars. I don't know how to do any of that crap."

"But you know people who do."

He gave Severin a dubious look. "Maybe. But I don't have any investigative experience either."

"It isn't rocket science. We aren't going to be processing any crime scenes or performing any autopsies. Go with your gut. Or just follow my lead. At any rate, it's always good to have two brains. Things will occur to you that won't occur to me."

"What about licensing and jurisdiction?"

"We're just going to be talking to people. Having conversations. That's it. No interrogations. No waterboarding. If folks don't want to talk to us, so be it. We'll say we tried. Think of it as akin to us being journalists. We're just writing our article for the Thorvaldssons instead of *The Seattle Times*."

Zhang looked skeptical. "What's your plan of attack?"

"The family suspects the husband, of course. And he worked with her at the U.S. Department of Commerce. So I figured, if they're willing, which is a big question mark, I'd talk to the government people who were involved in the investigation, Kristin Powell's friends and coworkers, and the people who last saw her alive over in China. Then, once we have a clearer picture of what might have gone down, we can rattle the husband's cage a bit to see what kind of feel he gives us. In general, I want to talk to as many people in the U.S. as possible before worrying about going to China. Maybe we won't need to."

"Why doesn't Thorvaldsson just hire a private detective in China?"

"And pay a Chinse detective instead of us? Come on. Who knows and who cares? Let's make some money." Severin took a big gulp of his beer. "Although that does remind me, there is one other aspect."

"What other aspect?"

"It doesn't make a lot of sense that these people would hire me, a washed up burnout, if everything was truly above board. For that matter, there's a lot of information blacked out or left out of the U.S. State Department's report of investigation. It could be—or rather, it's *probably* just your basic run-of-the-mill sensitive information. Stuff the State Department doesn't want to have advertised to the general public for whatever reason. To keep the names of their own personnel out of the media shit-storm. To keep their personnel from getting into hot water with the Chinese where maybe their visas are revoked or they're put on the blacklist and denied future entry. Maybe to protect the job security or even safety of Chinese nationals who agreed to talk to the State Department investigators. That type of thing."

"But . . . ."

"But it's at least a little bit odd—something diligence demands we learn more about."

"What else could it be?"

"I don't know. And admittedly, I've been out of the game for a while so my intuition is rusty."

"Never knew you had any."

"But when I channel my inner Sherlock Holmes, it tells me that Thorvaldsson is holding something back. Maybe something embarrassing about his niece. Maybe something else he knew about the government investigation. I can't put a finger on it. Assuming there even is an *it*. But my gut tells me there's definitely more to the story here. So I suppose that before I do anything else, I'll want to talk to any government types who might be able to paint a fuller picture of the circumstances of the investigation, explain why the report is so small, and so forth—starting with the U.S. Department of Commerce official who signed off on the State Department report. She should be able to shed some light."

"What part of China is this company, Yin . . . ."

"Yinzhen Sorghum Processing, or YSP for short."

"What part of China is YSP in?"

"Shandong Province. It's on the edge of the town of Yinzhen, 50 or 60 miles inland and southwest of the port city of Qingdao. You know where those are?"

"I know Qingdao. My mom's people were from around Jinan, which isn't too far away."

"So they'll speak the same dialect as you?"

"That's why I asked. But yes, I think so. They should speak Mandarin there."

"Oh, that reminds me," Severin said, drawing his smartphone from his pocket. "Take a look at this." He showed Zhang a photograph of one of the documents he'd found during his break-in of the night before. "Can you tell what this deals with?"

"It looks like an order from a construction company in Taipei, Taiwan, to another Taiwanese company of some kind. For plastic pipe, I think. Yes, I'm pretty sure it's for plastic pipe. Does that help you?"

"Are either of the companies called Sun Ocean Trade or Yinzhen Sorghum Processing?"

"No. Not even close."

"Anything to indicate that something is being imported or exported?"

Zhang looked closely. "No. These are domestic Taiwanese transactions."

They looked through Severin's photos of the other sample documents only to discover that they were similarly irrelevant. Severin was frustrated by the apparent dead-end, but encouraged by what he took to be a look of puzzle solver's curiosity on Zhang's face as he eyeballed the documents. "So you're interested?" Severin asked at last. Zhang looked thoughtful for a moment. Severin couldn't hold back. "Wallace, what's to consider? You're living in your parents' basement, for Pete's sake."

"Hey now."

"Probably still driving that piece of crap white Volkswagen Golf."

"No, old White Dog finally gave up the ghost. Timing belt broke. Trashed the engine."

"So what are you driving now? Wait—I'll take a stab. Former DJ, former drug dealer, clubber, living in his parents' basement. Poser. Clothes horse. Exotic ancestry. Let's see. If you made a little more money, you'd be driving a BMW 3-series. But you're doing bit contract work. So I'm going to go with a Honda Accord with some sort of ridiculous aftermarket spoiler and probably a corny blue LED light decoration in the rear window or on the license plate. Trying to make your car look like KITT."

"KITT?"

"Come on, Wallace. The car with artificial intelligence from Knight Rider? Eighties TV show starring David Hasselhoff?"

"Yes, Lars. I remember Knight Rider, thank you."

"So did I nail it?"

Zhang looked mildly irritated. "They teach you how to do that in racial profiling class back at redneck police academy?"

"Ha! I nailed it, didn't I?"

"Ass."

"So you'll do it, right? You can use that $5,000 to tint your car's windows."

"They're already tinted."

"Of course they are. So?"

"It's a hackneyed plot."

"It's a what?"

"This whole thing. It's unoriginal. Former lawman, his life a mess, looking for redemption or whatever? I can get 20 different movie versions of that on my TV right now, on-demand, without so much as getting off my couch."

"Redemption? I just want the money, Dr. Freud."

"Only cartoon characters have singularity of motive."

"And maybe a little change of scenery," Severin added.

"That's it? Private investigators are supposed to be driven by a unique sense of justice or whatever."

"Where are you getting that?"

"I took a creative writing class that covered the attributes of the major mystery subgenres. Hard boiled. Police procedural. Cozy. That sort of thing."

"You gonna be a mystery writer?" Severin asked before tipping his glass back and finishing the last third off his beer.

"Nah. There's no money in it."

Severin half slammed his empty glass down on the table. "Alright. Quit playing hard to get. Are you in or not? It's not like you have anything else worthwhile going on, right?"

Zhang gave him a long stare. "Sure. Why not?"

"Why not, indeed. With me leading the way, what could possibly go wrong?" Severin said with a grin. "Good. I'll book you a ticket to D.C. With any luck, we'll stumble across what we're looking for there. Then we won't even have to go to China. Speaking of which, do you have a valid passport?"

"Of course."

"Bring it by my place, and I'll mail it with mine to an express service that can get our Chinese visas on an expedited basis, just in case we do end up having to go."

"I'll get it to you today."

"So there aren't any issues with you going to China?"

"Because my folks were émigrés? No. Word in the expat communities is that the Chinese government doesn't really give a crap anymore. And I was born here anyway. They shouldn't have anything against me."

They left the brewpub, walking down the sidewalk until they came to Zhang's car—a lowered, white Honda Accord with an aftermarket spoiler and an LED light array clearly visible through the rear window.

"Good lord, Wallace. Next Christmas, I'm going to get you a custom license plate that says *douchebag.*"

"There's a limit of seven characters for vanity plates."

*****

Going back over the State Department report at his apartment that evening, Severin noted that the Commerce Department investigator who disappeared along with Kristin Powell was a young man named Bill Keen. Using nothing more than Google and a couple of internet social media networking pages, Severin was able to track down a phone number for Keen's widowed mother in Minneapolis. He asked the usual battery of questions. Was her son in any sort of trouble that she was aware of? Did she know of anyone with any antipathy toward him? Did he owe anyone money? Could she think of anything unusual about her son's behavior or activities leading up to his departure to China? But the call was unproductive. "You know boys," she'd said. "They never tell their mothers anything. I was clueless about his personal life." Indeed, she didn't know the names or phone numbers of any of his Washington, D.C. friends. All she had was a handful of names of his old high school and college friends, none of whom had been more than minimally involved in his life for many years. At best, he might have met a couple of them for a quick evening beer in one of those odd years when he'd even bothered to come home for Christmas.

Then Keen's mother, sounding lonely and grateful for the conversation, went on and on about her five cats, the University of Minnesota Golden Gophers hockey team, and the weather in Minneapolis, before at last offering a little bit more about her son. Prior to taking the job at Commerce, he spent nearly two years working as an engineer at a shipyard in Groton, Connecticut. Before that, he did a four-year stint in the U.S. Navy, in something called MASINT—measurement and signature intelligence—whatever that was. He also graduated with honors from the University of Minnesota with a commission via NROTC and a double major in Arabic and electrical engineering—an interesting combination. With a double major like that, how did he end up at the Commerce Department working on international trade investigations, Severin wondered?

Severin gathered that the Keens had never been a terribly close-knit family. But with her husband long dead, and her son disappeared, the widow's sense of loss, of profound loneliness, weighed down her every word. Severin knew the feeling. Her mention of Christmas took him back to that first Christmas after his parents were gone. None of his acquaintances had thought to invite him over. He had an aunt, an uncle, and two cousins back in Vermont, but he was the last known member of his family west of the Mississippi. And though he'd tried to mentally prepare himself for it, Christmas Day was an emotional black hole. He'd loaded it with non-stop activity. He went skiing up at Stevens Pass. He watched two movies at the local, tastelessly designed megaplex. And, when he finally had to bite the bullet and go home to his tiny apartment, he mixed himself a bunch of classic cocktails he'd never tried before—like the mint julep, Sazerac, and old fashioned—hoping the alcohol would soften the emotional pain he felt, or better yet render him incognizant, until the next day. Later, still unable to sleep, and at an entirely indecent hour, he went so far as to try to call two ex-girlfriends on the slim chance that they were sitting in their apartments and not off at happy family gatherings of their own. But neither picked up. Their phones rang and rang. Their voicemail messages played. And after each beep, Severin sat listening to the silence for a moment before hanging up. Nothing he did that Christmas came anywhere near to filling the void in his heart.

EIGHT

Three days later, Severin and Zhang flew from Seattle to Washington, D.C., their airliner banking this way and that as it descended through the winding, hair-raising upriver approach to Reagan National Airport, dodging invisible zones of restricted airspace along the way. Having never been to D.C., Zhang was glued to the left-side window as they passed Georgetown, the White House, and the Lincoln and Jefferson memorials while the pilots more or less followed the path of the Potomac River.

By the time they checked into their concrete monolith of a hotel in Arlington, it was too late to get anything accomplished, so they settled down in the sterile, dark hotel bar for a few Manhattans and an unimpressive plate of hot wings before calling it a night.

*****

The next afternoon in the hotel lobby, Zhang, who was wearing thick glasses because he couldn't find his contacts, was surprised to see Severin emerge from the elevator wearing a relatively stylish suit.

"Wow," Zhang said. "You clean up well."

"I'm glad I could surprise you."

"Go ahead. Let's get it out of the way."

"Get what out of the way?" Severin asked.

"You're looking at my glasses. Go ahead and make some smart comment about all Asians being myopic or whatever."

"All I was going to say was that I appreciate your dedication."

"My dedication?"

"To our job. It must be traumatizing for someone who's as vain as you are to appear in public with those ridiculous Bill Gates glasses."

"I can't find my contacts."

"So I assumed."

They headed for their rendezvous with the former U.S. Department of Commerce official who signed off on the State Department's report, boarding a Blue Line subway train at the Rosslyn Metro station after walking down the staggeringly long but non-functional escalator. Every seat in the train car was taken, so Severin and Zhang had to stand, holding a floor-to-ceiling pole for balance as the train started moving. They passed under the Potomac River, crossing from Virginia into D.C. At the next stop, Foggy Bottom, a woman boarded who was clearly at least eight months pregnant. She grabbed the same pole Severin and Zhang were sharing and wobbled as the train jerked forward. Severin looked around, double-checking for a seat for her. All around them, the seats were taken up by perfectly able-bodied 30-something-year-old men, their noses glued to their smart phones and notebook devices as they pretended not to notice there was a pregnant woman standing in their midst.

Severin scrutinized the closest of the seated men, and when he found the one he thought looked the most uptight, the one with the shiniest shoes and most ridiculously oversized and showy wristwatch—in this case, a Versace—he made his move. "Pardon me, sir. Would you be kind enough to let this pregnant woman take your seat?"

The man met Severin's eyes with a look that would freeze water.

"Oh, of course," the man said, rising and grabbing a handrail.

Oh, of course, Severin repeated in his mind, having an inward chuckle over his long-held belief that oversized wristwatches were to D.C. what oversized pickup trucks were to the rest of the country.

As the woman sat down, thanking the Versace guy, Severin muttered another degradation of Shakespeare: "So shines a good deed in a city of self-centered schmucks."

Zhang broke into a wide grin.

"What was that?" Versace guy said, turning his eyes to Severin.

"What was what?"

"Did you say something?"

"*Did* I say something?" Severin gave Versace guy a hard stare until Versace guy decided Severin wasn't somebody he should challenge and looked back down at his smartphone.

Severin scanned the faces of the other seated men. Having picked up on Severin's vaguely menacing tone, they glanced at Versace guy, then at one another, and finally back up at Versace guy. And Severin swore that they were each acknowledging the shared telepathy he always suspected the tightest of Washington assholes had the power to send and receive. The presumed message: *Sorry you lost your seat, sucker. But better you than me.*

As the train rumbled along its track, Zhang caught Severin eyeballing the other riders with a funny, almost disgusted look on his face. "What is it?" Zhang asked, under his breath.

"All these people. I mean, look at them. The suits. The intensity. The ambition."

"What of it?"

"Where does it come from? Why are we so different from them?"

"You mean why are we such losers?"

"Nice. Really, though. What's it about?"

"Power, grasshopper. A lust for power."

"I know *that*. I mean what drives it?"

Zhang thought for a moment. "They have an above average fear of the dark."

"And?"

"And nothing."

"An above average fear of the dark," Severin echoed, shaking his head. "Whatever that means."

*****

They got off the subway at the McPherson Square station and emerged on the surface in the heart of the capital. There wasn't anything particularly noteworthy about the block they were on, as it consisted of nothing more than midrise office buildings that would have looked normal in any U.S. city. But as they walked down 15th Street toward the Old Ebbitt Grill, location of their lunch meeting, they crossed Pennsylvania Avenue and were afforded impressive views of tree-lined Lafayette Square and the block-long, Greek Revival-style U.S. Treasury building with its massive granite columns. They also caught peek-a-boo views of the White House, a mere two blocks to their right, as well as the headquarters for the U.S. Department of Commerce, a few blocks straight ahead of them.

As they walked, Severin sensed the frenetic pace of the city. Cars racing this way and that, their drivers accelerating to close any gap between themselves and the cars in front of them. Cars at traffic lights jerking forward, inch-by-inch, in momentary false starts as their drivers sat in taut anticipation of sustained forward progress, of a light turning green. Car horns honking with unfathomable frequency. As he remembered from his time living there, D.C. seemed to encompass an almost constant state of urgency, of people bursting at the seams to get ahead of each other—in traffic, on Metro station escalators, in the ordering lines of the innumerable chain sandwich shops.

"Why does everybody honk their horns so much here?" Zhang asked. "It's insane."

"It's a hostile town."

"Hostile to what?"

"Anything that gets in its way."

"Charming."

"I'll tell you, Wallace, this place is hard on people. Chews them up. Sucks the humanity out of them. A lot of folks can't stay here long-term without blowing a gasket."

*****

At the Old Ebbitt Grill, a smartly dressed host led them past the long mahogany bar, through a room decorated with old paintings, antique chandeliers, and even the mounted heads of animals allegedly shot by Teddy Roosevelt, back to a booth where Tracy Fiskar, former bigwig with the U.S. Department of Commerce, waited for them. Severin didn't expect to like her. He thought of D.C. movers and shakers as a largely tiresome breed. Usually too self-absorbed and focused on whatever they were striving for to have any facets to their personalities that might be of interest to people who lived outside the Beltway. Overachievers with more flash than substance.

"Ms. Fiskar?" She rose to shake hands, revealing her power suit. She had keen eyes, a sly grin, and an aura of boundless energy about her. No doubt the frenetic pace of D.C. suited her to a T. "I'm Lars Severin. This is my associate, Wallace Zhang."

"Ms. Fiskar is my mother. Call me Tracy, please."

"Tracy then. Thanks for agreeing to meet."

"Hey, people in my line of work are always looking for a free lunch. Speaking of which," Fiskar said, picking up a menu as they all sat down. "If you're an oyster fan, they have local Chesapeake Bay oysters today. Some from Apalachicola too."

"No, thanks," Severin said. "I prefer my oysters to come from water I can see through."

"Huh?"

"Water that's blue instead of brown."

"Ah, so you're a West Coast oyster snob," she said, smiling.

"Unapologetically."

"Me too, truth be told. I grew up in the Pacific Northwest. Washington State."

"How refreshing. Us too. Federal Way for Wallace, La Conner for me."

"I'm from Tacoma."

"Oh, I'm sorry."

She laughed. "Yes, but that's just one of many factors contributing to the inferiority complex that drives my type-A personality. Anyway, I see that there are some oysters on today's list that come from Maine. They have clear water, don't they? Wallace? You in?" Zhang gave a nod. "Two dozen?"

"Works for me," Zhang said.

"Dirty martinis?" she added

"Marry me," Severin said.

They made a bit of small talk about the weather and what new exhibits at the Smithsonian they should see while in town before their drinks and large tray of shucked oysters on crushed ice arrived.

"So, how are you two involved in this again?" Fiskar asked.

Severin grinned. "It won't sound any more plausible than it did when I told you over the phone. Not to me, anyway."

She gave Severin a good, long look, then shrugged her shoulders. "Alright. I'll take it on faith. I guess if you have a secret evil agenda, it won't be the first time someone tells me I told you so."

"This is D.C.," Severin said. "So you never really know."

"I don't know anything that's classified, anyway," Fiskar said. "So screw it. Fire away. I'll tell you what I can."

"Well, as I mentioned on the phone, Kristin Powell's family has asked us to cast a wide net. I suppose the threshold question, assuming she was killed, is whether or not it was random. If it wasn't—if there was more to it—then the next thing we need is a better idea of the context. Given that you were the Commerce Department official who signed off on the State Department's report, we figure you're the one to ask."

"I can see how you'd think that," Fiskar said. "But I'm afraid I'm going to have to probably lower your expectations a bit. For one thing, I didn't know Kristin Powell or Bill Keen personally. I knew *of* them. And I'm sure we attended some of the same meetings. But it's a big administration, and I really only knew the people I worked with every day. Another thing is that my signature on the State Department report was, unfortunately, nothing more than a formality. It might as well have been a rubber stamp that said *Commerce acknowledges receipt of report and deems it satisfactory, regardless of content, because it doesn't want to make waves.* I wasn't involved in the investigation, wasn't privy to anything special, and nobody was interested in my genuine opinion of the substance of the report. They didn't so much as give me leeway to correct the State Department agents' crap grammar and spelling errors."

"So how was it that you were the one to sign off on it?" Zhang asked.

"An excellent question, Wallace. There was certainly nothing in my background or job description that would seem to qualify me. At the same time, dealing with an investigation into the disappearance of our employees was, thankfully, something of an unusual if not entirely novel problem. Something Commerce doesn't really have an office to deal with. But we had to be involved on some level, simply because they were our employees. So, for reasons unknown, they tapped me. Maybe they figured I'd keep my mouth shut. Poor judgement on their part." She chuckled. "I take it you've already seen the public version of the report."

"Yes."

"Then I hate to say it, but you probably know as much as I do."

"You mean they didn't give you the full, classified version?"

"Nope."

"Do you have any idea why there was so much redacting, or what was contained in the classified annex that wasn't included in the public version?" Severin asked.

"Not a clue. Apparently I'm important enough to sign off on it, thereby concurring on its adequacy, but not important enough to actually know its full contents. Welcome to my world."

"Do you have any reason to believe it involved any sort of national security or espionage matter?"

"Anything is possible in this town. But I really have no idea. And if I were in the know on such a thing, I'd have to pretend to not know anyway, right?" she said with a wink.

"Your title at the Commerce Department was special assistant?" Zhang asked.

"That's right."

"What is that, exactly?"

"Some would probably say office plant waterer. There's no standard definition. For me, it meant that I was the high chamberlain—essentially, the senior policy advisor and cutout—to Byron Edwards, former Assistant Secretary of Commerce for Enforcement and Compliance. In layman's language, he was the ranking political appointee of our division. Probably the hottest position in the world of U.S. international trade law enforcement."

"But Edwards no longer holds that position?"

"No. Now he's over at the Office of the United States Trade Representative. USTR for short. An outfit that barely has the budget to keep its building heated. Bunch of prima donnas who steal credit for other people's work. Edwards should fit right in. He was never good for much more than reading talking points and looking pretty."

"Why did he get demoted?"

"He wasn't. He wanted the position. It's a lesser job in an intellectual sense. But it gets your lips a little bit closer to the President's butt. And the closer their lips come to the President's butt, the cooler the USTR folks think they are—by association, anyway."

By now, Severin wore a wide smile. "Such irreverence."

"Well, I'm in the private sector now. So they can all bite me."

"You aren't a fan of Byron Edwards?"

She shrugged. "He's an archetype of the male D.C. striver."

"What does that mean?" Zhang asked.

"He's a power-hungry, womanizing slime bag. A purebred egomaniac."

Severin nearly laughed. "You know, Tracy, at the end of the day, men are simple creatures with simple needs. All we want is total power and control over everything, constant reassurance that we're great in bed, and immortality."

"Is that all?"

"Really, just those three things."

"So you left government and now you're with a consulting firm?" Zhang asked.

"Yes. We lobby on behalf of various Chinese business and trade groups."

"The irony."

"Economic necessity. It's what we do here in D.C., Wallace. Build up experience, connections, and clout working for the government—then go mercenary, selling our knowledge and influence to the highest bidder."

Severn nodded, pondering Fiskar's seeming hypocrisy, and finished his martini. "Well, we've come this far, so I suppose we'll ask you our little questions even if you didn't get to read the full classified version of the report."

"Do I think the disappearance was random? Like the team just happened to catch an airport cab being driven by a Chinese serial killer or whatever?"

"Or whatever."

She looked away, toward a painting behind the bar. "Well . . . ."

"Let me put it another way. Do you have any reason at all to even begin to suspect that it *wasn't* random?"

She took a breath. "I don't believe it was random. But I don't have anything concrete for you. I don't have anything specific to base that on. It's just a gut feeling. A funny smell that I might just be imagining."

Severin nodded, thoughtful. "There was surprisingly little substance to the State Department report."

"Oh, I agree with you. A handful of superficial interviews. A few paragraphs of conjecture. It's an empty document masquerading as a legitimate report. It screams *we don't really care. We just want this to go away.*"

"Why would they want that?" Severin asked. "And why would they want the signatories to be people who'd keep quiet?"

"They didn't want it to rock the boat. It was a sensitive time with respect to trade agreement negotiations that were underway with the Chinese. Negotiations being spearheaded by Byron Edwards."

"For what trade agreement?"

"A deal that would protect our soybean exports to China by setting annual export quantities and prices. Long story short, China was threatening to slap punitive tariffs on our soybeans in a thinly veiled retaliation for our imposition of punitive tariffs on unfairly priced Chinese steel exports to the U.S. The tariffs we slapped on Chinese steel were a result of what's called an antidumping investigation. Incidentally, it was an antidumping investigation of Chinese sorghum syrup exports to the U.S. that Kristin Powell and Bill Keen were working on when they disappeared."

"What's an antidumping investigation?" Severin asked.

"In layman's language, it's an investigation into unfair, anticompetitive pricing by foreign companies. Where prices on imported foreign goods are set so low that it seems they're intended to destroy a U.S. industry."

Zhang looked perplexed. "Let's see if I'm tracking," he said. "One: at the end of an antidumping investigation of Chinese steel exports to the U.S., the Commerce Department determined that Chinese companies were exporting steel at anticompetitive prices and slapped tariffs on Chinese steel. Two: In retaliation, China threatened to slap tariffs on U.S. soybean exports to China. Three: you were in the process of negotiating a trade agreement to protect U.S. soybean exports to China."

"There's more to it, of course. But, essentially, yes. You've got the idea. Now then, if anything had derailed the soybean agreement negotiations, the very powerful U.S. soybean lobby would have gone completely ape shit and threatened to cut off campaign contributions to every senator from a soybean producing state. After changing their underwear, each of those senators would have then threatened every executive branch loser they could find a phone number for with budget cuts, permanently stalled careers, and un-anesthetized castration. Byron Edwards would have been the first one in line to lose his testicles."

"So, bottom line," Zhang said, "because of the soybean agreement negotiations, everybody was walking on eggshells with the Chinese?"

"Which is why the powers that be, including Edwards, wanted the State Department investigation into the disappearance of Powell and Keen to just go away?" Severin added

"That may not be an entirely unreasonable way of interpreting the facts," Fiskar said.

"Was the soybean agreement really so important?" Severin asked

"At the big picture level, it was huge. China is our second-largest trading partner when it comes to trade in goods. In the past 12 months alone, the U.S. goods trade deficit with China has run over $300 billion. To put that into perspective for you, that's just a hair below the entire annual GDP of Denmark. A lot of money coming out of our wallets. Now, over that same period, the U.S. exported around $120 billion in goods to China. And guess what? About $13 billion of that total was accounted for by the humble soybean."

"So soybeans are big time," Zhang said.

"They are, indeed. And as you can imagine, for Byron Edwards personally, the soybean agreement negotiations represented career life or career death. Failing to get an agreement finalized would probably have doomed him to a life of overseeing Department of Education school desk booger removal programs left over from the Carter Administration. Getting it signed, on the other hand, made him a political appointee superstar. All of a sudden all those senators up on Capitol Hill owed him a favor. *Thanks a million, old boy. You saved our vegan soy bacon.* The next time a white hot political appointee position opened up—in this case, a slot at the Office of the United States Trade Representative—Edwards was automatically put on the short list. Those were the stakes. So to hell with the disappeared Commerce investigators. Nothing was going to get in the way of Edwards cutting the soybean deal before the end of the term. No. It was his big chance. And time was short. So to hell with everything else."

"So what became of the sorghum investigation of YSP?"

"It was never completed, meaning we never sent a team back to redo the on-site examination of YSP's personnel, facility, and records over in China. Normally, a company sends us data, business records, and detailed responses to our investigative questionnaires, and then we send a team of investigators to the company to check what they've sent us against the in-person testimony of their company officials, their original business records, and so forth. In other words, the investigators go over to make double-sure a company isn't bullshitting us, giving us false information, or whatever. But in the case of YSP, because of the circumstances, we based our findings on the unverified, uncorroborated data and investigative questionnaire responses their American attorney submitted to Commerce. In other words, we took what they gave us on faith."

"So you let them off easy?"

"I can't say that with any certainty. I mean, YSP *was* assigned an uncommonly low tariff rate. In fact, I think we might even have given them a zero tariff rate—the holy grail of antidumping investigations. Whatever the case, it was the lowest tariff rate assigned to any Chinese sorghum syrup company by far. But we'll never know whether the on-site part of the investigation would have changed the results because the information Powell and Keen's report would have contained vanished right along with them."

"Is it common for the on-site part of the investigation to turn up information that leads to a higher tariff rate for the company being investigated?"

"Very. Companies make major accounting mistakes. Companies manipulate data wherever they can argue that there's wiggle room. Companies sometimes even commit outright fraud, cooking their books and so forth. Often, we can sniff that out during the on-site part of the investigation."

"So then why didn't Commerce send another team and re-do the on-site part of the investigation?" Severin asked.

"Ostensibly—and I'm paraphrasing Edwards here—it was because we didn't have enough time before the statutory deadline for the final case results, didn't have spare personnel, and didn't have the budget for it. But I know for a fact that that's a lot of bull."

"So you think Edwards didn't want to give his investigators a second chance to find any dirt on YSP?" Zhang asked. "That he didn't even want to see the findings of the on-site part of the investigation out of fear that it might paint YSP in a bad light?"

"In so bad a light that it would force Edwards to take firm action in the sorghum case, which could, in-turn, antagonize the Chinese and torpedo the soybean agreement. Yes. That's exactly what I think. Mind you, it's a guess on my part. He didn't trust me enough to share his secret motives."

Severin wondered whether Fiskar's martini had gone straight to her head for her to be talking so openly.

Fiskar looked thoughtful for a moment. "And I'll tell you something else that may be meaningful, or may mean nothing. Just before Powell and Keen disappeared, the director of their office asked for a closed-door meeting with Edwards. Nobody knows what they talked about. But the rumor is that, just before asking for the meeting with Edwards, the office director received an email from Powell and Keen in China."

"An email saying what?" Severin asked.

"Nobody knows. Whatever it said, Edwards kept it under his hat, and presumably ordered the office director to do the same. But my hunch is that something unusual was afoot."

"Any theories?"

"Maybe the investigators found something that would have rocked the proverbial boat. I wish I had a clue."

"Sounds like we need to talk to Edwards," Zhang said.

"He won't talk to you unless you have some way to compel him. There's nothing in it for him. All talking to you might do is get him dragged into something he surely wants no part of."

"What about the office director? What did you say his name was?"

"*Her* name. And I didn't. It's Elaine Danielson. Been there for 30-plus years. You stand a better chance with her. But I'm sure she's been briefed to keep her mouth shut."

"Why would she care?" Zhang asked. "Edwards doesn't work there anymore."

"No, but she's an institutional woman. Living for her pension. Going along to get along. If they put the fear of God in her, she isn't liable to open up."

"So why are *you* talking to us?"

"Like I said, I'm out of government. Plus, Byron Edwards can kiss my ass."

"You aren't golfing buddies?"

"He's just another Beltway ass-clown. One of your dime-a-dozen political appointees who got his job not because he knew anything about the work of the agency, but because he helped out on some other ass-clown's election campaign. That's D.C. for you."

And his womanizing burned your fingers once too, didn't it? Severin thought as he finished his martini, guessing at the origin of Fiskar's apparent hatred.

NINE

Roughly four hours later, after making several unsuccessful attempts to contact Byron Edwards at his new office at USTR and finally being told by his blunt and rather rude secretary that she could think of no worthwhile reason they should speak with him, Severin and Zhang were shown into the large corner office of Ben Holloman, the American attorney for the Chinese sorghum syrup company YSP, a newly-minted partner of the Manhattan-based law firm of McElroy, Steen & Duff, and one of the last two people known to have seen Powell and Keen alive. Holloman was also one of the few American witnesses interviewed by State Department investigators. His secretary indicated that Holloman would be with them shortly, that he was just finishing up a teleconference, and that he was very sorry for making them wait.

They took seats in the two expensive looking, extraordinarily comfortable leather chairs that faced Holloman's empty desk. Behind it, a floor-to-ceiling window framed a corner of the Herbert C. Hoover Federal Building—the sprawling Classical Revival-style building of quarried limestone that served as headquarters for the Commerce Department. The higher ground of Arlington National Cemetery, across the Potomac and in full autumn glory, could be seen in the distance beyond it. Behind the chairs they sat in, another glass wall looked out on an open area where Holloman's secretary sat at her desk watching them.

"I'm surprised they let us wait in his office instead of a conference room or something," Zhang said. "I'm sure he has all sorts of sensitive or proprietary client information in here. Think of the liability."

"Maybe the conference room is in use. Anyway, his secretary is watching us like a hawk. We're fish in a tank in here."

"Tracy Fiskar was certainly interesting," Zhang said.

"Yeah?"

"The contradictions. Her claim that unfair trade practices are such a huge threat to the U.S. economy. Seemingly an important issue to her. And yet in practically the same breath, she tells us she's now a lobbyist for the Chinese."

"Wasn't it F. Scott Fitzgerald who said that the test of a first-rate intelligence is a person's ability to hold two opposing ideas in mind at the same time and still be able to function?"

"I'll take your word for it. And maybe I should give Fiskar the benefit of the doubt and assume she's lobbying on behalf of ethical businesses."

"Yeah. You should definitely try to rein in all your redneck xenophobia."

"I'm Chinese-American."

"That's what makes it so weird."

"Shut up."

"By the way, Wallace isn't your real name, is it?"

Zhang gave him funny look. "You've known me for, what—15 years? And you've just now decided to ask if Wallace is my real name?"

"Is it?"

"No."

"So what is it?"

Zhang looked reluctant. "It's Wei."

"Like Little Miss Muffet eating her curds and whey?"

"See, I knew you were going to say that. No, like W-E-I. It means great."

"Great?" Severin said with a grin. "*Great* Zhang. Yeah. So great that you're living in your parents' basement."

"Please. At least I'm not named after a fictional Ukrainian masochist."

"The hell are you talking about?"

"The name Severin. They didn't make you read *Venus in Furs* in comparative lit class at UW?"

"*Venus in Furs*? You trying to tell me you're a pervert?"

"Never mind."

"I'll grant you, Wei is catchy. But I think I'm going to just keep calling you Man Pretty. You *are* a pretty man, after all. Such pretty, pretty hair."

Turning to his left, Severin noticed that the wall was half taken up with various framed proclamations of Holloman's greatness. A giant, gilded diploma from the University of North Carolina School of Law, indicating that Holloman graduated with 'highest honors' and as a member of the Order of the Coif. Various certificates of appreciation. One from the U.S.-China Friendship Society. One from the District of Columbia Bar Association, recognizing his contribution to some sort of panel convened to address contemporary law practice ethics issues. A portrait of him shaking hands with the previous Senate majority leader. Another of him shaking hands with the Chinese ambassador to the United States. Cover pages of law review articles he'd authored. A picture of him in a bar association journal article bearing the headline *Rising Stars of International Trade Law*. The wall was Holloman's monument to himself. He'd probably have one of those ridiculous Versace watches, a fake tan, manicured nails, and perfect hair. Severin was ready to dislike him. But he'd do his best to hide his personal feelings for the man as he worked to establish the rapport that was so important to successful witness interviews.

"Oh, no—how embarrassing," Holloman said as he loped through the open door with a slight slouch, wearing common khakis, a plain linen shirt with the sleeves rolled up, and clearly unfashionable eyeglasses. He wore no watch at all.

"Pardon?" Severin said, as he and Zhang rose to shake Holloman's hand.

"As I came in, I saw that you were looking at what I call the Wall of Me. A collection of every meaningless award and accolade I've ever been given."

"It's impressive," Severin said blandly.

"It's distasteful and ostentatious," Holloman replied. "But clients—and more importantly, potential clients—seem to love that stuff."

"You meet with clients in your office instead of a conference room?" Zhang asked, still hung up on something Severin thought utterly irrelevant.

"Not all that often. But sometimes it's necessary. So my Wall of Me is what I have instead of Yelp reviews. I guess it makes a certain amount of sense," he said, taking a seat behind his massive hardwood desk. If they don't already know you personally, they're looking for any clues as to your quality as a lawyer. It's like buying a bottle of wine because you like the label. But in all honesty, it embarrasses me. I've never felt comfortable with the necessary evil of self-promotion. It's all just feels so, I don't know, silly."

Severin was surprised at Holloman's self-deprecation. "Highest honors and Order of the Coif? There's nothing silly about that."

"You're very kind. To me, that diploma is more of a daily reminder of the fact that I'll be paying off student loans until I'm almost 50 years old."

"I thought state schools were supposed to be cheaper."

"Ah, but I didn't grow up in North Carolina, so I had to pay non-resident tuition. No, sir. I am pure Central Florida white trash." He took a sip from a coffee cup that had been sitting on the desk when they were first shown in. "Really, I shouldn't gripe. Most of the people in this firm went to places like Stanford, Princeton, Harvard, and so on. Their loans make mine look like peanuts."

"I can imagine," Severin said.

"The funny thing is that I really wanted to go to Duke. Got admitted too. But there was just no way I was going to be able to afford private school. In retrospect, from a financial standpoint, I suppose I'm lucky that I couldn't. Ended up in the same place as all those rich kids anyway."

Severin thought he'd detected the slightest hint of bitterness, of envy, when Holloman mentioned the Ivy League credentials of his colleagues. It could have been his imagination.

"Anyway, I'm sorry to have kept you both waiting, and I hope I can be of help."

"We appreciate your time," Zhang said.

"So, my secretary said that Kristin Powell's family hired you to try to find out more about what happened to her. Is that right?"

"It is," Zhang said. "The State Department report isn't very thorough."

"They issued their report?"

"You haven't seen it?"

"No. I didn't even know they'd released it," he said, clearly irritated. "You'd think they'd at least let me know, or even send me a copy. I mean, I spent time with those folks. I had a relationship with them. You can't help developing a sort of emotional bond, even where the situation is somewhat adversarial with respect to our work." He shook his head. "I suppose it doesn't surprise me that it wasn't very thorough though. I got the impression the State Department wanted the whole thing to go away. Probably because of the soybean agreement negotiations."

"So we've been given to understand," Severin said. "We were hoping you could flesh out the report of your interview a bit."

"Sure. If you have it in your folder there, I can look over it and let you know if they left out anything important."

"That would be very helpful," Severin said, handing him a copy.

As he removed his glasses and polished them with a small cloth, Holloman said, "A couple of the State Department's special agents came by and interviewed me about a week after I got home, and I told them everything I knew. Talked to them for an hour or so. They were pretty coy, by which I mean it was an irritatingly one-way street with respect to the flow of information. Aside from those two, I had a *Washington Post* reporter calling to request an interview. But because of the sensitivity, I declined, thinking the *Post* would be able to get hold of anything State thought was appropriate to release to the public once the report came out. I'm assuming State didn't solve the crime. Or the family wouldn't have hired you to learn more."

"The State Department theorized that it was a random abduction and killing for money. That the investigators missed their flight to Shanghai, then caught the wrong cab to take them to the Shangri-La Hotel in Qingdao."

"I suppose that's possible, if hard to believe," Holloman said. "It's a generalization, but I don't think of Chinese cab drivers as being particularly dangerous folks."

They waited as Holloman read State's report of their interview of him. It didn't take him long, as it was barely a page long. An hour of transcript whittled down to just the information State considered relevant.

Holloman took a breath, removed his glasses, and looked up from the page. "They don't even mention the company driver," he said, sounding exasperated.

"Company driver?"

"Their van driver. He ferried us back and forth between the factory and the small hotel in Yinzhen where we all stayed, and also to and from Qingdao. I never got his name. But I mentioned to the State Department investigators that I thought he was acting a little bit funny. This was just my gut feeling now. And to be honest, even though I work with them all the time, I have a hard time reading the Chinese. Interpreting their facial expressions and body language and so forth. No offense," he said, glancing at Zhang. Zhang shrugged, seeming unconcerned. "At any rate, I emphasized to the State guys that the van driver seemed unusually tense. He was normally about as emotional as a cup of yogurt. But the day we drove back to Qingdao from Yinzhen, he was noticeably tense. Of course, he could have just been rattled by the heated argument between the Commerce Department people."

"Wait—heated argument? Maybe we should back up a bit," Severin said.

"Yeah. If this is all you know of all the testimony I gave the State guys, then we should definitely back up."

"How about if we go over the whole day?"

"I only have about 15 minutes before my next meeting, but I'll do my best. The day started out well enough. It was a Monday. Everybody was in good spirits because we were almost done with the on-site phase of the investigation of YSP, and everyone had had a nice time at Laoshan Mountain the day before."

"Laoshan Mountain?" Zhang asked.

"We'd taken Sunday off. One of the Commerce investigators was all fired up about visiting this place called Laoshan, up along the coast, past the big naval base just north of Qingdao. It's a mountain with ancient and quite famous Taoist temples carved out of exposed stone on its slopes. Stuff dating back to the Song dynasty. It was only a couple of hours drive from Yinzhen. And the investigator's description and excitement had gotten me interested too, so I arranged for YSP to give us a car and driver to take us up there for a little day-off excursion. It was a different driver, by the way. Not the van driver. Anyway, we headed up there, even making a quick stop at the famous Qingdao a/k/a Tsingtao brewery on the way." Holloman grinned, then gave a little chuckle.

"What?" Zhang asked.

"Nothing. Silly memory." When Severin and Zhang sat silent waiting for more, he went on. "We got stuck in a bit of traffic after touring the brewery. The same investigator who'd suggested we go to Laoshan had consumed so much beer that he had to urinate. Said he couldn't hold it."

"I assume you're talking about Bill Keen," Severin said.

"Yes. We had to let him out on the side of the road along the coast there, between Qingdao and Laoshan, so that he could hike up over a little knoll to relieve himself. Must have had an abnormally small bladder." He smiled wider. "I was half worried he'd get arrested because we were practically on the perimeter of the big navy base up there. That would have made for a good story, right? Chinese Navy base perimeter patrol arrests lanky, white U.S. government employee for pissing on their hill, sparking international incident." He shook his head. "Anyway, Laoshan turned out to be a beautiful place. Little ancient temples all over the forested mountainside. Sweeping views out over the Yellow Sea. Like something from a dream." Holloman was staring off into space, clearly lost in a pleasing memory. Then he snapped out of it, his eyes returning to Severin and Zhang. "That probably isn't what you came to talk about."

"No worries."

"Anyway, it's back to business Monday morning in Yinzhen, and we're all hoping to finish up. The YSP people and the Commerce investigators met me for breakfast in the hotel restaurant. Strange, antiquated little place. Lousy food. As usual, the van showed up around nine to take us to the factory to continue with the investigation. The factory is on the periphery of the town. We'd been working in their little conference room, going over the accounting records, discussing the company's history and sales practices with their officers and accounting staff. Things had been going well enough. But on that day, one of the investigators figured out that something was fundamentally wrong with one of the monthly accounting ledger books he was examining. The invoices, sales slips, the monthly totals—none of it matched what had been previously reported to Commerce in YSP's investigative questionnaire responses and data submissions. It took quite a while to figure out what had happened. But in brief, the YSP people had mislabeled the account book with the wrong year. It took them a long time to locate the right one. I won't dress it up. Trying to sort it out was a mess. Company minions running this way and that way, shouting at each other, trying to find the right records. And because it was the last scheduled day of their visit, the Commerce team didn't really end up having time to look at it. It caused a lot of confusion. A lot of angst for YSP. We had to manually reorganize a bunch of records on the spot. Match the right invoice and voucher books to the accounting ledgers. Double-check that the monthly figures totaled up properly. A pain. And in all honesty, I don't know how

Commerce would have ruled once the investigators got home."

"What do you mean?" Zhang asked.

"I mean Commerce has the discretion to penalize a company for being so disorganized that they submit the wrong information to the investigative record. If they'd wanted to, it might have been within the Commerce Department's authority to conclude that, in screwing up the presentation of their accounting records, YSP quote-unquote failed to cooperate to the best of its ability. In that case, Commerce would have hit YSP with a crushing tariff."

"But that didn't happen," Severin said.

"No. Because the investigators disappeared, they never had a chance to file the report that could have led to that. So in the tragedy of their disappearance, YSP may have dodged a bullet."

"Are you saying it may have been in your client's interest to make the investigators disappear?"

"If this were a Hollywood movie, sure. But in reality, the YSP people are a pretty docile bunch. They really are. Most of them are aging farmers who saved their pennies and put them all together to buy this little tin can of a factory out in the countryside. I can't picture them hurting anyone." He shrugged his shoulders. "But, then again, I suppose anything is possible. I'm sure it would have put them out of business if Commerce had put a punitive tariff on their sorghum. At the same time, it's just as possible—probably more so—that Commerce would have chalked up the accounting book errors as an innocent mistake and let YSP off the hook. In fact, that's exactly what I told the YSP people, to reassure them. Anyway, I only mention all this because I think the intensity of the last day, workwise, left us all a bit tense, a bit tired. It might have contributed to the way things went later."

"What happened later?" Severin asked.

"We wound things up at the factory and went back to the hotel to pack. The van was going to take us back to Qingdao. The Commerce team was going to try to catch the last flight from Qingdao to Shanghai. Their flight back to the U.S. originated in Shanghai the next evening, so they figured it would be smart to try to get there that night to have a little more buffer of time to catch their plane home. I was going to debrief the company officials at their freight forwarder's office that evening in Qingdao and then fly to Beijing the next morning to meet with a potential new client. But after I packed and came downstairs to the lobby, I was surprised to see Kristin Powell's husband, Wesley. Apparently he was supposed to investigate another sorghum company down in Jiangsu Province the following week, but flew in a couple of days early to attempt a surprise rendezvous with his wife. And when I say surprise, I mean she clearly had no idea he was coming. It was a huge surprise to me. I mean, this town, Yinzhen, is out in the middle of nowhere. It's miles from any major city. I don't even know how Wesley got himself there, but it must have taken some serious motivation. At any rate, his appearance on the scene was flat-out weird."

"How so?" Severin asked.

"I don't know anything about the Powells' relationship, and I don't know what had been going on just before I arrived in the lobby. But it would be an understatement to say that things were suddenly quite tense. Clearly, Wesley was expecting the team to be there another night. But when he found out they'd finished up and were headed to Qingdao in an attempt to catch the last flight to Shanghai, he asked if he could ride along. I told him that would be fine. We were in two vehicles. The company's president and accountant and the Commerce team's interpreter rode in the president's private car with his personal driver. All three Commerce employees rode with me in the company van. So we're out on these back roads, zig-zagging through farmland, and everybody's mood seems to be darkening as quickly as the twilight sky. I'm up front with the driver, trying to think about the things I needed to debrief the YSP company people on that evening. In the back, the Commerce people have been engaged in awkward, forced-sounding small talk, when suddenly Wesley demands to know why his wife didn't return any of his calls. I can only assume he'd tried to contact her several times from the States. Keen jumped to her defense, explaining that she hadn't been feeling well and had been going to bed right after dinner each evening. This was news to me, which is to say it wasn't entirely accurate. I saw her up late at least half the nights we were there, usually out walking the town with Keen or having a beer with him in the hotel restaurant. Regardless, Wesley's voice shoots up 20 decibels as he tells Keen to keep out of it. Then he really lays into his wife. Why hadn't she returned any of his calls? Did she have any idea how disrespectful that was? Did she have any idea how worried he'd been? I'll spare you the cuss words. Suffice it to say it was vitriolic. And I gathered from the argument that, unable to get Kristin on the phone, Wesley had called Keen on several occasions, asking that he find her and have her call him back. So he was also ticked that Keen hadn't gotten her to call home. Things kept getting uglier. Kristin was in tears. Then Keen finally exploded, calling Wesley crude names and threatening to beat the tar out of him if he didn't quiet down and leave Kristin alone. He used a number of expletives that I'll leave to your imagination." Then Holloman grinned a weak grin. "He even told Wesley that he needed therapy. I was of more than half a mind to voice my concurrence. Finally, Wesley demanded to be let out of the van."

"Out on some country road?" Zhang said.

"Exactly. Out in the middle of nowhere. Not even in the tiny town of Yinzhen anymore. We were out on some lonely road between farm fields. At this point, I intervened, asking everyone to please stop talking and cool off. I would have just had Wesley transfer to the other vehicle. But they were out of sight somewhere ahead of us, and we were in an area with no cell phone coverage, so I had no way of getting them to stop. I told Wesley that we weren't going to abandon him in the middle of nowhere as it was getting dark. That his request was ridiculous. He told me . . . ." Holloman paused, his face flushed with seeming embarrassment. "He said some indecent things to me and demanded, once again, to be let out of the van. I'm embarrassed to say that my anger got the better of me. I figured, okay, this jerk speaks enough Chinese to get by. And he managed to get to Yinzhen on his own. It's summer, so he isn't going to freeze to death. He'll probably be able to flag down a passing vehicle and pay them to drive him out to the nearest highway where he could catch a bus or something. So to hell with him, right? Worst case scenario, he could follow the road back to Yinzhen. I had the van driver pull over, and we let him out. I don't know what his plan was or where he was headed, and by then I really couldn't have cared less. I wasn't his number one fan to begin with."

"You already knew Wesley?"

"We worked together years ago. At the Commerce Department, actually. I spent two years there, getting what I still consider priceless hands-on investigative experience before making the move over to the private-sector law firms. Matter of fact, Wesley was on the interview panel that recommended hiring me."

"But you weren't buddies?"

"He was decent enough at first. We'd sort of bonded in the wake of meeting in my interview because we both had law degrees from UNC. But it seemed like things got weird between us when things started going well for me at Commerce. I did a few things right on a high-profile case, and the high command took notice. They fast tracked me for some special work in the assistant secretary's office. Gave me some choice assignments. As corny as it sounds to say it of a grown man, I always suspected that Wesley had grown jealous of me. Suffice it to say, he developed a habit of talking down to me at meetings, in front of our co-workers and managers. It chapped me, but I didn't think it was worth addressing head-on. Before long, I was out the door to the law firms anyway. Still, a couple of years ago, he was the lead investigator in a case I was involved with. When he dealt with me he was always professional to my face, but cold. And while I don't have any hard evidence to prove it, it seemed to me that a certain animosity surfaced in his treatment of my client. In his questions to them. In his analyses. In his conclusions. I mean, in antidumping cases, there is a lot of room for discretion and flexibility. Granting extensions to deadlines. Allowing respondent companies multiple opportunities to provide all the information and data the investigators request. That sort of thing. But Wesley was entirely inflexible. It was frustrating. I'm digressing."

"Your comments may prove illuminating, nonetheless," Severin said.

"Anyway, back to the story. After a few pointless minutes of Kristin pleading with him to get back in the van, we left Wesley on the roadside and sped off to try to get Kristin and Bill to their flight at Qingdao Airport. Now, as I mentioned, the driver seemed tense. Kept giving me funny looks. Maybe he was worried about Wesley. I don't speak more than a few words of the language, so I couldn't ask him if there was a problem. Anyway, it took us a long time to get to the airport. I told the team they weren't likely to make the last Shanghai flight, and that they should just let us take them to the hotel. But they insisted they'd be fine, and that if they missed the flight, they'd just take a cab to the hotel. I wished them a safe trip home at the airport drop-off curb, and the driver and I continued on to the hotel. That was the last time I ever saw them."

Severin thought Holloman looked genuinely sad. "Did you work with Kristin or Bill when you were at Commerce?"

"No. I've been in the private sector for 10 years. I don't think they were hired until long after I left. Nice enough people though. Reasonable. Polite. Quick studies. I'm not a terribly sociable person, but I liked their company."

"What were Kristin and Bill like, physically?"

"Sorry?"

"Were they big, small, athletic, weak-looking?"

"Oh. Keen was probably, I don't know, 5-foot-9. Not overly muscular, but not slight either. Not intimidating, but not an obvious pushover. Average, I guess. Seemed coordinated enough. Kristin was about the same height, but meek."

"How about Wesley?"

"Maybe 6 foot. Wide frame. I don't remember him being particularly athletic or strong when we were both at Commerce. And I didn't have much time with him in China. So I guess I really don't know."

"And the company van driver?"

"Short, but thick. It stands out over there. Most of them are so slight."

"Capable of throttling Keen?"

Holloman's face looked all the more troubled at Severin's question, as though it underlined a possibility he hadn't wanted to think about.

"Maybe. I don't know. I'm not sure I'd be a good judge of something like that."

They had Holloman go back over his story, filling in more detail as he went. But it didn't give them any more useful information than they already had. Then they thanked him for his time, and made to leave. But something in Holloman's expression held Severin in his chair.

"Is there something else?" Severin asked. Holloman, who'd been staring through his own desk, looked up to meet Severin's questioning gaze.

"I'm not certain that I . . . ."

"You have a hunch you're reluctant to voice because you're so unsure of it?"

"I suppose so."

"I'd encourage you to share it. In my experience, gut feelings prove relevant, often as not."

"Well, it's about Kristin and Bill." His face flushed again. "I feel half silly mentioning this, because the truth is I'm not good at reading people. And I have limited experience with, uh . . . ." His eyes looked to the ceiling. "It's just that I think there might have been something going on between them."

"Of a romantic nature? Between Kristin and Bill?"

He nodded. "Really, I have nothing concrete to base it on. Just maybe body language. Their facial expressions. A familiarity. But to be honest, romantic relationships aren't really my province."

"I'm glad you mentioned it," Severin said, bolstering him.

"Just—I would ask that you not tell the family. It's conjecture, after all. Conjecture on my part. I wouldn't want them to think something was going on if there wasn't."

TEN

"Of a romantic nature?" Zhang said to Severin as the elevator doors closed and they descended to the lobby of Holloman's office building. "Are you kidding me? Is that really how you talk to people?"

"Holloman is the awkward, proper, bookworm type. How would you have had me ask the question? If I'd used your crude dialect, he'd probably have clammed up out of embarrassment."

"Uptight guy."

"You'd be uptight too if you'd been a bookworm playground wimp who had to claw his way from white trash Central Florida to a corner office and partnership at McElroy, Steen & Duff. He's alright."

"Whatever. I didn't like him."

"Of course you didn't. He represents everything you and I don't. Goals. Follow through. Accomplishment. Living somewhere other than your parents' basement."

"I just realized something."

"What?"

"You're an inferior remake of Travis McGee."

"A what of who?"

"Travis McGee. Hard-drinking philosopher and unlicensed, world-weary private investigator of the John D. MacDonald mystery novels. A knight errant who has a deep understanding of just about every personality type in the world."

"Must have missed that one."

"There are more than 20 of them. Some of the best ever of the mystery genre."

"Who reads anymore?"

"I do."

"Well, I guess I'm just culturally illiterate."

"That's the least of your problems. Where the hell are we going?"

"The Office of the United States Trade Representative. Workplace of eager beaver Byron Edwards, former Assistant Secretary of Commerce."

"His secretary stonewalled us, probably on his instruction. And Tracy Fiskar said she was sure he wouldn't talk to us."

"Unless we have a way to compel him."

"The guy may be a self-concerned political jackass," Zhang said, "But you can't seriously suspect him of being involved with the killings."

"Don't jump to conclusions. Anyway, he can certainly tell us what Elaine Danielson told him. He can tell us what was said in the investigators' email from China that got Danielson so freaked out."

"How are you going to compel him to talk to us?"

"I'm not sure. I suppose, as a last resort, we can always twist his scrotum. Always works in the movies, right?"

They zig-zagged a few blocks to Pennsylvania Avenue, then passed between Lafayette Square and the White House. Zhang insisted on pausing at the White House fence so that Severin could take his picture there. Then they turned down 17th Street, finding themselves at the main entrance of the USTR building after walking another short block. It was an ancient Italianate building of white painted brick, clearly of 19th century construction, with an unusual wrought-iron balcony wrapping around the second of its five floors.

"Okay," Severin said, whipping out his smartphone. "Let's see what this son of a bitch looks like." He Googled Byron Edwards and found several official photos of him. In one, he was giving a speech at a podium in front of a large American flag. In another, he was shaking hands with some foreign dignitary across a long table surrounded by other suits. In yet another, he was touring a seaport's intermodal container yard, wearing a hardhat, trying to look like he understood what his host/tour guide was talking about. Trying to look like he gave a crap. Yet despite his power suit, good posture, and probably bleached teeth, he retained, in each photo, the facial expression of a half-wit. Severin and Zhang studied the photos so that they'd be able to spot Edwards when he emerged from the building.

"So you think a big cheese like Edwards is just going to walk out the main entrance like a regular Joe?" Zhang asked. "You don't think some black Lincoln Town Car with tinted windows is going to whisk him home after emerging from a secret underground garage?"

"You heard Tracy Fiskar say this agency is strapped for cash. That they can barely afford to keep the heat on. I seriously doubt anyone other than the USTR himself gets to have a private car. No. Edwards may be too good for the Metro. He may take a cab. But he won't be in any Lincoln Town Car with tinted windows."

"Why not just wait for him at his house?"

"I tried to Google his home address as we were walking here. There are enough B. Edwardses in this town to fill a bus."

For the next hour and half they sat on the edge of an immense concrete planter box that probably doubled as a car bomb security barrier, keeping their eyes locked on the USTR main entrance. Dozens of people came and went, none of them looking happy, many of them looking downright miserable. Finally, just after 6 p.m., they spotted Edwards, looking as unhappy as any of his colleagues. He strode out the door, turning north up 17th Street, ignoring a panhandler who asked him for spare change before telling him to have a "blessed day." Severin and Zhang followed behind at a distance of about half a block as he led them through town, across the George Washington University campus, and into a residential area around the intersection of 25th & I streets. Worried Edwards would suddenly duck into a house or apartment building, Severin and Zhang closed the gap, nearly catching up with him just as he turned up the front steps of a skinny red brick row house.

"What do we do?" Zhang asked.

"Mr. Edwards," Severin said as they came to a stop 10 feet from the man, not wanting to frighten him.

Edwards stopped and turned. "Who are you?"

"We've been hired by—"

Apparently Edwards had already heard enough. He turned away, quickly making for his front door, his right hand reaching into his overcoat pocket, presumably for his keys. Before Severin knew it, an overexcited Zhang was in pursuit.

"Wallace, wait," Severin said. But it was too late. He'd made it as far as Edwards' front porch, brashly clapping a hand down on Edwards' shoulder, before Edwards, looking startled, turned around, pulled his right hand from his overcoat pocket, reached out and pressed a stun gun right into Zhang's unguarded rib cage. Severin heard the zap, then heard Zhang make a sound that reminded him of someone trying to spit bile residue out of their mouth after vomiting. He fell to the ground. Edwards pocketed the stun gun, then pulled a pepper spray canister from his other pocket and blasted Zhang in the face. Zhang's shout of agony got Severin laughing so hard he almost couldn't focus on what was happening. But through the blur of his hysteria, he saw Edwards open his door, retreat into the dark hallway of his home, and slam the door behind him. Trying to breathe between fits of laughter, Severin climbed the steps to help get Zhang to his feet. Zhang's face was as red as a Bing cherry. Water poured from the corners of his swollen shut eyes. Snot poured from his nostrils. Drool ran off the protruding lower lip of his open mouth.

"I guess Edwards didn't want to talk to us," Severin said, barely able to finish his sentence before laughing again.

"Mah! Wuh!"

"Come on, Mike Hammer. Let's get out of here before the cops come."

"Bah! Thah fuggah son of a bih!"

"Yeah, yeah. Just put your arm over my shoulder and I'll guide you out of here. Keep walking."

Severin half dragged Zhang several blocks until he found a drugstore where he left Zhang just outside the front door with instructions to try to keep his inflamed face turned away from passers-by. He purchased a pair of large aviator sunglasses, a can of lidocaine spray, and a travel size bottle of baby shampoo. Then he led Zhang into a bathroom at the rear of some sort of cheesy, dark sports bar. There, Zhang used all the baby shampoo, spending 10 minutes doing his best to wash his face and hair in the sink. After that, Severin sprayed his face with the lidocaine.

"Look at my hair," Zhang said. "Let's go back to the hotel."

"No."

"It hurts," Zhang said, his nose still running, his eyes reduced to inflamed slits.

"I know. Best thing for it now is to get a drink."

"Give me a break."

"Really. It'll help. Aside from that, we've done everything we can for now. It just takes time for everything to calm down." He put the sunglasses on Zhang. "There. Now you look like a Sigma Chi frat boy," he said, grinning. "You'll fit right in in this cheeseball bar." Severin shook his head and almost started laughing again. "Damn, Wallace. You're a piece of work. What were you thinking grabbing hold of that guy?"

"He was going to get away."

"Are you out of your mind? You're lucky he didn't have a gun."

Severin bought them both double bourbons on the rocks, and they sat in a booth in a dark corner, sipping their drinks as Zhang's face slowly returned to normal. Zhang sat silent, scowling. "Well," Severin said. "I have to thank you. I don't think I've laughed that hard in 20 years."

"That's great, Lars."

*****

Once Zhang regained his composure, they walked to the Farragut North metro station and boarded a Red Line train.

"Where are we going now?" Zhang asked.

"Our day is done. I'm going to take you to an old haunt where we can decompress. A bona fide hole in the wall. You'll love it."

The rumble of an approaching train filled the station, which seemed as though it were designed to magnify the echoes and noise. A compression wave of air blasted them as the front of the train roared by. It finally screeched to a stop, and they got on, sharing a side-by-side seat and facing the same direction.

"So," Severin said. "Aside from you having your own ass handed to you by pencil-neck Byron Edwards, we made some headway today, didn't we? The plot thickens."

"You don't think Powell and Keen were picked up and murdered by a random taxi cab driver."

"No."

"Do you think Wesley caught up with them and did them in?" Zhang asked.

"If Keen and Kristin were really having an affair, and if Wesley was aware of it, then he'd have motive. But those are two big ifs. And what opportunity would he have had? If he managed to catch up with them at the airport in Qingdao, he couldn't have killed them there, with people everywhere."

"Maybe he caught up with them at the airport after they missed their flight, was apologetic, and talked them into sharing a ride to the hotel. Then he did them en route."

"Or maybe the company driver doubled-back, tracked them down at the airport, and offered to take them back to the hotel—all the while intending to knock them over the head and take their money, passports, and credit cards."

"Yeah, but he was probably handling their bags all the time, loading and unloading the van wherever they went. Why not just grab their wallets out of their luggage, hand the luggage over to them at the airport curb, and take off. They'd never have been able to pin it on him."

"News flash, Wallace. Most criminals are gap-toothed morons. Plus, we're talking about a couple of sheltered Americans traveling in rural China. They were probably paranoid enough to be carrying their money, passports, credit cards and whatnot in money belts. Or somewhere on their person, at the very least. No, if the driver wanted their stuff, he would have had to take it off of them."

"But could the driver have overpowered Keen, let alone both of them?"

"Maybe he had a weapon."

"What about Holloman's feeling about Kristin and Keen having something going on?"

"Like I said, it would give Wesley a motive. I think we'd be remiss if we didn't look into it. Speaking of which, I think it's time we had your hacker friend take a stab at a few email accounts for us. Both Powells, of course. And let's throw in Keen, for grins."

Zhang looked uneasy. "Their federal government email accounts, or just their private ones?"

"Both, if he can manage it."

"I take it the words *federal prison* don't worry you?"

"Ask your guy to be careful. If he can do it without undue risk, great. If not, he can stick to their private accounts. And what did you say your guy's name is?"

"I didn't."

*****

They ascended yet another unbelievably long but broken escalator at the Dupont Circle station, turning north once they reached the surface of the earth, and, after pausing to catch their breath, made their way to a block of 18th, just north of U Street. There, Severin stopped in front of the old brick façade of what appeared to be a very small sports bar. He stared in perplexity. "Damn."

"What? Is this it?" Zhang asked.

"It used to be. Used to be a joint called The Common Share. Great place to unwind. Cheapest drinks in the city. A fixture."

"Should we go in anyway?"

"Not really what I had in mind. Well, no worries. I know another place close by."

They strode a few blocks up 18th Street, where Severin came to a stop in front of another doorway. Again, he looked chagrined.

"And this used to be Asylum. Damn."

"World keeps turning, Lars. Time waits for no man, or whatever the expression is. Speaking of which, my stomach waits for no man. So let's figure something out. What are you in the mood for?"

"Japanese."

"Why Japanese?"

"Why? Because I like it, that's why. Plus, my stomach is acting up. Rice and miso sounds good. Some light Japanese beer."

"You could get rice at a Mexican place."

"You don't want Japanese?"

"A Mexican place has rice and light style beers for your stomach."

"It's okay to admit that you want Mexican instead of Japanese."

"No, I'm just saying. Mexican makes sense. But what do *you* want?"

"I told you, Japanese."

They ended up at Mexican restaurant in the same general area, and proceeded to get thoroughly drunk on Sauza tequila and Pacifico beers over plates of bland, greasy enchiladas—Severin electing to ignore the warning signs of his upset stomach. They sat in a cramped booth decorated with a torn bullfighting poster and red chili Christmas lights. An obligatory oversized black sombrero hung from the wall above them. Canned mariachi music played over tinny ceiling-mounted speakers.

"So why do you always sabotage your relationships?" Zhang asked.

"Huh?"

"With women."

"I don't sabotage my relationships with women."

"Then why did you say you did?"

"I didn't say that."

"You—those were your exact words. At Big Time Brewery."

"Wallace, see, all those years of abusing ecstasy turned your brain into Swiss cheese."

"Maybe you drank so much at the pub that you don't remember saying it. And anyway, I told you, I was a dealer, not a user."

"A dealer. I've always loved how that word is used in the context of the drug trade. Like you were the owner of a dealership. Come on down to Wallace's, ladies and gentlemen, for limited time 4th of July savings. Ninety days same as cash. Prices 3,000 percent below MSRP." Zhang ignored him and went on. "See because usually, people who have a tendency to torpedo their own relationships have some sort of heartbreak in their past. Their fingers have been burned, and they don't want to feel it again, right? That sense of loss. So you avoid getting into meaningful relationships. When things get serious, you bolt. You self-destruct. Blow the relationship up. It's easier that way."

"You're a lay psychologist now?"

"So did your steady high school gal break your heart? Leave you for the captain of the football team?"

"I *was* captain of the football team."

"Of course. But seriously, what did it to you? Your folks died after your graduation from UW. But by then you were old enough that it shouldn't have caused long-term damage the same way that trauma in early childhood might."

"I lost my baby sister to crib death when I was four. Does that count?"

"Are you serious?"

"No, it's something I just tell people for a laugh."

"You never told me about that before."

"I don't think I've ever told anyone about that before." Zhang was speechless. "What about you, then, Dr. Phil?" Severin asked, eager to end Zhang's line of questioning. "No long-term relationships, despite your J. Crew catalogue good looks. Wait—you're a closeted metrosexual."

"I'm a what? What does that even mean?"

"You're an urban, politically progressive, asexual male with an interest in grooming, fashion, and men's beauty treatments."

"Asexual?"

"Still coming to terms with it. Worried about how your conservative parents will take it."

"I'm not metrosexual."

"You're definitely metrosexual."

"Lars—"

"Relax, Wallace. Do I look like a cave man? I'm totally, totally cool with it. But I have to say, now everything makes sense."

"Lars, you're full of sh—"

"Look at yourself. Look at all the evidence. You've always been up on all the latest fashions. Your clothes. Your shoes. Your hair. You drove a white Volkswagen Golf in college."

"It had a turbo charger."

"It had a Depeche Mode CD stuck in its stereo."

"Oh, I get it. We're back at redneck bigot police academy profiling class, right? Asian dude with a cool car, Depeche Mode blaring out of his 2,000 watts worth of Blaupunkt speakers—must be metrosexual."

"That's not a rebuttal. And the white VW Golf was most certainly not a cool car."

"Huh. Well, setting aside the question of whether or not I liked Depeche Mode, for the record, that CD wasn't even mine. My ex-girlfriend jammed it in there."

"Your Canadian ex-girlfriend from that trip to Niagara Falls? The one nobody we know has ever met? What was her name again?" Severin was grinning, shaking his head. "A lowered, white, Depeche Mode playing Volkswagen Golf with an oversized aftermarket spoiler."

"You're not even remembering your profiling lessons correctly," Zhang said. "White Volkswagen Golf either means old lady who thinks she's a friend of the earth because she drives a small European car and grows her own tomatoes, or a male 20-something, small-volume cocaine dealer who likes to act all gangster but is actually a white valedictorian Jewish guy from a happy middle-class family in New Jersey."

"*She* wouldn't have had a spoiler, and *he* wouldn't have had a Depeche Mode CD."

They ordered another round and drank half of it in silence as they each fiddled with their cell phones.

"Why did you decide to quit Customs?" Zhang finally asked, his sense of restraint having been further washed away by tequila and beer.

"I didn't exactly decide to quit."

"You were fired?"

Severin shrugged. "Let's change the subject."

"Oh, come on. You're going to get all reticent on me now? We've known each other for a hundred years. You already know I live in my parents' basement. What could be worse than that?" Severin just stared back at him, looking unhappy. "So, you were fired?"

Severin rolled his eyes. "I was encouraged to leave. They were going to demote me on the basis of some trumped up insubordination nonsense."

"Why would they do that?"

"Some of the higher ups didn't like me. One in particular. The Deputy Chief of Mission of the U.S. Embassy in Seoul. Grumpy old asshole. Bitter because, like so many of those State Department guys, he'd joined the Foreign Service as an idealistic young man. Then he discovered that instead of negotiating treaties and having a say in policy-making, he was doomed to a life of kowtowing to headquarters, cleaning up after whatever faux pas the ambassador was committing, and dealing with menial consular bullshit." A grin appeared on Severin's face.

"What?" Zhang asked.

"Looking back, I almost feel sorry for the son of a bitch. All those years of hard study at Harvard's Kennedy School of Government or whatever, all that student loan debt, mastery of a foreign language, and all just to end up a glorified lackey trapped in a lousy overseas posting with nowhere else to go except maybe an adjunct position at Backwater State University, Crapville campus." He shook his head. "Anyway, the guy hated my guts."

"What did you do, hook up with his wife?"

"That was the rumor."

"Really? Damn, Lars. Good one."

"He was a bastard. And *she* was miserable. Like 25 years younger than him. No exaggeration. He kept her as a trophy wife. She was fun."

"Well, if she was fun, then I guess it was okay."

"Yeah, well."

"So then what? You told them to screw themselves after they threatened you with demotion, then ended up at that crap organic certification gig in Seattle? You had intelligence training. Investigations experience. Why didn't you go to one of those big international, high-paying private investigative or business intelligence firms or consultancies, or whatever they call themselves?"

"Because, Wallace, as a part of the screw-Severin package they'd put together, Customs pulled my security clearance. All those private sector outfits want people who already have security clearances."

"How could they do that?"

"Submitted a form to U.S. government lords of security clearances. In essence, it said I couldn't be trusted with secret information because I partied too much. As if I went around showing people the blueprints for the F-22 fighter at consular cocktail parties or some nonsense."

"Well, dude."

"Well dude, what?"

"You're pretty much an alcoholic, right?"

"Screw you, Wallace. I like to have a drink to take the edge off. My life isn't all rainbows and lollipops."

"*A* drink to take the edge off."

"It's not like I'm Don Draper."

"Isn't it?"

"I don't drink *that* much. I don't."

"The loser doth protest too much, methinks."

"I don't drink any more than I did in college. No more than you did."

"That was college."

"So?"

"It was different then," Zhang said.

"How was it different?"

"We drank for fun."

"Why do we drink now?" Severin asked.

"You mean why do *you* drink now? I don't know. But it isn't for fun. And what does 'taking the edge off' really mean?"

"Don't shackle my buzz, Wallace. One more round?"

"Of course." Zhang flagged down the server. "So, going back a bit further, why did you quit being a cop in Anacortes?"

"Oh, Wallace," Severin said with a sigh. "Can't a man just relax and enjoy his evening in our glorious nation's capital?"

"Don't be like that. Come on, now. What happened? You were a patrolman for a few years, then a detective, right? You burn out?"

Severin's gaze dropped to his glass of beer. "There was a case . . . ."

"A case."

"With kids. Two kids."

"Juvenile delinquents?"

"A five-year-old boy and a three-year-old girl."

"Oh," Zhang muttered, already wishing he hadn't asked. Severin's face was as somber as he'd ever seen it.

"I'd worked several homicides in my time up there. Adult male and female victims from all walks. It was grim work. But for whatever reason, it never really got to me. This was different. I'd dealt with this family a handful of times as a patrolman. They lived in a little old white Cape Cod house near Cranberry Lake, just off Highway 20, on the way out to the ferry terminal. The father was a civilian electrical engineer down at Whidbey Island Naval Air Station. A very decent man. Loved his wife. Loved his kids. But he was mentally ill. I don't know the finer details of it. Bottom line, when he didn't take his meds, he got psychotic. But whenever I got called to the house by the wife or an alarmed neighbor, they'd convince me that they could handle him if I just helped them make him take his pills. That there was no need for the State to intervene. Of course I knew, deep down, that that was wrong. But every time I went out there, I gave in. I didn't want to arrest the poor guy. I'd look into the sad, wet eyes of his beautiful little daughter, Olive, worrying that I was there to take her dad away, and it would just crack my fool heart right open. So I'd help his wife get him to take his pill, leave them the number for our go-to psychiatrist at the hospital, and depart with my fingers crossed."

"Once they promoted me to detective, someone else had to deal with them. I didn't see or hear about them for a long time. But," he took another breath, "around the end of my third year as a detective, the same guy, after telling his clueless co-workers that he knew he could handle it, and unbeknownst to his wife, decided to go off his meds again." He shook his head. "It was an insidious quality of his disease, you see. It itself convinces you it isn't there. Convinces you that it's a waste to keep taking the meds and dealing with their bothersome side effects. So he flushed his pills, and inside of a week, he killed his wife and children as they slept. Cut their throats with a razor blade, then went to an all-night coffee shop and explained to a random, utterly mystified server that he'd finally built up the courage to fight back against the dark angels, whatever the hell that meant. I got the call at about 1 a.m. Having met the wife and kids a bunch of times years earlier, having formed the inevitable emotional bond with them, I was wrangling with a huge fear of what I would see. So I drove out to their little white house . . . ." He paused. "Shit, Wallace." He shook his head again. "Their eyes were open. It was . . . ." He turned and stared across the restaurant in the direction of the bar. Just then, Zhang noticed that Severin was squeezing the edges of the table with both his hands.

"Hey, Lars, forget it. Never mind."

Severin gulped. "It was their faces, Wallace. The look on those kids' little faces. With their eyes open and all."

"Lars, really."

"It's weird. I mean, I've never had kids. Don't want to have kids. Don't even really like kids."

"The innocence, right? Makes it all the more tragic."

"Sure. I mean, to some extent. But I think what got me—what *really* got me—was the idea of their helplessness. I mean, with adult homicide victims, I could always tell myself, *oh, they'd been stupid to get themselves into this or that situation,* or *I would have made different choices,* or whatever. But with the kids, it just hit me how helpless we all are. We're all so utterly damned helpless in the face of death." He exhaled. "The vision of those kids' faces are a daily—and I mean daily—reminder of that."

"I'm speechless."

"Yeah, well. Anyway, that was it for me. I decided I'd seen enough. I marketed my investigations experience to our good old federal government, and Homeland Security picked me up by my bootstraps, gave me six months of training down in Georgia, and dropped me in Customs as a special agent. Criminal investigations, but no homicides. No more kids. No more death."

"I can understand you not wanting to get back into local law enforcement. But there must be other lucrative options out there for you. I mean, you aren't a *total* moron. You're maybe even marginally capable. Why do you stay in that crap-paying organic certification job when you hate it so much?"

"I don't know."

"You don't know?"

"Honestly? I just have trouble caring anymore. No motivation. For anything, really."

"You're a bit young for middle-age malaise."

"It's strange, Wallace. It's like my sensory capacity, my passion for things has faded. Foods I used to love don't taste as good anymore. Things don't smell as good—feel as good. Things that used to excite me now feel run-of-the-mill. Things that used to make me laugh out loud now just draw a half-baked smile."

"You know what will help?"

"What?"

"Another tequila."

*****

That night, in his hotel bed, Severin's eyes popped open. Again, he had a racing, pounding heartbeat that he could feel in his neck and head. Again, his extremities felt cold and he had trouble swallowing. What the hell was going on? Had he had his recurring nightmare about being frozen in the doorway, having run from the murdered family, but afraid to step forward into the dark void? He couldn't recall. Was this all a precursor to cardiac arrest? He felt for his pulse on his carotid artery, and what he discovered made him sit bolt upright in bed. It seemed to him that after a series of beats that came in rapid succession, his pulse rate suddenly dropped. Was it his imagination? He kept his fingertips on his artery, monitoring. Indeed, his heart rate was changing abruptly. It seemed to slow down when he exhaled, and speed up when he inhaled. Was that normal? Was his heart failing?

All of a sudden, he didn't feel a beat where it was supposed to be. It just didn't come. *Holy shit!* In the frightening pause, he wondered if his heartbeat would resume. When it did, it was with a heavy thump of a beat that seemed to send an electric shock through his limbs. He felt light headed. Should he call an ambulance?

His heart continued to beat. His pulse rate was still rapid, but at least his heart was beating rhythmically. He sat there with his fingers on his carotid artery for another 20 minutes, his full attention focused on every beat, until his arm grew tired. He worried that if he went back to sleep—if he didn't stay awake to monitor his pulse—whatever his condition was could get worse without his knowing it, possibly endangering his life.

Were these episodes getting more frequent? More intense? If they were, then it had to be cancer. A tumor growing in his brain, pressing against the medulla, or whatever the hell part controlled heart rhythm. Or could it be ALS? ALS was progressive, wasn't it? Was it ALS? Or maybe the progressive failure of his heart's sinus node?

It took him a terrified hour and a half to get back to sleep.

ELEVEN

Despite a pounding hangover headache, Severin forced himself to rise at 9 a.m. He made a pot of sour coffee with the foil-sealed pouch of oxidized grounds provided by the hotel, drank it down, and fired up his laptop. The first thing he did was try to track down the lead State Department investigator who'd penned the report on Powell and Keen's disappearance. He dialed the Washington, D.C. number that was in the report only to be informed that the lead agent, Don Allen, had been transferred to the U.S. Embassy in the small South American nation of Guyana. His replacement regretted to say that she didn't have Allen's new phone number. That was telling.

Severin hung up. "Guyana?" he muttered aloud. *A malaria-ridden diplomatic backwater if ever there was one. Must have pissed somebody off to get exiled to there.* After a quick internet search for the number, he dialed the main switchboard for the U.S. Embassy in the Guyanese capital city of Georgetown, and was then promptly transferred to Allen's desk.

"Agent Allen?"

"Yes," he said in a tone that gave Severin the impression he'd interrupted the man as he was reading the sports section of *USA Today* and about to take a bite of a jelly doughnut.

"Morning. Lance Johnston with Political Affairs."

"Okay."

"The undersecretary has to brief a Senate subcommittee tomorrow on everything China, and she tasked me with putting together her briefing book which is to include talking points about the disappearance of the Commerce personnel you led the investigation of, just in case it comes up. I apologize for the urgency, but I'm drafting the talking points as we speak, and the undersecretary and I would be grateful if you could help me flesh this out for a minute. I have just a handful of follow-up questions."

"As long as they don't concern classified information. For that, you'll have to use proper channels, no matter how much of a rush you're in."

Severin was able to confirm that Kristin's husband Wesley had been cursorily interviewed approximately two weeks after the disappearance of the Commerce team. He'd seemed cooperative enough. But he was hard to read. He'd been an emotional wreck. Seemed profoundly angry, which was to be expected. Regardless, the agents were told by their political appointee, non-law enforcement trained superior that because YSP's lawyer, Holloman, had already confirmed that Wesley had parted ways with the group several hours before the Commerce team disappeared, it wasn't necessary to trouble him with any further questions in what was clearly a difficult time for him. In other words, they'd taken Wesley at his word and dropped the line of inquiry. It was astonishing. But then again, State Department agents probably weren't used to investigating homicides. Any homicide detective worth the price of his clip-on tie would have turned Wesley inside out before even thinking about tossing him back into the lake. Would have grilled him. It would have been one of the absolute top priorities.

"A couple of the interviews you wrote up mention a van ride from the involved manufacturing facility to an airport in the city of Qingdao."

"Right."

"I didn't see a report of the interview of the van driver in the attachments. Did you have any discussions with the driver that perhaps didn't merit inclusion in the final report?"

"No. We didn't interview the van driver."

Severin was momentarily staggered by the apparent incompetence. In the pause, Allen picked up on the unasked question.

"He'd disappeared. Nobody could locate him," he said, already irritated.

Now Severin found himself tempted to ask how hard Allen and his Chinese liaisons had bothered to try. He was quick to assume that Allen had that despicable indifference so common to the lesser members of federal law enforcement. It was a personality type that drove Severin crazy back when he was a Fed. If such people didn't give a damn anymore, regardless of the legitimacy of their reasons, then they should quit, sell insurance, and make room for someone good. That they hung on, that they lingered, contagiously miserable and useless, made him furious.

"I see. Do you happen to have a phone number or last known address for the van driver? A list of known associates maybe? Anything that might be of use in tracking him down?"

"Chinese police handled all of that."

"Do you at least have his name?"

"You're writing talking points. What do you need the van driver's name for when he isn't even mentioned in the report? What's the relevance?"

Alright, schmucko. "He was one of the last people to see the Commerce investigators alive, unless the undersecretary and I are misunderstanding something."

Severin's repeated mention of the title *undersecretary* silenced Allen. Unhappy though they might be, the last thing lingerers like him wanted to do was give their superiors any reason to notice them. Severin knew exactly what Allen was thinking, and knew the best thing to do would be to use this new leverage to extract more information from him. But his irritation got the best of him. "Mr. Allen, I have to ask, how long ago did you graduate from training? I mean, are you new to this sort of thing? New to basic investigative work?"

"Who the fff—I've been . . . . What did you say your name was again?"

Click.

Next, he tried the other, junior State Department agent listed on the report. The man was earnest but inexperienced—barely a year out of training, even now. Severin had a relaxed conversation with him, but was able to glean very little useful information. He was at least able to confirm beyond any doubt that the powers that be wanted the investigation to be as short and superficial as possible. The agents had been instructed not to press the Chinese for anything that wasn't offered unbidden. They'd essentially been spoon-fed whatever information the Chinese had seen fit to give them. They'd been allowed to sit in on a handful of interviews in China, had conducted a handful more in the U.S., but had been compelled to make quick findings as to whether there were any suspects. With what little information they'd either been given by the Chinese or had been able to compile on their own within the short time frame, they couldn't conclude that there were any viable suspects—though the junior agent claimed he would have slept better had they been given time to gather a few more facts concerning Wesley. *No kidding*, Severin thought.

So State had assigned the case to an incompetent burnout and a wet-behind-the-ears rookie, and then hobbled them from the get-go. Apparently, Byron Edwards wasn't the only one who didn't want the investigation to lead anywhere.

Getting back on his laptop, Severin searched Powell and Keen's names paired with the terms antidumping and commerce. In barely over a minute, he found Keen's name and former office telephone number in the introductory paragraph of a year old Federal Register notice publishing the findings of an antidumping investigation involving steel from Indonesia. In the same paragraph, he found the name and number for Keen's partner on the case—a man named Sergey Vladimirovich. The same paragraph gave the name of the specific division and office of the Commerce Department for which Keen and Vladimirovich worked. With that, Severin used a telephone directory on the Commerce Department web site to collect the names and phone numbers of 10 more of Keen and Kristin Powell's officemates, as well as the numbers for their director, Elaine Danielson, and Wesley.

Impatient for progress, and casting caution to the wind, Severin started dialing the numbers. Nobody answered for the first three, so he left voicemails requesting a call back. On the fourth number, an investigator named Jane Smiley answered. Severin gave her a quick and honest explanation of why he was calling, and asked if she'd be willing to meet with him to talk about Kristin Powell.

"I don't—I'm sorry, what's your name again?"

He told her, and reiterated that the family simply wanted to know more about what might have happened to Kristin. For closure.

"I didn't work with her on that case."

Severin thought she sounded, quite suddenly, scared. As if she'd just realized or remembered something deeply troubling. "I realize that. But I still think it would be helpful to my big picture underst—"

"No, I don't think I can help you."

"I wouldn't take more than 10 or 15 minutes of your time. I'd buy you coffee. A cappuccino. A mocha. Whatever you like."

"No. I'm sorry. I'm going to have to hang up now. Goodbye."

Calls five and six went to voicemail. Call seven, to Sergey Vladimirovich, hit the mark. Vladimirovich, who sounded to Severin like a man with a serious chip on his shoulder—an authority problem—said he'd be happy to meet. Happy to tell him everything he knew.

The rest of his calls were unproductive. Severin didn't attempt to contact Elaine Danielson or Wesley Powell. He had other plans for them.

*****

Severin found Zhang finishing his breakfast in the hotel restaurant.

"My head is killing me," Severin said as he strode up to Zhang's table.

"Bring me a violin and I'll play you a lament."

"Be a little kind," Severin said, sitting down and then waving an empty coffee cup at the unsmiling server across the room.

"I had a crazy vivid dream last night that I was going bald," Zhang said. "My hair was coming out in big clumps."

"Your pretty, pretty hair? Must have been traumatizing."

"Yeah, well. I went back over the State Department report this morning."

"You're kidding. You're a go-getter, Wallace. Aren't we supposed to still be on Pacific Time?" Zhang didn't bother to answer. "Anything at all about the company van driver?"

"All it says is that the investigators and their Chinese police liaisons were unable to locate him for an interview."

"So he dropped off the face of the earth?"

"Possibly."

"Or, just as possibly, State didn't really want to find him."

"Why wouldn't they want to find him?"

"Who knows? Anyway, I got nothing of value out of the State Department investigators. But I talked one of Powell and Keen's colleagues into meeting us for lunch. Guy named Sergey Vladimirovich."

"A Highland Scot."

"No doubt. I tried the others, with the exception of Wesley and Elaine Danielson, but it didn't get me anywhere. Only one besides Vladimirovich even answered the phone. And none of the others have called me back."

"It's still morning."

"Well, if I don't hear from them, maybe we can chase a couple of them down as they leave Commerce at the end of the work day. Danielson, at least."

*****

They met Vladimirovich on his lunch break in the enormous, sprawling food court of the Ronald Reagan Federal Building, across the street from Commerce headquarters. He brought an officemate he introduced as Andrew Bergman. Severin remembered leaving Bergman a voicemail. They were young—late twenties or very early thirties. Bergman was dressed in smart business casual, but Vladimirovich looked like he dressed as shabbily as he thought he could get away with. Testing the limits. Measured disrespect, in this case indicated by jeans with a hole in one of the knees and a hooded sweatshirt bearing the logo of a hip brand of skateboard. They both wolfed down plates of chicken fried rice as they talked to Severin and Zhang.

"Thanks for meeting with us," Severin said. "Your other officemates won't even return our calls."

"It doesn't surprise me," Vladimirovich said. "Way back, just after Kristin and Bill disappeared, the whole division was ordered not to talk to anyone about it."

"Well, we appreciate your willingness to talk to us all the more then."

"We liked Kristin and Bill," Vladimirovich said. "And we hate our jobs."

"And our bosses," Bergman added. "Anyway, they can't fire us. We're federal employees," he added with a wink.

"So you guys both work for Elaine Danielson?" Zhang asked. They both nodded. "Were you close to Kristin and Bill?"

"We hung out with Bill a fair bit," Vladimirovich said. "I wouldn't say we were close to Kristin. Wesley wouldn't let anyone get within arm's length of her. But they were both nice people."

"So you know Kristin's husband?"

"Oh, yes."

"What can you tell us about their relationship?" Severin asked.

"Kristin and Wesley's?" Vladimirovich asked. "Well, he's a head case. I'll tell you that for free."

"A 21-gun salute head case? Or just a run-of-the-mill head case?"

"Nobody likes the bastard. He's insecure. Condescending. Steals credit for other people's work. Blames other people for his own screw-ups. A backstabber. I could go on and on, but we've all seen the type, right? He used to be what's called a program manager. But the people under him staged a full-scale revolt. And somebody higher up had the balls to do the right thing for once. They let him keep his pay grade, but made him what's called a technical employee. Non-managerial. People still have to be teamed up with him on cases, but nobody has to work under him anymore. Anyway, Kristin got hired, oh, maybe a year ago. They put her in the only vacant cubicle in the office, which was next to Wesley's, of course, because nobody wanted to sit by the bastard. Sweet girl. An introvert. Had framed pictures of cats on her desk, if that tells you anything. Wesley was on her like white on rice before she knew any better. Grabbed her up and got all possessive. They were rarely apart. Arrived together each morning. Lunched together. Went home together. Only socialized with others if it was an official staff event. Christmas party. Somebody's birthday or whatever. Wesley would get all weird on anybody who tried to do anything with her—especially other men. You couldn't even get a coffee with her without Wesley giving you the stink eye. Psycho jealous type. Anyway, within six months of her arrival, they were married. There was no lead-up. No engagement period. No parties or showers. No save-the-date cards. Just all of a sudden, after a three-day weekend, they arrived at the office married. Kristin's other office suitemate, Jane Smiley, finally pried it out of her that Wesley proposed and talked her into going straight to the courthouse with her on the previous Friday. And that was that."

"Was he ever violent toward her?" Zhang asked.

"Not that I saw," Bergman said, with Vladimirovich shaking his head in concurrence. "Although he was definitely what I would call psychologically abusive with her. Hypercritical. Belittling. Then again, that's how he is with everybody."

"Did you ever see him get violent with anybody?" Severin asked.

"No. That being said, I have the definite feeling he is capable of going crazy on someone—attacking them—if sufficiently taunted or provoked. He just seems like one of those guys who's always on the edge of exploding."

"Did either of you notice anything out of the ordinary in the lead-up to Kristin and Bill's trip to China?" Zhang asked.

"Not in the lead-up," Vladimirovich said. "But while they were in China, Danielson got an email from one of them."

"Saying what?"

"No idea. But whatever it said, it got her wound up. This is all second-hand, though."

"From whom?"

"Danielson's secretary. Told us Danielson was all wigged out. Asked her to arrange an urgent meeting with the assistant secretary. Subject matter undisclosed."

"What's Danielson's secretary's name? Sounds like we should have a word with her."

"You mean what *was* her name. It was Tyreesha Harris."

"She's dead?"

"Robbed and shot to death walking to her car at the Anacostia Metro Station."

Severin and Zhang glanced at one another. "Then we'll have to talk to Danielson," Zhang said. "Is there anything you can do to help us facilitate a rendezvous with her?"

"She won't agree to a meeting," Bergman said. "I can pretty much guarantee that. She doesn't do anything she considers the slightest bit risky. And she's the type who considers driving at night risky. No way she's going to agree to be seen anywhere near you two." He thought for a moment. "But you know what? She takes the bus. An express to Alexandria. She waits for it every day, just after 5, down by the corner of 14th and Constitution. It might be worth trying to ambush her there."

"What does she look like?"

"Late 50s. Heavyset. Maybe 5-foot-3. Brown hair that looks dyed. Today she's wearing a kelly green dress. And she always wears a tan, full-length rain coat, even when it's sunny outside."

"Aside from whatever happened on the team's trip to China, was there anything else unusual about the case they were working?" Severin asked.

"Nothing too weird," Vladimirovich said. "I mean, I guess it's somewhat weird that the company they were investigating was looking like it wasn't going to get a punitive tariff rate applied to their goods."

"What do you mean?"

"In these investigations, if we determine that a foreign company's sales to the U.S. weren't priced anti-competitively, then they don't get penalized with an extra tariff on their imports. They get what we call a zero tariff rate."

"Right, but you're saying it's unusual for a company to get a zero tariff rate?"

"It is for cases involving Chinese companies. I won't bore you with all the reasons why."

"And you're saying that the sorghum syrup manufacturer Powell and Keen were investigating was going to get a zero tariff rate?"

"It was looking that way," Vladimirovich said. "I mean, anything can happen in these cases. New information can be discovered that changes our analysis or calculation. But yeah, they were looking like they were in good shape."

"You sound skeptical," Zhang said.

"Their lawyer, Holloman . . . ."

"What about him?"

"He's sharp."

"Definitely one of the smart ones," Bergman added, nodding.

"I mean, a lot of the lawyers we deal with are smiling meatheads," Vladimirovich said. "Guys who got into Harvard and Yale because of connections instead of merit. Better at slapping backs than understanding the nuances of our investigations and the underlying law. Anyway, Holloman definitely read chapter two of the manual, as they say. Definitely knows his stuff. He does really well, consistently. Has clients in a bunch of different antidumping cases. And they all tend to come out in pretty good shape."

"What's wrong with that?" Zhang asked. "The cases are fact-driven, right? And I gather that Holloman's services are in demand. Maybe he can afford to be selective in who he takes on as a client. Maybe he only accepts clients who he reckons are charging fair prices on their U.S. sales."

"Sure. That's possible," Vladimirovich said.

"But," Severin said.

"But we see a lot of fraud out there. Or at least what you might call compelling circumstantial evidence of fraud. Schemes you wouldn't believe. And some of it can't have been brought about without the deliberate ignorance, or even active assistance or guidance, of these foreign companies' American lawyers."

"Don't you catch that when you go do the overseas, on-site part of your investigation or whatever?" Zhang asked.

"Not if a company is good at cooking its books or forging supporting documentation like raw material and utility bills, payroll records, invoices and shipping paperwork," Bergman said. "I just had a case where we figured out the company we were investigating was the same company we'd penalized two years earlier. All the same people. They'd just changed their company name, moved to an office and warehouse two miles from their original address, and pretended they were new to avoid paying the cash deposits for tariffs that were slapped on them the year before. It's a fraudulent way of getting yourself a clean slate and new investigation."

"How did you figure that out?"

"They accidentally included letterhead with the old company name in some of their submissions to the new case record."

"Oops," Severin said.

"Yeah. And between you and me," Bergman said, "it's all the more suspect when a foreign company fares as well as YSP did in one of our investigations because there's a lot of room for discretion in how we apply our statutes and regulations. A lot of gray area. And when we have the option, we don't tend to rule on issues in a way that benefits the foreign companies. Especially Chinese companies. To put it bluntly, the deck is usually stacked against them—if their American adversaries in the case have any influence on the Hill, that is. It's political."

"Like everything else in this town," Severin said.

"So much so that sometimes it's hard to figure out who the good guys are," Vladimirovich said. "I mean, if you're a foreign company, is it okay to commit fraud to get around a law if it's being applied unfairly?" He shrugged. "Sounds like a question for undergrad philosophy class, right?"

"So, bottom line, you're suspicious of Holloman because of his success?" Zhang said.

Vladimirovich shrugged. "I'm suspicious of everyone. It's the nature of the business. The foreign companies. The American companies. The lawyers on both sides. Our own political masters. They're *all* working their angles, if you ask me. All bullshitting us. All scratching the backs of congressmen and senators who, in-turn, scratch the backs of the campaign contributors who own the foreign or U.S.-based factories involved in our cases. All twisting the law and facts to fit their ends. Undermining the legitimacy of our work until our efforts are practically meaningless. A dirty business, all the way around."

"I take it you aren't concerned about your potential future in politics, throwing around blunt statements like that," Zhang said.

"No. And you know what? You think any of these bastards gives a crap about the American or foreign workers they're supposed to be fighting for? Hell no. They're all in it for themselves. For the billable hours. The power. The ego trip. This whole business is nothing but a three-ring weasel circus."

"Hey, there's numb nuts right there," Bergman said, pointing to a tall but slouching, scowling, dark-haired man crossing the food court, a paper-wrapped sub sandwich held in the crook of his arm as if it were a football, making his way for the entrance to the pedestrian tunnel that led back under 14th Street to Commerce.

"Numb nuts?" Zhang asked.

"Wesley."

As he walked, Wesley's roaming eyes chanced upon Bergman. He stopped in his tracks. His gaze moved from Bergman to Vladimirovich, then to Severin and Zhang. His dark eyes smoldered as he took in the scene. There wasn't a doubt in Severin's mind that Wesley had been told someone was attempting to contact and interview Kristin and Bill's other coworkers, and that Wesley was guessing, correctly, that he was looking at the culprits. In a vain attempt to look disinterested, he nodded an acknowledgement at Bergman, then resumed his course without looking back.

"So what else?" Bergman asked.

"Who else might know anything?" Severin said.

"I'm not sure. We can ask around for you. Course, the other problem is getting people to talk to you. Our office is sort of a weird bunch. Easily intimidated by the political chain of command, you know? Most of them were pretty spooked by what happened, and probably all the more spooked by the bosses telling them to keep their mouths shut—half implying that discussing it was somehow a federal crime."

"At some point, we may have to go to China for a bit of follow-up," Severin said. "With that in mind, if there is anything you can give us that might help us figure out who to talk to over there, such as the names of people at the company they were investigating, that would be enormously helpful."

"No problem," Vladimirovich said. "The sorghum case got handed off to a new hire. Nice enough guy. If you give me your email address, I'll ask him to send you the public version of the company's investigative questionnaire responses. The amount of useful information in those things varies from case to case, but they should have some public information about the organization, management, and even maybe a little bit about the ownership of the company. Anything that isn't proprietary."

"That would be great. Thank you."

Severin gave both of them his cell number, email address, and the name of their hotel in Arlington, asking that they do whatever they could to encourage their colleagues to reach out.

As they rose to leave, Bergman paused. "I just thought of one other thing. It's probably nothing."

"In movies," Zhang said, "when they say *it's probably nothing*, it always ends up being the clue that breaks the case."

"What is it?" Severin asked.

"The day before they dropped off the radar, Keen texted me a picture to my smartphone. No text. Thing is, I can't even make out what it's a photo of. It's a huge image. Takes forever to load. And when it finally does, I have to scroll all over the place to find the edges. All I can make out is a big black and gray blob. I figured it was, you know, like an unintended or accidental text. Probably an accidental photo, too. Touchscreen buttons activated by accidental contact, in his pocket or whatever."

"That happens to me all the time," Vladimirovich added. "Once, when I was in a bar hitting on this Hill intern, I pull my phone out of my coat pocket to find that my mother has been on the other end for almost 15 minutes."

"Did she hear anything incriminating?" Severin asked.

"She claimed she couldn't hear a thing. Just bar noise muffled by the fabric of my coat pocket. Said she stayed on the line just in case I'd been kidnapped and gagged or was having a heart attack. But who knows. She might just have been trying to avoid embarrassing me."

"Would you mind forwarding me the photo Keen texted to you?" Severin asked Bergman. "You never know with these things. Did you tell State about it?"

"State?"

"The investigators from the State Department."

"Are you kidding? We're a couple of nobodies. They never bothered to meet with us."

TWELVE

The same afternoon, Severin and Zhang turned the corner of 14th Street and Constitution Avenue, striding into the shadow of the massive Commerce headquarters building, to find Elaine Danielson, waiting for her bus in her kelly green dress and tan raincoat, right when and where Bergman told them she would be.

"Ms. Danielson?" Severin asked softly. She flinched anyway, then gave a furtive glance up 14th in a desperate search for her bus. "My name is Lars Sev—"

"I can't talk to you." She hardly made eye contact before taking two steps closer to the curb and scanning the area as if looking for a means of escape.

"You already know who we are."

"Please go away."

"We'd only ask for a moment of your time. We'll be completely discreet. Nobody ever has to know you spoke with us."

"No." She gave up on the bus and made for the crosswalk, walking quickly. Severin guessed she was heading for the Federal Triangle Metro Station. Striding alongside her, he noticed tiny droplets of sweat forming on her hairline. But it was only 49 degrees out, and she'd barely walked 20 yards.

"If you'd even answer just a couple of quick questions for me. Just a couple." Her pace quickened. "What did the email from Keen and Powell say? Did they find something? Did they think they were in danger?"

"Go away."

"Ms. Danielson, what are you afraid of? Did someone threaten you?"

She didn't answer. Didn't slow down. Didn't so much as turn her head to look at Severin. And a few moments later, she turned into one of the auxiliary pedestrian entrances to the Ronald Reagan Building. A brawny security guard stood just inside the door. Severin and Zhang gave up their pursuit. But just as they were turning to head up the street, a man in a cheap gray suit appeared, seemingly out of nowhere, directly in front of them. It looked to Severin as if the man was puffing his chest out.

"Mr. Severin?"

"Who are you?"

With a jerky quickness, the man flashed his federal credentials and badge. Severin was 90 percent certain they bore the seal of the State Department, and entirely certain of the reason the man was so quick to return his credentials and badge to his pocket.

"Why are you questioning people about a U.S. government matter?" the man asked.

"You know something? You were so quick to tuck your credentials away that I didn't catch your name."

"You're questioning people about an overseas matter under federal jurisdiction."

"I am? Who gave you that idea?" Silence. "Nobody, huh? Well, well. Special Agent No-name, sent forth by nobody."

"You don't have an investigator's license valid in this jurisdiction. So your activities are illegal."

"Is that right? Well, isn't this a little outside your jurisdiction too? I thought you guys were all about diplomatic security. Holding the schlongs of foreign diplomats while they pee or whatever."

"I'll be happy to bring along one of my friends in the D.C. police next time. And I can assure you that this *is* within *their* jurisdiction."

"Oh yeah? What's your name, buddy? Let's see those credentials again." The man stood unmoving, his expression suddenly less commanding. "I thought so. So what's the story? Friend of a friend ask you to hassle us? To try to scare us off? What are you going to do, arrest us because some douche you've never met asked a friend of yours to ask you to tell us we're working as PIs without licenses?" The man stood silent, now looking entirely unsure of himself. "Need me to say that again, but slower? Tell you what—$50 says your boss doesn't even know you're out here doing this. Am I right? Is that kosher with your chain of command? No, it isn't. So get lost." As Severin turned to flag down a taxi, he saw that Zhang had been standing behind him grinning.

"Hey, I'm not—"

"And get a real job, schmucko."

The man didn't follow them.

*****

"What do you think that was about?" Zhang asked as they sat in the back of a worn-out cab that smelled like day-old chicken curry, headed back across the river to their hotel.

"Someone doesn't like us being here. Could be anyone. But there was absolutely nothing officially sanctioned about that dimwit approaching us, rest assured. Favor by a Sigma Chi frat brother of a cousin of a friend of a friend of a friend type of thing. Guy's name was probably Chet. Or Chad. He looked like a Chad."

"If he's just some chump, then how did he find us?" Zhang asked.

Severin was wondering that himself. "Maybe Wesley saw us from his office window, as we were pacing back and forth out there watching for Danielson, and called the guy," he said, now quite unsure of himself.

"Does Wesley have an office on that side of the building?"

"How should I know?"

THIRTEEN

As Severin opened his hotel room door, eager to get to his toilet, he stepped over a standard white business size envelope with his last name on it. It wasn't marked with the hotel's letterhead.

Five minutes later, he was standing in Zhang's doorway, holding the open note in his hand. It was written on a sheet of printer paper. "I think we have a dime-store spy on our hands here. Look at this thing." The note read: *Go home, Severin. More going on than you know. You are playing with fire. Friendly warning.* "Looks like someone did it with their non-dominant hand so the writing wouldn't be recognizable."

"How banal," Zhang said. "Isn't that a trick from one of the Hardy Boys stories?"

"Wallace, your comments are starting to make me feel like my whole life is one big rerun."

"A remake, you mean. An inferior remake."

"First, you tell me this whole affair has a hackneyed plot, or sounds like *The Girl with the Dragon Tattoo*, and that I'm just the latest clone of the redemption seeking former lawman from dozens of crap movies you've seen. Next, I'm a lesser knockoff of Travis McKee."

"McGee."

"McGee then. Unlicensed PI—"

"And excessive drinker."

"—from 20-plus mystery novels. Old hat. Now you're telling me we're re-enacting elements of a Hardy Boys story from, what, 70 or 80 years ago?"

"And let's not forget that even your name is stolen from a 19th century novella about a Ukrainian pervert."

"See what I mean?"

"Well, you know what they say."

"No, but I bet you'll tell me."

"Everything has been done before."

"Then save me some time by telling me how this story ends."

*****

Lacking motivation to find a good place to eat, they settled for another unimpressive meal in their hotel. Afterward, though it was barely 7:30, Zhang said he was too tired to go out, so Severin headed back up to his room with a tentative plan to pour all the little vodkas and gins in his mini-bar into a cup with two ice cubes, add a splash of tonic water, kick back in bed, and maybe watch a pay-per-view movie. A comedy. As he arrived at the elevators on Zhang's floor, he found another man already waiting there. Both the up and down elevator buttons were pushed. Severin figured the guy wasn't watching what he was doing and hit the wrong button first. Maybe he was drunk. The up elevator came, and they both moved toward it—the man starting to move a split second after Severin. Once inside, the man pushed the button for the top floor. "What floor?" he asked Severin. For reasons that escaped him, the hairs on the back of Severin's neck stood up. "Seven please," he said. As the elevator ascended, Severin had the peculiar feeling that the man was studying him with his peripheral vision. Of course, he couldn't tell for sure. But the feeling was definitely there.

He got out on the seventh floor and walked down the corridor as if everything was normal as could be, looking over his shoulder a couple of times as he went. Nobody was behind him. Reaching the fire stairs, he climbed to the eighth floor, peeked out the cracked fire door to see whether the man was anywhere to be seen, then walked to his room, smiling over what he was certain—or at least nearly certain—was just silly paranoia.

Before mixing his drink and turning on a movie, he decided to check his email one more time. He was pleased to see that the new Commerce investigator who had taken over Powell and Keen's sorghum case had, presumably at the request of Bergman or Vladimirovich, emailed him several dozen files that hopefully included the promised public versions of the company's voluminous investigative questionnaire responses. He'd look at them later. In the meantime, he forwarded copies to Zhang.

He was about to shut down his laptop when the tiny white envelope icon symbolizing a newly received email appeared in his in-box. It was from an anonymous Gmail account—the email address a nonsensical combination of letters and numbers. Someone had probably set up the account just to send this one email. There was nothing in the subject line but an exclamation point. Nothing to suggest there were any computer viruses attached. Opening it, he found a simple four-sentence note. *I was a friend of Kristin Powell. I have information for you. Meet me at Galaxy Hut on Wilson*

Boulevard in Arlington this evening at 9 PM. I already know what you look like.

Wishing the email contained a little more information, Severin was nevertheless pleased to learn that at least one of his old watering holes was still in business. A place where he could always find a good beer on tap. He wrote back a plain reply. *Galaxy Hut. 9 PM. See you there.*

Back on his feet and staring out his 8th floor window, across the Potomac River and western edge of D.C., he called Zhang and told him to hold off on changing into his jammies. He remained there after hanging up, gazing down on the labyrinth of office buildings that housed the government agencies, law and lobbying firms, and embassies comprising the privileged but never satisfied core of the most powerful city on Earth. Innumerable entities pressing innumerable causes with cleverly veiled disregard for the desires or best interests of the electorate. Desperate people vying, clawing for seats at the top table. For power. Just looking at it conjured up memories—some exaggerated, some dead on the money—from the time he lived and worked there. In his bitter and cynical eyes, it was a corrupting snake pit that slowly but surely brought out the worst in people.

Severin caught himself nearly shuddering. Snapping out of it, he pondered the fact that there were a disconcerting number of gaps in his understanding of what happened to Powell and Keen, and perhaps more importantly, why it happened. If anything, the number of unanswered questions was growing, not shrinking. It was his understanding that the precious soybean trade agreement was signed, sealed, and delivered. In other words, it was, in theory, no longer a factor. So why was there still so much apparent push-back? Why were people still so afraid to talk with them? For that matter, why was so much of the State Department report blacked out in the first place? Was there something else going on? Something that he had yet to discover? He really began to wonder. And was he truly just being paranoid about the man in the elevator? Perhaps not.

He turned away from the window, walked over to his suitcase, dug out a small notepad that contained nothing more than a few pages of irrelevant, nearly week-old notes encompassing his search for D.C. flights and hotel rooms, and set it on the small desk. Then he did something he hadn't done since his days in the diplomatic service in Korea. Using a simple trick from his basic counter-surveillance training manual, he opened the notepad to its second page, took three of his own hairs, and laid them across the first, 10th, and 15th lines on the page. He closed the notepad once again, slowly and carefully, making sure the hairs didn't move from where he'd placed them. Making sure they couldn't be seen unless the notepad was opened. Then he messed up his bed and hung the do-not-disturb sign on his doorknob.

*****

As they got into the elevator, Severin pushed the button for the 4th floor instead of the lobby.

"What are you doing?" Zhang asked.

The door opened at the 4th floor. "Come on," Severin said. They walked to the far end of the hall where a floor-to-ceiling window framed a view of the Lincoln Memorial across the river, and further off, the Washington Monument and Capitol Building. All three reflected the rapidly fading purple-magenta light of the evening sky. "I want you to assume that people are going to be listening to anything you say in your room or on your phone."

Zhang smiled. "You're joking."

"No."

"Then you're paranoid."

"Probably. But if there's one thing I've learned over the years, it's to trust the hairs on the back of my own neck."

"And they're standing up?"

"Yes."

"Why?"

"I'm not sure. There was a guy in the elevator earlier . . . . Never mind. Just humor me."

"Whatever."

"There's one other thing. There's a small room just outside the elevators and stairwell on the underground parking level. At one end, there's a marble table with a decorative vase of fake flowers on it."

"So?"

"I want you to set up your smart phone to take a video in there. Lean it against that vase, in the shadow of the fake flowers, and hit record. Make sure it's set up to cover enough of the room that the video will catch anyone coming out of the elevators or stairwell."

Zhang gave him a dubious look.

"Just do it. Then walk to the far end of the parking garage, conceal yourself behind a minivan or something, and wait for me. I'm going to get off in the lobby, pretend to wait for you by the couches, and then head down the stairs to meet you in the garage."

*****

A little while later, as they were walking up Wilson Boulevard toward Galaxy Hut, and with Severin eyeballing window reflections to check for followers on foot, they watched the short video on Zhang's smart phone. For the first two minutes, they saw nothing but the empty room. At the 2:17 mark, the elevator doors opened and Severin strode through the room. Then it was back to nothing. 2:30. 2:40.

"This is silly," Zhang said.

"Wait."

At the 2:47 mark, the door to the stairwell appeared to move. They both stopped mid-stride on the sidewalk.

"Did that door just—"

"Wait, I said." Then the door opened, but only three or four inches. There, it stayed for a moment before a slouching man in what looked like khakis and a blue raincoat burst from the dark doorway and flashed across the screen in a blur of rapid movement. "Replay that," Severin said. They watched it three more times before Severin asked if Zhang could freeze it as the man crossed the field of vision. Zhang tried several times, pausing it in a number of places. But no matter what he did, they couldn't get a clear image.

"Probably just some random guy," Zhang said.

"Probably."

"Maybe dropped his phone as he was trying to open the door from the stairwell."

"Maybe. But after he walked half way across the parking lot, looking all around, I watched him reverse course and go back to the elevators."

"Might have forgotten his car keys."

"Might have."

"Who would be following us?"

Severin shrugged. "One of Wesley Powell's buddies. Someone from State. The Gestapo. Who knows?"

*****

Having walked just over a mile from their hotel, they entered the Galaxy Hut bar and took a small table in the corner. The place was barely half full. But the music playing on the house stereo would be loud enough to mask their conversation from anyone who wasn't seated at their table.

"So," Zhang said, "man or woman?"

"The email didn't say. But from what we know of Kristin's personality, and of her husband's jealous protectiveness, I'm guessing any close friend of hers would be female."

"Mr. Severin?" a female voice asked, right on cue. "I'm Chloe Kellar."

Severin turned to see a tall, confident looking, red-headed woman looking down at him. Her hair was tied back in a simple athlete's ponytail, and she wore no-nonsense jeans and a T-shirt. "Lars, please. And this is Wallace. Join us?"

She plopped down with her half-empty pint of dark beer as the server strode over from the bar.

"What are we drinking there?" Severin asked.

"Porter," Kellar said.

"Brilliant." Severin and Zhang ordered the same.

"Sorry for the cloak and dagger," she said. "I just wanted to make sure you were who you said you were before I gave you any name or real contact information."

"You checked on us?" Zhang asked.

"I called Kristin's cousin, Anna, out in Oregon. Kristin, Anna, and I met for a little girls' night out a few months ago. Anna, in turn, called the uncle who hired you to make sure you were for real."

"Well done," Severin said. "And speaking of names, I don't remember seeing yours in the directory for Kristin's office."

"No, I work in another part of the building. National Oceanic and Atmospheric Administration. Totally different sub-agency of Commerce. Anyway, like I said in my email, I was friends with Kristin. Loved her. And I play soccer with Bergman. At practice after work today, he told me you're here gathering more information for the family. That they think there's more to the story."

"Did you see the report from the State Department?" Severin asked.

"No. But I heard it's worthless," Kellar said.

"I can't say we disagree with you. Still, its conclusions—if they can be called that—are entirely plausible."

"Well, I don't know whether you've met her husband, Wesley, or not. But I can tell you right now that somebody should be taking another look at him."

"Not terribly well liked, I take it?"

"A controlling, psychologically abusive creep."

"Physically abusive too? Ever see him get even just a little bit rough with Kristin?"

She shook her head. "No. But I'm sure he had it in him."

"Did she ever hint at it? I mean, that he was rough at home maybe? Behind closed doors?"

She shook her head again. "Still, the guy was primed to explode. Total jealous psycho."

"Why do you say that?"

"He was crazy possessive with Kristin, for one thing. Wouldn't let anyone near her."

"I'm surprised he let Kristin join you for a girl's night out."

"We literally had to sneak her out of the building while he was in a meeting."

"I know the type. So how did *you* get to know her?"

"We were in yoga class together in the Commerce Department gym. It was practially the only time all day long when Wesley wasn't right next to her. She was a sweetheart. Needy. No confidence. Wouldn't stand up for herself. But a real sweetheart."

"Why did she stay with him?"

"Usual story. Like I said, she was needy. She had no self-esteem. He doted on her. Gave her the strokes she craved. Worshipped her in his creepy way."

"Attention is the heroin of the emotionally deprived," Zhang said. Severin gave him a questioning look.

"Still, there are plenty of possessive, jealous men out there who don't necessarily merit suspicion along the lines of what you might have in mind," Severin said.

"Yeah, but I think he knew. I mean, he always looked paranoid—like the whole world was out to get him, to steal his case work, steal his woman, steal back credit that he already stole for the work of someone else. But his body language and facial expressions the week before Kristin left for China—I really think he knew."

"Knew what, exactly?"

"That Kristin and Bill were in love. That they were having an affair."

"How did they manage that?" Zhang asked. "I mean, with Wesley sticking to Kristin like her Siamese twin all the time?"

"Where there's a will," Severin muttered. "Did Kristin confide in you?"

"She didn't need to, though I think she tried to once. Poor thing was trembling. Looked like she was going to have a stroke. That was around a month before she left for China."

"And Wesley was on to them?"

"That was my read," Kellar said. "He was suddenly that much more possessive. That much more venomous and suspicious of everyone around him. I imagine he was reading the same body language between Kristin and Bill that I was, and knew that if something wasn't already going on, it would be soon. I'm sure the idea of Kristin and Bill flying off to China for two weeks had Wesley apoplectic."

"But you're not absolutely certain that they were having an affair? Or that if they were, that Wesley was aware of it?" Zhang said

"Not 100 percent, no. I'll say I'm 95 percent sure. How's that?"

"It's helpful. But the more concrete evidence you can give us, the better," Severin said.

"How about this? I heard that Wesley made a series of increasingly anxious, increasingly demanding, increasingly belligerent early-morning phone calls to China, trying to contact Kristin when she and Keen were over there. But he never got in touch with her. Not once. He connected with Keen a handful of times, demanding that he get Kristin on the phone. Keen always told Wesley that Kristin was already asleep, or hadn't been feeling well and was in her room after giving Keen instructions that she wasn't to be disturbed, or whatever. There was always a plausible excuse. I mean, of course it was reasonable that she was in bed by the time Wesley called, given the 12-hour time difference. Of course it was reasonable that she might not be feeling well, since a lot of folks get crazy diarrhea and whatnot when they're in the back country overseas. But she never obeyed Wesley's command that she return his calls. That would be very out of character her, unless she had a secret reason."

"How do you know about Wesley's phone calls?" Severin said.

"From Kristin and Wesley's office suitemate, Jane Smiley. She'd be there in the morning when Wesley was trying to call."

"Is she a friend of yours?"

"Not really. I know her from stopping by their office to see Kristin. But we bumped into each other in the cafeteria just after Kristin and Bill disappeared and got to talking. Speaking of which, she won't talk to you in case you're wondering. I already asked her if she'd come along tonight. She's terrified the boogiemen will come get her if she talks. That, or she'll get fired and Wesley will sue her for defamation."

"Can you think of anyone else who might know about any of this and who might actually be willing to talk to us?" Zhang asked.

She stared at the ceiling in thought, then shook her head.

"What about this," Severin said, pulling the *Go home, Severin* note from his coat pocket and unfolding it to show her. "Recognize the writing?"

"No. It looks like someone wrote it with the wrong hand. Isn't that an old trick from the Nancy Drew stories?"

*****

As the door to his hotel room closed behind him, an exhausted Severin stood in the entryway, giving his senses a chance to process the scene. Did anything look like it had been moved? No. Were there any odd smells in the air, like the trace of an alien shampoo, aftershave, or antiperspirant—vestiges of an uninvited guest? No. He walked over to the desk and, with great care, opened the note pad to its second page. There, his three hairs remained on the lines of the paper. One on the first line, one on the 10th, one on the—16th? He recounted the lines carefully, touching and making a slight indentation in each with his thumbnail. Sixteenth line.

Oh, no.

He sat down on edge of his bed and considered the probabilities. It was entirely possible that he'd miscounted the number of lines on the paper when he set up his surveillance detection trap before going to Galaxy Hut. It was also possible that, despite his hanging the do-not-disturb sign on his doorknob, a housekeeper had come into the room on some errand and somehow moved or fiddled with the notebook. But that made less sense.

For one thing, if a housekeeper had come in, he or she would probably have done something else that was noticeable, like made his deliberately messed up bed. But there was no trace of housekeeping activity. Also, if a housekeeper had done something with the notebook that caused one of the hairs to move, then why didn't the other two hairs move?

That left the possibility that he was under surveillance. Professional surveillance. For not only could they get into the room—presumably without a key—they'd apparently also been *watching for* just the sort of counter-surveillance detection trap Severin had set for them. They'd opened the notebook slowly and carefully. And if they'd been able to turn to the second page without disturbing that one hair, or had been able to return it—that single, small hair—to its proper spot, there'd have been no trace of their visit.

The implications yanked Severin back into secret, buried memories of when he'd been strong-armed into using his overseas Customs position to deliver and retrieve messages for one of the more obscure organs of the U.S. intelligence apparatus. Playing the innocent tourist on the free Sundays before more than a dozen legitimate Pacific Rim trade shows or customs and intellectual property issue consultations between U.S. and Asian government officials. Wondering if he was being followed. Through dark, narrow, ancient alleyways of Beijing's hutongs and Forbidden City. Along the crumbling wharfs and gray Soviet-era apartment blocks of Vladivostok. Through the crowded, colorful open-air markets and steamy, disorienting neighborhoods of Ho Chi Minh City. Wondering whether his counter-surveillance maneuvers had succeeded in losing any unseen followers. Wondering if, somehow, they'd nevertheless seen him make the drop or pick up the envelope or flash drive from its prearranged hiding place under the garbage can, in the stack of discarded newspapers, in the basket of a parked bicycle. Wondering whether an unmarked van would round the corner at any moment to block his path, or whether the door to his hotel room would fly open in the middle of the night. Whether the oft-dreamed of mob of plainclothes goons would surround him, handcuff him, inject him with a sedative, pull a black hood over his head, and drag him away to some dark hole where he'd be tortured for his pathetic few secrets and then shot—his disappearance officially attributed to an ill-advised stroll in a bad part of the city.

Back in the present, Severin realized his palms were damp and his heart was racing. He went to his bathroom to splash water on his face, then thought long and hard about making himself a strong drink to take some of the force off the shockwaves of his resurrected memories of sheer terror. Instead, he turned out the lights in his room, turned on the camera on his smartphone, and scanned the room with it. Then he walked down to Zhang's room. When Zhang opened his door, Severin stepped in and turned out the lights.

"The hell are you doing? Don't be trying to kiss me."

"Shhh."

Severin scanned Zhang's room with his smartphone camera. Then he turned the lights back on. "Grab your laptop and follow me."

They went downstairs and sat down in a pair of wingback chairs they found outside the monstrous double doors of a banquet room on the mezzanine level.

"So what was going on up there?" Zhan asked.

"All but the oldest, crappiest surveillance cameras have night vision capability," Severin said as he turned on Zhang's laptop. "Their weakness, from a detection standpoint, is that they put off an infrared flare that you can often see with a digital camera."

"Surveillance cameras?"

"I didn't see any flares in either of our rooms."

"Thank goodness. I was so worried."

"Don't be sarcastic."

"Why would we even care if someone was watching us?"

"Because if someone is, then the who and the why could lead us to an explanation for Powell and Keen's disappearance."

Severin told Zhang about the moved hair as he searched the internet before downloading and installing a free program he seemed to already be familiar with.

"What are you putting on my computer?"

"This software will scan the area and detect wireless interfaces. More importantly, it can detect wireless bugs."

"I didn't know you were such a computer whiz. Maybe *you* should do our hacking."

"I can download and run a program. I don't know if that qualifies me as a computer whiz. You don't happen to have a GPS receiver connected to your laptop, do you?"

"Why would I?"

"Tomorrow we'll find you a USB tuner and SDR kit."

"SDR?"

"Software Defined Radio. Most audio bugs operate between 10 megahertz and 8 or 9 gigahertz. With an SDR kit and this software, we can use your laptop to detect signals covering most of that range."

"Okay, Howard."

"Howard?"

"Hughes. And after we get your bug detector, maybe we can make aluminum foil hats to keep the NSA from controlling our minds with beamed satellite signals."

Severin went back to his room, dragged his desk over to and up against his door, and stacked a bunch of empty beer cans and bottles on the edge of it in several tall, precarious columns. It probably wouldn't stop anyone from getting in. But it would slow them down, and make it impossible for them to get in without making a racket and, hopefully, waking him.

Finally, utterly exhausted, he got into bed and turned off the light.

*****

Severin had just nodded off when the hotel telephone rang, startling him. "This had better be good, Man Pretty."

"Lars Severin?" a deep, unfriendly voice asked.

"Who's this?"

"You know who this is. Don't say my name over the phone. I want to talk to you. Set a few things straight. Can you be at the main entrance to my building tomorrow morning at 7 a.m.?"

"Why so early?"

"Is that a problem for you?"

Severin sighed the special sigh he reserved for people who irritate the hell out of him. "We'll be there."

"I'll send someone down to meet you at the security checkpoint and escort you though."

FOURTEEN

The next morning, Severin turned his cell phone back on to discover that Bergman had forwarded the photo that Keen has texted him from China—probably by accident—the day before he disappeared. Severin looked at it, and found that Bergman's description had been on the money. A blurry, gray-black blob, seemingly out of focus and totally unidentifiable. He sent it on to Zhang, instructing him to see if he could find someone—one of his tech buddies—who could shrink down and clean up the image so that they might be able to discern what it was. Then he showered, once again messed up his bed, and once again hung the *do not disturb* sign on his doorknob. But just as he pulled his door shut to leave, he set up another simple, old, but harder to foil surveillance trap. He placed a small wedge of folded-up paper in the crevice between the door and the doorframe, just below the middle hinge. If anyone tried to open his door, the wedge would, if all went as planned, drop to the floor before they could see precisely where it was placed. If it was gone when he got back, or if it was repositioned, he would know someone had been in his room.

*****

On the Metro train ride to Federal Triangle, Severin scanned the faces of those who shared their train car, searching his memory for a hint of recognition of any of them, and doing his best to commit each to memory so he'd know if he ran into them again. He told Zhang how he thought they should play their interview of Wesley.

"Generally, I like to go into these sorts of things with a lot more information than we have, on my own timeline and on my terms. But he initiated the contact. He may not give us another chance. And we can't compel him. We have to jump on it."

"Makes sense."

"If the circumstances were ideal, and if we were sworn law enforcement officers, we'd go in there already knowing almost everything, and with an eye toward getting a straight confession out of him. We'd take command of the conversation from the get-go. Empathizing. Conveying our understanding of his reasons. But also making it absolutely clear that we already know he did it. That he wouldn't stand a chance at trial. That any attempts at subterfuge would only run against his own interests. We'd lay out the list of evidence if we had to, and then tell him this is his one last chance to come clean and to tell his side of it. That by doing so, by being cooperative, he'd make the prosecutor much more inclined to reduce the charges, request the lightest possible sentence, and encourage the judge to agree to the same."

"And that the opposite is true as well?"

"Exactly. Try to mislead us, and the system drops the hammer. No mercy. Maximum penalty. Maximum sentence."

"But."

"But, unfortunately for us, we don't have near enough factual information to take that tack."

"And we aren't sworn law enforcement officers."

"Right. We can't offer a carrot, and we have no stick. So I propose that we do two things here, in particular order. One, we just let him talk. He's already indicated a desire to quote-unquote set a few things straight. So, great. We let him run. Let him feel like he's in control. Let him believe we think his words are sincere. He'll bullshit us, and we'll hold back. We won't be aggressive. We might even be well-advised to play it a bit obtuse. Act like semi-retired mercenary versions of the ubiquitous in-house agency security nincompoops these guys deal with in getting their various clearances signed off on. Guys who aren't quite bright enough to be out on the street working cases. In short, guys of the type Wesley has learned to not take seriously. To that end, I won't mention my background unless he asks about it. If he does, I'll be vague."

"We'll follow up with a few innocuous seeming questions. He'll bullshit us some more. But the shape of his bullshit will tell us a lot. Will help us deduce. Everything a person says tells you something, even if it's lies. So this, Wallace, is the subtle, indirect fact-finding phase. You follow me?"

"Like you said, it isn't rocket science."

"Part two is where we shake him up a bit and see how he reacts. Ask him some questions that poke at his sensitive parts. See if he looks honest, evasive, terrified, or whatever."

"Got it. Incidentally, my computer wizard acquaintance got back to me with some pertinent and very timely information."

"The hacker?"

"Let's stick with computer wizard. And again, let's not use names."

"You're right. The less I know about your little ring of Amerasian computer geek friends from high school, the better."

"Actually, he's Pakistani. Here on an EB-5 visa."

"Oh, good!" Severin said with a laugh. "I'm sure the folks at the NSA aren't watching for Pakistani nationals here on visas trying to break into U.S. government email networks."

"Hey, if I had any redneck Bible Belt WASP friends who knew how to do this sort of thing, I'd have gone to them. Anyway, my guy had some success."

"Did he indeed?"

"With one email account. Non-government."

"Well, that's good news."

"A private email account for Keen. My guy sent me a file of all of Keen's emails from the three months leading up to his disappearance, and a month after."

"Excellent. And?"

"And, though I haven't had time to conduct a thorough examination of the whole file, when I scanned his emails for the week before they left for China, one jumped out at me."

"Don't leave me in suspense, Wallace."

"It was an itinerary confirmation from Singapore Airlines for passengers Kristin Powell and Bill Keen for a nonstop flight, one-way, from Shanghai to Denpasar, Bali. No return flight to the United States."

"Huh! Running off to Bali, eh? Well, toot my whistle. I guess Holloman and Chloe Kellar were right."

"But then why would they bother to go to China at all? Why not pretend to leave for China and then just disappear?"

"Maybe it wasn't a sure thing yet. Maybe Keen planned to use the trip to convince Kristin to run away with him."

"Or maybe they wanted to get the job done and email their report off before jumping ship so that they wouldn't totally screw over their boss."

"Maybe, maybe, maybe. Were there any logins or emails sent from his account after the date they allegedly disappeared?"

"I don't know about logins. But, after they disappeared, there were no more emails sent from that account. It went dead."

"That isn't encouraging."

*****

They stepped through the bronze main doors of the Commerce headquarters building to see that its entry foyer was even more grand and spectacular than its columned, Neoclassical, Greek Revival-style exterior. Walls of granite and limestone climbed from the marble and travertine floor to a high, vaulted ceiling with golden coffering and enormous bronze chandeliers. After pausing for a moment to let Zhang gawk, Severin checked in at the relatively quiet security desk. The security officer made a phone call, and around 10 minutes later, a short, slouching, meek, and thoroughly broken looking middle-aged man arrived to escort them upstairs subsequent to their going through an antiquated magnetometer—probably inherited from a recently renovated airport. Aside from confirming Severin and Zhang's identity with the morbidly obese security desk officer, the man didn't speak. He just turned to walk away, and Severin and Zhang, assuming it was appropriate, followed.

Their escort—who Severin thought bore an unfortunate resemblance to one of the elder hobbits from the *Lord of the Rings* films—led them to the far side of the building where they rode an elevator to the seventh floor before emerging on a hallway that Severin guessed had to be a thousand feet long. "How big is this building?" he asked the hobbit.

"Herbert Clark Hoover Federal Building has 3,300 rooms, 36 elevators, and an area of 1,812,102 square feet. Largest office building in the world at the time of its completion in 1932. Pentagon is bigger now."

Severin revised his moniker for their escort. He wasn't a hobbit. He was the savant character from the movie *Rain Man*.

Rain Man led them to a door to an office suite, knocked, opened and held the door open for them, then departed without a sound. They stood in a cramped, stuffy, windowless, colorless room containing two unoccupied gray cubicles, one against either side wall, each stacked high with documents and random office detritus. Another door stood open in the opposite wall. They approached it and looked in to see Wesley Powell, whom they recognized from the day before in the Reagan Building food court, sitting behind a large wooden desk and staring out tall windows that framed a view of the Ellipse and White House South Lawn across the street. He had a phone pressed against his ear and appeared to be in a state of deep thought. "Mmm-hmm," Wesley was muttering into the phone. "Yeah. Well, I need that memorandum by Tuesday at the latest. So figure out how to get it done." He glanced up at them for a moment, raised an insolent *just wait right there* finger, then resumed his conversation as he stared down through the surface of the desk. Classical music played from hidden speakers.

Several things occurred to Severin. First, there probably wasn't really anybody on the phone with Wesley. It was too early in the morning for him to be in a work conversation. Indeed, there was hardly anyone in the building yet. Plus, his tone struck Severin as contrived. Second, this wasn't Wesley's office. He'd probably removed and hidden somebody's nameplate, maybe Elaine Danielson's, just prior to their arrival, hoping they'd think it was his. They already knew he shared a suite of cubicles with other workers. In short, Severin figured that Wesley was trying to make himself look more important than he was, driven by some kind of insecurity or fear. Or that he was trying to hide his guilt behind of a façade of busyness and authority. Or both. After another minute of occasional mutterings into the phone, Wesley hung it up.

"Sounded like an important call," Severin said.

"Well. They'll have to get by without me for a few minutes."

Going back to verse one, chapter one of his law enforcement training introduction to interrogation course—get your interviewee talking—and banking on his read of Wesley as being someone who liked to go on and on about himself and what he did, Severin, feigning ignorance, fired off an open-ended question that he already knew the answer to. "So what do you do here?"

"What do I do here," Wesley echoed in an altogether pedantic and pompous tone of voice—more as a statement than a question. "I save the U.S. economy."

"Wow. Awesome. How do you do that?"

"By enforcing U.S. antidumping law."

"Anti-*what*?"

"Antidumping."

"You mean, like, toxic waste?"

"No. Not, like, toxic waste," Wesley said with a sigh, nearly rolling his eyes. "Have you ever read anything written by James Fallows?"

"The sports writer from Winnipeg?"

"Sports writer? No. Never mind. Let's see if I can explain this without confusing you. Dumping is an old-school international trade law term for strategic anticompetitive pricing. It's a classic unfair trade practice and a massive threat to the U.S. economy. Foreign companies cutting prices to undercut U.S. companies—not just to compete for sales in the U.S., but to instead drive the U.S. companies to extinction. To prevent that, to prevent foreign companies from purposely destroying U.S. industries by *dumping* super cheap goods into the U.S. market, we have a body of federal law designed to stop it. In a nutshell, a U.S. industry brings us a complaint that alleges dumping by their foreign competition. We investigate those foreign companies, and if we find that they are dumping their products in the U.S., then we place a tariff on those foreign companies' imports into the U.S. It levels the playing field."

"And that saves the U.S. economy?" Severin asked. "Must be a big deal."

"You're skeptical."

"No. Well, I mean, I guess it seems weird that I'd never heard of antidumping until just now," Severin lied. "I mean, I read my hometown paper."

"Let me illustrate it a different way. What's an industry you think of the U.S. as leading the world in?"

"I don't know," he said, shrugging. "How about computer stuff. Microchips and so forth."

"Ah, semiconductors. Perfect example. Did you know that there would be no Intel, no Motorola, no AMD computer chip manufacturing companies today—probably no Apple, no IBM, no Dell or Hewlett-Packard—if it weren't for us?"

"Is that right?"

"I'll tell you a story. This was a long time ago, so I may not have my facts 100 percent right here. But with that caveat, in the 1980s, Japanese semiconductor manufacturers like Hitachi, NEC, and Toshiba, probably under the direction of Japan's Ministry of International Trade and Industry, began dramatically cutting the prices of the memory chips they sold to U.S. computer makers. *Dumping* them in the U.S. market. The prices were ridiculous. In fact, they were often below the cost of production. As you can imagine, after several years of this, the U.S. memory chip makers were on the verge of bankruptcy. Even though U.S. technology was absolutely, positively superior, the U.S. manufacturers, following free market principles, couldn't stay in the game. They couldn't afford to sell at a loss just for the sake of being competitive and maintaining production. By 1986, roughly 9 out of every 10 of the most popular types of memory chips were made in Japan. And one by one, as the U.S. chip makers bowed out, the aftereffects began to take down the U.S. companies that made the machinery that made the chips. Then, the U.S. computer makers began to falter because the supply of the chips they needed began to dry up as the Japanese chip makers, who now largely controlled the global supply, were suddenly favoring Japanese computer makers. Restricting the flow."

"Needless to say, the result was a domino effect. In a few short years, U.S. high tech went from leading the world to facing extinction—even though, with respect to free market principles, they'd done everything right. Even though they made the best stuff. U.S. manufacturers were on the brink of utter collapse, from end-to-end of the supply chain. And you can bet that U.S. microprocessor producers were next on Japan's list of targeted industries." He leaned back in his chair. "So how did the Japanese pull this off?"

"No idea," Zhang said.

"They offset their losses on their U.S. sales by overcharging their customers back in Japan. In short, they were using high prices back in Japan as a sort of subsidy so that they could undercharge customers in the U.S. All with an eye toward destroying their U.S. competition over the long term. All with an eye toward eventually taking over and completely dominating the U.S. and world semiconductor and computer industries. They didn't care about short-term profits. They were playing the long game. Once Intel, Motorola, and AMD were out of the memory chip game, Hitachi, NEC, and Toshiba would be able to charge whatever they wanted. They could favor Japanese computer makers with greater availability of the most cutting-edge chips, and with better, lower prices than what they charged U.S. computer makers. Then, once Apple, HP, Dell and IBM were gone, Japanese computer companies Sony, Fujitsu, Toshiba, and so forth would be king. Japan would be king. Every U.S. product with a silicon chip in it would need to get that chip from Japan. The U.S. military would be utterly dependent on Japan for critical components of its weaponry. And a lot of American high-tech workers would now be picking cabbage outside of Modesto."

"But you came to the rescue."

"Happily for Apple Computers, happily for U.S. Steel, American wheat and honey farmers, battery and solar panel makers, timber workers, shrimp fisherman, and so forth, this anticompetitive pricing, this *dumping*, violates U.S. law. In the computer memory chip case I was describing, our investigation led us to impose tariff rates as high as 35 percent on the import of Japanese memory chips into the U.S. As a consequence, the Japanese surrendered in their trade war against us. Thanks to us, the U.S. industry rebounded. So today we still have Apple. We still have Intel. Our high-tech industry is once again the envy of the world. And truth be told, without the antidumping laws that we enforce here, there would probably be no U.S. steel industry left, no solar panel industry, no commercial uranium enrichment, no tomato or salmon farming, less wheat farming, less domestic lumber production, no domestically manufactured batteries, diamond saw blades, lined paper, washing machines, laminate flooring, wind turbine towers, or oil pipe. The list goes on and on."

"Well then, thank you," Severin said. "I guess maybe I shouldn't always hate on the federal government."

"Indeed. What we do here protects our economy from something that's a greater threat than terrorism and narcotics combined."

"I had no idea," Zhang said, shrugging.

"Nobody does. Our investigations don't sell newspapers. They don't capture people's attention the way hijackings, bombings, and cocaine do."

"I suppose you can't expect an unfairly low-priced computer chip to frighten people the same way 9/11 or Pablo Escobar did," Severin said.

"Unless they happen to work in one of the targeted industries."

"Can I ask you a quick question on an entirely different subject?"

"Certainly."

"Just out of curiosity, why didn't you want me to say your name on the telephone when you called me last night?"

"I'm not at liberty to say."

"Really? Alright. Well then, why did you want to talk to us?"

"Because people always suspect the husband. Because I don't know what other bull people might be feeding you—what lies you've heard. Because I'm not," he paused. Cleared his throat. "Because I'm not well-liked by some people here. So they might be inclined to draw conclusions against me."

"Well, we're not biased. We're here to get as much information for Kristin's family as we can, so we'd be happy to take down whatever you'd like to tell us."

"I'm not sure how to begin. Kristin's family never liked me, so there's no limit to what kinds of crazy theories they've come up with."

"Why didn't they like you?" Zhang asked.

"Because I'm not a millionaire businessman. Because Kristin preferred me to them. Because I don't eat lutefisk and refused to wear their ridiculous Norwegian bunad folk costumes for their annual family Christmas photo. But whatever," he said, waving a hand as if swatting away a fly. "What would you like to know?"

"Well, we skimmed the State Department report," Severin said. "It says you were over there at the end of the team's trip."

"Yes."

"Then for starters, maybe we could flesh that out a little."

"Fair enough."

"So why were you there?"

"I was investigating a different company in China the following week."

"In the same town?"

"Not—no."

"But nearby?"

"In Jiangsu Province. Town called Jinhu. Not nearby. Not on the way. They were in a town called Yinzhen. Well off the beaten path, to say the least. It was quite a journey. Planes, buses, taxis. I won't say it was easy. But I speak Chinese, so that facilitated things. I went to compare notes. To see what they learned that could help me in my own investigative work the following week. A lot of times, it turns out these companies are secretly related. Multiple storefronts of the same entity, owned by the same people. Sometimes, when they know there will be different Commerce teams at each location, you'll even catch them using the same personnel in the investigations of allegedly different, unrelated manufacturers. That sort of thing."

"I see. So your visit to Yinzhen was, in essence, for purposes of making your own investigative efforts more effective?"

"Yes."

"So it was officially sanctioned," Severin said. "You were sent there by your superiors."

"Well, I mean, I had permission to take an acclimation day. Permission to fly over there with enough time to take a 24-hour break before my own work was scheduled to begin. To get over the jet lag and so forth."

"So your supervisors didn't send you. But they knew you were meeting the other team?"

"No."

"But you went there for work reasons. Not for personal reasons."

"I wanted to see my wife, too. Is there something wrong with that?"

"Not at all. Just trying to get the complete picture."

"Fine."

"And you got to see her? Your wife?"

"Yes."

"And how did that go?"

"Fine."

"No discord? No arguments or anything?" Zhang asked.

"What would we argue about?"

"And you were able to talk to them about how things went on the on-site part of their investigation?"

"Yes."

"So how did their investigation go?"

"Fine."

"Anything noteworthy about it?" Severin asked.

"How so?"

"Well, I'm no expert on what you people do here, so I'd leave it to you to decide whether there was anything, say, at all out of the ordinary about how it went."

"Actually, as we were about to get in the van to go to the airport, I asked how it went. Kristin said 'weird.' I asked how so. But she said that she'd explain later, and nodded toward YSP's lawyer who was standing nearby as the company people loaded our luggage into the van. When we got in, the lawyer was sitting right there with us and could hear everything we were saying to each other."

"So after all your efforts to get there and discuss how their investigation was going, you didn't really end up talking to them about how it went?"

"There was a rush to get to the airport. I mean, by the time I got there they'd wound up their work and were trying to get to Qingdao to catch the last flight to Shanghai. And on-site investigations in China are almost always weird. That's the norm. I didn't see any reason to press the matter."

"Okay," Severin said. "You arrived to find that they were already done and rushing to depart. Kristin said the verification was weird, but you didn't ask for details because it didn't seem warranted and because the company's attorney was always close by."

"Exactly. We never want to give lawyers clues about what our findings will be once we get home and analyze everything. It just gives them a chance to screw with us. Try to apply political pressure and so forth."

"I see. Who was their attorney?" Severin asked, playing dumb, wanting to see Wesley's expression as he said the name.

"Holloman," he said in a tone of distaste. "Benjamin R. Holloman of the law firm of McElroy, Steen & Duff. A weasely bastard. Used to be a subpar employee here, actually."

"You rode with them to Qingdao airport?"

"Part of the way. Then I realized it made more sense to take another route. They were driving east. I needed to head southwest, to Jiangsu Province. So I made other arrangements."

"After going all that way, going to all that trouble, to see your wife?"

A hint of dilemma flashed across Wesley's face. A crack in the façade of total confidence. "It wasn't a pleasant—I mean . . . ." Severin waited, watching him deliberate, formulate. "There was an argument. Keen," he said, his voice suddenly venomous. "Keen kept butting in. I was just trying to have a conversation with my wife." He shook his head.

"Why would Keen care about your conversation with Kristin?"

"That's how he was. He liked to get into other people's business."

"What was the conversation about?" Zhang asked.

"I don't even remember. Nothing. Just husband-wife stuff." He paused. "She hadn't returned some phone calls I made, and I was expressing the fact that I'd been worried. Worried over whether or not she was alright. As any husband would be."

"So it was an argument," Severin said.

"No!" he said too loudly. "I mean, it became that with Keen. He kept trying to answer for her. Like I said, butting in. It wasn't any of his business."

"You were angry."

"Yes, but come on."

"So then, what, you had them take you to a bus station?"

"No, I needed to take a walk. Take a breather. I just got out. Isn't all this in the State Department report?"

"I'm afraid we haven't had a chance to look at it all that closely yet," Zhang lied.

"You got out where?" Severin asked.

"Hell, I don't know. Out on some two-bit, potholed country road. Farm fields all around. Middle of nowhere."

"And then what?"

"Then I flagged down a passing farm truck. Big flatbed loaded with empty pig cages. Gave this fella around $10 worth of Yuan to drive me over to Zhucheng, which was, I don't know, six or seven miles to the east. From there I caught a bus south. Made my way to the manufacturer I was investigating down in Jiangsu. That's all I know."

"Okay," Severin said. "Now if you don't mind, if you could walk us through the facts just one more time, we can make sure we understand exactly what you've told us. Got to be sure we don't screw it up."

Wesley retold the story, with Severin listening closely for any and all changes, however slight—any of which could be signals that the story was fabricated. But the story was the same the second time around. Again, it ended with Wesley heading southwest by bus. At that point, Severin decided to test the waters in earnest. "So you never saw Kristin again," he said, watching Wesley's face. His hostile expression didn't change. He just shook his head, then turned and looked out the window as if he were taking a moment for somber reflection. Was it an act?

"So what do you think happened to them?" Zhang asked. "Any ideas?" Wesley shrugged. "Do you buy State's theory that they were killed in a random robbery gone bad?"

"It's possible. But so are other things. That company driver, for one. He disappeared, right? State couldn't find him? That's suspicious. I'm sure the company didn't pay him squat. And what an opportunity, right? Cash and credit cards. American passports. Can you imagine what those fetch on the black market in China?"

"Probably a fair chunk of change," Zhang said. "Still, sounds a bit extreme for the size of the payout."

"Then look at the company people."

"Why them?"

Because of all the money at stake as a consequence of the antidumping investigation. Because of how much depended on the results."

"But the company would expect the case to go on regardless of the team's disappearance, wouldn't it? Didn't it?" Zhang asked.

"Yes, but maybe the on-site investigation didn't go well for YSP. Maybe the team found something that was going to sink YSP's ship, so to speak. Something YSP could sweep up after they got rid of the team. Something they could re-hide before Commerce could send another pair of investigators."

"Like what?"

"Could have been anything. Something as innocent as a systemic bookkeeping error. Something as sinister as outright fraud. Who knows?"

"Well, you would know, if anyone," Severin said. "If there was dirty work afoot, it would have been headline news, right? The team would have told you the moment you got to Yinzhen. Stands to reason it would have been among the first things they mentioned."

"Yeah, I mean—but things . . . ." Wesley looked profoundly

uncomfortable. "Like I already told you, the YSP people were right there with us. Their lawyer, Holloman, rode in the van with us. The team could hardly tell me anything sensitive under the circumstances."

"Couldn't you have snuck around the corner with them before everyone got in the van? Asked for a private word with your wife? Pretended you had to go to the bathroom, asked Keen to show you where it was, then slipped away to get the thumbnail report?"

"I didn't know there was any real reason to. And if Keen or Kirstin did, they didn't make it happen. That's on them."

Cold, Severin thought. "So you think it's possible, if things weren't going their way, that the YSP people might have effectuated the team's disappearance?"

Wesley shrugged again. After a quiet stretch that seemed to make him fidgety, he said, "Is there anything else I can help you understand, or any information I can help you get? All you have to do is ask."

Severin decided that Wesley, while clearly uncomfortable, wasn't quite uncomfortable enough. That maybe it was time to see where a different tack took them. Maybe time for the gloves to come off. "That's very generous of you, Wesley. May we look at your email account?"

Wesley looked surprised. Then, for a moment, troubled. He re-mastered himself before answering. "I wish I could let you do that. There is proprietary information in there that you have to be on a protective order clearance list to look at."

"Of course," Zhang said. "We'd settle for your private email account then."

"Don't have one."

"You don't have a private email account? In this day and age? Really?" Wesley shrugged his shoulders again.

"Do you know anything about our run-in with a State Department flunky yesterday?" Severin asked.

"You mean one of the State Department investigators who worked this case?"

Severin sat quiet for a moment, letting the silence do its work, all the while watching for telltale signs the man was playing dumb. He didn't see any, but that didn't settle the matter. "Wesley, I'm going to be honest with you. It's our understanding that you were spitting mad when you got to Yinzhen. That you completely lost your cool in the van. Blew up. That it wasn't as minor as you are trying to make it sound."

"Holloman told you that, right? Another jerk. Fine. Yeah. Maybe I lost my cool a little bit. But gentlemen, come on. I'd just traveled all the way there from D.C. I was worried about my wife. I was tired. It's only natural I'd be on edge or whatever."

"You blew up, you got out of the van, and then you just threw your hands up and went on your merry way to Jiangsu Province, right? Walked it off and carried on like it was nothing, even though you'd just traveled 7,000 miles, a day earlier than you would have otherwise, by subway, airliner, bus, taxi, ox cart, and/or who knows what, in order to see your wife. Can anyone corroborate your story?"

"Corroborate?"

"Any witnesses who can put you on the bus south. Anyone who can confirm the time at which you arrived in Jinhu. A coworker? Hotel personnel? Anyone?"

"I don't actually think—"

"Or documentation? Receipts? I'm sure you have to keep all your receipts and ticket stubs for claiming your travel expenses when you return home, right? Bus ticket stubs with departure and arrival times, maybe? Taxi receipts?"

"I didn't keep any of that for in-country travel until I got to Jinhu. It was personal. You can't claim expenses for personal travel."

"Personal credit card bills then? Your monthly statements?"

He shook his head. "I negotiated cash transactions for the tickets. That's how it works over there. So no."

"Anyone or anything, Wesley, to show that you didn't decide to chase Kristin and Keen down, confront them at Qingdao Airport or wherever, give them a piece of your mind?"

"You mean anything to prove that I couldn't have killed them."

"Phone or hotel bills showing that you tried to call Kristin every day, because you missed her so much, the following week?" Zhang asked. Wesley just stared. "Something, anything, that shows you tried to call her, even just once?" Zhang asked.

After a pause, Severin stepped in again. "Why did you take two months off after you got home?"

"I was mourning. I was depressed. Is that unreasonable?"

"Tell us more about this explosion on the van ride." Wesley was flushing, but his expression remained stone steady. "Were you upset about anything in particular?"

"I already told you. Keen kept butting into our conversation."

"When you were asking Kristin why she didn't take or return your calls from the U.S.?"

"I've told you that twice now."

"Was that was the primary source of your anger with her at the time?"

"I wasn't angry with *her*."

"Okay, then let's say you were emotional."

"I was just expressing my disappointment in her communication because I'd been worried that something had happened to her."

"But you were able to make contact with Keen, right? More than once, we understand. Keen certainly would have told you if you had any reason to worry about her health and safety when you spoke to him each day, right?"

"I didn't—look, he said she wasn't feeling well."

"Sure," Severin said. "Well, look, whether or not you had logical grounds to be worried about her safety doesn't really interest me. Because honestly, looking at this as an outsider, I've got to tell you that, by far, Kristin and Keen's relationship, and especially the whole Bali thing, had to have you more upset than anything else. If I had been in your shoes, a little communications hiccup would have felt petty compared to *that.*" Severin stopped to watch Wesley's face for reaction and response. Wesley looked caught between emotions. His lower lip quivered, just perceptibly, as if he were fighting to contain profound sadness. Yet at the same time, his eyes burned with naked fury.

"Can't say that I have either the time or inclination to pay attention to the dynamics of all of my coworkers' relationships," he said, doing a poor job of feigning obliviousness. "Anyway, I'm going to need to get back to work here, so . . . ."

And you don't even bother to ask what I meant by the Bali thing, Severin noted.

Wesley's lip quivered again, and for a split second, Severin felt sorry for him. Pitied him for his low self-esteem and the sad childhood that had no doubt crushed it. But Severin had no time for pity.

"I imagine you must have felt pretty damned low whenever you caught one of your friends or coworker's furtive, knowing glances," Severin said.

"Their obvious changes of subject when you came through the door," Zhang added. "The whispers."

"I'd like you to leave."

"Look," Severin said, his eyes still locked in its study of Wesley's facial expression, "I'm sorry to have to bring up something so unpleasant. But I'm of course talking about the romantic relationship between Kristin and Bill. I mean, I don't care how tough a guy is. Under those circumstances, any man would feel a terrible—an absolutely terrible sense of betrayal and loss. Of humiliation. Especially with your colleagues knowing." Wesley's mouth hung open, but no sound emerged from it. "When did you figure out that they were running away to Bali?" Severin let the silence hang once again. Then he asked a final question of Wesley. "Are you sad that she's gone?"

Wesley's eyebrows slowly furrowed as his face grew dark—darker, angrier, more hateful than it had yet appeared. "You need to leave."

FIFTEEN

"By the end of the interview, that guy wanted to rip your eyes out," Zhang said as they sat on the edge of the wide steps, away from the crowd, at the Iwo Jima Marine Corps Memorial, back across the river in Arlington. "I figured he might try to stab you through the heart with his pencil"

"The thought may have crossed his mind," Severin said, constantly scanning the area, scanning the faces of the other people at the memorial, doing his best to detect any surveillance.

"Did you notice that his office was on the opposite side of the building from where the State Department flunky jumped us on the sidewalk yesterday?"

"That wasn't Wesley's office."

"You don't think? Well then it's probably at least on the same side of the building, assuming they cluster offices of the same unit close together."

"Maybe."

"He was certainly evasive."

"But evasive because he's the killer, or because he's horrifically embarrassed about being cuckolded?"

"He definitely knew about his wife and Keen."

"Yes, he did."

"So we now know he had the motive," Zhang said. "And being in China on a legitimate U.S. government mission? What a great opportunity."

"But when did he have the opportunity exactly? Let's think this through. He got out of the van many miles from Qingdao. That much we know for certain. But then what? He lucks out and hitches a ride to Qingdao Airport to catch his wife and Keen, and then?"

"And then Kristin and Keen miss their flight to Shanghai, as expected. Then Wesley is all apologetic and talks his way into sharing their cab back to the Shangri-La Hotel. But they don't go to the hotel. Remember, he speaks Chinese and they don't. So maybe he bribes or coerces the taxi driver into taking them somewhere else. Maybe he even talks Kristin and Keen into going somewhere. *Let me show you this beautiful park I visited when I was here investigating mung bean exporters last year.* Cab drops them off somewhere and he kills them."

"With what?"

"His bare hands. A length of wire. I don't know."

"Overpowers both of them?"

"Knocks Keen out first, with a cheap shot, rock to the head or whatever. Takes him out by surprise, so he only has to worry about overpowering Kristin. Kills both of them, then buries the bodies in a recently plowed farm field."

"Qingdao is a major city."

"Throws them in a dumpster then. Tosses them off a wharf and into the ocean."

"Without being seen? In a city of 9 million?"

"In a dark alley. In an empty parking garage. On an abandoned pier. I don't know."

"Without the bodies ever being found?"

"That sort of thing happens in the U.S. all the time. Point is, it's feasible." Not getting any further challenge from Severin, he went on. "So he's our guy, right?"

"He's certainly at the top of my list of suspects for the moment," Severin said.

"What about the other theories Wesley threw at us?"

"They look like red herrings from where I sit. Smokescreen. Like you said earlier, do you really think the company van driver killed them for a couple of passports, credit cards, and loose change?"

"Maybe the van driver's mother needed medicine he couldn't afford," Zhang said. "And if Wesley did it, then who used the credit cards?"

"Wesley could have taken the wallets and passports off the bodies and then left them in plain sight where someone random was likely to pick them up and try to use or sell them. All to make it look like a robbery. To throw us off. And as for his suggestion that someone from YSP killed them . . . ." Severin shook his head. "No matter how badly the investigation may have gone for them, it seems even more improbable that they would have done something as stupidly bold as bump off two U.S. government employees who were in China on an official mission. People who were, technically speaking and in the diplomatic sense, there at the invitation of the Chinese government. Too much risk. And for what? A difference in their tariff rate of a few percentage points? I don't think so."

"Yeah. And what was with the *I'm not at liberty to say* comment when you asked him why he didn't want you to use his name on the telephone?"

"Posturing. More red herring bullshit. Maybe trying to muddy the waters by getting us wondering whether there is some sort of espionage angle here. Probably B.S."

"So it doesn't bolster your concern that somebody might be surveilling us?"

"No," Severin said, only half believing it. "Wesley is full of crap. As for the surveillance, I'm probably imagining things. I probably miscounted the lines on my notepad. I don't know."

"So you don't think there could be something bigger afoot that we're clueless about?"

"There could be. But I'm tending doubt it," Severin said.

"What about the shooting death of Elaine Danielson's secretary, Tyreesha Harris? Just a coincidence?"

"In Anacostia? That neighborhood's a war zone, if memory serves. Sad though it may be to say so, a shooting there can hardly be called suspicious."

"Okay, but what about that State Department oaf who accosted us on 14th Street?"

"Again, probably Wesley's buddy from the local chapter of the Oprah Book Club, called in for a favor. Believe me, if we'd stumbled into something of a sensitive nature, they wouldn't throw a solo man at us on the street with a half-baked warning like that."

"And the hand-written note?"

"Wesley again. But now that we're reflecting, I have to admit that one thing does intrigue me a bit. That Bali flight itinerary."

"You think they ran off to Bali after all?" Zhang asked. "Dropped off the grid? Now they're, what, selling beads to Australian beach bums and living on wild bananas and mangoes?" Severin didn't respond. "According to the State Department report, Chinese customs said there was no record of them ever leaving China."

"Yeah, but China's customs records probably aren't quite as reliable as some. In fact, Kristin and Keen could very well have just slipped the customs officer at passport control $20 to not process their departure. Twenty dollars to just waive them through," Severin said, opening the web browser on his phone. He looked up the 800 number for Singapore Airlines, instructing Zhang to retrieve the Bali flight itinerary obtained from Keen's hacked email account. Once he got a ticket agent on the line, he pretended to be Keen, providing the itinerary confirmation number, and asking how he could go about getting a refund for his unused ticket from Shanghai to Denpasar, Bali. After a review of the itinerary, the agent regretted to tell him that, even though the ticket was not used, the fare was nonrefundable.

"I guess that's life. Thanks anyway," Severin said, hanging up. "Well, that probably settles that," he said to Zhang. "They didn't make their flight."

"So now what?"

"I doubt very much Thorvaldsson is going to hand us $50,000 just for telling him it's our hunch that Wesley did it. That's already *his* hunch, after all."

"Wait, $50,000? I thought you said we were splitting $10,000."

"Oh."

"Oh?"

"I mean, uh—"

"Et tu, Brute? You piece of sh—"

"Wallace, come on."

"Wallace come on yourself, asshole. Is this the part where I crack you in the jaw and walk away? That's what usually happens in the movies we're reenacting."

"Hold on, hold on. Look at it as us being even now."

"Even? What did I owe you for?"

"Remember our sophomore year, when you took my mountain bike without asking and it got stolen from out in front of Kane Hall? Remember how you refused to admit you'd taken it until we were seniors, and it had all blown over. You never paid me back."

"That bike was a clapped out piece of junk."

"It was an original, first-generation Specialized Stumpjumper. A piece of history."

"You're comparing me getting your rusting, $50 student bike stolen to you holding out on me over a $50,000 payoff?"

"You have to factor in inflation. You have to factor in the cost of a bike relative to the budget of your average college student."

"My budget is still that of an average college student."

"Wallace, come on."

"Admit that you're an asshole."

"I'm sorry. Really."

"Say it."

"Wallace."

"*Say* it."

"I'm an asshole."

"And?"

"I'll split the $50,000 with you."

"Yeah, you will," Zhang said, glaring, but not with enough intensity to suggest that, given their long relationship, he didn't half expect such a move by Severin all along. "So I'll ask again: now what?"

"We keep digging. Keep asking questions."

"Of whom?"

"I don't know about you, but I'd like to have a chat with the team's interpreter. She wasn't in the van, right? Wasn't she in the other car?

Regardless, she might at least be able to tell us about the lead-up to their departure from Yinzhen. We can also take a swing at running down that company van driver. Maybe even a couple of the head honchos at YSP, to eliminate them as suspects if nothing else."

"So we're definitely going to China then?"

"Interpreter lives in Shanghai. The van driver and any other YSP people we might want to talk to probably live in Yinzhen or somewhere nearby in Shandong Province. We need to talk to some folks who were closer to whatever went down."

"What do you think you're going to learn from them?"

"Well obviously, if the van driver did it, we're hoping his guilt will shine through as it does with most moron criminals. If it was Wesley, maybe somebody overheard him make a threat, saw him pocket a big knife, or who knows what. If it was somebody else, like one of the company people, hopefully we'll be able to sniff it out. Honestly, I don't know what we're looking for exactly. But we aren't going to learn anything if we don't go over there and mix it up with the locals. Stir the pot a bit. See what floats to the top."

*****

They spent the rest of the day taking cabs all over Arlington and Fairfax counties, on a wild goose chase of a search for the bug-finding SDR kit Severin insisted they get hold of. They tried calling various stores first. But the minimum wage clerks who answered the phones never seemed to understand what Severin was asking for. So they had to resort to going to each store and digging around in their shelves of equipment. The quest took them from Alexandria to Annandale to McLean before they finally found what they were looking for at a tiny electronics shop in Dunn Loring.

Upon their return to the hotel, they went straight to Zhang's room, where Severin fired up Zhang's laptop, installed the SDR kit—which looked just like a USB flash drive—and clicked the "run" button on the scanner software's control screen. The software churned out several columns of alphanumeric data under headers labeled access point MAC address, associated station MAC address, signal level, channel, and so forth. Then he and Zhang went back out into the hallway.

"What does all that mean?" Zhang asked.

"It means there are a lot of wireless signals beaming through your room. The hotel's WiFi. Personal WiFi hotspots on guests' phones or laptops. Nothing that looks like it could be from hidden micro-cameras or microphones. Nothing suspicious. Still, if your computer had a GPS receiver, we could pinpoint exactly where each of the signals are coming from and—"

"I get it," Zhang said. "So, we're in the clear?"

"Probably. No guarantees."

"You going to scan your room too?"

"Later."

"Where'd you learn how to do all that?"

"Here and there."

"Here and there?"

"YouTube."

"YouTube, my ass." Zhang waited for Severin to offer more of an explanation. He didn't. "But really Lars, you probably miscounted the lines in your little notebook hair trick. You watch too many movies. Seriously, who would give a crap that a couple of irrelevant blockheads like us are chatting with people about Kristin Powell?"

"What about the guy in the parking garage?"

"Lars, if I listen hard enough when I'm at home in bed in the middle of the night, I can usually convince myself that I hear someone outside my parents' house trying to break in. Probably a serial killer. Of course, it always turns out to be the heating ducts flexing and pinging, or the breeze-blown branches of their plum tree tapping against the vinyl siding."

"Look, Wallace, just . . . ."

"Just what? What am I missing? We're talking about a rank and file employee of a U.S. government department that every Republican on Capitol Hill wants to dissolve, who worked in a sub-agency that nobody has ever heard of, and on a case that nobody cares about anymore. Am I on target?"

Severin was half tempted to reveal a few of the many espionage related secrets of his Customs career—half tempted to enlighten Zhang as to the intelligence community's love for pressing straight government employees into using the cover of their legitimate positions to facilitate spying. Half tempted to explain that this might have happened to Bill or Kristin. But gruff, grave voices of indoctrinators and instructors echoed from the training courses of his past, warning him, in no uncertain terms, of the many wicked penalties that could be brought to bear were he ever to reveal anything about his training and accumulated secret knowledge. So he held back. Told Zhang that it was up to him, but that he'd definitely recommend implementing a few precautionary measures. "A little heightened awareness," he said, "never hurt anyone. We probably don't know the whole story here, Wallace. And keep in mind that sometimes what you don't know *can* hurt you. There could be more going on here than we think."

*****

When Severin returned to his room, he was moderately relieved to see that his door wedge was still in the position in which he originally placed it. But then again, he thought, a really good operative would probably have been looking for door wedges as well as notebook hairs, and could have opened the door slowly, just a crack, before spotting the wedge and recording its position for future replacement. At least he knew that if anyone was indeed watching him, they were pros. That whittled down the list of possible suspects.

After turning on Zhang's laptop, he scanned his room with the SDR program with similar results. Then he slid his desk over against the door, reassembled his stacked empty beer can break-in alarm system, and dove into bed, utterly spent.

SIXTEEN

Over the next day and a half they booked flights, received their passports and visas from the express visa service via overnight mail, made a rough outline of their plan for China, and took a couple of hours to blow off steam by touring the Smithsonian National Air and Space Museum. They constantly checked behind themselves for followers whenever they were outside the hotel. Severin obtained the telephone number of the Shanghai-based interpreter, Ms. Yu Lin, from Sergei Vladimirovich, and Zhang began a preliminary examination of the case files they'd been sent by the new hire who took over the YSP case, looking for names of any YSP personnel who might be able to help them locate the missing van driver, or who may have witnessed any interactions between Wesley, Kristin, and Keen. "Some of those case files are hundreds of pages long," Zhang complained when they met for lunch following his initial look.

"Lucky for you, it's going to take us almost 20 hours to fly from here to Shanghai tomorrow. You'll have plenty of time to give them a good look."

"Great. Thanks."

For reasons he refused to explain, and despite Zhang's troubled perplexity over it, Severin insisted that Zhang, on the promise of reimbursement, book and pay for his flights separately. He also told Zhang that when they arrived in China, Zhang was to go through customs on his own. From the moment they unbuckled their seatbelts, under no circumstances was Zhang to acknowledge or in any way indicate that he was traveling with or even knew Severin. They would clear customs, take separate taxis, and then rendezvous at the hotel.

"You're giving me the creeps," Zhang had protested.

"It's just a basic precaution," he'd said as nonchalantly as possible. "In case one of us, for any reason at all, gets held up, at least the other of us won't get entangled."

"For *any reason* such as what?"

"I have no idea. You just never know when traveling abroad," Severin said. "Especially in security-conscious places like China."

Severin was relatively confident that if his cover had ever been blown—that is, if the Chinese had ever figured out that he was facilitating espionage operations way back in his customs days—their security services would have grabbed him then. Still, there was a little voice in his head imploring him not to take the risk—not to tempt fate by going back. But it wasn't loud enough to deter him from going after his big potential payday. All the same, he wasn't about to let Zhang get taken down with him in the unlikely event that they were ready and waiting to arrest him at the airport.

SEVENTEEN

Severin woke with a stiff neck in his coach class window seat, nearly six hours into the second leg of their journey. The cabin was dark, but for a few overhead lights illuminated above passengers who were reading. He was tempted to ask for a couple more vodka tonics to take the edge off his discomfort and growing sense of unease and hopefully knock himself back out. As he thought about it, a little girl peeked over the seat back in front of him. He could only see her eyes, nose, and the top of her head. But she looked Chinese, and couldn't have been more than 3 years old. Severin smiled at her. Her facial expression—what he could see of it—changed, her smiling eyes making her look as though she was about to laugh. She quickly dropped back down, only to slowly rise and peek over the seat back again. Severin waved, and she dropped down. They went through this cycle several times, with Severin leaning forward and lowering his head to hide from her until he thought she'd be up and trying to see him. Then he'd pop up and smile at her again. She began to giggle. "What's your name?" Severin asked her, unsure whether or not she spoke English.

"Lulu," she said, rising up on her tiptoes so that Severin could see her whole face above the seat back.

"Hi Lulu. I'm Lars. How old are you?" She held up three fingers. "Are you going to China?"

Lulu nodded. "To visit my nainai."

"Your nainai? Is that your grandpa?" She shook her head. "Your grandma?" She nodded.

"Do you like candy?"

Lulu nodded again, and Severin pulled a hard starlight peppermint candy from his bag that he'd saved after his meal at the airport. At that point, the mother turned around.

"Oh, please don't give her that. She could choke."

"What? Oh. I'm sorry," Severin babbled, his face turning red. "I don't have kids. It didn't occur to me."

"It's okay," she said, giving him a skeptical look, then getting Lulu turned around and buckled up.

Probably worried I'm some creep, handing out candy to kids like a serial killer, Severin thought.

Lulu burst into tears. "I want the candy," she cried. "Candy!" Sleeping passengers all around them began opening their eyes, annoyed.

Severin shrunk down in his seat, put his headphones on, and started once again listening to his favorite Sonata Pathétique by Beethoven. Then he raised his window shade to reveal bands of violet and indigo stretching across the horizon of the otherwise dark and vast Arctic sky, and a line of jagged, snow-covered mountains—maybe Alaska's Brooks Range—drifting by below their starboard wing, lit purple by an anemic, distant, invisible sun hidden just below the curve of the earth. The music and the moving view conspired to improve Severin's mood. He savored the beauty of the moment until Zhang ruined everything by plopping down in the empty seat next to him.

"I thought I saw movement over here. You're alive."

Zhang's breath was an eye-stinging fume of sour airliner coffee and decaying bits of meat.

"Shall I compare thee to a summer's New Orleans seafood restaurant dumpster?" Severin asked.

"Huh?"

"You have rot breath," Severin said. Did you floss after that steak last night? You need a Tic Tac or something."

"Good morning to you too."

"Is it morning?"

"Actually, it's still late afternoon of the longest day of your life. It's as dim as it is out there because we're taking the polar route."

"I'm not an idiot."

"What are you listening to?"

"Ludwig van."

"Right. And I'm the king of Spain."

"Look at the *now playing* window on my iPod."

Zhang did. "Well I'll be damned. Beethoven? You? Really?"

"I love it. There's so much more to it than what passes for good music today."

"That's very Alex DeLarge of you."

"It's what?" Severin asked.

"Alex DeLarge. The sociopath Beethoven fanatic from the film *A Clockwork Orange*?"

"Are you saying I'm a sociopath, or just making another point about my life being one giant retread?"

"Maybe both. Anyway, I've been checking out the case files on my laptop."

"Do we have to talk about this right now?"

"The new guy on the YSP case who Bergman and Vladimirovich had email the public version of the file to us either misunderstood what they asked him to do, wasn't being careful, or just doesn't get it."

"What are you talking about?"

"He sent us the full case file, including the proprietary information. The trade secrets. Not just the public stuff."

"That could get him fired."

"Well, I'm not about to report it to anyone. Anyway, it's not like we're from some competing company that's going to use YSP's business secrets to our advantage. No harm, no foul."

"I suppose makes sense."

"At any rate, it gives us lots of information we can use to locate or contact YSP company officials. Names of the officers, owners, and key management."

"And YSP's address?"

"I'm sure it's in there somewhere. Anyway, how hard could it be to find a factory in the one-horse town where it's supposed to be located?"

"You get a gold star for the day, Wallace."

"And YSP's accounting records show what they paid Holloman, in case you're curious what big-time D.C. lawyers make in these cases."

"Lay it on me."

"A flat fee of $35,000."

"For the whole thing? That doesn't seem like that much."

"I know. For an investigation that generates hundreds and hundreds of pages of documents, takes many months to conclude, and requires that Holloman and his assistant fly to China for three weeks?"

"I wonder what Holloman's hourly wage is when you break it down that way," Severin said.

"Maybe he's still trying to get established in the market for Chinese clients. Offering bargain prices to get his foot in the door," Zhang said.

"I would have thought he was pretty well established already. But what do I know?"

They were both quiet for a minute. But Severin saw out of the corner of his eye an expression on Zhang's face that made it look as though he were debating whether or not to say something. Severin hoped beyond hope that he wouldn't, and that he and his foul breath would leave him alone so that he could try to get back to sleep.

"So why aren't you happy?" Zhang asked at last.

"What?"

"Back at Big Time Brewery, when I asked if you were happy, you said you were too smart and well-informed to be happy."

"Wallace, I'd love it if you would just leave me the f—"

"I can tell you exactly what your fundamental problem is."

"My fundamental problem? This should be good."

"You're not feeding your soul."

"And you're not the Dalai Lama."

"You hate your job. You hate your apartment. You sabotage your relationships. You have no friends. You're disconnected."

"And you're telling me this because?"

"Maybe the universe sent me to help you."

"Good."

"You need to rediscover a modicum of spirituality. A way to reconnect with humanity. We're all on the same ship, you know."

"Where's the ship's bar?"

"Let me ask you something. What are you going to do when we go home?"

"I don't know. Go beg for my old job back I guess."

"You aren't going back to that crap job."

"What else am I going to do?"

"Anything. You hate it there."

"It pays the rent."

"Barely. Listen to you. You're just treading water. What, are you going to do that job, living paycheck to paycheck, until you die? Is that your life plan?"

"I don't know, Wallace. What's *your* life plan?"

"See, this is part of your problem. Part of why you're unhappy. You need to at least do something you can derive meaning from. Think how much meaning we all derive from what we do. You need to do something you love."

"I don't love to do anything."

"Something you like, then."

"I like to sleep. In fact, I'd really like to sleep right now."

*****

Several hours later, Severin woke once again—this time to the jostling of considerable turbulence—to see the magnificent snow-capped cone of Mount Fuji passing underneath them. If they were over Japan, it wouldn't be too much longer, he thought. He was dying to get up and stretch his legs. But the final stretch felt much longer than it was, and ongoing turbulence kept the seatbelt sign on for the duration. Severin grew so restless he could hardly sit still.

*****

At last, they were descending into Shanghai from the north, over flat lowlands comprised of innumerable rectangular rice paddies that had probably existed for hundreds, even thousands of years. Diffused sunlight glinted off the pooled water they held. It occurred to Severin that in crossing the vast Pacific, he was jumping from a society in which school history texts measured long stretches of time in decades or centuries to one in which texts measured them in millennia. Even the air, thick with an orange humid haze, looked old.

By the time they parked at the gate at Shanghai's gleaming Pudong International Airport, Severin was so fidgety he thought he would lose his mind. He deplaned without so much as a glance in Zhang's direction, then followed the mob to customs. There, doing covert breathing exercises in an inadequate effort to keep himself calm, he stood in line, half expecting to feel a hand grip his shoulder from behind as a team of Chinese counterintelligence operatives—having finally caught their elusive and long-sought-after quarry—prepared to take him away to somewhere terrible. And suddenly he realized his insistence that Zhang buy his own plane ticket and go through customs separately was pointless. Like a fool, he'd mailed their passports and visa applications in the same damned envelope. The Chinese already knew they were traveling together.

The line moved forward, person by person. He could feel another one of his episodes coming on. His heart was pounding. Skipping beats. His face was flushed. Was anyone looking at him? If they were, they'd surely see the fear in his eyes.

Finally, it was his turn at the customs officer's window. Severin felt his armpits sweating. The officer looked him in the eye. Did he have a photo of Severin tacked to the side of the window? Something his superior had given him at their morning briefing. "When you see this guy coming off Flight 484 from the U.S., push your alert button." Could the officer tell his façade was about to crumble under the pressure of his now hardly-contained terror? They were trained to recognize the signs, weren't they? But suddenly Severin's passport was laying on the narrow counter in between himself and the customs officer, and the officer was already summoning the next person in line with a disinterested wave of the hand.

*****

His immaculate, brand new cab sped along the new expressway toward downtown Shanghai, toward a wall of skyscrapers that had marched, with jaw-dropping rapidity, far further east, toward the airport, compared with the last time Severin had been there. Gleaming glass and steel buildings, each one more impressive than the last—symbols of an ancient nation's resurgent pride, confidence, and capability. With an unexpected sense of awe, it struck him that China had to have risen, at least in terms of economic development, farther and faster than any other country in the history of the world—surpassing even post-war Germany and Japan.

As they crossed a high bridge over the Huangpu River, Severin looked to his right. There, in the distance, he saw The Bund—a riverfront strip of venerable if eclectic Romanesque Revival, Beaux Arts, and other Western architectural-style buildings that could easily have been mistaken for the older quarter of any number of European cities. A once-impressive vestige of the era of western colonial occupation, now utterly dwarfed and outshone by the nearby forests of magnificent, shining New China skyscrapers that seemed to stretch for miles in every direction.

Severin had to repeatedly shake off his sense of wonder and remind himself to peek out the back window to check for a tail. But after a few looks, he decided it was an impossible task. For, as he remembered from previous trips to China, there were so many cars and trucks of the same make, model, and color on the road that, barring unique signage, dents, or other markings—which professional surveillance personnel would be sure their chase vehicles did not have—the effort to single any of them out was futile.

*****

The cabs disgorged them in the large circle drive of the Portman Ritz Carlton Hotel. As they passed through the sliding glass doors, the abrupt transition from humid, still Shanghai air—smelling of a mix of cooking food and the sulfurous, metallic emissions of nearby factories—to the lightly perfumed, crisp, refrigerated air of the hotel slapped them from their post-flight daze. Severin marveled at the hotel's opulence as he checked in. Once upstairs in his 24th floor room, he placed a call to Zhang who, curiously, turned out to be only two doors down on the same floor. Were they on the same floor because it just happened to be tailored to the needs of Americans or other English speakers? After all, everything in the room—from the fire alarm evacuation instructions right down to the room service menu—was in English. Or was there a less innocent reason for their proximity to one another in a hotel that must have had at least 600 rooms? Were they, by chance, on a special floor and in special rooms wired for surveillance, complete with microphones, pinhole cameras, and tapped phones? He wasn't about to take any chances. He scanned each of their rooms with his smartphone camera and the SDR kit on Zhang's laptop. Finding no signs of surveillance, he told Zhang to meet him in the bar downstairs in half an hour. "And for pity's sake, brush and floss your teeth."

Before going downstairs, Severin repeated the trick of placing a paper wedge in the crevice between his door and doorframe, messing up his bed, and hanging the *do not disturb* placard from his doorknob.

EIGHTEEN

Severin found Zhang in the bar at the appointed time. He already had a tall, bright yellow, creamy looking drink in hand.

"What's that pretty thing you're sipping on, Man Pretty?" Severin asked as he scanned the bar to see that there were no other patrons.

"A mango milkshake."

"You gonna go ride your tricycle after you finish it?"

"This is the best milkshake I've ever had in my life."

"Let me taste that thing." Severin took a sip. "Damn. That's a damned good milkshake."

"Get you one."

"I think I'll make mine a Scotch. My neck aches from that flight." He waved the bartender over and ordered a smoky double Ardbeg.

"How can you drink that stuff?" Zhang asked. "Tastes like a bus station ashtray."

"I like it. It's great with raw oysters." His drink came and he took a long sip. "So. Notice anything weird on the drive in from the airport?"

"No. But I wouldn't know what to look for. By the way, this is a seriously fancy hotel. Are you sure it's kosher with Thorvaldsson that we're staying in a place like this? I mean, it must cost a lot."

"The cost is surprisingly low. And Thorvaldsson insisted that we stay in top-notch places. So I say we relax and enjoy it."

When they finished their drinks, Severin suggested they take a walk to keep themselves awake until a locally appropriate bed time.

*****

They made their way east, down the historic, tree-lined Nanjing Road, toward the heart of the great city. The sidewalks were thronged with people. It was like an American city, but with all those slight differences you notice overseas. Slightly different cars, clothing styles, smells, traffic signage. Skyscrapers, their tops barely visible through a pervasive gray-orange haze, towered above them. In the space of five blocks, they passed multiple construction sites—each of them crawling with poor migrant laborers in quilted jackets and dirty work pants—wedged in between immaculate banks, cafes and boutiques serving thoroughly groomed businesspeople in smart suits.

"Once again, assume you're being watched 24/7," Severin told Zhang. "Don't discuss anything of a sensitive nature on any phone, in your hotel room, or in cars. Walking outside is best. Let's work out an innocuous code phrase we can use when one of us sees the need for a talk."

"How about if I ask you what the temperature is supposed to be outside today."

"Perfect. Now then, we need Chinese cell phones."

Before long, the road turned into a wide pedestrian mall somewhat reminiscent of Times Square or the famous shopping districts of Tokyo. Narrow, vertical, brightly lit signs adorned with Chinese characters made of elaborate neon lights. Vivid reds, blues, greens, yellows. All the paraphernalia of American or European malls: Zara, Louis Vutton, H&M, Christian Louboutan and, of course, McDonalds. All the western institutions intermingled with massive Chinese department stores, jewelers, restaurants, tea shops, cafes, and label-specific stores of high fashion. A shopper's paradise. But Severin hated shopping.

They came to a sparkling new mall where they found a cell phone store. With what struck Severin as an absurd amount of discussion and haggling for the amount of money involved, and after unhappily learning that they had to register their passport numbers in order to get them, Zhang procured two Chinese smartphones and a one-month service plan with unlimited voice and data minutes.

"So now our passports are linked to these phones?" Zhang said.

"So it seems. Better be careful what we say on them. Big brother may be listening."

"How Orwellian. By the way, I'm hungry again," Zhang said as they left the mall.

"You eat like a horse. How are you not 400 pounds?"

"What do you feel like?"

"I wouldn't mind going back to the hotel and eating in the bar," Severin said. "Get a couple drinks. They had a Reuben sandwich on the menu. Might be our last chance to get Western food for a long time."

"We just got to China. How about Chinese?"

"We're going to have nothing but Chinese for days. Maybe weeks."

"Yeah, but Chinese restaurants always have lots of choices."

"Why do you even ask?"

"Huh?"

"What I want. You ask, but we always end up doing what you want."

"No we don't."

"You're a deft manipulator."

"I am not. The hell are you talking about?"

"I tell you I want Japanese, we end up at Mexican. I tell you I want a Reuben sandwich, you're steering me toward Chinese."

"We're in China. What better place to get it? Plus, the only time you get sick in China is when you eat Western food."

"Exactly. You always explain exactly how it makes more sense to do what you want. You've always been like that, ever since college. I don't know why you ever bother asking my preference on anything—especially when it comes to food. We always end up doing what you want."

"We eat what you want all the time."

"Name one time."

Zhang couldn't. And a few minutes later, Zhang was leading them through the front door of a lavishly decorated Chinese restaurant on Nanjing Road where they were dealt with in short manner by a rather grumpy female server as they ordered and gorged on too many platters of traditional but not particularly good Chinese food.

*****

It was still only 7 p.m. Shanghai time when they finished their meal, so they decided to hop a cab down to the Bund and the Huangpu riverfront for another walk. It was a short ride. All along the riverside walk fronting the old European buildings of the Bund, proud, smiling families were posing to take pictures with the spectacular Pearl Tower—Shanghai's answer to Seattle's Space Needle—in the background, across the river.

The river itself was roughly the breadth of the Potomac where it flowed between the Lincoln Memorial and Arlington National Cemetery. The water was muddy and brown, giving off a complex, organic aroma that formed an exotic mishmash with the terrestrial smells of frying food, the diesel exhaust of passing trucks, the perfume of passing businesswomen, and the body odor of passing laborers. Unlike the quiet Potomac, the Huangpu teemed with a haphazard, seemingly endless parade of vessels motoring up and downriver. Skinny barges and one-off, makeshift craft of all sorts, carrying machinery, stacked crates, livestock, or exposed piles of bulk goods—produce, grains, raw ores, chemicals, soil, the crumbled concrete and bent rebar of demolished, outdated buildings. The river thronged with life, much as it probably had for millennia. Watermen scratching together an existence working on any sort of improvised, jimmy-rigged boat they could weld or nail together and keep afloat. Working with whatever they could get their hands on to make ends meet—to get ahead. In a moment of fanciful silliness, Severin imagined that they all came from some sort of Wild West, pirate-run port hundreds of kilometers upriver, inland, in the ancient interior of China. A dusty, desert town akin to Mos Eisley from *Star Wars*, complete with a raucous cantina where one could find China's version of Han Solo. A place where captains and crew drank away their paychecks with reckless disregard, only to set sail again the next day, looking for a new load of cargo to carry back down to Shanghai.

Then Severin remembered the river was only 70 miles long.

*****

Darkness had fallen by the time they got back to the hotel, so they figured they'd return to their rooms and at least try to sleep despite the 12-hour time difference from D.C. and the complicating factor of their intermittent slumber on the flight over. After checking to see that his door wedge was still in place, Severin stretched out in his bed and remained there for two hours, wide awake, before getting up and, in another fit of paranoia, getting right up close to both the dressing and bathroom mirrors and attempting to peer through them. Testing whether they had any gaps in their backing to facilitate one-way observation or filming. He found nothing and got back in bed, where he once again found himself thinking back to his days as an undeclared spy and courier with diplomatic cover as a legitimate U.S. Customs agent. He'd never met any of his contacts—merely dropped messages for them and collected the products of their treason. He wondered how many of them there had been, whether they'd had families, whether they'd been young or old, male or female. He wondered whether they were truly committed to freedom and capitalism, or whether they had instead been blackmailed or strong-armed into service by one of the American or other western intelligence agencies somehow. He wondered whether they were still alive, or whether their lives had ended in horrific fashion after their fingernails were torn off in one of the many the damp, dark, subterranean, hell-on-Earth concrete dungeons of the dreaded Chinese Ministry of State Security—the MSS.

*****

Eventually, between 2 and 3 a.m., he decided a hot bath might help make him drowsy. He soaked for a good half hour, then wrapped himself in a hotel robe that was a foot too short. With his mind a jet-lagged, whacked out, paranoid whirlwind of incongruous thoughts, he switched on the television to see some sort of Chinese musical play or opera on the first channel he turned to. Players ran about the stage in brightly colored costumes, bearing wicked-looking painted-on masks with exaggerated facial expressions, dancing around to the odd pinging and banging sounds of unfamiliar, unseen instruments, pausing periodically to recite lines of dialogue in highly stylized singsong tones of voice. The old cop in him reflected that all the color and sound and weirdness of it would probably have sent someone under the influence of psilocybin mushrooms or LSD into a terminal fit. He sat on the edge of his bed for nearly 10 minutes, somewhat disturbed but utterly transfixed by the show, bizarre and novel as it was for him. A quick return to the television service's channel guide revealed that the program was the Beijing Opera's presentation of something called Journey to the West: Legend of the Monkey King.

*****

Just after 4 a.m., Severin gave up, dressed, and went downstairs to the bar, where he found Zhang reading a magazine and drinking a pot of tea.

"This is ridiculous," Severin said. "We need to find some sleeping pills, or we're not going to be able to function during daylight hours."

"I haven't slept a wink," Zhang said. "Any ideas?"

"You already know what I'm going to say."

"That we should drink? I'm inclined to agree." Without another word, Zhang went to the bar and came back with two shot glasses filled with a colorless spirit.

"What is it?" Severin asked, sniffing at his, pulling a face of revulsion. "Smells like chemicals."

"I've never known you to turn down a shot. It's called Baijiu. The national firewater. Also the most consumed spirit in the world. It's distilled from fermented sorghum."

"Sorghum again. The stuff of global conspiracy and intrigue. Not just for Tennessee biscuits anymore."

"Indeed. Now then, you need to learn how to say cheers in China. Could come in handy."

"How do you say it?"

"Gan bei!" Zhang said, downing his shot.

"Gan bei," Severin echoed with less enthusiasm, tossing his own shot back with an all-too-well-practiced flick of the wrist.

"It translates to *dry the cup*, which basically means don't stop until it's gone."

"Ugh! This is awful. I remember drinking something like this when I was stationed in Korea. Goryangju, I think it was called. A few more of these and I'll either be ready for bed or a trip to the emergency room."

"It's better than Jim Beam."

"Please." Severin scratched his head. "I saw the craziest thing on television a little while ago. They said it was the Beijing Opera. But it didn't look like any opera I've ever seen."

"Legend of the Monkey *King*?"

"How did you guess that?"

"It's probably *the* opera here. China's *Barber of Seville* or *La Bohème* or whatever."

"Why is it so popular? I found it mildly disturbing. All the weird faces and sounds and whatnot."

"I don't know. Why is *La Bohème* so popular?"

"You have a point. So what's the legend then?"

"Of the Monkey King? I can't remember the story exactly. Something about a clever monkey who is happy until he realizes he's mortal and that the gods don't have any respect for him. Then he pulls a bunch of tricks on the gods to gain power and immortality. The gods still don't take him seriously though, which royally pisses him off and motivates him to grab for more and more power until he becomes a genuine threat to the gods' hegemony. Then he wreaks havoc. Or something like that."

"Huh. Greed, anger, arrogance, and a yearning for eternal life. The pillars of human existence."

Zhang made quick trip the bathroom. As he got back to the table, Severin said "I like to cook."

"Good for you."

"No, jerky. On the plane, you were asking what I like to do. I like to cook."

"You cook? Really? That's hard to picture."

"Thanks. Truth is, I'm a great cook."

"What do you cook?"

"Anything."

"What's your signature dish?"

"It's hard to pick one. Maybe my brined and alder planked salmon. Or my beef Wellington. It's the best in the world."

"So be a chef."

"I have no formal training. Can you picture them reviewing my resume down at Dahlia Lounge or Canlis? Hey Pierre, get a load of this. This guy's claim to fame is that he cooks for himself, like a big boy, and likes to watch the Food Network." Severin shook his head. "Nobody would take me seriously."

"Who takes you seriously now?"

Severin was struck dumb.

"Go to chef school," Zhang said.

"Costs too much."

"Use the money you get from this job."

"If we ever get paid."

"Well, what's wrong with starting on a lower rung of the ladder? Don't apply at Canlis. Apply at an Olive Garden or Spaghetti Factory or something."

"Screw that."

*****

Four rounds later, they were starting to float.

"Can we switch to something else?" Severin asked. "Anything else. Really, anything."

Zhang watched Severin contemplate and then gulp down his drink with a frown.

"That business with the dead kids in Anacortes," Zhang began.

"What about it?"

"It still haunts you."

"Where did *that* come from?"

"It does, doesn't it?"

Severin sighed and nodded. "Yes. Didn't I already tell you that?"

"Does it affect your health or mental wellbeing?"

"I don't know. Maybe."

"Have you ever talked to anyone about it?"

"I talked to you about it."

"You know what I mean."

"My captain referred me to a headshrinker who was supposed to be a specialist in recovery from traumatic experience or whatever."

"Did it help?"

"Maybe a little bit. At first, anyway. I only went a few times. It didn't really click for me. Plus, she wanted to put me on meds, which would have meant I'd have had to take a leave of absence. Wouldn't have been allowed to carry a gun. Wasn't going to happen."

"Well, now that you aren't carrying a gun, maybe you should try again with somebody else. Maybe a behavioral psychologist or therapist instead of a shrink. Maybe they can teach you some coping methods or whatever."

"They'll just tell me the same crap."

"You don't know that. It's worth a try."

"Is it? I tend to think that things are what they are, and you either carry on, or you don't. Hopefully, over time, the edge comes off."

"That's a crock. Let me tell you something. You're one of those types who think they know more than they do. I am too. But someone once convinced me to talk to someone—someone professional—and it made a huge difference in my life. In my state of mind."

"Did you talk to them about your innermost feelings, Wallace? About how your parents only loved you when you got A's in math?"

"I'm being sincere. Try again. If it doesn't click, then try somebody else. Keep trying until you find the person who gets you. Who tells you things that make sense to you. Things that actually help."

"Who has time for wild goose chases?"

"It's like hiring an architect or something. Just because you don't like the designs the first one gives you doesn't mean you give up and just design your own house. We'd all be living in leaning shacks with leaking roofs."

"Do you know how expensive psychiatrists and psychologists are? Do you know how much of that kind of thing my crap medical insurance would cover? Jack squat."

"Then go to a therapist, like I said. They're less expensive, right?"

"I was raised to think of therapists as the chiropractors of mental health."

"That's an outdated way of thinking. There are good ones out there. You just have to keep trying until you find one you like."

"Right. Thanks for the lecture, Sigmund. It's exactly what I needed four Baijiu shots into a self-prescribed insomnia recovery regimen after a 20-hour flight."

*****

Sometime later, just after falling asleep, Severin woke from his recurring nightmare of the murdered family and the dark void to yet another episode of heart palpitations. This time, it took him nearly two frightening, obsessively pulse-checking hours to get back to sleep.

NINETEEN

The next day, Severin rose just before noon, ordered a pot of coffee from room service, and took a long, hot shower. Once dressed, he took the elevator down to the lobby and went out into the bustle of midday on Nanjing Road. As he walked, he dialed the number Andrew Bergman had given him for the Commerce team's interpreter, Yu Lin. On the pretext of being an American tour operator who, having heard good things, was interested in possibly contracting with her to serve as interpreter and guide for periodic Shanghai bus tours, Severin set up an afternoon meeting with her at a café conveniently close to her home in the nearby French Concession neighborhood.

*****

As Severin and Zhang walked from the hotel to the café in the French Concession, they crossed, rather abruptly, from a zone of modern Shanghai into a markedly older neighborhood with buildings that looked as if they belonged in a Western European city of the early 20th century. It was relatively quiet—extremely quiet compared to Nanjing Road. Large, old plane trees lined the avenues, their enormous branches leaning out over the pavement, creating a tunnel-like canopy of leaves. Narrow alleyways led off to courtyard gardens and restaurants. There were numerous French and Belgian-style bistros and sidewalk cafes. There were antique stores, quaint boutiques, and art galleries.

"I was digging through more of the case record earlier," Zhang said as they walked.

"Anything interesting?"

"As a matter of fact."

"Don't make me beg."

"Well, first of all, you know how I told you the new kid assigned to the YSP case accidentally emailed us the full proprietary version of the case file?"

"I do."

"Well, it included a big analysis memorandum the Commerce Department put together. The memo includes a bunch of customs data covering several years of U.S. imports of sorghum syrup, and goes into detail describing and analyzing the total U.S. sales volumes and per-kilogram prices for each of the four Chinese companies that were being investigated."

"And I give a crap about such minutia because why?"

"Last year YSP was the Goliath."

"Again, so what?"

"It's just weird. I mean, YSP had by far the highest sales volumes of any of the four companies Commerce investigated."

"That's weird?"

"It's weird because, according to the data in the memo, in previous years the four Chinese sorghum manufacturers had roughly equal U.S. sales volumes. It's weird because all of a sudden, last year, YSP rocketed ahead of the other three. And it's especially weird because YSP did this after almost doubling the prices of its U.S. sales. Basic economics, Lars. Have you ever heard of a company's sales figures suddenly jumping way up after they double their prices?"

"Maybe they have a superior product."

"Lars, it's sorghum syrup. A product that's about as sophisticated as canned corn. How much variation could there possibly be?"

*****

A smartly dressed, middle-aged Chinese woman immediately rose from her table as they entered the very European café.

"Mr. Severin? I am Yu Lin. It is my pleasure to meet you."

"And you. This is my associate, Wallace Zhang."

"A pleasure to meet you, Mr. Zhang. May I order something for you?"

Though they each requested straight black coffee, she asked them a bunch of questions about whether or not they might like this or that natural or artificial sweetener, this or that dairy product—running through the list from skim milk, to whole milk, to cream, and finally non-dairy creamer—perhaps in an effort to impress them with her knowledge of English. Then, the moment they sat down, probably with the idea of making a good impression as a potential tour guide, she jumped straight into a thumbnail history of the French Concession neighborhood in which they sat.

"You probably noticed the European-looking architecture on the blocks between your hotel and this café."

"We did," Zhang said, tempted to get to the point, but restraining himself in accordance with Severin's instruction to let her talk, establish rapport, and get comfortable with them before they raised the curtain on the real reason they were there.

"Those buildings and houses are remnants of the era of European imperialism in China. At the time of this neighborhood's construction, Shanghai was divided into zones of French, British, and American control. Concessions, as they were called. Many European powers, with their advanced weapons and militaries, forced the Imperial Qing Dynasty—which was weak at the time—into signing what we refer to as the Unequal Treaties, granting to foreign powers these so-called concessions of territory, or even outright colonies, to force China into trade with the West. Forcing foreign laws, even religions, on Chinese citizens who lived in these places. It was a part of what Chinese call our Century of Humiliation. Can you imagine what such a surrender of sovereignty would do to a nation's psyche?"

"I don't imagine Americans would be very happy about it if the situation were reversed," Zhang said.

"Indeed," she said. "Britain, France, Germany, Portugal, Belgium, Italy, Russia, Japan, and even the United States. All these countries had their occupied territories. The Shanghai French Concession was established in 1849, and existed until the Vichy French government handed it over to China's pro-Japanese wartime occupation puppet government in 1943."

"I'd like to think the world has grown up a bit since then," Severin said. "But I may be kidding myself."

To that point, Yu Lin's face had borne no hint of feeling, and her passionless contribution to the conversation had been delivered as if it were a speech she'd read from notecards many hundreds of times. Something oft repeated to busloads of tourists. Something used to demonstrate a knowledge that might favorably impress a potential employer. Severin smiled inwardly as it crossed his mind that he could be talking to an android.

"So my acquaintances have told us that you do a lot of work for the U.S. Consulate," Severin said.

"That is correct. I am acknowledged by your consulate as an expert English interpreter, and I have been vetted to handle sensitive and proprietary material."

"And one of your jobs involves providing your services as an interpreter to antidumping investigation teams from the U.S. Department of Commerce?"

"Yes," she said, as a look of confusion and concern appeared on her previously expressionless face.

"We have a small confession to make," Severin said.

"Confession?"

"We aren't tour operators."

Lin rose to leave. Severin and Zhang followed. "Ms. Lin, let us explain ourselves," he said as they emerged from the dark coffee house back onto the street. They followed her at a comfortable distance so that she'd know they had no intention of apprehending or restraining her. "There's nothing to be at all worried about."

"No."

"It's just that we've been hired by the family of one of the Commerce investigators you worked with to find out anything we can about the circumstances surrounding her disappearance. The family just wants to know what happened to their little girl."

At this, she glanced back at them for a brief look. And when she did, they could see the conflict, the regret, the genuine sadness in her eyes.

"Kristin," she said quietly.

"Yes. Kristin Powell."

"She was very nice person," Lin said, dropping the article 'a' in her distress. "I like her very much."

"She had a kind heart," Zhang said for effect.

"I should not talk to you," she said, still walking, though not as briskly. Then she stopped. She was looking through the windows of some sort of shop front. She glanced up and down the street, then opened the door of the shop. "Come in here," she said, disappearing through the dark doorway.

Severin and Zhang followed her in. It was some sort of foot massage or pedicure shop, inadequately lit with bare fluorescent tubes. A row of five massive massage chairs ran down one side of the narrow, low-ceilinged room. It smelled of nail polish. A single customer sat in a chair with her feet soaking in a shallow glass tank of water. As he looked closer, Severin could see innumerable tiny fish swimming around the woman's feet. They appeared to be biting at her toes. Severin elbowed Zhang, gesturing toward the fish.

"The fish exfoliate your feet," Zhang said.

"Now I've seen everything," he muttered as Lin exchanged a quick word with the receptionist—the only other person in the room for the moment.

"It's okay," Lin said.

"What is?" Severin asked.

"She does not speak English. Neither of them do," she said, taking up position just inside the shop window, behind a lace curtain, in a spot from which she could watch the street. "I like Kristin very much. I try to help you. But quick. Then I go," she said, her eyes never leaving the street.

"What are you worried about?"

"If somebody see me, or know I talk to you, it could jeopardize my work for the consulate."

"Why would the consulate care if you talked with us?"

"After your State Department people talk to me, another man order me never to discuss the matter again."

"Someone at the consulate told you that?"

"Yes."

"Well, if anybody asks, you can just tell them we were tour operators after all," Zhang offered.

"Periodically, they check such things. Double-check. Sometimes they have people follow me. Because of the sensitivity of my work for U.S. Department of Commerce. Because of the sensitive information I see."

"I understand," Severin said. "We can be very brief." She didn't say anything, so he pressed on. "The person who ordered you not to discuss the case—was he your regular contact for contract work?"

"No. Not him. I don't know who the man was. I never see him before."

"An American?" Zhang asked.

"Yes."

"From the State Department?" Severin asked.

"I don't know. I don't think so. The State Department men came earlier."

"Did this man say why you couldn't discuss the case?"

"No."

"Do you have any idea why anyone would order you not to discuss it?"

"I don't know."

"We understand that Kristin's husband, Wesley, arrived as everyone was preparing to depart the hotel in Yinzhen," Zhang said.

"Yes. I do not like him."

"Why not?"

"His face. I could see that he was not a kind person. Not kind to Kristin."

"Did he make any comments or gestures you perceived as indicating that he was a danger to Kristin or Bill Keen?"

"No. I was in my room packing when he arrive. I only see him for a few minutes while we wait in lobby for the vehicles. But I do not like his face."

"Did you overhear anything he said? Anything at all?" Severin asked.

"No. He was whispering to Kristin when I come down to lobby. His face was angry as he whispered. Then we got in the vehicles and depart for Qingdao Airport. Bill Keen, Kristin and her husband were in van with Mr. Holloman. I ride in sedan with YSP company people. Once we depart hotel, I never talk to them again."

"But you saw them. You saw them in the van."

"The van was behind us on the road as we leave Yinzhen. Then it disappear, so we pull over to wait a few minutes. Then it pass us and we follow it to the main highway."

"Where did you pull over?"

"Maybe 5 kilometers from Yinzhen. Small road between farm fields, somewhere between Yinzhen and the national express road. I am not sure where. It was getting dark.

"Could you see them in the van as they passed? Are you sure they were still in the van?"

"Too dark."

"What about the van driver? Anything odd about the behavior of YSP's van driver?" Zhang asked.

"I don't remember paying attention to him. He loaded everyone's bags. After that, I don't know."

"Anything on previous days, like when he was driving the team back and forth from the hotel to YSP's factory?"

"No. He was quiet. I didn't pay attention to him."

"Did you catch his name?"

"I heard them call him Fang."

"Fang what?"

"I don't know. Maybe Xu. Fang Xu. Yes."

"Did *anyone* put off even the slightest hint of antipathy toward Kristin or Bill? The YSP company people? Anyone?" Severin asked.

"Antipathy?"

"Hostility or dislike."

"The YSP people were upset over how the investigation had gone. But I could not tell if their feelings were directed at Bill and Kristin or just at the situation."

"Did they seem worried that the confusion over the dates of their records would have a negative impact on Commerce's findings?"

"Dates of their records?"

"The YSP attorney, Mr. Holloman, told us there was a lot of confusion. That it took a lot of time to sort out. Something about the ledger books being accidentally labeled with the wrong months."

She turned to face them. "Accidentally? I am not sure what you mean."

"Well, what do *you* mean? Why were the YSP people upset?"

"I mean they were upset about the way the investigation ended. Upset that Keen ended the procedures prematurely because of the closet."

Severin shot Zhang a perplexed look. "The closet?"

She glanced out at the street again, scanning with frightened eyes. "I told your investigators. From State Department." Severin and Zhang stood speechless, so she went on. "On the examination tour of the factory. Bill and I were with YSP owner examining factory while Kristin stayed in office with YSP accountant and Mr. Holloman to keep reviewing records. We split up to save time. So Bill turns corner in factory and sees woman he never see before emerge from a door carrying what looks like one of the ledger books they had been examining. She looks surprised and nervous. She walks away into factory, but Bill catches door before it close. He look inside. It's a closet full of cardboard boxes. On top of one box is ledger book labeled for one of same months Commerce team was examining. But original ledger books were already supposed to be in conference room for the Commerce team to inspect. This ledger book look exactly the same. Bill come out of the closet and walk over to me on other side of hallway and told me to go get Kristin and Mr. Holloman. But as he talk, somebody close the door to closet. Bill runs back to door and door is locked. He has me ask YSP people to unlock door. They apologize and say they didn't know he wanted to go in closet or they would not have closed door, so now they must go find key. So Bill and I walk back to conference room where he tells Holloman that he must have immediate access to that closet or he will terminate investigation. Holloman ask him to calm down and says he will make all YSP personnel look for key." The pace of Lin's speech quickened the further she got into her story. "Bill says we will all wait by closet until key is found. But as we leave conference room and go into factory, we find door to hallway in which closet is located is now locked too. No window. No way to get in or see in to where closet is. Five minutes later, YSP owner comes with both keys and opens hallway door, then closet door. Bill goes into closet and starts to pull leger books out of boxes, but then realizes they are not for the same months that we are there to audit. They are from previous years. But Bill believes he previously saw one ledger book for one of exact same months he was auditing."

"He was sure?"

"He was at first. But then when he began to doubt himself, he told Holloman that he wants to see woman who came out of closet so he could ask her about it face-to-face. But YSP people say they don't know who he means. That no woman works in company offices. Bill says that is not true, and that if woman does not show up in conference room in five minutes, investigation is terminated. Five minutes go by. No woman comes. Bill ends investigation and says they will report what happened when they return to Washington, D.C."

"Did Holloman seem worried when Bill first returned to the conference room and said he wanted in the closet?" Zhang asked.

"Hard to say. He was agitated, certainly, because Bill's demand was very threatening. Later, after we return to conference room to wait for woman Bill saw, I had to use restroom, so I miss part of conversation. But when I return, Mr. Holloman is frustrated, telling Bill that YSP had been cooperating, that Bill was mistaken, and that he would sue Commerce Department for unreasonable termination of investigation and would win in court. Maybe Bill make accusations while I am in restroom. I do not know.

YSP officials were very upset and were in animated discussion with Holloman through company's interpreter." As she said this, her eyes seemed to lock on someone walking outside.

"Could you hear what was said?"

"No, they went out into hall," she said, backing away from the window as if retreating from a predator. "That's all I know."

Another customer opened the door to the shop, letting in the bright outside light. Lin slipped out as the door closed, refusing to meet Severin or Zhang's eyes.

"Let her go," Severin said. They turned their attention back to the tank of skin-eating fish and watched for a moment.

"Funny," Zhang said.

"What is?"

"The name of that suspect van driver. Fang."

"Creepy, right? Like a vampire."

"No, dumb-ass. It translates to honest. Virtuous."

"Ah. Well, you can't judge a book by its cover. Honest Xu. I love y'all's names."

*****

"So what do we make of all that?" Zhang asked as they took their time strolling back through the French Concession neighborhood to their hotel.

"Sounds like YSP was up to no good. Had a second set of books. Maybe the records they showed Bill and Kristin were fakes."

"But maybe not. It sounded like Bill wasn't 100 percent certain. Maybe he was wrong about the date of the ledger book he found in the closet."

"And wrong about seeing a female emerge from the closet? I don't think so. Plus, it's fishy that YSP claimed it didn't have any female employees. It's even more fishy that all these doors suddenly closed and locked and that the company people took a long time to get them open again—probably just enough time for them to clear out any accounting records that might indicate fraud. No. YSP was definitely bullshitting them."

"Wouldn't it be awfully hard to pull off creating a complete second set of books? I mean, if the Commerce team was performing an investigative audit, YSP would have needed fake invoices, raw materials purchase receipts, bills of lading, and so forth. Full fake accounting records."

"All you need is a printer and some forms," Severin said.

"A lot of forms."

"Everyone has told us that fraud schemes are common in this arena. So if the records were fake, I'd guess the prices on the *real* invoices for YSP's U.S. sales were much, much lower than the prices they declared to U.S. Customs or reported to Commerce. For that matter, they were probably undercutting their competition. I imagine that's how they doubled their U.S. sales volume last year."

"So on paper, YSP looked like it was playing by the rules. But in reality, it was selling its sorghum into the U.S. at anticompetitive low prices? Issuing a second set of invoices or something?"

"Exactly. I'd also guess that Keen's termination of the investigation is probably what prompted his mysterious, wave-making email to Danielson. I wish we knew what the hell he told her."

"Why would Holloman keep this from us?"

"He did say it was a bad day. He said there was a lot of confusion over the ledger books."

"Yeah, but he didn't come out and tell us that Keen ended the investigation early, did he?"

"Maybe he took advantage of the Commerce team's disappearance to let the whole thing just go away."

"Or maybe *he* killed them."

"For the sake of a minor client? A sorghum syrup processor in rural China that paid him a grand total of $35,000 when he's probably pulling down at least half a million a year as a partner in a big D.C. law firm? Anything is possible, I suppose. But it seems improbable."

"Well then, maybe someone from the company killed them. There was a lot more at stake for them, right?"

"That makes a little bit more sense. But still . . . ."

"And what's the story with the mystery man ordering Ms. Lin to not speak with anyone about the case?"

"Now *that* is an excellent question. A troubling question."

"And?"

Severin shook his head. "I don't know. It's a blank space in the story."

"So now what?" Zhang asked.

"I suppose we go to Yinzhen. Maybe try to track down that van driver."

"Maybe *he* killed them."

"Maybe, indeed. Maybe on orders from the company, or maybe just for himself."

TWENTY

The next morning, they woke relatively early to give Zhang plenty of time to figure out transportation. They learned it was roughly six hours driving time from Shanghai, up through the coastal province of Jiangsu, to Yinzhen. In the alternative, they could spend two hours getting to the far side of town and through security to an airplane, fly almost another two hours to Qingdao, negotiate for another car, and then drive an hour and a half from Qingdao to Yinzhen. They decided to drive the whole trip. It would probably take a hair longer, but would be less of a hassle.

Following the advice of the concierge, Zhang hired a regular Shanghai taxi to take them anywhere they wanted to go for $150 a day. As in the cell phone store, it took forever for Zhang to negotiate what should have been a very simple arrangement with the driver. At one point, with the driver looking on eagerly after making his latest argument, Zhang turned to Severin to complain that the Shanghainese loved to haggle, and that the negotiation was beginning to feel like a *Monty Python* sketch. When the deal was finally struck, all the cab driver had to do was disconnect the taxi light from the roof of his vehicle to avoid being ticketed for working in a city where he wasn't licensed, and they were on their way.

The driver had a permanent smile on his face, seemingly thrilled at the idea of setting off on a cross-country adventure with two crazy Americans. He hadn't even asked for time to go home to pack a change of clothes. All he had, aside from what he wore, was a large thermos full of hot water for his tea. His car was some type of Volkswagen that looked like a stretched version of a late 90s Jetta. The back seat was roomy and comfortable, and the driver was clearly skilled—darting between narrow lanes to avoid traffic, taking advantage of every gap. It made Severin happy. He had a huge appreciation for professional driving that went back to his days as a police patrolman.

Before they'd gone far, Severin had the cab driver circle one of the less crowded blocks in the neighborhood, double back, then proceed for several blocks down an empty alley—all while Severin watched out the back window. Satisfied that they weren't being followed, he told Zhang to give the driver the go-ahead to take them to Yinzhen.

They flew across town, heading north. As they reached the edge of the city and merged onto a modern expressway, Severin found the transition abrupt. One moment, they were zipping along new streets flanked by gleaming, newly-constructed high-rise buildings of steel and glass, the next they were passing between farm fields. There was no gradual change, as one might see in the U.S., from urban to suburban to rural areas. They seemed to go from 40-story condos to soybean fields in a stretch of 20 yards.

The other thing that struck Severin was the obvious difference in standard of living. Shanghai was a rich city by anyone's measure. It was an economic engine. A center of investment, development, and great wealth. Its breakneck growth, towering new skyscrapers, fancy cars, stores, restaurants, museums, and parks were a testament to this. But as they crossed the first farm fields on the edge of town and approached a farmers' village, the difference was stark. Houses in the village were extremely humble. Small. Unadorned. Some had no front door—just an empty door frame. Severin couldn't help wondering whether the farm families who lived there grew at all jealous, bitter, or angry as they looked across the fields to the incredible wealth of Shanghai. He imagined it would be the sort of anger that eventually led to rebellion. To revolution. If the government wasn't careful here, if it didn't address the obvious income disparity in a big way, Severin figured history might very well repeat itself—with armies of pissed off farmers rolling into the cities to reset the balance, spilling a lot of blood in the process.

*****

Soon they were out of sight of the city, amidst fields that had probably been tended for thousands of years. Severin was watching the cab driver pour himself a third cup from his thermos while keeping the steering wheel steady with his knee. "Everybody drinks tea here."

"You're a gifted detective, Lars. When did you first notice?"

"Hardly anybody seems to drink coffee."

"Tea is the second most popular drink on Earth, after water. And it originated here. China is the top producer in the world."

Severin saw that the driver had a box full of loose leaf tea sitting on the front passenger seat. Yet he hadn't seen the man change out the tea leaves. The same tea leaves sat in his cup which he had now refilled a third time. "I should learn more about tea," Severin said. "Coffee makes my stomach hurt sometimes."

"Sure," Zhang said, sounding uninterested as he gazed out the window.

"Can you ask the driver if that's a good kind?" he said, gesturing to the fancy box, adorned with an orange and white foil wrapper and a ribbon seal.

Zhang did. "He says it's a good pu-ehr tea."

"Pu-ehr?"

"It's an aged, fermented tea that they make in the Six Great Mountains region of Yunnan Province, along the Mekong River, down by the borders with Myanmar and Laos. He says he will get a cup when we stop to get gas so that you can try some."

The driver was still talking. "What's he saying now?"

"He's complaining that his tea has gotten much more expensive the past few years. He has been drinking this brand since he was a child. He says it used to come in a simple, orange cardboard box. Now it comes in a fancy box decorated with foil, and the price has gone way up. But the tea inside is still just the same."

"Maybe that's why he's reusing the same tea leaves over and over. Sounds like things in China are just like they are in the U.S. Fancier packaging, higher prices, same old mayonnaise."

*****

Zhang elbowed Severin awake as the car was ascending a long, high bridge. "Behold, Lars. The mighty Yangtze River. One of the cradles of ancient human civilization. Longest river in all of Asia."

"You're like an encyclopedia. A walking, talking, annoying encyclopedia."

"Born in the high Himalayas, flowing all the way to the Pacific Ocean. Home of the Three Gorges Dam—largest hydro-electric power station in the world."

"Impressive."

"Nanjing is just up river from here. Or Nanking, as it's known more notoriously."

"Isn't that where that massacre thing went down?"

"That 'massacre thing'? Yes, Lars. How awe-inspiring, your knowledge of Chinese history."

"Oh now, Wallace. You can't fool me. That was a fake compliment." Zhang sat silent. "What? What's your problem?"

"It's a pet peeve of mine."

"What is?"

"Americans don't know shit about Chinese history. The country with the largest population and second-largest national economy on Earth. The U.S.'s second-largest trading partner, after Canada."

"I just told you Nanking was the massacre place."

"Is that the extent of your knowledge of it?"

"I—well, I mean, I don't know the details."

"Let me ask you something. What's the most memorable event of your life?"

"Probably the first time I saw a full-frontal, naked—"

"No, jackass. Excluding all of that."

"9/11, I guess."

"Of course. And do you know how many people died on 9/11?"

"Three thousand or so."

"That's right. And do you know how many were murdered by invading Japanese troops in the Nanking massacres?"

"More than that."

"More than 300,000. Three hundred thousand, Lars! Most of them civilians, including women and children. The rest were surrendered and unarmed Chinese soldiers. And yet I doubt more than 1 in 50 Americans has a clue about that."

"You have a point."

"What do you know about the Boxer Rebellion?"

"Was Muhammad Ali involved?"

"A massive uprising against all those occupation imperialist forces the interpreter mentioned. Even the U.S. About 140,000 Chinese killed in that one, from 1899 to 1901."

"I'm pulling your leg. I *have* heard of it."

"Right. Because the U.S. was involved, it gets three or four sentences in our high school history books. But it was a drop in the bucket compared to the Taiping Rebellion. Don't know about that one, do you? The Chinese civil war that raged from 1850 to 1864, started by a millenarian Christian who claimed to be the younger brother of Jesus. Twenty million people died in that one. No wonder the Communist Party isn't a big fan of religions, right? Twenty *million*. That's almost twice as many as were killed in the Holocaust. Thirty-two times as many as were killed in the American Civil War. And nobody in the U.S. has ever heard of it."

"Come on, Wallace. We have 700-plus cable channels in the U.S. Between television and internet porn, who has time to learn about Chinese history?"

"That's in bad taste."

"You're right. I'm sorry. But you're ranting." Severin turned and looked at Zhang. "So tell me about some of the good things."

"Good things?"

"Not just the genocidal, homicidal massacres. Good things I should know about Chinese history. It's contributions to civilization, for example."

"How about the invention of rockets, suspension bridges, gunpowder, magnetic compasses, paper, fireworks, parachutes, noodles? How about the world's first planetarium? How about the first utilization of natural gas as fuel? In the 10th century, the Song Dynastic capital of Bianjing was arguably the most modern city in the world. For hundreds and hundreds of years, China outpaced the rest of the world in the sciences, in invention, in the arts, in philosophy, in *civilization*. And now look. China is in the midst of the fastest and largest scale period of economic growth of any country in the history of the planet. How about that for good things?"

"Except for the bigger carbon footprint, yes. Very good. And in all seriousness, I think this is an incredible country."

"And in all seriousness, you're a typical arrogant, ethnocentric American to think you have any right to judge China or any another country."

"Oh, Wallace. Honestly. You need to lighten up."

They drove on, passing innumerable soybean fields and villages where farm families probably lived much as they had for many centuries. There seemed to be a village every five miles—each consisting of a cluster of old houses and one or two larger brick buildings with tall smokestacks invariably emitting curling columns of yellowish smoke that seemed to hang in the heavy, humid air. Some of the buildings could have been tiny, coal-fired power plants. But most were probably small, low-tech factories, cranking out agricultural byproducts, iron rebar, industrial chemicals, plastic thingamabobs, or something along those lines. Eventually, the crops began to vary. But most of it appeared to be low-lying leafy green vegetables or beans of some sort.

Severin took a long drink of cold green tea from a liter-sized plastic bottle he'd purchased at a small grocery attached to the hotel. Looking for a way to kill time on the long drive ahead, he put on his headphones, stretched his legs out as much as he could in the back seat, leaned back, and played his Sonata Pathétique. As the music played, his mind wandered back to Zhang's mention of the Nanking massacres. World history was full of similar horrors. But in Severin's mind, the thing that always stuck out about Nanking in particular was the bizarre contrast, the seeming disconnect, between the culture of the Japanese perpetrators and their horrific actions. It was beyond dispute that Japanese soldiers—and not just a handful of deranged maniacs, but thousands of regular soldiers—had committed unspeakable atrocities against the city's unarmed men, women, and children. Yet these soldiers had come from a country of exceeding politeness, perfect little bonsai gardens, cute tea ceremonies, beautiful watercolor paintings, and graceful calligraphy. From a culture that encouraged keeping one's opinions to one's self in accordance with the traditional honne–tatemae, private mind-public mind divide. How could the bloodthirsty homicidal monsters of Nanking have come from a culture of tea parties and dainty bonsai trees? It made no sense to him. Was it that they were emotionally repressed? Did they so need to vent that when they finally had a chance to do so in Nanking, their expression conflagrated into an orgy of war crimes? Even more perplexing was the fact that it took the Japanese government until 1995 to apologize and accept responsibility for what happened there, and that even in the 21st century, more than 70 years later, a considerable number of the more lunatic nationalist Japanese politicians still refused to acknowledge that it had happened at all. The Far East's version of Holocaust deniers. Perhaps the world hadn't grown up after all.

TWENTY-ONE

Several hours later, having passed hundreds of farms, dozens of villages, small factories, and smokestacks, they were at last approaching the town of Yinzhen. Emerging from an area of small coastal mountains and out onto a floodplain, they exited the main highway and drove a two-lane country road between wide, tilled fields, across numerous drainage or irrigation canals. Twice they had to pass slower vehicles: in one instance, a very slow truck overloaded with timber, and in the other, an honest to goodness ox cart.

The road narrowed as they reached Yinzhen proper, and farm fields gave way to blocks of dusty, indistinguishable, single-story houses with reddish terracotta tile roofs, all built of a seemingly ubiquitous cream-colored brick. Severin guessed there was a little brick factory on the edge of town that had supplied building materials to everyone for countless generations. As they continued down the street, Severin kept seeing men in white tank tops standing in open doorways, leaning against the frames, some of them with their elbows propped high and armpits exposed, many of them smoking, all of them watching the vehicles that drove down the road. Traffic increased dramatically, with small motorcycles and scooters overloaded with multiple passengers—many of them holding onto the bike or driver with one hand while holding bulging shopping bags or holding down a hat with the other—zig-zagging between cars, in and out of side streets and alleyways. And though the main road they came in on was paved, a good number of the intersecting streets were dirt.

As they neared the city center, such as it was, they began to see small businesses of all sorts. But overall, there didn't appear to be much to Yinzhen. In its entirety, it was maybe 500 smallish blocks of houses, small fluorescent-lit shops, light industrial buildings, and warehouses. If it weren't for the fact that the shops each seemed to have a colorful, modern rectangular sign of the style common to stores in American strip malls, and that people were driving cars instead of riding bicycles, Severin would have thought he'd taken a time machine back several decades. The main street and its flanking buildings probably hadn't changed appreciably in many years. And judging by the number of enormous potholes, it hadn't been repaved in the current century.

They pulled up at a gas station, and the driver and Zhang asked the attendant about suitable lodging. Minutes later, they were unloading their bags at a three-star state-run hotel fronted by a compound of concrete slabs in which several elderly people were doing tai chi. The driver assured them the hotel had Wi-Fi. Severin thought the air quality was a lot better out here in the countryside. But there was still something slightly metallic in the way it smelled.

Despite the hotel's dated appearance, it was very clean and well-appointed. A restaurant adjoined the lobby. Of its 20 tables, only one was occupied—by a lone businessman. Regardless, three servers, dressed in white, stood at different points along the wall, waiting to meet the sole customer's needs. A buffet of rice, vegetables, and various steamed buns sat in a rack of eight warming trays, and the air smelled of steaming tea. The front desk was staffed by two smartly dressed young women who got them checked in after an improbably long discussion with Zhang and their taxi driver. Severin once again scanned both of their rooms for cameras and bugs—Zhang's was directly across the hall from Severin's. Not finding anything, he nevertheless reminded Zhang, via hand-written note, that their detection capabilities were limited, and that not finding anything didn't necessarily guarantee the rooms were free of surveillance equipment. He told Zhang to meet him in the lobby in an hour, then went to his room to shower and rest.

Entering his room, Severin discovered that the air was uncomfortably warm—probably in the mid-80s. But he was pleased to see that it was clean and bright. And to his absolute delight, he found a dock for attaching his smart-phone to a small stereo system that was housed in a wall-mounted shelf between the two twin beds. He turned down the thermostat, showered, plugged his phone into the dock, and dozed off on top of his extremely firm bed to the soothing and welcome notes of another Beethoven sonata.

*****

An hour later, as Severin was once again setting his door wedge surveillance detection trap, Zhang opened his own door across the hall. His shoes were shined, his clothes looked clean and pressed, and his hair was once again glossy and perfect.

"You're looking pretty again, Man Pretty," Severin said. "What's your secret?"

"I took a shower."

"Do you use a moisture-balancing, volumizing conditioner with plant-based emollients?" Zhang ignored him. "How's your room?" Severin asked. "Mine is really clean."

"Do you realize how ethnocentric and basically racist you sound?"

"What?"

"The underlying message is that you're surprised your room is clean."

"No, I was . . . . Well, alright. I see your point."

They descended to the lobby where Zhang asked the front desk for directions to YSP. He hadn't yet been able to find a street address for YSP in the multitude of Commerce case file documents that was any more specific than "edge part of Yinzhen." But the girl had never heard of it. She shouted through the open doorway of an office to ask her coworker, and then, when her coworker didn't know, called her manager on the phone. No luck.

"How could nobody have heard of it?" Zhang said. "This town is the size of a postage stamp."

"Screw it," Severin said. "Let's drive around. How hard could it be to find a factory? By the way, is your room hot?"

"Temperature wise? No. Why?"

"Mine's a damned oven. I turned down the thermostat, but I don't know if it made a difference."

"You'll live."

They had their Shanghai cab driver drive them back and forth around the periphery of the town, up one street, down another, sometimes on unpaved alleys. Not seeing any signs for YSP, nor anything that was obviously a sorghum factory, they began stopping at random shops and gas stations to inquire. Still, nobody had ever heard of YSP nor any of the YSP officers, owners, or managers named in YSP's response to the Commerce Department's investigative questionnaires. After two unfruitful hours, at Zhang's suggestion, they widened the radius of their search, reasoning that a factory that processed an agricultural product would probably be located a bit farther outside of town, near the crops. They drove and drove, covering every country road they could find. But still, they had no luck. Finally, after more than six hours of fruitless searching, having inquired with dozens of locals, and driven every muddy and potholed excuse for a road they could find, they called it a day.

"This is ridiculous," Severin said as they made their way back to the hotel. "You're sure there isn't a street address for this place in all of those documents you have?"

"No, I'm not sure. There are hundreds and hundreds of pages. But there's no street address in any of the places you'd expect to find one—on copies of YSP's invoices, in the company description section of their investigative questionnaire responses, or anywhere else I've looked."

"Well, look harder."

"Why don't *you* look?"

Severin shook his head. "Do you think that maybe YSP was just a front? Something that never really existed as a viable company?"

"You mean did they borrow some old factory building and trump it up to make it look legitimate for the Commerce investigators' visit? Wheel in some machinery, some accounting records, and some barrels of sorghum to make it look real, and then wheel it all back out again afterward? I guess if they could have been working from a fake set of records, then it isn't unreasonable to think the whole operation was fake. But why would they fake that part?"

"Remember how Bergman and Vladimirovich said that when they start selling their stuff to the U.S., new companies can avoid paying high tariff rates that were already slapped on other companies during previous investigations?"

"Vaguely."

"I suppose that if YSP was just a front, and the real company is located somewhere else, then if YSP got slapped with a punitive tariff at the end of the investigation, the real company could just change the location of its front company the next year, change the name, and request that Commerce conduct a new investigation. It would give them the so-called clean slate that Vladimirovich was talking about. Another chance to get a low or zero tariff rate. Another chance to export to the U.S. without having to fork out a bunch of cash to pay for tariffs previously imposed on a quote-unquote different company."

"So the same guys just rename their fake front company, relocate their fake factory, and reboot their quest for a zero tariff rate with the Commerce Department?"

"With all of those potential customers over in the U.S.? I would. Wouldn't you?"

*****

When they got back to the hotel, the front desk receptionist waved Zhang over and explained that the gas station attendant who'd directed them to the hotel had come by to invite "the American giants" to his family's house for dinner.

"What do you think?" Zhang asked Severin.

"Guy could be a serial killer."

"It will probably be awesome. The Chinese rival the Italians when it comes to kick-ass family dinners."

"Why not."

The receptionist told them they were to meet the attendant at his gas station at 7 p.m. if they accepted. So they did, walking the few short blocks from the hotel. The attendant, whose name was Rong, was talking a mile a minute as he removed a used tire from the back seat of his car—one of the ubiquitous Volkswagen almost-Jettas—and ushered them in. They drove to the edge of town and across a mile of open farmland, the roads turning to dirt as they did, before arriving in a small village, perhaps four blocks square. Rong's house was on a corner. It was a one-story place that was attached to the rest of the block of residences, much as row houses are in the U.S. It was constructed of the ubiquitous cream colored brick and terracotta roofing tiles, but had an unusually tall, brown wooden door that looked ancient.

Rong pulled to the curb, opened the car door for Zhang with a flair one might expect of a royal footman, then ran ahead of them to open his home's door with a similar panache and proud expression of welcome. Severin entered to see a small family room in which a middle-aged woman, presumably the mother, sat painting her fingernails on a small couch while a boy, maybe 10 years old, played with a toy ship on the floor. She looked up at Severin as he entered and her jaw fell open. She sat frozen, staring. Then the boy did the same. A chattering female voice emanated from a small doorway, probably to a kitchen. A moment later, an old Chinese woman—maybe Grandma—appeared in the doorway, made eye contact with Severin, made a choked *ah!* sound of surprise, then froze along with the rest of them, staring at Severin as though he had green skin and had just emerged from a flying saucer.

By now, Rong was coming in the house. He spoke in very emphatic Chinese, no doubt explaining that they would be feeding guests from the United States. And as he did, the expressions on each of his family members' faces changed from one of perplexity and utter surprise to one of excitement, welcome, and wonder. All of a sudden there was a flurry of activity, with the women jumping around, tidying up, pushing Severin and Zhang to sit on the couch—the best seats in the room—as the boy disappeared into another room, only to re-emerge a minute later wearing a Seattle Seahawks T-shirt. Introductions were made, everyone smiling and nodding politely. Severin and Zhang were brought hot black tea to sip while being more or less interrogated by Rong and his wife and son while his mother finished cooking dinner. The scent of garlic and frying onions drifted in, making Severin's mouth water as he was peppered with questions. They wanted confirmation of their suspicions that everybody in the U.S. was rich. It was relative, Zhang told them. Had they ever been to the Grand Canyon? Had they ever been on TV? Where were they from? Did they know the Seattle Seahawks quarterback Russell Wilson? Did they know Bill

Gates? Did they have big Buicks?

Before long, they were seated at a round table in the dining room. It was cramped, lit by nothing more than a single, bare light bulb in a simple, ceiling-mounted porcelain light socket. But the Spartan atmosphere was more than offset by the bounty of food the grandmother had set on the table. There were eight different dishes, leaving Severin to wonder whether they ate like this all the time. There were two different dishes of leafy greens that could have been bok choy, one sautéed with garlic, the other with peppers and scallions. There was, of course, rice. There was a dish of chicken thighs in a savory brown sauce, a dish made up of a medley of fresh vegetables only half of which Severin could identify, and a thick, rich looking soup. There were pork and ginger dumplings floating in a pot of wonderful smelling clear broth. Then there was a dish of something that looked like goose feet.

"Are those goose feet?" Severin asked Zhang.

"Yes. They have good meat. After the famines of the 1950s, nothing goes to waste here. Try them. They're good."

Severin did, and was happily surprised to find them delicious. Then he tried the soup, which reminded him of Ivar's clam chowder. It was delicious too. In fact, everything was. Though aside from the dumplings and bok choy, none of the dishes remotely resembled anything Severin had ever eaten in a Chinese restaurant in the U.S. Everything was fresh, the flavors a perfect balance of salty and sweet.

"What's in that soup?" he asked Zhang. "It looks like clam chowder."

"I'm sure it isn't."

"What's the meat in it then? It looks and tastes like chopped clam."

Zhang asked, got his long-winded answer from the grandmother, then didn't say anything.

"So? What is it?"

"I'll tell you after you eat it."

"Wallace."

"She says it's good for a man."

"Good for a man? The hell does that mean?"

"Just eat."

They lingered over the meal for more than two hours, their happy hosts peppering them with questions about America. As the dishes were cleared, Rong got out three small glasses, then set a bottle of Baijiu on the table that had so much dust on it Severin was sure it was only broken out on very special occasions. They were guests of honor. And Severin did feel honored. He had a great time, filled with that tingle—that childlike sense of excitement, awe, and wonder that often came when he made meaningful personal contact with people in countries and cultures that were foreign to him. He even had, for a fleeting moment, a faint twinkling of hope for the human race.

TWENTY-TWO

After their superb dinner at Rong's house, and over another bottle of Baijiu back in the empty hotel restaurant, Zhang scrolled back through the electronic case record on his laptop while Severin peered over his shoulder, both of them looking for an address or phone number for YSP or any of its personnel. They scrolled through dozens and dozens of pages, covering YSP's accounting records, company structure, shipping documents, production processes, and all sorts of perplexing measures of production costs. His eyes red and aching for a break, Severin spotted something as Zhang was about to scroll to the next document. "Wait." He was looking at a page full of YSP's answers to written investigative questions posed by the Commerce Department. Part way down the page, a narrative response included the name and street address of YSP's Seattle-based U.S. importer, Sun Ocean Trading. The paragraph containing Sun Ocean's name and address was enclosed in hand-drawn brackets. "What do those brackets mean?" Severin asked, already guessing the answer.

"The information between the brackets is proprietary. That means all parties to the case basically treat it as a trade secret under the terms of a protective order. In other words, only each party's lawyers are supposed to be able to see it. They aren't allowed to share it with their clients, or they get disbarred and thrown in federal prison. That way, they have all the information they need to make their legal arguments, but nobody's trade secrets are given to the competition."

"And because the name and address of Sun Ocean are in brackets, they're supposed to be treated as trade secrets?"

"Must be. I mean, think about it. Nobody wants to reveal who their customers are, right? Nobody wants them published in the findings of a U.S. government investigation. The competition would be liable to swoop in and try to steal the customers away."

"So Sun Ocean's name and address would have been excluded from the public versions of these documents?"

"Right. And I can tell you from looking through all these documents that they *were* excluded from the public versions. Blacked out, deleted, or whatever."

"Can you think of any reason why Orin Thorvaldsson would have had access to the proprietary portion of the case record?"

"He wouldn't have. Like I said, only the Commerce investigators and the lawyers for the parties to the investigation have access to that."

"Then how did Thorvaldsson know the name and address of YSP's importer, Sun Ocean?"

"Oh. That's—that's a very good question."

"The plot thickens once again."

"Yes it does. Do you think Kristin might have told him?"

"What, over Christmas dinner back on Lopez Island? By accident, after one too many glasses of wine? Both the importer's name *and* its street address?"

"Yeah, it doesn't add up."

"It sure doesn't. Unless . . . ."

"Unless what?"

"Come on, Wallace. Channel your inner Sherlock Holmes."

"Why don't you channel your inner guy who isn't a condescending ass?"

"Does the case file have a list of all the importers?"

"What do you mean?"

"I mean a list of all the U.S. companies that are importing sorghum syrup from the Chinese companies that are under investigation."

"Actually, yeah. I think so. Hold on a minute."

Zhang scrolled through the record until he found a different document—one he recalled seeing before, during their flight to Shanghai. It was a memorandum that listed the names and addresses of each of the importers allegedly purchasing sorghum syrup from the Chinese companies under investigation. There were seven. Not counting Sun Ocean, there was one in Flushing, New York, one in Newark, New Jersey, one in Portland, Oregon, and three in greater Los Angeles."

"Let me use your laptop for a second," Severin said. "I want to Google a few things here."

"You can't."

"I'm not going to hurt your precious laptop. Come on."

"No, I mean Google is blocked in China. There is no Google."

"No Google? That's like saying there's no oxygen."

"It's part of how the Communist Party keeps information from the people."

"Oh. Nice. So then how do you search for stuff on the internet?"

"They have their own state-filtered, state-monitored search engine called Baidu."

"Whatever. It's not like I'm looking for information on how to join the Falun Gong Tabernacle Choir. I'm sure Baidu will do the trick."

One by one, Severin searched the business filings of each sorghum importer through the official government records web site of the U.S. state in which each allegedly existed. When he got to the second of the three Los Angeles-based importers, he muttered, "That sneaky son of a bitch."

"What?"

"Look." Severin turned the laptop so that Zhang could see what he'd found. It was a page from the California articles of incorporation of an importer called Marshall Quotient Trading. The company had been in existence for 15 years.

"What am I supposed to—"

"Here," Severin said, putting his fingertip on the edge of the line labeled "Incorporator." Next to it, in beautiful and perfectly legible cursive, was the signature of Orin Thorvaldsson.

"That sneaky son of a bitch."

"Like I said."

"What did he tell you his business was again?"

"Trading. So I guess I can't call him a liar. Still, it's awful funny-like that he wouldn't mention this little tidbit," Severin added, wondering if he were, in fact, serving as Thorvaldsson's marionette in a play that was bigger than he'd been led to believe.

"So he owns a competing sorghum importer?"

"That's the way I read it. So maybe the attorneys representing Thorvaldsson's company broke the law by sharing Sun Ocean's name and mailing address with Thorvaldsson. Ballsy. They could get disbarred and go to prison for that."

"Bergman and Vladimirovich warned us that these cases were dirty," Zhang said.

"This whole system of protecting trade secrets depends on the ethical character of the involved lawyers. They have to be trusted not to pass the information on to their clients. That's a laugh."

"And there's nothing in the State Department's report to indicate that they knew anything about this, is there? I mean, it doesn't look like the State Department connected the dots that Kristin's uncle owns one of Sun Ocean's competitors."

"I don't think so."

"What are the implications?" Zhang asked.

"Well, for one thing, it sheds new light on Thorvaldsson's possible reasons for hiring me to learn more about what happened."

"Was Kristin acting as her uncle's operative? Getting an unfair peek at the opposition's books and operations? Trying to see what they were up to? Or worse, working to get Commerce to drop the hammer on them when they might not otherwise have done so? Did YSP figure it out—figure out who she was and what she was up to—and then knock her over the head?" Zhang asked.

"Could be. And given what the interpreter told us about what went down at the factory—that the Commerce investigators might have uncovered activities that were going to sink YSP's ship—considering the money that might have been at stake over YSP's sales to the United States, I hate to say it, but maybe it gives legs to Wesley's suggestion that somebody from the company got rid of them."

"Over sorghum syrup imports?"

"I'll grant you, it isn't cocaine," Severin said. "But really, what kind of money are we talking about here? Assume I'm dumb for a moment and walk me through the consequences of YSP getting slapped with a high tariff because of the Commerce investigation."

"Well, if they were caught *in flagrante* with a set of fake accounting records, Commerce would drop the hammer and the company's imports would be subject to the maximum punitive tariff rate."

"I know. But what *is* the rate? How much money are we talking about?"

Zhang spent several minutes searching for the final investigation findings that covered all the sorghum producers in China. "Okay, here we go," he said, scrolling to the conclusion section. "Holy crap."

"Holy crap, what?"

"YSP could have been facing a tariff rate of 354 percent."

"Wow. I thought we were talking about peanuts here."

"So did I. And get this: According to the memo we were just looking at, YSP sold $7.2 million in sorghum syrup to the U.S. last year. In other words, if Powell and Keen actually caught YSP committing fraud, and if they'd had a chance to report it, I think YSP and/or its importer would have ended up owing the U.S. government more than $25 million."

"Wait—twenty-five *million* dollars?"

"Unless my math is off."

"But you're Asian, so—"

"Exactly."

"Did the goal posts just move?"

"They may have."

"But we still don't know where this damned factory is. Here, take my cell phone."

Severin had Zhang make a several attempts at calling the interpreter on the theory that she could at least tell them what road the YSP factory—fake or legitimate—was on, and maybe give them a description of the building. She never answered.

"Maybe she recognizes your cell number," Zhang said.

"Good point." With that, Zhang rose and went to the front desk where he called up to their Shanghai taxi driver's room. In minutes, the driver was in the lobby loaning his cell phone to Zhang for the equivalent of about $5 in Chinese currency. Zhang tried the interpreter's number again and, when she promptly answered, was able to keep her on the phone just long enough to learn that the factory was on something called Jinan Road, and that it had corrugated tin walls that were painted white.

"Jinan Road?" Severin said. I remember seeing that just a mile or two north of town. In fact, I might even remember the building."

"Can we please wait until tomorrow?" Zhang asked.

Without answering, Severin smiled, refilled both of their glasses with Baijiu and raised his to his lips. "How you say?"

"Gan bai, stupid white man."

"Gan bai. I'm feeling more optimistic by the minute."

They drank.

"Another round?" Severin asked.

"No, I want to get a decent night's sleep for once."

"Come on."

"You need to cut back, Lars. Seriously. You're going to die young."

"Maybe *you* need to cut back."

"Nice redirection."

"I'm not as bad as a lot of people."

"Nice rationalization."

"Look, Wallace. Do I not handle it? I do."

"Wow."

"Wow, what?"

"In just this week, you've already gone through more than half the classic alcoholic's top-10 list of excuses."

"Quit being an ass. Let's celebrate our find. You know you want it."

"'Tis one thing to be tempted, another thing to pass out in a public dining room and urinate in one's pants."

"*Hamlet*?"

"*Measure for Measure*."

"Look, you can't leave me to drink alone."

With a sigh, Zhang sat back down as Severin refilled their glasses.

"By the way, you going to finally tell me what was in that soup back at Rong's place?" Severin asked.

"Did you like it?"

"Yeah."

"Then don't worry about it."

"Wallace. I'm not messing around. What was in that soup?"
"Something that's good for a man."

TWENTY-THREE

The next morning, Severin shuffled into the dining room to find Zhang already sipping tea and chewing on a small white bun of some sort. He also had a bowl of something steaming hot. There were two other men in the room, chatting quietly, dressed in white, short-sleeve, cotton and polyester blend collared shirts of the sort half the men in China seemed to wear. Along one wall, a row of a dozen or so warming trays held a variety of breakfast items, none of which Severin immediately recognized. Most of the stuff looked like it had been sitting for a few hours. "This doesn't look that great," he said to Zhang.

"It's the Chinese equivalent of the limp bacon and oily waffle free breakfast you get at your typical two or three-star motel in the U.S. Common Chinese breakfast foods, but not of the best quality."

"What's that bun thing you're eating?"

"Baozi."

"Thanks. That helps me a lot."

"It's a steamed bun, made of rice dough."

"A dough ball."

"This one is filled with pork. There are plain ones, and egg-filled too."

"What's in the bowl?"

"Congee."

"Okay, again, your level of helpfulness is—"

"It's a rice porridge. You can get different toppings for it. Fermented tofu, pickled vegetables, eggs, meat, peanuts."

"How about brown sugar and cream?"

"Ah, no."

"Great."

"I thought you said you'd lived in Asia before. Don't be a baby. Try it with eggs. It's good. The tea is good too."

"Where's the coffee?"

"Get real."

"Don't fool with me, Wallace. I'm from Seattle. I could die if I don't get my morning coffee."

"No coffee."

After rolling his eyes to the sound of his own subtle groan, Severin worked his way down the buffet line of warming trays, taking a sample of everything but a deep fried fish dish that didn't appeal to his alcohol-ravaged stomach. In addition to what Zhang told him about, there were deep-fried dough sticks with soybean milk, steamed buns with bean paste or custard, spiced wheat noodles with scallions, and what looked to Severin like thin little egg and onion frittatas. He ended up liking the pork-filled steamed buns the best. And the tea, which Zhang explained was a well-known Chrysanthemum variety from Anhui Province, was excellent.

*****

Later that morning, an exceptionally heavy rain fell from a cast-iron sky as they sat in the taxi cab on a muddy shoulder opposite the only building with white-painted corrugated tin walls along the entire length of Jinan Road. The building was shaped like the letter 'L,' the base end consisting of what looked like a high-ceilinged warehouse, with the long end comprised of three floors of manufacturing areas and offices. It was flanked by other timeworn industrial properties—one that appeared to be a metal scrapyard, another a facility for storing or distributing barrels of paint—and fronted by a parking lot with weeds growing up through the many cracks in its pavement. A tall, dark smokestack rose from the middle of the building, but no smoke came from it, and there was no signage or anything else to indicate that it was indeed the facility of YSP. In the half hour they'd been watching the alleged YSP factory, they'd seen occasional activity at both of the neighboring properties. But they'd seen none at YSP. Despite the fact that it was well into the work day, there didn't appear to be anyone on the premises at all. There were no parked cars, no lights on, no sounds emanating from within.

"How's your optimism now?" Zhang asked.

"Be patient, Wallace. Maybe it isn't sorghum season, so maybe they only come in for half days or whatever."

"Or maybe this is a red herring. Maybe YSP only exists on paper, like we theorized yesterday. A front. People will show up a few days before the Commerce Department's next audit to make the place look legit."

"We've only been here half an hour. Relax."

Zhang sighed. "Fine."

A large truck full of thoroughly unhappy looking pigs rolled by, dark exhaust billowing from its oversize tailpipe.

"So the air in your room isn't hotter than hell?" Severin asked.

"It's fine."

"I can barely sleep in mine."

*****

The hours clicked by. Hard rain continued to pound on the roof of the car, and they took turns getting soaked in order to urinate on the roadside. Because of the rain, they kept the windows shut, and the cramped cab became a steam bath—the air warm and humid to the point of being stifling, the windows fogged and in need of constant wiping. But there continued to be no observable activity at the alleged YSP building. As the stiffness and eventual ache in his inactive joints grew, Severin began to despair. At sundown, they called it a day and went back to the hotel, back to their usual spot in the empty dining room, back to the Baijiu.

*****

The next day was essentially the same, with one notable exception being that they left the cab driver at the hotel after assuring him—through the handover of another $50 worth of Chinese currency—that they were both competent drivers and that his cab would come to no harm. Also, Severin had begged Zhang to ask the hotel staff to fix the thermostat in his room.

The heavy rain continued. Their muscles and joints ached from sitting, and there was no activity at the YSP factory. But today, instead of taking turns urinating on the roadside while the driving rain soaked them, they were crawling up into scrubby wet bushes to relieve themselves of diarrhea—caused by their breakfast, tainted water, or heaven knew what—that had hit both of them just after noon.

"Today's word of the day is *lassitude*," an irritated, bored Severin said, not really expecting a response.

"Lassitude?"

"Weariness, mental or physical." His butt sore from sitting, he tried, without success, to stretch—extending his feet under the dash as far as they would go, arcing his torso up over the headrest until his face pressed against the roof of the car. But he couldn't quite straighten his body. Frustrated, he plopped back down in the seat. "What the hell is the deal with this endless rain? I don't think I've ever seen it rain this hard for this long. Not even in Florida."

"It's the remains of a tropical cyclone."

"A cyclone?"

"The remnants. Its winds petered out before it made landfall. But it still packs plenty of moisture. The news said it'll be parked over most of the northeast coastal provinces for at least another 24 hours."

"If it goes any longer than that, I'm going to start building an ark."

*****

As they sat, time seemed to stretch out. Seemed to slow. They grew more grumpy and miserable and sick of each other by the minute.

"So let me ask you something, since you're so full of unsolicited sage advice," Severin said.

"Be my guest."

"What would you do if you were me?"

"What are you talking about?"

"If you were living my life."

"You mean if I were a rudderless alcoholic in denial?"

"Ah. Point taken. I should have known better than to ask."

"I'm just trying to understand your question."

"You know what? You're an ass. An irritating, lactose intolerant, pontifical—"

"Foul words is but foul wind, and foul wind is but foul breath, and foul breath is—"

"Please—please, just stop talking."

*****

Finally, as the sky grew dark at the end of the day, emboldened by their impatience, they moved the taxi to another street, parking around the corner and out of sight, and approached the factory on foot. Half concealed in the semi-darkness, they snuck around the back of the building and peered through each of the ground-level windows. In the manufacturing spaces, they saw what looked like a large drill press, a rack of basic hand tools, a bundle of brooms, and several dozen woven polypropylene sacks stuffed with some sort of bulk good and stacked seven to eight feet high against one of the interior walls. There was nothing that jumped out at them as being obviously designed for the processing of sorghum—or any other agricultural product, for that matter. Nor did there appear to be any barrels of sorghum syrup nor any remnants of sorghum cane. The building could have been used for anything.

The office spaces each housed desks. One had an antiquated, dust-covered copy machine. Another contained a stack of three cardboard boxes. While none of this grabbed Severin's attention, there certainly could have been something worth seeing somewhere in the building. But they could only see a portion of the interior spaces by peering through the first floor windows.

They tried the two doors on the back side of the building only to find they were both locked tight. But in fiddling with the windows, Severin found one he didn't think was latched—one he might be able to pry and slide open. It was only three or four feet above ground. He shook it and pushed at it, but couldn't get enough leverage to get it open. "Go find me a stick or pry bar or something," he told Zhang as he continued to monkey with it. As Zhang was kicking around the property looking for a suitable tool, Severin was able to slide the window open just enough to get his fingers in the gap. Then he pulled it as far as it would go—maybe a foot. He stuck his head in the dark gap and took a look around. The room was empty. There was a chalkboard with traces of partially erased Chinese writing.

When Zhang returned, Severin had him give him a leg up. Turned on his side, he wriggled through the window, giving himself a long, deep, zig-zagging scratch on the side of his rib cage as he pulled himself through, dragging his torso across the raised edge of the window frame. As Zhang held his legs, he lowered himself to the floor, head first, before finally pulling his feet through the window and somersaulting into a sitting position. He lifted his shirt to look at the scratch.

"You bleeding?" Zhang asked.

"Not bad. Stay here and keep an eye out," he told Zhang as he stood up and, using a metal chair for leverage, pried the window wider open.

"In the rain?"

"It will help wash the diarrhea off your shoes."

"Great."

"Give a shout if you see anybody coming."

"Alright."

Using the flashlight feature of his smartphone, Severin exited the room, emerging in a long, empty hallway with office doors lining each side, a broad stairwell at its midpoint. He climbed the stairs to begin his search on the 3rd floor, making his way from room to room, searching desks, cabinets, and closets, looking for anything helpful. In room after room, he found nothing but furniture and office supplies—if anything at all. Finally, in the last room at the end of the hallway back down on the main floor, he opened one of the three cardboard boxes he'd seen from the window to find it full of documents. Printed in English, they appeared to be invoices and bills of lading for dog food shipments destined for a U.S. importer called Yang & Lui Trading of Seattle, Washington. The header, however, was in Chinese. The other two boxes contained empty three-ring binders labeled by month and year.

He grabbed a representative sample of each of the documents and moved down the hall to the manufacturing floor, where he took a closer look at the woven polypropylene sacks stacked against the wall. As he expected, they were labeled as dog food, the labels including the same set of Chinese characters as on the headers of the documents. On the floor next to one of the stacks, he found a pile of large adhesive labels of the exact same dimensions as the labels already affixed to the dog food sacks. But there were no Chinese characters on these labels. Instead, the company name was written in English. It read Zucheng Pet Food Products Co. Ltd. Severin guessed that whoever worked here was simply relabeling the feed bags for shipment to an English-speaking country so that the ultimate customers would be able to read the company's name. Still, a sense of suspicion rose in his gut. He grabbed a screwdriver from a rack of hand tools in the corner, came back over to the sacks, and used the screwdriver to tear one of them open. Brown pellets spilled from the hole. He cupped his hand under it and, catching a few, raised them to his nose and took a whiff. Dog kibble.

Great.

Severin sighed, not knowing where else to look, beginning to think the whole journey to Yinzhen was a dead end. He gazed around the manufacturing floor, feelings of dejection taking hold of him. As he moped back through the doorway and into the dark antechamber that separated the offices from the manufacturing floor, he stopped before a small door he hadn't previously noticed. It was steel framed. But the door itself was wood. He tried the knob and found it locked. Inspecting it with his light, he saw that it had no deadbolt and was held in place by nothing more than a standard latch and strike-plate assembly. He had a strong suspicion that this was the infamous closet Keen had found—the closet that may have contained a second set of books that would have been irrefutable evidence that YSP was committing fraud to fool the Commerce Department.

Giving himself a moment to ponder other options, but unable to come up with any of promise, he raised his right foot and gave the door a powerful kick just below the knob. It held fast. But after five more strong kicks, the wood around the latch cracked and the door broke open, with splinters flying this way and that. Severin shined his light in to have a look. Though it might have been the very closet Keen was concerned about, it was empty now. It didn't hold so much as a broom and dustpan. But as Severin turned to leave, he saw that there was a small safe in the wall with a combination lock. Could it contain some critical piece of evidence that would set them on a course toward learning what had happened to Kristin? He doubted it. Regardless, he had neither the tools nor the know-how necessary to get into the safe. Any attempt at breaking into it would have to wait.

Emerging back into the hallway, he started walking toward what appeared to be an exit door at its far end when a tiny red light caught his eye. It was up in a corner of the ceiling. As he got closer and shined his flashlight up at it, he saw that it was a motion sensor. Just as he began to wonder whether anybody was actually monitoring its readings, he heard the sound of tires crunching on gravel on both sides of the building.

"Lars!" he heard Zhang shout through the window.

"Coming."

Severin scrambled back out the window to find Zhang backing up toward him while retreating from three Chinese men with hostile expressions advancing on him from around one corner of the building. Then two more came around the other corner. Severin and Zhang were trapped between the building, a high chain-link fence, and the men.

"You can fight, right?" Severin asked Zhang.

"I was a Golden Gloves semi-finalist. Can you?"

One of the men took a lazy swing at Severin, who deflected the fist as he stepped forward to meet the man nearly chest to chest, simultaneously delivering a powerful uppercut palm-heel strike to the man's chin. The sickening sound of the man's teeth crashing together was followed by a sort of shocked sigh as the man crumpled to the ground unconscious.

"Okay then," Zhang said, as he raised his fists to the two men nearest him. They appeared to study him for a moment before backing up a few steps—perhaps recognizing from his stance and body language that he knew how to fight. The men on Severin's side, dropping their aggressive posture, grabbed their unconscious comrade by the arms and legs and circled around to regroup with the other two. This left a path of escape open to Severin and Zhang—a path they promptly used. Exiting the property, they saw two newly arrived black sedans parked to either side of the building. They took the long way around the block in an attempt to hide the fact that they were going to their parked taxi cab, hopefully keeping secret the fact that they had one at their disposal for surveillance purposes.

"Should we get their license plate numbers?" Zhang asked.

"To do what with? Call the cops and then have to explain to them why we'd like a registration trace?"

"Well, I mean—"

"Let's get the hell out of here."

TWENTY-FOUR

Upon their return to the hotel, Severin had Zhang inquire as to whether the thermostat in his room had been repaired, and was assured by the desk staff that it had. Resuming their positions in the dining room, Severin insisted they drink something other than Baijiu. "They have beer," Zhang said.

"Let's stick with spirits."

"The only other spirit they have is cognac."

"Whatever. Fine."

As they each sipped their first glass, they simultaneously pulled faces and looked at each other with disgusted surprise.

"This is not cognac," Severin said.

"No."

"Let me see that bottle." Zhang handed it to him. "This is made in Georgia. The country, not the state. Former Soviet republic. The French would shit a collective brick if they knew the Georgians were calling this stuff cognac."

"Back to Baijiu?" Zhang asked.

"Back to Baijiu. But let's mix it with something."

"Coke?"

"How about beer?"

"We'll have wicked hangovers."

"I'll take my chances."

Zhang went and got them a bottle of Baijiu and a couple of large, cold Qingdao beers from one of the servers.

"Now then, what do you make of these?" Severin asked as he handed Zhang the documents he'd stolen from the factory.

"Invoices. Shipping documents. For dog food."

"I can see that. What about the Chinese characters in the header? I found hundreds of sacks of dog food in the factory with the same characters on the label. Does it give the name of the company? Zucheng Pet Food Products Company, right?"

"No."

"No?"

"Ningbo Animal Feed Company Limited."

"Ning what?"

"Ningbo. It's a city. That's odd."

"Odd? Why?" Severin asked, holding his hands to his head as if he were having a migraine.

"The name of the company. And the Ningbo business address here in the header. I mean, Ningbo is hundreds of miles from here. It's well south of Shanghai, near the coast. Why would their documents and products be all the way up here?"

"The labels they were putting on the sacks of dog food said Zucheng. New labels that were going over old Ningbo labels that were in Chinese."

"Trying to make it look like the dogfood was made by Zucheng instead of Ningbo?"

"I guess."

They both sat quietly pondering the significance. Finally, Severin huffed, slapped his hands on the table, then poured them each large servings of Baijiu. "This stinks. We're never going to get that $50,000." Severin turned up his glass, dumping the Baijiu down his throat."

"You don't think they'll still pay us?"

"For telling them we found a big pile of dog food where YSP was supposed to have been?"

"There has to be more to this."

"Sure there's more to it. But we don't have anywhere else to go for answers."

"What about down to Ningbo? There's a business address on these invoices."

"We won't find anything there."

"Why not."

"Because if it isn't a legitimate company, they won't have a legitimate facility there. We'll find another empty warehouse of another long-vanished, fly-by-night outfit like YSP. If it is a legitimate company, then it seems they've recently relocated from Ningbo to here."

"Maybe they'll still have an actual office in Ningbo."

"Even if they do, we have no reason to think they have anything to do with YSP and aren't simply the next tenant of the building we just burgled. There's always a chance, I suppose. We could check it as a last resort. But it's probably another red herring."

"What about busting into that safe you found?"

"And how do propose to do that, Butch Cassidy? With dynamite? It's a tiny wall safe. Even if we could open it, what do you think we're going to find in there? The YSP CEO's secret personal diary saying *here's what I did with the bodies*? Anyway, assuming YSP was a front, a fake company, then they would have cleaned everything out of there a long time ago."

"Maybe YSP was a real company."

"If they were, then they went out of business. Either way, their stuff would have been removed before the dog food company took over the building."

"If there's nothing there worth hiding, why did five goons show up to drive us off?"

"They're probably just security toughs, paid to keep thieves out of all these little factories and storage yards."

"Their cars were black. They could have been official."

"If they were official, it wouldn't have gone down like that. Plus, since it's obvious we're foreigners, they'd have known to check the hotel. And even if there is more to it, even if they're being dispatched by some evil overlord who wants to keep people away so that they can't discover that it isn't really a sorghum factory, it still doesn't get us anywhere, does it? It doesn't change the fact that there was nothing there."

"We're at a dead end then."

"So it would seem."

*****

They drank and drank, Zhang getting silly, Severin getting gloomy.

"Let's stop," Zhang half slurred. "Or I'll end up puking all over myself in bed."

"You know something, Wallace?"

"What?"

"I don't have shit."

"For brains? I beg to differ, sir."

"No, seriously. Look at it. I'm rocketing toward middle age. Our contemporaries have homes, families, stable lives. I'm up to my ass in debt, living paycheck to paycheck. I have a piece of junk old car that barely runs. I live in a rat-hole apartment that overlooks Interstate 5. I have no retirement account. No wife. No girlfriend. No friends, really."

"Would you feel better if I gave you an uppercut to the jaw?"

"Maybe."

"Don't be such a mope. It's a choice, you know."

"A choice?"

"You choose to wallow in self-pity. You choose to be unhappy."

"Why would I do that?"

"You tell me."

Severin stared at him for a moment, his eyes glassy. "I'm going to bed," he said, finally.

"That's a great idea. Oh, wait." Zhang pulled a small brown bottle from his pants pocket. Its colorful label bore the face of an old Chinese man surrounded by Chinese writing. "Here, take this before you go to bed."

"What is it?"

"Chinese medicine. I got it at a shop down the street. It will help keep you from feeling hung over."

As they strode to the elevator, Severin noticed a Chinese man sitting on a small black vinyl sofa opposite the adjacent stairwell. He seemed to be watching them. Was it because of the novelty of seeing a Caucasian in Yinzhen? Or were his interests more sinister? If he were a professional, Severin rationalized, he wouldn't be staring straight at them. In fact, he probably wouldn't be sitting there in plain view at all. Still, it worried him.

"Wallace," Severin said once the elevator doors closed. "Slide your desk in front of the door of your hotel room tonight, alright?"

"You're being paranoid again. Nobody followed us from D.C. to Shanghai, and nobody followed us from Shanghai to here."

"There's no harm. Just do it."

"You just told me there was nothing official about our goon encounter at the factory."

"It doesn't necessarily have anything to do with that. And anyway, official or not, somebody isn't happy about our being here."

"I think you need an enema."

*****

That night, Severin woke with a jolt to the sensation that he hadn't been breathing. His room was hotter than ever. He was in the grips of yet another episode. But this one was the worst yet. Checking his pulse, he found that it was up near 160 beats per minute and that the rhythm was irregular—his heart skipping numerous beats. *This is really it. My heart is giving out. I'm dying.*

With alcohol spins giving him the feeling that he was sinking into the mattress, he jumped from bed. But as soon as he was vertical, he was overcome with nausea. Running to the bathroom, he knelt on the floor in front of the toilet, grabbed hold of the urine stained rim, and vomited. For a long time he knelt there dizzy, the odors of bile and dried pee mingling in his nostrils, his heart pounding, his abdomen convulsing as he repeatedly retched or dry heaved. Finally, he curled up in the fetal position on the relatively cool tile floor next to the toilet. *I'm dying.*

He lay there frightened, monitoring his heartbeat, listening to his breathing, fighting to stay awake, to stay aware. At last, more than an hour later, his heart seemed to return to normal. And with his mortal terror now paired with a depressing certainty that he'd never get the $50,000 from Thorvaldsson, utter exhaustion claimed him and he fell asleep in his underwear beside the toilet.

TWENTY-FIVE

The next morning, a thoroughly dehydrated Severin woke to a terrible headache, sour stomach, sticky eyes, and tacky tongue—his room still 85 degrees. He rose from the floor at the base of the toilet and staggered back into his bedroom looking for a bottle of water. Both his bottles were empty. At least he was alive. A line from *Hamlet* forced its unwelcome way into his aching head. "What should such fellows as I do crawling between Earth and heaven?" He turned on his phone and went back to the bathroom to splash water on his face, brush his teeth, and put on clothes. By the time he came back to his bed and picked the phone up off the nightstand, he could see that he had a text message from Zhang from the previous night. Zhang's mysterious computer genius/hacker buddy had gotten back to them about the photo Keen had texted to Andrew Bergman. Apparently, the photo had exceptionally large dimensions indicating that Keen had taken it using an extremely powerful digital camera that he must have later connected to his smart phone so that he could upload and send the photo. Zhang's friend had used a simple photo-editing software package to shrink the image down to a size that enabled viewing on a normal-size computer, tablet, or smart-phone screen so that it wasn't simply a black-and-white blob encompassing one small part of what was, in fact, an extremely large and extremely high-resolution image. The hacker's conclusion, after doing a bit of follow-up research and finding some artists renditions of the expected hull shape and conning tower position, was that the photo was of a brand new type of Chinese ballistic missile submarine.

Holy shit.

The first of its class, the new sub was called Type 096 by the Chinese, or Tang Class by NATO. It was thought to be awaiting initial sea trials at the large navy base just north of the port of Qingdao. To the great consternation of other Pacific Rim nations, including the United States, the Type 096 was believed to carry 12 more missile tubes than the generation of missile sub preceding it.

Severin sprang from his bed and began pulling the desk away from his hotel room door as implications spun through his head. Was Keen a spy? Was Kristin? Was their employment with the Commerce Department just cover? A way for them to get into China? Perhaps they were planning to go to Bali to be debriefed by their Western Pacific regional intelligence handler before heading home to D.C. But if that were the case, Keen wouldn't have had his Bali flight itinerary sent to his easily-hacked personal email account, would he? It made no apparent sense. Regardless, whatever their intent, the only thing Severin was reasonably sure of was that Powell and Keen never made it to Bali. Maybe they were in a Chinese prison. Maybe the MSS has already killed them.

It was still possible that they'd been killed by YSP company goons, by Wesley, or in a random robbery. Regardless, he and Zhang were quite possibly in grave danger, as it seemed they might have unwittingly stumbled into a blown U.S. spying operation. Had Keen's seemingly comical need to urinate on the coast road from the Qingdao Brewery to Laoshan Mountain that Holloman told them about actually been a trick—a ruse to get himself a chance to climb over a knoll where he could photograph this new submarine at its base for the CIA, DIA, or whoever the hell? Maybe the shooting death of Tyreesha Harris at the Anacostia Metro station was part of a cover up. Maybe Severin's sense that he and Wallace were under surveillance—in D.C. and in China—was all because of this. Were they being watched now? Did the Chinese think he and Wallace were spies too? If so, why hadn't they been arrested?

As he threw his door open, he was surprised to see Zhang's open as well. The frame of Zhang's door was all scratched and dented up, as though someone had been using it for leverage, trying to pop the door open with a makeshift pry bar. Inside the room, he caught a glimpse of a bloody, badly beaten body just as med techs were draping a blanket over it as it lay on a gurney flanked by police.

No!

Afraid to acknowledge that he was with Zhang until he had a better idea of what was going on, Severin took one step backward into his room, closed the door, and leaned against the wall, his mind overwhelmed by horror. Before he could take a breath, his cell phone rang. The call was coming from Zhang's phone. This was it. His time had come. It would be the leader of the Chinese counterintelligence team that had been tracking them, calling to tell him it would be easier for him if he surrendered without a fuss. Imploring him not to resist, as Zhang presumably had, and end up beaten until his head was an unrecognizable, shapeless, bloody pulp. Despite his fear, despite his rising nausea, he somehow managed to answer the call.

"Good morning sunshine." It sounded like Zhang. "Hello?"

"Wall . . . ."

"What? Were you still asleep, you alcoholic bum? Did you see my text message?"

"Wallace."

"Good guess. What's the matter with you?"

"Where are you?"

"Oh, sorry. I couldn't sleep with the street noise, so I had them move me to a room overlooking the courtyard after you sacked out last night. Room 204."

"Stay where you are."

"Why? What's going—"

Severin hung up. As he was slipping out of his own room, taking care to make his move when the attention of the police, medical personnel, and gawkers in the hallway was directed away from him, he noticed the same pry bar marks on his own door frame. He was certain they hadn't been there last night. Someone had tried to get in, but couldn't with the desk wedged up against the other side of the door.

Half a minute later, he was in Zhang's room, explaining what he'd seen.

"You think that was supposed to be me, but they gave my old room to somebody else who checked in last night? Somebody who was mistaken for me in the dark?" Zhang asked.

"I think someone came for both of us last night."

"The goons from the factory?"

"Or poorly trained MMS agents. Have you considered the implications of the submarine photo from Keen's phone?"

"You don't think Keen just thought it was something cool to take a picture of when saw it moored in the harbor as he was taking his beer piss?"

"An unusually high-res photo?"

"But why would anyone send him? Can't satellites photograph all that stuff these days?"

"From overhead, sure. But from the side? At high-res? I don't know."

Zhang looked astonished. "If Keen was a spy, would he really have just sent the picture in an unencrypted text message?"

"Maybe the circumstances dictated the method. Maybe he knew he was being pursued, knew they were closing in, and only had once chance. Maybe in his haste he sent it to the wrong contact number. How should I know?"

"Do they really still send people in on the ground to take pictures?"

"Do you really want to stick around to find out? Do you know what they do to suspected spies in this country?"

"I guess, uh, no and no."

"Let's go."

"Give me a minute to pack."

"Leave it. Just grab your passport and the keys to the cab."

"Wouldn't our passports be compromised?"

"We can always sell them for the cash we may need to get smuggled out of the country. And there's still a chance my espionage theory is off target. At any rate, we'll cross that bridge when we come to it. Let's go."

They slipped out of Zhang's room, down the dim and empty hallway, and into a fire escape stairwell.

"Do you know how to hotwire a car?" Severin asked as they flew down the stairs.

"Why would I know how to hotwire a car?"

"I don't know. Because you're an Asian guy who went to Federal Way High School?"

"Nice. Aren't you law enforcement types supposed to know how to do all that sort of stuff?"

"Hotwiring was an elective course at the academy. I took a second semester of racial profiling instead."

They popped out a back door of the hotel and out into the still pouring rain. "I'm sure they've figured out the cab is ours. It may even have a tracking device on it. But since you can't hotwire a car, it's our only option for now. Hopefully we can slip away unnoticed. We'll ditch it as soon as we can. Maybe once we get to a bigger city—Zucheng, or even Qingdao—we can lose ourselves in the crowd. You drive. You're less conspicuous."

"What about the cabbie?"

"Never mind about the cabbie. Let's get the hell out of here."

Sneaking along the outer wall of the hotel, they made their way toward the back end of the grounds until they could peek around a corner to observe the parking area. There didn't appear to be anyone around—though it was hard to tell because heavy rain was pouring down so hard that it largely obscured their view of whomever might be inside nearby cars. Crouching between two rows of cars, they ran for the cab, flung open the doors, and jumped in. Driving as fast as they could go without attracting attention to themselves, they were soon out of the parking lot and headed down the street away from the center of town. Severin, mindful of how he stood out in a rural corner of China that rarely saw westerners, crouched as low he could while still being able to peek out the rear window—which he constantly did, watching for followers.

"Turn on the radio and select AM," Severin said.

"Another one of your counter-surveillance tricks?" Zhang said, turning it on.

"Some types of tracking devices mess with AM radio. If one is on our car, we might hear a loud tone if the radio is on. Not a sure thing though.

Depends on the type of tracker."

They listened to the radio but didn't hear anything out of the ordinary. As they neared the outskirts where the main highway was located, they found a row of orange cones blocking the road. Beyond the cones, floodwaters covered the road where a culvert had been two days earlier.

"Oh, crap." Zhang said.

"There's another ramp on the other side of town. Stick to the side streets. But wait. Give me your phone. I don't trust the delete function on these things. And neither of us wants to be caught with a phone containing texts or emails about a new submarine." Severin took it, got out of the car, and threw both of their phones out into the overflowing drainage canal.

They made their way back across Yinzhen, Severin still constantly scanning for followers. He didn't see any. But that didn't necessarily mean there weren't any. They could just be that good. He tried to commit car types and license plate numbers to memory. But his hungover brain wasn't cooperating. Regardless, as they reached the outskirts of the other end of town, they ran into the same problem. The road was awash in floodwater. They were cut off from the only two highway on-ramps they were aware of.

"Okay," Severin said, his pulse racing. "We'll try the country roads. Smaller and slower, but at least they'll get us the hell out of here. Let's head north. When we were looking for the factory, it seemed to me that the roads didn't cross as many drainage canals out that way, and the land was a bit higher."

The first road they tried got them out into farmland nearly two miles outside of town before it came to a flooded and impassable bridge. The second barely made it a mile. As they crisscrossed through the northern reaches of Yinzhen, they found themselves on the road the YSP factory was on. Approaching it, Severin spotted a van in its otherwise empty parking lot. "Pull over," he said.

"Are you nuts? Let's get out of here!"

"Let's watch that van for a minute."

"I thought we were about to be arrested as spies."

"Take three deep breaths. For the moment, nobody's following us, at least as far as I can tell. And I've finally had a non-frantic moment to think."

"You said yourself there's probably a tracking device on the car. They're just sitting back waiting for us to stop so they can swoop in and bag us."

"Wallace—"

"$50,000 isn't going to do us much good if we're both dead."

"We're trapped, Wallace. If these roads on the north side are flooded, then all the damned roads out of here are flooded. Also, if it was the MSS that came for us last night, they'd have us, don't you think? They wouldn't have given up on my door after having a little trouble prying it open, and they wouldn't have just up and left after killing a man they thought was you.

The place would have been swarming with agents. They would have locked down the hotel. And they would have taken us alive, for interrogation. They wouldn't have wanted to beat you to death."

"You sure about that?"

"No, I'm not sure. It still could have been an MSS operation. An inept operation run by a fifth-rate, blockhead agent who got his job because of family connections. Or maybe YSP thugs were behind the break-in last night, but MSS is still out there surveilling us. What difference does it make? What choice do we have? We can't get out."

"This is bad, Lars."

"Breathe, Wallace. Let's just watch the van for a minute while we think about what to do."

As they sat in the car, the rain pounding on the roof, Severin considered their options. They could ditch the car and hide. Zhang could certainly blend in well enough if he changed out of his Seattle clothes and into something more common to the area. They could set off on foot, and possibly swim across the flooded channels. If they didn't drown and made it to one of the roads on higher ground, they could try to flag down a passing motorist and pay them anything to just get them to a city. Maybe one with a U.S. consulate they could take refuge in. He tried to remember what the nearest city with a consulate would be. Probably Shanghai, hundreds of miles to the south.

"My heart is racing," Zhang said.

"Not as bad as mine was last night. Woke up at midnight or something. Heart pounding in my ears. Skipping beats. Pulse rate up around 160 beats per minute."

"Trouble swallowing? A vague feeling that you're gonna die?"

"Yeah," Severin said with a tone that all but asked *how did you know?*

"You had a panic attack."

"Screw you."

"No, really. You're describing the exact symptoms of a panic attack."

"Why would I have had a panic attack last night?"

"With all the anxiety we deal with as a species, the better question is why aren't all of us having panic attacks all the time? We're all afraid of the dark on some level, Lars."

"Right. How about we change the subject. Let's think about what we should do."

"Wait, how many of those pills did you take?"

"I don't know. Seven or eight, maybe."

"Eight?!"

"They were small."

"You're supposed to take two."

"You could have mentioned that."

"The pills could have been a contributing factor. There's some weird stuff in Chinese medicine."

"What was in those things?"

"I don't know. The bottle just listed the symptoms it was good for."

"And what symptoms were those?"

"Hangover."

"Is that all?"

"Stuffy nose, excessive bile, lethargy, and impotence."

"Oh my g—"

Just then, Severin spotted a man emerging from the YSP factory. He carried a large umbrella and wore an unusual jacket. It appeared to be white leather. Under one arm, he was carrying a small cardboard box as well as what appeared to be a hotplate. He jumped in the van, started up, and headed out of the parking lot and down the street.

"Follow him at a good distance," Severin said.

The van zigzagged through Yinzhen's industrial zone, passing other small factories and warehouses, making several turns along the way, as if the van driver were, like them, trying to find a way out of town. Finally, it came to a stop at the curb on a random stretch of road alongside a grass lot strewn with slabs and blocks of what looked like broken concrete. Perhaps the fragments of a demolished foundation.

"Why is he stopping there, of all places?" Zhang asked as he too pulled over.

"Maybe he's pouring a cup of tea."

"Or maybe he spotted us tailing him."

The van sat, running. And they sat, watching. One minute, two minutes, five minutes. Suddenly, two familiar looking black sedans came racing around the same corner they'd taken. One pulled in at an angle, just in front of them, blocking all possibility of forward motion. The other pulled right up to their rear bumper. They were trapped. The van fled.

"I'm guessing he spotted us."

"You think?"

"And called his goon buddies."

Four men jumped out of each car. Some of them held lengths of iron pipe. Severin recognized at least two of them from their confrontation at the factory the night before.

"Here we go," Severin said.

They threw their doors open and stood for battle. The eight men advanced on them. Those with iron pipes held them high in the air. Severin and Zhang were each able to disable the first man to attack with hard punches to the face. But then the remaining men gang-tackled them. Severin fell to the ground and immediately employed the ground-fighting defensive tactic of spinning on his back and keeping his feet and legs directed at his attackers, kicking at them whenever they moved forward. But they quickly figured out that if one of them kept Severin occupied, the other two could flank him and approach unopposed. As he kicked at one of them, landing a blow on the man's knee and dropping him, he lifted a forearm above his face to shield his head from a pipe one of the others was swinging down on him. He watched in horror as the pipe came down on his arm, breaking it so thoroughly that he could see a new odd angle in it resembling a second elbow. With his broken arm, he was only partially able to block the next blow, which caught the edge of his eyebrow, opening a huge cut that immediately bled into his eye, half blinding him. With his good eye, he turned to see Zhang already flat on his belly on the concrete on the far side of the car, unconscious, his arms pinned under his torso, blood pouring from his nostrils. Then he heard loud voices coming from elsewhere, and his good eye was drawn to the image of four more men—in plain clothes, but of a rigid bearing that suggested military or law enforcement discipline—emerging from two newly-arrived cars with small guns drawn, seeming to shout commands at the attackers. Some of the attackers began backing away from the men with the guns. It was the last thing Severin saw. A brilliant flash of blinding white light shot across his consciousness from somewhere in the back of his skull. Then all went dark.

TWENTY-SIX

All at once, Severin was aware of pain. Two kinds of pain—a sharp pain and a throbbing pain—both originating from the right-rear quadrant of his skull. In heavily accented and halting English, someone said, "You squeeze finger please," and Severin realized he was reclined and that his right hand was indeed closed around someone's finger. He gave it a quick, weak squeeze, then tried to open his eyes. Painfully bright light pushed another dagger of pain through the back of his head, and he quickly shut his eyes against it. An interrogation light? Had someone decided that he was a spy, there to gather information on the new submarine? Was he imprisoned in one of the dungeons of the MSS?

How had he gotten here? What had happened? His memory was a jumbled mess, distorted and barely visible across a black abyss of pain. Despite it, he tried, once more, to open his eyes. Holding them open for an agonizing couple of seconds, he was able to see that he was in a bed in an immaculate, ultramodern hospital room. That much was clear. His broken arm was already in a cast. A man in medical scrubs stood at his side, looking at a clipboard. Another man in street clothes sat in a chair opposite the bed staring at him intently. His face struck Severin as familiar. Perhaps he was from a surveillance team that had been shadowing them. Perhaps he was an MSS counterintelligence officer. Someone to be wary of. Someone to fear. As he wondered, nausea hit him like a ton of bricks. He sat up straight, feeling his head go light as he did so, turned, and vomited to his right, losing consciousness as he heaved.

*****

"Mr. Lars Severin," a gentle, accented voice said—presumably that of the man who had been sitting in the chair, as it seemed to come from across the room. Severin opened his eyes once again, briefly, to confirm his suspicion. "Good afternoon. I'm one of your rescuers. You've had a busy day. Do you remember what happened?" English fluency. Another worrying sign that this mystery man was a professional. Severin didn't speak. "Maybe it's better that you not try to talk right now. The doctors have said that, above all, you need to rest. That you should not strain yourself in body or mind. You are in a hospital in the port city of Qingdao, in case you're wondering. We had to bring you here because the facilities in Yinzhen and Zhucheng weren't equipped to handle the situation. They don't have CT scan or MRI machines out there. We had to get you out of there in the back of a dump truck," he said with a faint hint of a smile. "It was the only thing we could find with sufficient clearance to ford the flooded road."

"Anyway, you ran into some rough boys today, and one of them gave you a glancing knock on the back of the head with a metal pipe. But you're lucky with respect to the head injury. It seems you have only a mild concussion. However, you also have a compound fracture to your arm, and a good set of stitches on your eyebrow."

Severin pursed his lips to speak, but the sound didn't want to come out. The man seemed to anticipate his question. "Wallace Zhang was not so lucky. He's alive, but he has a serious concussion. The doctors thought he might have bleeding on the surface of his brain. What they call a subdural hematoma. They had him prepped for surgery to drain the blood, then did one more scan with the MRI machine and decided he didn't have a hematoma after all. They called off the surgery. So he is fortunate in that respect. But it will be some time before he is able to speak or receive visitors, and he isn't going to be very happy with the pre-op haircut they gave him. Still, the doctors assure me his prognosis is good. And we have very good medical personnel at this hospital. So not to worry. Rest. You are safe here."

Severin didn't believe him. He wanted to call Thorvaldsson and tell him what had happened. Wanted to tell him that things had gone well beyond the scope of what he'd signed on for and that he and Wallace needed to get the hell out of China and go home. But he had no phone. Even if he did, he didn't think it would be secure to call from the hospital.

*****

Shortly after waking the next morning, Severin sat up in bed, looking around the Spartan, fluorescent-lighted room, utterly amazed that he was still alive, not in a cinder block interrogation cell, and that he wasn't even so much as handcuffed to the bed. The door to his room was open. He considered getting up and making a run for it. But a wave of weakness, lightheadedness, and nausea shook him as soon as he half-attempted to lift his legs over the edge of the bed. He wasn't going anywhere. At least not yet. As he let his head fall back onto his pillow, a uniformed police officer glanced in, then shouted down the hallway. A moment later, the plain-clothes man from the day before strode through the doorway, carrying himself with a posture of command.

"You're awake. Very good," the man said, taking a seat on a chair beside Severin's bed." Severin eyeballed him. "My name is Joe."

"Joe," Severin repeated dubiously, his voice weak.

"That's the anglicized version, anyway. Much easier to say and spell. It's actually Jianquo."

"Let's stick with Joe."

"Works for me."

"Tell me, Joe. Am I under arrest?"

Joe looked surprised. "No. Should you be?" Severin just stared at him, silent, knowing from experience that a feigned look of surprise at such a question was an old interrogation trick to keep from spooking a suspect when you wanted them to keep talking to you.

"Where's Wallace?"

"In the ICU. He's still more-or-less unconscious."

That struck Severin as a sinister excuse for not being able to see him. Was Zhang instead being interrogated? Tortured? As for his own predicament, were they just playing nice to see how much information they could get out of him before bringing in the bruisers?

"Who are you, Joe?"

Joe straightened in his seat. "Well, I'm a type of policeman. I think it's in both our best interests that we just leave it at that."

"A policeman," Severin echoed, thinking *a policeman who happens to speak perfect English, despite living in a remote and tiny village of a rural Chinese province where a knowledge of English is probably about as useful as tits on a boar.*

As if reading Severin's thoughts, Joe said, "I was in Yinzhen on a temporary assignment. I'm based here in Qingdao. It's a major city, at least by U.S. standards. I moved here for my wife. I actually lived in the States for many years. Went to grade school and college there."

"Grade school and college where?"

"Grade school in San Marino, California. L.A. County. College at UCLA."

"Really," Severin said, two-thirds sure this was some sort of trick to get him talking. "I had the best doughnut of my life there after a campus tour. A buttermilk bar," he said, waiting and watching Bill's face.

"At Stan's, right? Stan's Donuts? Off of Weyburn Avenue? That place has been there since California was part of Mexico."

Severin gave him a close look before answering. "Yes. Stan's." Maybe this guy was for real after all. Or maybe the MSS counterintelligence bureau was so good that it could quickly summon and brief an operative who really had studied at UCLA.

"Anyway, I'm here more or less temporarily. We moved from Los Angeles to Beijing seven years ago. But my wife's family lives in Qingdao, and her mother is ill. So she wanted to be close to home. My father-in-law is a big cheese in law enforcement here. He was able to call in a favor to get me transferred to this job."

"Which you don't want to describe."

"Well, I can tell you that in Beijing I was a sort of general detective. Assault, theft, murder—all within my purview. Let's just say that I now have a certain specialization in anticorruption investigations."

"Business must be good."

"You have no idea. Last year alone, there were more than a hundred thousand government officials found guilty of corruption in China. Not suspected—*found guilty*. Over a hundred thousand! And that's according to an official government report, so you can assume the true figure is much higher."

"Wow," Severin said, thinking that was close to the total number of employees in the entire U.S. Department of Justice. "But why come back to China at all?"

"Well, for one thing, it was taking my wife forever to get a U.S. visa. But I also wanted to contribute."

"What do you mean?"

"This is the country of my birth. My heritage. I wanted to help."

"By being a cop?"

"I majored in economics at UCLA. Studying econ and living in the U.S. drove a point home to me. Economic miracle that this country is, it won't last unless we can do something about all the corruption. The income disparity. The lack of consistent legal recourse for common people. If the rich and powerful and corrupt keep getting richer and more powerful off the backs of cheap labor and decent honest people, one day it will all come crashing down. History will repeat itself. But it doesn't have to go that way."

"No? It seems to be going that way in the rest of the world. Why not here too?"

They studied one another for a quiet moment.

"What's your interest in the man you were following?" Joe asked, changing tacks.

"Who?"

"The driver of the van you followed all over Yinzhen. The buffoon in the ridiculous white leather jacket."

"We weren't following anybody. We were trying to find a clear road to the highway. One that wasn't flooded."

"I assume your real interest lies with the driver's employer."

"Who is his employer?"

Joe smiled. "I thought so."

"Fair enough. So really, who is his employer?"

"I'm afraid I'm not at liberty to say."

"In other words, he's under investigation, this mystery employer."

"Let's call him a government official, and leave it at that." He sat back in his chair and studied Severin intently. "Are you from one of his competitors perhaps?"

"Do government officials have competitors?" Joe just stared, waiting. "I really don't know what you're talking about. But I'm beginning to wish I did."

"I'll ask politely. What are you doing here, Mr. Severin?"

Severin saw no real alternative to answering the question, and no plausible lie came to mind. "We were hired by the family of a female U.S. government official who disappeared after departing Yinzhen, at the conclusion of an investigation of a company called Yinzhen Sorghum Processing. The family just wants to know what happened to their girl. We spotted the van at the alleged sorghum factory and, hoping to learn something, followed it until we got waylaid. We didn't have a chance to learn anything about the driver."

Severin was certain that, at best, this would be the end of his endeavor to find answers. If this officer didn't arrest him for breaking some sort of Chinese law against private vigilante investigations being conducted by foreigners, then he would, at a minimum, expel him from the country immediately.

"What was her name? The woman who disappeared?"

"Kristin Powell."

Joe just nodded. "Okay. Okay." He closed his eyes as though for the first time in days, his eyelids dropping slowly, ponderously. "Is there really nothing you can tell me about the driver's employer? Nothing, for example, that any law enforcement official would naturally be interested to know?"

"Could you be even a little bit more specific?"

"I'm afraid not."

Having assumed he was in the custody of the MSS, another possibility began to take shape in Severin's mind. There had been no questions concerning his phone, Keen, or the photo of the new Chinese ballistic missile submarine. And if they had been with the MSS, then surely the men who attacked them would have been more careful to capture them in interrogation-ready condition—not beaten within an inch of their lives. Plus, they would have been armed with guns instead of lengths of pipe. Perhaps he and Zhang weren't suspects after all. Perhaps the Chinese hadn't known Keen was a spy. Perhaps this man really was a police officer. Perhaps he and Zhang had simply stumbled into a genuine Chinese anticorruption investigation.

"I'm not sure that I know anything helpful," Severin said. "Are you able to tell me whether the driver's employer owns Yinzhen Sorghum Processing?"

Joe raised his eyebrows and smirked as though on the edge of laughing. "What an interesting question."

"I see," Severin said. "Are Chinese government officials allowed to own private business entities?"

"Another interesting question, Mr. Severin. And no, technically speaking, government officials are not permitted to hold positions in private enterprises."

"So if I'm an anticorruption investigator, I'm guessing that one of my bigger challenges is going to be gathering enough evidence to prove that a government official is also secretly the owner of a business."

Joe was still smirking. "Life is full of challenges, Mr. Severin."

"Did you arrest the men who attacked us? Did they tell you anything?"

"I'm afraid that I'm not at liberty to discuss that either." He studied Severin a moment longer, then reached into the inside pocket of his jacket. "Here is my card. I know you can't read the Chinese characters. But that's my cell number at the bottom. I would very much appreciate it if you would give me a call if you happen to come across anything you think might be of interest to me. We'll leave it vague for the moment. Now rest. They'll probably discharge you tomorrow. You'll find that in Qingdao, unlike in Yinzhen, there are many very comfortable and opulent hotels to stay in while you wait for Wallace Zhang to recover. Excellent restaurants too. See you around."

After Joe left, Severin sat there thinking. Why hadn't he been arrested? Even if they didn't think he was a spy, surely his fact-finding mission violated some tenet of Chinese sovereignty, law, or etiquette. He could still be the target of an elaborate and well-orchestrated MSS operation—one in which this Joe guy was pretending to be a cop, pretending to be unaware of Powell's possible spying, and leaving Severin free, but under constant surveillance, hoping that Severin would try to contact other operatives who might be helping or working with him. If there were an MSS operation, then they were surely assuming that Severin had traitorous co-conspirators or facilitators on the Chinese mainland. In that case, their goal would be to identify and roll up the entire network.

Then again, if Joe truly was a policeman, and if he was high-ranking enough to command a squad of men at least as big as the group that rescued him in Yinzhen, then whatever case he was working was probably a relatively big deal. Which meant that the government official he was investigating was probably a big cheese. And if the government official was also the invisible puppeteer controlling YSP, then he probably had a government position involving international trade. In customs, maybe.

Was Joe perhaps thinking that Severin and Zhang's continued freedom of movement—or more specifically, their meddling, their hornet nest kicking—might be, in some obscure way, helpful to his investigation? Was Joe thinking that they might provoke the hidden target of his investigation into making an ill-advised move that he could use to his advantage—maybe even as justification for making an arrest? At this point, all Severin could do was theorize.

TWENTY-SEVEN

That afternoon, shortly before being discharged from the hospital, Severin shuffled his sore body down the hall to Zhang's room. Seeing Zhang was a shock. Asleep—or in any case, unconscious—he had an IV in his right arm, an oxygen cannula in his nose, and a huge bandage wrapped around his head. His face was ashen where it wasn't black and blue. He looked dead.

Severin sat in a visitor's chair against the opposite wall. For several minutes he remained silent, horrified, at a loss for what to say. Sometimes he would stare at Zhang, sometimes he'd have to look away. A tremendous sense of guilt washed over him. It made him feel sick. Made him tremble as though he were somewhere terribly cold.

At last, Severin cleared his throat. "I remember seeing on TV that you're supposed to talk to people who have head injuries. Maybe that's B.S. I don't know." He looked up at the ceiling, then back down at Zhang. "You know, Wallace, I'll tell you something funny. I've never really related well to people." He shifted in his seat. "What am I trying to say here?" He paused, took a deep breath, swallowed. "Shit, Wallace. I'm so sorry." He began to choke up. "I'm so sorry that this happened." That was all he could manage to say as he fought back emotion. Had he been able to continue, he might have added that he was grateful for his time with Zhang. That having Zhang around reminded him of happier times in his life. Instead, he sat for several more minutes, silent, trying to master himself. Wishing to God he had a drink. At long last, he swallowed and cleared his throat once again. "I suppose you're a sort of link, Wallace," he muttered sadly, more to himself than to Zhang. "A faint link to how things used to be for me. A long time ago."

*****

Having checked into Qingdao's Shangri-La Hotel, Severin took a notepad and pen from the desk in his lavish room and took the elevator to the hotel's business center. There, he situated himself at a desktop computer at a small workstation in the corner and brought up the partially censored Chinese search engine, Baidu. First, he conducted a search for the terms *antidumping* together with *dog food*, and quickly found several news articles about a recently initiated U.S. antidumping investigation involving dog food from China. Next, he found a U.S. Federal Register notice containing a list of the 27 Chinese dog food manufacturers the U.S. was now investigating. Both Ningbo Animal Feed and Zucheng Pet Food Products were on the list. He ran searches on each company name. His search of Ningbo Animal Feed turned up a web-site for a company ostensibly located in city of Ningbo, which Zhang had said was hundreds of miles to the south. Its website looked legitimate enough. Searching Zhucheng Pet Food next, following a link to the company's web site, he found himself staring at a photo of the alleged YSP sorghum factory in Yinzhen.

The web-site was amateurish, looking like it had been thrown together in a couple of hours by someone who didn't really know what they were doing. Severin figured it was a good bet the web site had been set up simply for appearance's sake, and not for any legitimate marketing purposes. In broken English, it indicated that the company had been producing premium pet food for more than 20 years, and had long experience in exporting to customers in Japan, the European Union, and the United States. Aside from this statement, and a few low-resolution photos of piles of what appeared to be dog food, it provided the name and phone number of a purported sales agent. Severin wrote down the phone number, then spent two hours scrolling through the sorghum case record trying to find a matching phone number for one of YSP's officials. But he had no luck. Still, given the photo on the web-site, and recalling Andrew Bergman's statement that there was pervasive fraud in these cases, Severin suspected some sort of dishonorable connection between YSP, Zucheng Pet Food, and Ningbo Animal Feed.

Another idea occurred to him, and he ran searches of public business filings of the U.S. dog food importer named on the shipping documents he'd found at the YSP building: Yang & Lui Trading of Seattle, Washington. He did the same for Sun Ocean Trading. According to company LLC filings on record with the Washington Secretary of State's office, both importers were supposedly based in the International District of Seattle. That, by itself, certainly wasn't damning. And each importer had different owners and registered agents for service of legal process. However, when Severin ran searches of the attorneys each importer listed as their registered agent, he discovered they both worked in the same very small law firm in Seattle's Northgate neighborhood. For Sun Ocean Trading and Yang & Lui Trading to both be located in Seattle's International District neighborhood, to both be using the same tiny law firm for service of process, to both to be involved in the importation of Chinese products subject to antidumping tariffs, *and* for both of them to be working with Chinese companies that each shared some connection to the YSP building in the remote village of Yinzhen—well, that was just too much to ignore.

*****

Back in his room, Severin received a phone call from Joe.

"Sorry to bother you."

"No problem," Severin said, half wondering if Joe was going to tell him they'd recovered their cell phones from the drainage canal and found the texts about the submarine.

"I have some good news. Wallace Zhang has regained consciousness."

TWENTY-EIGHT

Back in the visitor's chair in Zhang's hospital room, Severin sat looking at him, feeling as guilty as ever. Zhang, still with an oxygen cannula in his nose, was visibly woozy, blinking slowly.

"Anyway, I'm sorry about all of this," Severin said, continuing an annoyingly long monologue of regret. "As soon as you feel mobile, I'll arrange to get us the hell out of here and on the first plane home. I spoke with Thorvaldsson. He said to stick it out if we could, but that he'd understand if we needed to come home. We won't get the rest of the money, of course. But screw it. I told him we were out of here." Zhang rolled his eyes and groaned. Severin took it as a sound of disapproval. "Don't worry. We'll wait until you feel fit to move."

"No," Zhang half whispered.

"No?"

"No."

"No, what?"

Zhang closed his eyes. "I'm still seeing double. My head hurts like hell. And look at my hair, Lars."

"Your hair." Severin thought that perhaps Zhang wasn't quite of right mind yet. Then he saw the slightest hint of a weak smile form at the corners of Zhang's mouth.

"My pretty, pretty hair."

There was a huge square patch shaved bare on the side of Zhang's head, put there when he was being prepped for the surgery he didn't end up having. He looked freakish and ridiculous.

"Clearly, you've lost your mind."

"I don't even remember what happened. Cop told me." He took several deep, slow breaths, then reached up with the arm that didn't have an IV in it and gingerly touched the deeply bruised square of bare scalp on his head. "Bastards. We're not going home yet."

Severin looked incredulous. "You sure about that?"

"What else are you going to do, Lars?" Zhang slowly croaked. "Go back to your debt, and your booze, and beg your boss for your crap job back?"

"Hey now. Be nice."

"Am I going to go back to my parents' basement? Screw that, Lars."

"I can appreciate you want revenge for them making your head look like the belly of a black Labrador that just had abdominal surgery at the vet. But what about the . . . ." He stopped himself over a sudden fear of microphones, and tried to pantomime using a submarine periscope.

Zhang shook his head. "Coincidence. If it were really a thing, we'd know by now."

"Unless they're waiting for . . . ." Severin stopped himself, but thought *unless they're waiting to see if we make contact with other operatives.*

"We have no real reason to think that," Zhang said, knowing what Severin intended to say.

"It's still theoretically possible."

"Anything is possible." He took a deep breath. "Are we going to give up on all that money over something so unlikely?"

"It isn't *that* unlikely. And the consequences—"

"We aren't going home yet."

Severin threw his hands up, looking uneasy. "Fine."

"But now you tell me something, and tell me true."

"What?"

"What's the real fee Thorvaldsson is paying you?"

"It's $50,000. I told you. Really."

Zhang just stared at him.

"Wallace. Really. And if he throws in any sort of bonus, I promise we'll split it 50/50. I'll even split my royalties with you."

"What royalties?"

"From the memoir I'm going to write. A memoir chronicling our adventure."

"Huh," Zhang said, his weak smile returning. He took another deep breath through his nose tube. "Okay. When I'm back on my feet, the gloves are coming off. You know what I'm saying?"

"The gloves are coming off. Yes."

TWENTY-NINE

When Severin entered Zhang's hospital room the next morning, it was immediately apparent that Zhang was feeling much better, so Severin brought him up to speed. "So, in a nutshell, what I've come to is this," Severin said. "It is not beyond the realm of possibility that there is some hidden octopus person or entity that owns or runs multiple, allegedly independent and unrelated manufacturers of goods that are subject to antidumping investigations."

"But why?" Zhang asked. "Why deal in products that are subject to high tariffs in the United States? Why not just deal in something that isn't subject to an international trade dispute?"

"Ay, there's the rub."

"To dump, or not to dump: that is the question. Whether 'tis nobler in the mind to suffer the slings and arrows of U.S. fair trade law, blah, blah, blah . . . ."

"Very good, Wallace. Especially for someone with a concussion."

"Thank you."

"Anyhooooo, it's possible that someone out there has simply figured out a scheme to game the system—one the Commerce Department hasn't wised up to yet—such that Commerce thinks they aren't exporting their products to the U.S. at anticompetitive low prices. In the context of the sorghum case, for example, if someone figured out a tricky way to reduce the high 354 percent antidumping tariff on sorghum down to a low level, or even zero, they could use their low tariff rate to become the only Chinese manufacturer of sorghum syrup able to export to the U.S. at a competitive price. That is, the *only* viable exporter to the U.S. market. You follow me?"

"I think so," Zhang said.

"So if YSP is the only viable exporter to the U.S. market, then if any other sorghum manufacturers want to sell their products to the U.S. at all, they probably have to funnel their sorghum through YSP. Probably having to relabel their sorghum as being produced by YSP. However it works, I'm guessing they have to pay YSP's phantom owner a hefty tribute in the process. And if such a scheme works with sorghum, it would probably work with anything. Dog food, steel pipe, textiles—anything."

"So you're saying that maybe whoever owns the YSP sorghum-hyphen-Zucheng dog food building has ties to all sorts of industries?"

"Exactly. And his angle is that he takes kickbacks from them for letting them use his companies' names so that they can avoid high U.S. tariffs. You could say he actually *specializes* in exporting goods that are subject to U.S. antidumping investigations. A secret cartel specializing in getting around U.S. trade law. Maybe Powell and Keen figured or ferreted the scheme out. Maybe their discovery brought down someone's—an invisible someone's—murderous wrath."

"Unless, of course, they were killed by Wesley, in a cuckold's jealous rage," Zhang said.

"Or were arrested and so forth because of . . . ." Severin said, pantomiming using a submarine periscope again.

"Or were abducted at random and killed for the value of their passports and credit cards."

"Or were able to stow away to Bali, undetected, to begin new lives as beach bums."

"Or to be debriefed by their—"

Severin cut him off with a zip-your-mouth gesture, then pointed to the ceiling to remind Zhang of the possibility that they were being listened to.

"But I really don't think they're in Bali," Severin continued. "And the only possibility offering leads to pursue is my new trade law cartel theory."

"Leads? What leads?"

"In the case record documents, I found the address for YSP's freight forwarder, or shipping agent, or whatever such things are called here. And guess what? They're located here in Qingdao."

"A shipping agent wouldn't be related to YSP, would it?"

"We shall see. I have a funny gut feeling, and a half-baked plan to stake out their offices."

"Looking for what?"

"I'm not sure. But whatever it is, I think we'll know it when we see it."

THIRTY

For the next several days, as he waited for Zhang to be released from the hospital, Severin accomplished very little. Using nothing more than hand gestures, head nods, and the words yes and no, he was able to negotiate the purchase of a bicycle from a street vendor for the equivalent of roughly $20. Following the directions of the hotel concierge, he used the bike to make his way to the address for the office of Qingdao Ocean One Logistics Company Limited—YSP's alleged shipping agent. Riding with one arm in a cast took some getting used to, and the bike turned out to be totally unnecessary as the office was barely a mile and a half from the Shangri-La Hotel. Regardless, Severin used the bike to make a few passes by the office to take a good look at it. He contemplated staking it out, but decided it would be too risky given that he'd stick out like a sore Caucasian thumb. So he spent a couple of days just riding his bike around the city. It was a fascinating and surprisingly beautiful place, with an old city center comprised of colonial-era German designed buildings and houses that looked like they belonged in an ancient Hanseatic seaport like Bremen or Hamburg. As in Shanghai, the old part of the city was surrounded by gleaming new skyscrapers. The whole downtown area was out on a narrow, rocky peninsula—flanked with wide beaches of golden sand—jutting out into the Yellow Sea. The geography very much reminded Severin of Spain's Costa Brava region, between Barcelona and the French border. He walked the beaches, bought two new pairs of compact binoculars as he wandered the extraordinary markets, and toured the excellent Qingdao Brewery

THIRTY-ONE

At last, the physicians released Zhang with a giant bottle of prescription pain killers that he kept hidden from Severin. He moved into the Shangri-La Hotel, one floor down from Severin's room. Zhang had a barber shave his head to even out the job the hospital did in prepping him for the surgery that never happened, hoping to make himself less conspicuous and hideous—though he still bore large bruises. Then he called the hotel in Yinzhen, leaving a message to tell their poor Shanghai taxi driver where he could find his borrowed/stolen cab—if he hadn't already done so. Aside from that, they took another 72 hours to let Zhang rest and get used to being back on his feet before resuming the chase. When they finally did, they hired another taxi for full-time transportation, then took up station on the roadside across and half a block up the street from the office of Qingdao Ocean One Logistics, just off Laiyang Road. From where they sat with their new binoculars, they could see out over picturesque Huiquan Bay. Two grand sailboats traversed its blue-brown waters. Severin imagined the golden sand beach along the bay would be packed with people come summer. But on this cool winter day, with temperatures barely touching 40 degrees Fahrenheit, it was deserted.

"At least this time we have a view for our stakeout," Zhang said.

"At least this time we don't have diarrhea."

"Amen."

"You know, depending on how our pursuit shakes out, you may need to follow someone on foot. I'd do it, except that I'd be hard to miss."

"Because you're a pale, hairy, round-eye Western barbarian?"

"Are you up to it?"

"I think so. I still feel a little fuzzy. But I think so. Though I had better get a hat to hide the giant bruise on my head, or I'll stick out like the freak that I am."

"We'll get you several hats."

*****

After they'd been sitting in the taxi watching the office of Qingdao Ocean One Logistics for three hours, their driver began to fidget.

"I don't know how long this guy is going to last," Severin said.

"Looks like he has restless leg syndrome"

"My parents called it shaky leg. Are you absolutely sure he's against just letting us borrow the cab?"

"He was adamant. We can try with a different cabbie tomorrow. Hey—someone just came out of the office."

"Finally."

"See that guy with the duffel bag?"

"I see him. Tell the driver to follow at a discreet distance."

They crawled along, watching the man make his way down the side street, turn left on Laiyang Road, and walk another few hundred feet to a bus stop. After a couple minutes, a half-empty bus picked the man up and headed north, inland. It being rush hour, traffic was terrible. It took them more than an hour to travel seven miles to the stop where their quarry got off the bus, in the Licang District. From there, it looked as though the man was headed to a high-rise apartment building—one of several identical buildings lining both sides of the street. At this point, Zhang jumped out of the taxi to follow on foot, trailing the man right through the front door of the building. A few minutes later, he was back in the cab.

"He lives there. He got his mail, read it in the lobby, then took an elevator to the fifth floor."

"Then he's not who we're looking for," Severin said.

"Why not?"

"This is a regular building in a regular working-class neighborhood, and he rode the bus home to it. We're looking for the el jefe. At the very least, the el jefe is probably going to have fancy digs and drive a Mercedes."

"Or a Buick."

"A Buick?"

"Buick is a big status symbol here."

"You're kidding."

"You don't even want to ask him any questions?"

"And have him turn around and warn the el jefe? No."

"You know, when you say 'the el jefe,' the *the* is redundant."

"Huh?"

"The article 'el' is masculine Spanish for 'the.' So when you say 'the el jefe,' you're saying 'the the boss.'"

"Don't—see, this is exactly why . . . ." Severin shook his head.
"I just thought you wouldn't want to keep sounding like an idiot."
"You live in your parents' basement."
"Yeah. That's mature."

*****

The next day, they set off early to find hats for Zhang, following the concierge's directions to a large open-air market—a maze of stalls offering everything from plastic buckets to tea to tires to medicines. In a section offering food, including an incredible variety of fresh produce, they saw cages containing several varieties of live animals that neither of them could identify. There was even a van that held several goats with a handler who was milking directly into milk jugs for a line of eager customers.

"I wonder if that's a civet," Zhang said, pointing to a cage that held a frightened animal that looked like a cross between a raccoon and a weasel or cat.

"What's a civet?"

"Some sort of nocturnal mammal. Remember the SARS outbreak? Some scientists thought the SARS virus crossed over to humans from civets." Zhang shook his head. "You know, over here, some people even thought SARS was created by the CIA, and that it was specifically engineered to infect only Chinese."

"Good lord. I guess there are paranoid kooks in every corner of the world. Not just in Uganda and the Idaho Panhandle."

*****

They found Zhang three nondescript baseball-style caps—one tan, one dark green, one navy blue. Then they got hold of another cab—this time successfully talking the cab driver into just giving them his taxi by promising him advance payments of $100 a day—and resumed their stakeout down at the offices of Qingdao Ocean One Logistics. But just over five hours later, they were foiled again, having followed—through more terrible rush hour traffic—another regular worker in his regular clothes and regular car to his regular apartment in the regular working-class neighborhood of Yingzi.

"Why did we bother following this guy across town?" Zhang asked.

"It's always possible the el jef—pardon me, *el* jefe, could wear humble clothes. Look at Bill Gates."

*****

A few hours into their third day staking out Qingdao Ocean One Logistics, a van pulled up in front of the building, the driver remaining within with the engine running. After a couple of minutes, a rotund man exited the office building and turned toward the van. His hair was styled, and he wore a dark blue Western-style business suit as well as a watch that was big enough for Zhang and Severin to see without the use of their binoculars. The van pulled away as soon as the man shut the passenger side door.

"That's him," Severin said.

"You sound so sure."

"He's overweight. Nobody here is overweight. Follow him."

A low layer of iron gray overcast darkened the sky from horizon to horizon. It was so low that the tops of some of the taller buildings were hidden in cloud as they followed the van into the heart of the city. It made several stops along the way. At each, both the driver and el jefe got out and went in the back doors of what turned out to be various import-export offices, each, according to the names on their respective office front signs, dealing in different products. Frozen seafood, chemicals, molded plastics, paint. Whenever the van stopped, Severin and Zhang also stopped—far enough away that they wouldn't be seen—and surveilled. El jefe and his driver never stayed at any one stop for more than five or ten minutes.

At the fourth such stop, they pulled to the side of the street opposite an alley the van had driven down. Once again, they watched through their binoculars.

"What do you think they're up to?" Zhang asked.

"Looks like collections."

"Like a Mafia protection racket type of thing?"

"Some sort of extortion, I would guess. Or maybe they're collecting kickback payments for the use of el jefe's tariff evasion schemes."

As Severin said this, el jefe and his driver emerged from the back door of a building and into the alley. But this time they were pulling someone with them. The driver held a small and terrified looking old man by his arms from behind as el jefe went to the van and came back with a pair of bolt cutters. The driver, still holding the little old man, forced one of the old man's arms out, then gripped one of his fingers and held it firm and extended. El Jefe aligned the bolt cutter blades so that if he closed the metal arms, it would clip the old man's finger off like a little hotdog.

"Oh, shit," Zhang said. "Look."

"Like I was saying."

There seemed to be a discussion underway. The old man, his face red, kept nodding in agreement with whatever el jefe was saying or demanding. Then they let the old man and his intact finger go and got back in the van. Message delivered.

Zhang and Severin followed the van a couple more miles, back out onto roads that more or less followed the contours of the coastline, past the old German section of the city, and around Qingdao Bay. Finally, it turned left off of the main road onto a street dead-ending at the shore. The van drove around the back of a brand new skyscraper of white masonry and blue glass, then pulled into a parking space adjacent to the main door. Zhang and Severin pulled to the curb a fair distance away, and watched as el jefe and the driver disappeared into the building.

"Should I follow them?" Zhang asked.

"That looks like the type of building that would have a security desk just inside the door."

"I'll take that as a no."

"The parking lot is full, all except for the spot that was waiting for them right next to the main door. What does that tell us, Grasshopper?"

"That el jefe is *the man*."

"There's a sign on a post at the head of the parking spot the van pulled into."

"Is there?"

"Want to go see what it says?"

"Be right back."

When Zhang returned, he was smiling.

"What's the verdict?"

"It says 'reserved for deputy commissioner of customs.'"

"Well, I'll be damned."

*****

It was nearly three hours before the pair re-emerged from the building and got back in the van. When they did, Zhang had to be hailed from behind the dumpster where he was urinating to scramble back into the taxi while trying to zip his pants. They followed the van less than a mile before it turned up a quiet residential street lined with brand new homes that each had to have been at least 4,000 square feet. The van pulled into the driveway, but nobody got out. Severin and Zhang waited on the curb at the end of the block.

"Why aren't they getting out?" Zhang asked.

"How should I know?"

"Do you think they spotted us? Do you think a bunch of goons are on their way here to beat our asses again?"

"It's possible. We won't loiter long."

They both switched back and forth between observing the van and examining the house.

"Wallace, take a look in the lower right window of the house. See the fancy-schmancy lighted floating wall shelves. Are those bottles of cognac?"

Zhang turned his attention to the set of three lit, wall-mounted glass shelves with a dozen or so bottles of cognac on display. The amber spirit in each bottle glowed warmly under the soft, focused beam of a shelf light. "Yeah. Real cognac—not that Georgian fire water we had in Yinzhen. XO grade cognacs from several of the best labels. Hennessy, Louis Royer, Courvoisier, Martell, Otard. Damn—there's even a bottle of Rémy Martin Louis XIII. That's at least $2,000 a bottle."

"El jefe is living a bit above his pay grade, isn't he?" Sevein said.

"For a humble customs official, a government employee, I should say so."

"I certainly don't remember drinking a whole lot of high-dollar cognac when *I* worked for the government. Unless it was at one of those notorious big law firm Christmas parties where they try to buy influence with fake good-fellowship and fancy snacks."

"I think we should leave," Zhang said.

"Look."

"El jefe emerged from the van and went into what was, presumably, his house.

"I think we're cool," Severin said. "They were just finishing up a conversation or something."

The van backed down the driveway, reversed direction, and came rolling down the street toward them. Severin and Zhang crouched down. As the van passed them, Severin snuck a look at the driver. He was now wearing a white leather jacket.

"I'll be damned a second time in one day."

"What?"

"That was the van driver from Yinzhen. The dude we were following when we got waylaid."

"Let's hope he didn't see us."

"He didn't. Let's see if we can't follow that son of a bitch."

They did, keeping a much healthier distance than they did when they were spotted, trapped, and pulverized back in Yinzhen. They tracked the van east, out of downtown, to the Laoshan District. It was an easy task, as the van stayed on the same main road for most of the way. The journey terminated at a luxury mid-rise apartment building that appeared to have an unobstructed view of Fushan Bay, and fronted, to Severin's considerable surprise, a first-class golf course. The building was part of a complex, access to which was controlled by an actively guarded gate. They pulled off the main road and watched as the van disappeared into the underground parking garage of one of the buildings.

"Once again," Severin said, "I'm thinking this guy is maybe, just maybe living above his pay grade."

"Assuming he's merely the company van driver."

"I just wonder about that."

"Do you want me to try to follow him in on foot? I don't think he saw my face in Yinzhen."

"I think we'll be able to see where he goes from here."

They watched the building through their binoculars, scanning from window to window.

"There he is," Zhang said. "Third floor. Second window from the left."

He had entered a corner apartment. Severin could also see a woman—probably his wife—in the kitchen cooking dinner, as well as a young boy watching television in an adjoining room.

"A stand up family man," Zhang said. "Who'd have guessed?"

"This is a welcome discovery."

"Why?"

"I don't see a family. What I see is potential leverage. Let's go back to the hotel and formulate a new plan."

THIRTY-TWO

The first thing they did the next day was get Zhang a couple of the ubiquitous short-sleeve, cotton-polyester blend, collared shirts they'd seen on half the men in every city and town in China—one white, one pale blue. Combined with the nondescript baseball hats covering his bruised and shaved head, Zhang looked like a regular resident of Qingdao. He'd blend in anywhere. Severin also bought a pair of cameras and large, 100-400mm zoom lenses that were remarkably cheap.

The next part of their plan involved following the van driver in the taxi until he stopped somewhere, anywhere public, at which point Zhang would attempt to follow on foot to learn anything he could about the man. Severin would stay with the cab because he was too conspicuous.

"Repeat after me," Severin said to Zhang as they sat in the hotel restaurant, discussing their game plan over breakfast. "You're going to be ridiculously careful and conservative in your surveillance."

"I'm going to be ridiculously careful and conservative in my surveillance."

"One, we don't want to spook our quarry, causing him to bolt. Two, we don't want him to call more of his goon buddies to finish you off. Three, I have a broken wing, and you have a dented skull, so we aren't in any condition to fight. Four, I don't think we can depend on being rescued by Officer Joe again."

"As if I didn't already know all of this."

*****

Their first day shadowing the van driver was rewarding. He took his wife and son straight to el jefe's house, where el jefe, who stood in what looked like a living room, grabbed the boy and raised him high in the air. The boy spread his arms as if he were an airplane as Severin and Zhang watched through their binoculars.

"Grandparents," Zhang said.

"But on Mom or Dad's side?"

"Mom's."

"Why do you say that?"

"Look at the resemblance. I realize we all look the same to you, but still."

"I'll take your word for it. So mister van driver is working for his father-in-law. That could be useful."

As they continued watching, Severin saw el jefe take a box down from a kitchen cupboard and place it on a countertop next to his tea cup before putting a strainer of tea leaves in the cup and filling it with water. It was the same brand of pu-ehr tea, in the same fancy box with its orange and white foil and ribbon seal their Shanghai-to-Yinzhen taxi driver drank. But after a few minutes, el jefe removed the tea leaves and appeared to toss them in a garbage can. No reusing tea leaves for this guy.

"It wasn't the pills," Severin said as they sat.

"What?"

"The hangover, stuffy nose, excessive bile, lethargy, impotence pills you gave me. It may have increased the intensity of my little heart-racing episode back in Yinzhen, but it didn't cause it. I've had them before."

"It's funny you say that, because I've been giving thought to your big question."

"My big question?"

"About what I would do if I were you, living your life or whatever."

"Don't jerk my chain."

"I'm being sincere. I've been thinking about it."

"And?" Severin said in a tone of suspicion.

"I really think you should find a good psychiatrist." Severin groaned and rolled his eyes. "No, hear me out."

"Fine."

"How often do you have panic attacks?"

"Do you have to call them panic attacks?"

"Lars, it's what they are. It doesn't mean you're a delicate flower. The causes can be genetic. They can be caused by changes in your brain chemistry or function. They can come on after long-term stresses in your life, like losing your parents. They can come on in response to your growing midlife angst about mortality. Things you have no conscious control over. Drinking doesn't help, either."

"Drinking calms me."

"Which is probably why you drink so much. But the depressive, relaxing effect is temporary."

"Well, obviously."

"No, I mean four to six hours after you drink, your body breaks the alcohol down into chemical components that actually have a stimulant effect. That's why you wake up at two in the morning sweating and irritated after you drink half a bottle of wine at dinner."

"How do you know all this? You subscribe to JAMA?"

"Because I've been treated for panic attacks. Mine came on during college. When we were roommates, in fact."

"I didn't know that."

"I kept it hidden from everybody. I was worried about the stigma or whatever."

"So what did your treatment consist of?"

"Some psychotherapy. Really, only half a dozen sessions. The guy taught me a few techniques for weathering stress. Getting through tough moments. And I was on meds for about a year. Selective serotonin re-uptake inhibitors. Greatest thing since sliced bread."

"Did that mess up your head? Make you feel fuzzy or whatever?"

"Not at all. They made me feel great."

"And the attacks never came back?"

"They didn't."

"So what caused them in the first place?"

"Beats me. I remember stressing about exams. Stressing about not wanting to disappoint my parents by telling them I didn't want to go to medical school. But that seems like pretty normal stuff. Maybe I'm just genetically predisposed. Not enough serotonin in my head or whatever. At any rate, it was something they taught me to manage the early stages of. Something they taught me to nip it in the bud."

"Hmm."

"The moral of my story is that I think whatever you are using alcohol to deal with—to self-medicate for—might be better dealt with by modern medicine. Plus, therapy and pills won't make your liver fall out your ass like booze will."

Severin fidgeted in his seat. "I suppose that's food for thought." He turned and made eye contact with Zhang. "Thanks, Wallace. Really."

"De nada."

*****

It was on their third day of following the van driver that they hit pay dirt. Instead of going straight home from the office, the van driver took himself to some sort of nightclub. Zhang followed him in and was able to sit close enough to hear occasional fragments of a conversation the driver was having with a young girl dressed in a short silk dress as they both drank bright green cocktails out of martini glasses, sitting close together at a tiny table, their knees touching.

A few minutes later, Zhang came flying out of the club, making straight for the cab.

"Give me the camera with the shorter lens on it," Zhang said.

"Talk to me, Goose."

"Mister van driver has a mistress."

"So he's cheating on el jefe's daughter. Well, well. Fish in a barrel."

"It gets better."

"How could it?"

"His name is Fang."

"The name of the van driver the State Department couldn't find?"

"And possibly the last guy seen with Keen and Powell, yes. Have the camera with the big lens ready for when he comes out."

"Rest assured, I will."

*****

That evening, Severin and Zhang sat in Zhang's hotel room, examining more than a dozen photographs spread over Zhang's bed. There were several that captured the driver and his mistress kissing at their club table, his hand on her bare knee. There were also several of the two lovebirds kissing as they stood outside the club, about to part ways. They were in perfect focus. There was no mistaking it was the van driver.

"These are fantastic," Zhang said.

"These are what we call dream leverage."

"So now what do we do?"

"Now we buy what will hopefully be the last cell phone either of us ever purchase in China. We'll write the phone number on the outside of a big manila envelope, put copies of the photos in it, then leave it under a wiper blade on the windshield of the van at a time when he'll be the first to see it. When he calls, you'll explain to him that copies of these photos will be hand-delivered to his wife and his boss/father-in-law unless he agrees to meet us in a public place for a short and happy little conversation."

*****

The next day, they left the envelope on the van's windshield when the driver stopped at a small market and ran inside for a pack of cigarettes. Zhang and Severin sat in the cab and watched through their binoculars, grins on their faces, as the driver came out and found it. He opened it, thumbed through the pictures, and with a thoroughly terrified look on his face, looked all around, up and down the street, frantic. Then he got in the van and drove away at an unusually high speed. Zhang and Severin sat tight.

Within seven minutes, their new cell phone rang. Zhang answered it and began a conversation in Chinese. His tone was one of reprimand, then of warning. Soon, he motioned for Severin's notepad and pen, then scribbled down what appeared to be directions. Then he hung up.

"Well?"

"It's on. Fang doesn't work tomorrow, so he'll meet us at 10 a.m. at a Taoist temple at the end of a short trail popular with tourists up on Laoshan Mountain. The trailhead is about 14 miles from here."

"Fourteen miles? I thought we were going to meet him nearby."

"His idea. He's worried about being seen."

"How very dramatic."

THIRTY-THREE

Zhang and Severin left the hotel at 7 a.m., wanting to make sure they got to the mountain well ahead of Fang or any goons who might lay in wait to sandbag them. On the way, they pulled off the road once more in front of Fang's apartment building to check that he hadn't left ahead of them. Severin trained his binoculars on the windows.

"There he is, gnawing on a banana. Looks like he's having a heated discussion with the missus."

"Maybe she's ticked that he isn't hanging out with her on his day off," Zhang said.

"He's going hiking. Looking to get healthy. She should give him some credit."

*****

A few miles farther down the road on their drive out to Laoshan Mountain, they began skirting the perimeter of the sprawling Jianggezhuang naval base—no doubt the base where Keen photographed the new submarine—and glanced at each other with sudden unease.

"Don't even say it," Zhang said.

A little further on, they came to a small, beachside fishing village of tan brick houses with red terracotta roofs. A dozen or so old wooden fishing boats sat at anchor in the calm cove. Severin wondered how many hundreds of years people had been doing the same things here—their lifestyle little changed. It struck him that China was so full of contrasts. Unbelievably rapid economic advancement juxtaposed with political backwardness. A society long influenced by the Buddhist philosophy of eliminating cravings, yet hamstrung by pervasive, debilitating corruption and materialism.

Incredible wealth and incredible poverty. Ancient temples within ultramodern cities. A centuries-old fishing village where the fishermen still used primitive, open-bow wooden boats just down the road from a ballistic missile submarine base.

The road hugged the sheer and rocky coastline until turning inland for a short stretch and then terminating at a parking lot that fronted a small tea plantation and a temple built in the grand, highly ornate architectural style of some lost, ancient dynasty. The front gate was comprised of massive, tall, red wooden doors and a flared tile roof of a blue-green color that reminded Severin of oxidized copper. It was flanked by immense stone sculptures of what appeared to be lions—which didn't make much sense to Severin, given that he was 99.9 percent sure there had never been lions in Asia outside of zoos or, perhaps, the private gardens of the absurdly rich and powerful.

They stopped for a moment to read a plaque explaining, in English, how Laoshan was perhaps the most important place in the Taoist religion. That Taoist monks had lived in the many temples dotting the sacred mountain for literally thousands of years. They called it the home of the immortals. The home of those who controlled the wind and the rain.

"What are the tenets of Taoism, anyway," Severin asked. "Is it similar to Buddhism?"

"No."

"So what's it all about?"

"I don't really know. The word Tao means the path. One of my uncles tried to explain it to me once. But I didn't get it."

"Maybe it's like the Force."

"Maybe you're, like, an idiot."

Following the instructions Fang had given them, they passed through the temple complex, emerging on the other side to find a trailhead that immediately began to climb up a ridge of the forested mountainside. It was paved and included stone steps on the steepest sections. But it was a largely relentless ascent, and Severin found himself winded in minutes. Though the sky was mostly clear, a small white cloud clung to the shoulders of the mountain, obscuring their view of the summit. They soon ascended into it, and their visibility was reduced to a few dozen feet. Thought it was morning, hawkers were already manning tables of food, drinks, and souvenirs that flanked the trail wherever there was available space on the ridge. Many of the tables had elaborate tarp covers strung up overhead for protection from sun or rain. It seemed that half the hawkers were selling bottled water that had come from a source on the mountain itself—indeed, it was the frequently mentioned, frequently praised, frequently pushed Laoshan Water served at their hotel and at the nicer restaurants they'd been to in Qingdao. The hawkers would appear out of the mist and, quickly pegging Severin and Zhang as English speakers, would half shout "Laoshan

Water! Laoshan Water for good health!" One of the hawkers sat next to an ice-filled cooler of bottled Qingdao beer.

"I'm getting one," Severin said.

"It isn't even 9 a.m. Don't we need to be sharp?"

Severin ignored him, bought a beer, and plopped down on a PVC chair, at a PVC table, under a giant blue tarp to drink it. Zhang shook his head and sat down next to him.

"This is a damn good beer."

"Great."

"I get that Fang is worried about being seen, but this seems a bit extreme." Severin said.

"Seeing this trail, I'm guessing he probably thought he could get here ahead of us and watch the approach to see who we are and how many of us he'd be dealing with. He also said there was just too much danger for him down in the city."

"Did he really use the Chinese word for danger?"

"Yes. And he sounded genuinely frightened."

"Does he know who we are?"

"He assumes we're the guys who were following him in Yinzhen. But beyond that, I don't think he has a clue."

"We'll enlighten him."

"You don't think he'll just shoot us?"

"Too public. And he'd only have one very long escape route back down the mountain. Too risky."

They resumed their ascent as soon as Severin finished his beer. The cloud at last moved off, revealing clear blue sky and the summit of the great granite mountain towering above them. Before long, they could see their destination: a cluster of what looked like half a dozen small, old stone buildings built on a ledge that looked like it had been chiseled out of the mountainside. Ten minutes later, they were there. It was a high shelf of stone, maybe 20 yards deep at best. On it sat the little stone buildings, and behind them, tiny temples carved into the mountain itself—ornate gates framing small doorways to man-made tunnels housing Taoist altars and religious decorations. The air smelled of burning incense, and innumerable little bells could be heard tinkling in the gentle breeze. A white-and-blue clad Taoist monk emerged from a narrow gate through a wall that ran from the edge of the cliff, clear across the shelf, to the sheer granite face of the mountainside. He strode past them silently, without so much as raising his gaze to acknowledge their presence, then disappeared around the corner of a tiny stone building perched on the edge of a great precipice. From where they now stood, they had a spectacular view out over the Yellow Sea toward Korea.

"Let's go hang out near the edge and keep an eye on our good friend

Fang as he makes the climb," Severin said. "Make sure he isn't accompanied by any of his goon buddies." They did so. And barely half an hour later, Severin spotted Fang through his binoculars, slowly making his way up the mountain path, alone. The only other people visible on the trail were a trio of young women with cameras—obvious tourists—and a Taoist monk who was descending with a pair of large plastic buckets.

After watching Fang for several minutes to assure themselves there wasn't any hostile muscle following him up the ridge at a discreet distance, Severin and Zhang hid themselves in a clump of trees from where they would be able to observe Fang from close up. Soon, Fang emerged at the top of the stairwell and, after pausing with his hands on his knees to catch his breath, strode to the exact same spot near the edge of the cliff where Severin and Zhang had just been observing his ascent. He pulled a pair of binoculars from a jacket pocket and trained them on the trail, below.

"Sorry, Fang," Severin whispered, "but the early bird catches the worm."

He and Zhang watched him for a couple of minutes—with Severin, still moderately concerned that Fang might be carrying a weapon, looking for telltale bulges in Fang's clothes. Then, as Fang bent down to scratch his leg, Severin saw that he had a handgun jammed into the waistband of his pants at the small of his back.

"Wait here," Sevrin whispered to Zhang. "Don't move."

Fang, having watched the trail through his binoculars for a couple of minutes, lowered them, rubbed his eyes, and then strode a few steps to his left, disappearing behind one of the small stone buildings. Severin emerged from concealment and slunk up to the corner of the same building. Peeking around it, he saw Fang, standing near the edge of the cliff not 10 feet away, once again watching the trail though his binoculars.

Severin knew a number of standard police takedown moves. The only problem was that they weren't designed for officers with a broken arm in a cast. He tried to think of which he could pull off, bearing in mind that he was quite a bit bigger than Fang. He took three long, quick steps forward and, as Fang just began to turn, put him in what amounted to an almost complete wedge hold, securing one of Fang's arms, and at least half-securing the other, before turning, locking a leg across Fang's shins, and dropping him face down onto the ground. Laying atop the smaller man, Severin immediately jerked one of Fang's arms up and behind his back, pinned it there with his cast, and took possession of the gun with his good arm. Tucking the gun in his own waistband, he then gave Fang a cursory pat down, making sure he didn't have any other hidden firearms. Satisfied that Fang was as clean as he needed to be for the moment, Severin called for Zhang, jammed the gun—some sort of compact .38—into his own waistband, pulled Fang to his feet, then stepped back and took a deep breath.

"Good morning, Fang," Zhang said in Chinese as he approached.

Several times, Fang's anxious gaze jumped back and forth between Severin and Zhang, who kept a decent distance—both to help Fang get over the initial shock of being taken to the ground and disarmed, and to maintain a buffer that would give them more time to react if he decided to attack them with a hidden knife or other undiscovered weapon.

Severin brushed off his dusty pants as he gave Fang a good, long look. "Start by reminding him that if he doesn't answer all of our questions to our satisfaction, we'll send copies of all of those photos to—"

"You don't have to speak Chinese," Fang said, his arms hanging at his sides, looking angry but resigned, not bothering to brush himself off.

"Oh, you speak English," Severin said. "How nice. And how did you come by that skill?"

"I was raised by my aunt and uncle in Singapore. They sent me to the American School."

"Do you know why we're here?" Severin asked.

"To blackmail me."

"There's a little more to it than that, isn't there?" Zhang said.

Fang sighed. "We know you're trying to use the system," he mumbled. "Trying to use American trade law for competitive advantage."

"Competitive advantage?" Zhang said. "I think you're thinking of someone else."

"You're looking for evidence to give to the U.S. Department of Commerce so they put an unfair high tariff on our products."

"Like I said, you got the wrong guys, pal."

"You know something?" Fang said with a new spark of bitterness and defiance in his eyes. "The unjust, protectionist antidumping laws are only there for China bashing."

"China bashing?" Severin said.

"We're not dumping. We're not being anticompetitive. We just have low labor and material costs so we can make products a lot cheaper than America can. That's all. The U.S. government knows this. There isn't even any such thing as dumping."

"Tell that to Hitachi, NEC, and Toshiba's computer chip subsidiaries," Zhang said.

"What is this, *Meet the Press*?" Severin asked.

"You think unjust American law will stop us?" Fang said, shaking his head. "It won't."

"Probably not," Severin said. "Because if Commerce slaps you with a high tariff, you'll just re-label your sorghum syrup as something else, right? What customs agent is going to know that it isn't corn syrup, light molasses, or buckwheat honey? U.S. Customs is too busy watching for terrorists and drugs. They don't have the time or money to test thousands of drums of syrup to see whether or not they contain sorghum. And even if they did catch you committing fraud, what do you have to worry about? When Customs tries to find your U.S. importer to collect the antidumping tariffs, are they going to find millions of dollars stacked to the ceiling at your bustling U.S. headquarters? No. They'll find a façade—an empty, dusty office you never used as anything more than a mailing address. And next year you'll just find a new mailing address and restart the game somewhere else, right? Did I score a bullseye?"

Fang glared at him. "We are *not* dumping."

"Well, you know what?" Severin said. "That's between you and the U.S. government. The only reason we're here is that a family wants to know what happened to their little girl who was here investigating YSP."

"You work for Marshall Quotient Trading."

"No," Zhang said.

Fang looked perplexed. "I don't . . . . Why—"

"Because you are one of the last two people on Earth known to have been with Kristin Powell and Bill Keen, the vanished investigators from the Commerce Department," Severin said.

"No."

"Both the American attorney, Ben Holloman, and the Commerce team's interpreter, Yu Lin, say you were. They said you were acting funny before you dropped them off at the airport, dropped Holloman at the hotel, and then mysteriously disappeared."

At this Fang smiled a bitter smile. "No. No, you have the wrong Fang."

"What?"

"I wasn't in the van with the Commerce investigators. I was in the car with the interpreter. Ask her. I am Fang Hou. The van driver is Fang Xu. I'm sure our names all sound the same to you, just as our faces all look the same."

"Now Fang, don't be cross," Severin said, tiring of the farce. "Why don't you show us your identification card so that we know you aren't trying to pull the proverbial fast one."

Fang frowned, muttered something in Chinese, then pulled his identity card from his wallet. Sure enough, his name was Fang Hou.

"Fine," Severin said. "If you aren't the van driver, then who are you? And if you're so innocent, then why the hell did you call for those pipe-wielding goons to maul us back in Yinzhen?"

"Somebody sent an email telling us that one of the competing importers in the U.S., Marshall Quotient Trading, had sent people to try to dig up dirt on YSP."

"Dirt?"

"Something they could give to the U.S. government. Something the Commerce Department could use to justify the imposition of a high tariff on our sorghum syrup, to destroy our business."

"Who sent the email?" Severin asked.

"It was anonymous. An email address made up of random letters and numbers."

"You thought we were from a competing importer?"

Fang shrugged.

"So if you aren't the van driver we're looking for, then what's your position in YSP?"

Fang held back. "Let's talk about those photos first."

"What about them?" Severin said.

"Are those the only copies?"

"What do you think?"

"So what guarantees are you offering for my cooperation?"

"We'll get rid of the pictures for you. No one—not your children, your wife, or your father-in-law—will ever be the wiser. Not because of us, anyway."

"How can I be sure?"

"You can't be sure, Fang. You have to take our word for it. But consider that we'd have no motive to do anything but destroy them if you give us the information we need. Now, I'll ask you one more time. If you don't answer, we're going back to Qingdao to mail some envelopes full of photos. What is your position in YSP?"

Fang seemed to deliberate before speaking. Looking very reluctant, he resumed. "There's no such thing as YSP. It's just a paper company. A name we'll use as long as Commerce has a low tariff rate assigned to it. When it doesn't, we'll give it a new name."

"What is your role in the bigger picture then?"

"On paper, I'm the vice-president for compliance at Qingdao Ocean One Logistics. It's an empty title. I'm really just a servant for Xiu."

Severin thought he caught a trace of bitterness in Fang's tone. "And who is Xiu?"

"The big boss."

"El jefe? The man you drive around in the van?" Zhang asked.

"Yes."

"And the owner of the sorghum exporter of many names?" Severin asked.

"Of that. Of lots of different companies."

"Running customs evasion and racketeering tribute schemes for all sort of products, right?"

Fang shrugged his shoulders, nodded.

"And he's a senior customs official with uniformed customs officers and any number of plainclothes goons at his beck and call."

"Yes."

"*And* he's your father-in-law. Well, well."

Fang just stared, looking furious.

"Look, all we care about is what happened to Kristin Powell," Zhang said.

"I don't know."

"Oh, Fang. Come on now."

"I really don't. Why don't you ask the American lawyer, Holloman."

"Why would we want to do that?"

"Because he was the last person to be seen with them who had any reason to make them disappear."

"Doubtful," Zhang said. "Holloman is a big-time attorney in Washington, D.C., where the average rate for big firm partners hovers around $1,000 per hour. What would have been his motivation to risk his neck like that for a client that only pays him $35,000 for a year's work?" Zhang asked.

"The $35,000 figure is just for the accounting records we put together for Commerce. It's for show. It has nothing to do with what Xiu actually pays him."

"How much does Xiu pay him?"

"Four million dollars a year, give or take."

"Four million?" Zhang said, sounding dubious. "To represent a two-bit sorghum processor?"

"Don't be obtuse," Fang said. "Four million to represent all of Xiu's companies. Holloman and Xiu specialize in taking on small companies in industries that have been targeted by U.S. antidumping investigations and are saddled with high tariff rates. They use their magic legal and accounting schemes to figure out how to get each company's tariff rate down to zero. Then that company becomes the main player for the industry, and all the other factories or suppliers pay Xiu to export to the U.S. through Xiu's companies because he has by far the lowest tariff rate, and nobody else can compete profitably in the U.S. market unless they go through him. He makes himself the necessary middle man for entire industries."

"Like what?"

"Sorghum syrup, composite roofing shingles, plastic bottles, applesauce—"

"Dog food," Severin added.

"Yes, dog food. Each industry is an income stream."

"And Xiu is Holloman's sugar daddy."

"No. It was all Holloman's idea from the beginning," Fang said. "He approached us five years ago, when our canned oyster company got caught up in an American antidumping investigation. He said he had this idea that would make us all rich. Before that, Xiu was just a regular exporter."

"And high Customs official," Severin said. "No conflict of interest there, right?"

"Still," Zhang said, "from Holloman's point of view, why would he take such a risk and go to such extremes when YSP is just one small piece of the pie? Why not just suck it up for a year, write off YSP, and start over with a new paper company with a new fake name in a new fake location the next year—especially when, as you say, U.S. Customs will never collect any tariffs from the importer anyway?"

"Because anyone who knows anything about these cases knows that the American lawyers have to come over here days—sometimes weeks—before the Commerce investigators show up to help their clients prepare," Fang said.

"In other words, there's no way Holloman could pretend he didn't know YSP was committing fraud," Severin said.

"Exactly."

"So if the investigators had been able to file their report, Holloman would have been disbarred. Probably imprisoned," Zhang added.

Severin and Zhang stared at one another.

"So," Severin said at last, "when you left Yinzhen, the van with the Commerce employees was behind you."

"Yes. But then it wasn't. I didn't know why, so I pulled over and waited for them to catch up."

"How far outside of Yinzhen?"

"I don't know. Five or six kilometers maybe."

"How long did you wait?"

Fang shrugged. "A few minutes."

"Then the van caught up and passed you?"

"Yes."

"When it passed, could you see that everyone was still in the van?"

"I didn't really look. Anyway, it was too dark. I wouldn't have been able to see them."

"Do you remember where you pulled the car over and waited?"

"Approximately."

"Then show us."

"I can't be seen with you! Xiu has people everywhere. Always watching."

"He's your loving father-in-law."

"He will have me killed. He will not hesitate."

"Look, Fang. If we're going to believe a single word you've told us, then we're going to need to find evidence that corroborates your story."

"What do you expect to find?"

"Bodies," Severin said. "If Holloman killed them, he probably did so on that lonely stretch of road where you waited for the van."

"I'm—no. I'm not going."

Severin nodded to Zhang, who pulled from his inner jacket pocket another 5x7 photo of Fang in a compromising position with his mistress and held it up to Fang's face.

"Will your loving father-in-law kill you if he sees these?" Zhang said.

"We'll put you in the back seat, with a hat, hood, and big pair of ladies sunglasses to obscure your face," Severin said, tossing Fang's gun off the cliff as the three of them turned to begin their descent of the mountain. "You'll be fine."

THIRTY-FOUR

Three hours and two traffic jams later, they were driving down a lonely stretch of country road that ran between two vast but fallow farm fields a few kilometers northeast of Yinzhen.

"I think it was right around here somewhere," Fang said.

"Where you pulled over to wait for the van?" Severin asked.

"Yes. But it was getting dark. I'm not sure."

"Okay. We'll keep heading toward town. You shout out when we get to where you last remember seeing the van's headlights behind you."

"You really think we're going to find bodies?" Zhang asked, sounding more than a little uneasy. "Even if they were killed here, they were probably disposed of someplace else, right? I mean, if they were killed here, nobody would have had time to dig graves and bury them in the time Fang was pulled over and waiting for the van to reappear. And if they weren't buried, somebody would have discovered them. Unless, of course, there was some other accomplice who came to bury them. But if that's the case, we'll never find their remains."

"Humor me," Severin said.

They drove on, heading southwest toward Yinzhen. But before they'd gone far, Severin spotted a narrow dirt service road perpendicular to the road they were on that led out into the farm fields.

"Turn onto that road," Severin said to Wallace.

They drove at a crawl, watching for anything that might pass for a clue. But half a mile from the main road they encountered an impassible water-filled pothole that was as wide as the service road itself. Severin and Zhang got out, skirted the pothole on foot, and spent the next half-hour walking up and down the rest of the short road, getting dark brown mud all over their shoes, searching every square foot. But they found nothing more substantial than a few dozen cigarette butts.

They got back in the car and resumed their drive toward Yinzhen. Within a couple of minutes, they spotted another service road, much like the other. Again, they turned onto it. There were no houses or other farm structures for many hundreds of yards in any direction. They motored along slowly—maybe a couple of miles per hour—as they watched for clues out of their open windows. A lightning bolt flashed within a wall of purple stratocumulus clouds rapidly approaching from the south. A few seconds later, deep rolling thunder rattled the car.

"Do you think we're going to get wet?" Zhang said, eyeballing the towering clouds.

Severin didn't answer. His eyes were locked on what looked like a large heap of agricultural refuse up ahead 50 or 60 yards on their right. As they got closer, they could see with certainty that it was a giant compost pile comprised of decomposing plant matter. Weeds, cuttings, reaped sorghum cane. It looked as if refuse had been deposited there season after season for many years. The pile was about the same height as Severin, had a more or less circular base of at least 20 feet, and had a fair degree of overall symmetry. But a flaw in its symmetry was what now held Severin's eye. A place where it looked like the side of the pile had eroded and collapsed—or been pulled down—into a shorter semicircle of debris that extended out from the larger pile.

"Stop the car," Severin said.

"You see something?"

Severin opened his door, got out, and walked slowly, apprehensively, toward the pile—toward the flaw. He stopped ten feet from the flaw and stared at it as Zhang came up behind him, then walked all the way around the greater pile, examining it as he went. As he expected, he found that the flaw was the only one of its kind in the pile. Stopping as he reached the flaw again, he noted what he was sure had once been deep grooves gouged out of the side of the pile by the heel of someone's foot. They were thoroughly eroded, but clearly recognizable as such. Someone had climbed up on the pile and either accidentally or deliberately pushed material down, creating the flaw.

"Check the car to see if there's something we can dig or probe with," he said to Zhang. "A shovel. A tire iron. Anything."

Zhang gave him a grave look before going. There was a bad smell in the air. Not just of decaying plants. It was more akin to putrid meat and reminded Severin of the stagnant air downwind of a pork slaughterhouse one humid summer day that he spent near his cousin's home in Louisville, Kentucky. As he drew slowly closer to the flaw in the pile, he saw that it wasn't going to be necessary to dig. The sole of a black leather women's shoe was exposed where compost had eroded away. A symbol imprinted in the rubber indicated that it was made by Cole Haan—an American brand.

Severin took out his phone and dialed Officer Joe as another thunderclap roared in their ears and a hard rain began to fall.

THIRTY-FIVE

By dusk, Officer Joe's men—half of them plain-clothes, half uniformed police—had exhumed the remains and were scouring the area for evidence with the help of one dog and two metal detectors. But to Severin's surprise, they hadn't found two bodies—they'd found three.

Momentarily satisfied with the progress being made, Joe did Severin and Zhang the courtesy of coming over to explain where things stood. "As you probably guessed, it looks like the perpetrator dragged the bodies to the edge of the compost heap, then got on top of it and shoved waste down the side to conceal them, quick and dirty. Two of the bodies are wearing clothes of American manufacture. One male, one female, each appearing to match the descriptions of Powell and Keen—at least with respect to approximate height and hair color. The third body appears to be Chinese."

"The van driver, Fang Xu," Severin said.

"Possibly. None of the bodies have any identification on them. Each has one kill shot to the skull. It's clear the female was also hit in the hip. I'm confident we'll find abdominal shots to both male victims as well, once we have a chance to carefully examine the bodies. My guess, under some pretext or threat, the perpetrator convinced the three victims to get out of the van. Then, before they could run, he got off at least three quick shots to hobble or incapacitate them. Then he finished each of them off with a shot to the skull and concealed the bodies. You might also be interested to see this," Joe said, holding up a small clear plastic evidence bag. It held a brass bullet shell.

".32 ACP?" Severin said.

"Exactly."

"Is the .32 ACP a common bullet in China?"

"Funny you should ask," Joe said, looking impressed. "First of all, while some nevertheless do, it's technically illegal for private citizens to have guns. So *no* bullets are common. That being said, the .32 caliber is that much more uncommon. And I dare say that in China this particular bullet," he said, turning the shell so that Severin could see its flat, round back end, "is unheard of." Stamped into the brass, in text that curved around the primer pocket, were the words *Winchester Super X.* An American bullet. "We've only found the one shell. It was in the irrigation ditch under 35 centimeters of water. My guess is the perpetrator tried to pick up his brass to minimize evidence, but couldn't find this one and gave up in his haste. But it looks like we'll recover at least three bullets. As I mentioned, each victim has an entry wound to the skull. But none of them has an apparent exit wound."

"I don't suppose we could borrow one of the bullets," Severin said.

"Quite impossible. But I can probably find a way to email you a copy of the analysis. Just don't tell anyone where you got it."

"We'd be grateful. And if there's ever a need to have the report submitted as evidence in an American court, an official copy would have to be requested through proper diplomatic channels anyway. So as far as we're concerned, anything you email to us will never have existed."

"Then of what use will it be to you?"

"That remains to be seen. But it's a start. Now I suppose we'd better get back to the hotel to call Thorvaldsson."

THIRTY-SIX

Back in Seattle four days later, Severin received the forensic report from Officer Joe indicating, among other things, that the gun that killed Powell and Keen was a .32 caliber Beretta Tomcat. "Very popular for concealed carry because of its small size," Severin explained to Zhang over beers at Big Time Brewery. "Perfect for an ankle holster."

"Strapped to the ankle of a shit-bag D.C. attorney," Zhang said.

"Methinks. And something else occurred to me last night."

"What?"

"When we interviewed him way back when, Holloman usually referred to Keen and Powell as *the Commerce team*, or *the Commerce investigators*. He didn't like to use their names."

"Because it made him uncomfortable," Zhang said.

"I just wonder."

"Do you think it was Holloman who made the anonymous call to Xiu's people, warning them that somebody from Marshall Quotient Trading would be poking around the fake YSP factory?"

"And do I think Holloman was hoping Xiu's people would kill us? Yes and yes."

*****

Early the next day, they once again flew from Seattle to Washington, D.C. That same evening, dull with jetlag and stinking of the fried crab cakes they'd had for a late dinner, Severin and Zhang sat in a rented Ford sedan, under a broad, ancient chestnut tree on a quiet stretch of Dumbarton Street in the Georgetown neighborhood. It was just after 3 a.m. on a clear, cold night. They were parked several doors down from the stately brick Federal-style townhouse of Ben Holloman, Esquire—hot-shot partner at the prestigious law firm of McElroy, Steen & Duff.

Three hours earlier, they'd stopped in roughly the same location to take a preliminary look at the house. Though initially frustrated to find that it bore window stickers indicating that it was protected—and no doubt wired with burglar alarms—by a private security company, they'd been pleased to see that the alarm system control keypad was mounted in the kitchen, clearly visible through the home's front windows.

"Part of me still finds it hard to believe that Holloman's our guy," Zhang said.

"Who else could have done it?"

"I don't know. Someone from the company?"

"Shooting American bullets from an American gun?"

"Maybe it was Holloman's gun in someone else's hand."

"Anything is possible, I suppose."

"Don't get me wrong. I didn't like him. Way too uptight. But still, he seemed pretty sincere. Pretty straight. One of those rare birds who come from nowhere and make it to the top table on merit."

"On the other hand," Severin said, "he's a highly successful member of a profession that has turned being two-faced and full of crap into a form of performance art. I'm sure he could make himself seem like whatever he wants. Maybe all his self-deprecation is a façade. Maybe it takes a viper to climb from where he started to where he is. Someone with no moral compass. Maybe he's twisted by envy of his privileged Harvard and Yale-educated colleagues. Who knows?"

"If it was Holloman, why on Earth would he have ever have agreed to talk to us in the first place?"

"He was under the not altogether unreasonable impression that by being cooperative and agreeable, he'd largely avert suspicion. Plus, I'm sure he had great confidence in his ability to act the sincere and concerned witness. Again, he's a lawyer."

"But you think he owns a gun and keeps it at home? Guns are illegal in D.C., aren't they?"

"That's funny, Wallace. You should do stand-up."

"Fine. But really, wouldn't he have been insane to try to smuggle a gun into China? The Chinese don't play around when it comes to stuff like that."

"When we arrived in Shanghai, did Chinese customs bother to unzip your suitcase and conduct even a cursory hand search?"

"I don't remember."

"They didn't. They ran the baggage through what looked like x-ray machines. But it didn't look like anybody was monitoring the screens."

"What are you saying?"

"I'd bet good money those machines aren't even operational. Just props for deterrence."

"You mean they were just running bags down conveyor belts for show, through unmonitored or otherwise dead x-ray machines?"

"Yup. And someone who travels there regularly would probably be aware of this. Or maybe he bribed a corrupt customs agent to help him circumvent the process. Or maybe he gets preferred treatment over there on account of his status as a highly respected defender of Chinese trading companies."

"You can take guns on airplanes?"

"In checked baggage."

"Okay, but airlines x-ray checked luggage for international flights, don't they? And they'd know guns aren't allowed in China. So wouldn't the airline have stopped it?"

"I don't know. Maybe he express-mailed the gun to himself there, addressing it to an alias just in case. Maybe he concealed it in a lead box. Who knows? Where there's a will, there's a way."

"But why would he take a gun to China at all?"

"Why does anybody carry a gun? He's afraid of stuff."

"Okay." Zhang shook his head. "But I still have my doubts."

"Well, we'll see if we can't put those doubts to rest shortly. Speaking of which, why don't you go ahead and take the lens caps off those binoculars."

"Alright, sir."

With that, Severin took hold of the hammer he'd purchased at a hardware store earlier in the day, opened the car door, and crossed the dark street, heading for Holloman's house. Once there, he popped on his tiny LED keychain light and examined the front windows until he saw what he was looking for: a window alarm sensor. It was on an old-fashioned multi-paned window with an ancient wooden frame. He would have to move quickly, just in case Holloman was a light sleeper—or even awake. With the blunt top of the hammer, he punched in one of the window panes, reached in, unlatched the window, and raised it a few inches, instantly triggering a shrill alarm siren. He ran for it, looking over his shoulder as he went around the corner of the block to observe, with satisfaction, that Holloman had, rather stupidly, turned on the interior lights of his house. That would make things much easier for Zhang to observe.

*****

Sometime later, he rendezvoused with Zhang down on M Street.

"His security system code is 7771," Zhang said.

"Excellent."

"And guess what he was brandishing when he rushed into the parlor in his pedophile silk robe."

"A cute little handgun."

"Es correcto. It was in his hand as soon as he appeared, and he appeared quickly. So I'm guessing he keeps it in the bedroom."

"Well done, Wallace."

*****

In late morning the next day, having insisted that Zhang stay behind at the hotel and not risk getting himself arrested—or worse—if things went wrong, Severin was strolling down Holloman's block of Dumbarton Street for the second time in 10 minutes, on the opposite side of the street from his house, making a quick and dirty reconnaissance. Holloman's house appeared to be unoccupied, but Severin couldn't be sure. He continued his walk, going around the corner before calling Zhang.

"His secretary said he isn't in the office yet," Zhang said.

"Crap. I wish I'd gotten here early enough to make sure he left for work."

"Want to wait until tomorrow?"

"Maybe. I'm going to have a closer look."

Severin gave it another few minutes before walking back down Dumbarton Street—this time on the sidewalk fronting Holloman's house. Reaching it, he marched right up to the front door as if his purpose were entirely normal, then made motions as if knocking on the door—without actually making contact—for the sake of any casual observers, all the while peering in the windows looking for signs of life. The house looked empty.

Screw it.

He scanned the street and nearby windows for potential witnesses. Then he reared back, and with all the force he could muster, knocked the door in in one powerful kick with the bottom of his foot. The deadbolt splintered what turned out to be a surprisingly weak and brittle doorframe. He stepped inside, closed the door behind him, and took two seconds to listen. All was quiet, save for the beeps of the alarm system's countdown. He ran to the keypad and punched in the code, 7771, deactivating the system, then went down the hall to find Holloman's bedroom.

*****

Back at the hotel, Severin strode into Zhang's room carrying a large paper grocery bag. He went to the bed and dumped its contents onto Zhang's comforter. A newly purchased hack saw, a small plastic card, a sawed open, hard-sided, plastic, portable locking gun case, and a small pistol.

"That, sir," Severin said, "is a .32 caliber Beretta Tomcat. And can you guess what's loaded in its seven-round magazine?"

"Winchester Super X bullets?"

"Ten points for Wallace. There's also this," he said, holding up the small plastic card. "It's a nonresident concealed carry permit issued by Fairfax County, Virginia. Might be useful to pull the application records, if they aren't sealed like they are in some jurisdictions."

"So now what?"

"Now I make a phone call and cash in on a favor."

Severin called Greg Carlsen, his old friend and colleague on the Anacortes, Washington, police force, explaining that he was going to send him the Beretta by overnight mail so that Carlsen could have a lab confirm that the Beretta fired the bullets described in a Chinese forensic analysis that Severin would be emailing him a rough translation of.

"You're pushing the edge of the limits of our friendship," Carlsen said. "But since I got you into this, I'll do it. I have a cold case I can assign the analysis to. Nobody will notice."

"In the meantime, why don't you run the serial number to see if any surprises pop up."

"You're a bold bastard. Give it to me." Severin gave it to him, and heard Carlsen keying it into the laptop of his patrol car terminal. "Nothing weird. Looks clean."

"It was worth a look. Thanks."

"Wait—when did you say this murder took place?"

"Last August."

"This gun was first purchased on September 4th."

"Are you sure?"

"Afraid so."

Severin pondered the possibilities. Had Holloman dumped the .32 he used to kill Powell, Keen, and Fang Xu while still in China? That would have made sense. He probably chucked it off a bridge, into some ancient, muddy river or canal, never to be seen again, and then replaced it with a new one upon his return. "Well, I guess you don't have to worry about having the gun tested. Thanks for nothing."

"That's what I'm here for."

He hung up and explained the situation to Zhang.

"So now what?" Zhang asked. "Are we at a dead end?"

"Let's get a drink to loosen up our thinking caps."

THIRTY-SEVEN

With a sense of *déjà vu*, Severin and Zhang once again sat in the rental car in the dark, under the broad chestnut tree, with two pair of binoculars trained on Holloman's house on Dumbarton Street. They'd just watched Holloman get home from work, pour himself a surprisingly low-quality bourbon, and plop down in front of his television to watch—of all things—an ancient rerun of the original *Muppet Show* with guest star Loretta Lynn.

"A hillbilly kid at heart," Severin said.

"A lonely one, a long way from the hills."

"Actually, I don't think there are any hills where he grew up in Florida."

"I sort of feel sorry for him."

"Even though he probably murdered three innocent people?"

"Well."

"I'll tell you what. Let's shake of your gloom with some fun, seat-of-our-pants subterfuge," Severin said, dialing Holloman's home number on his cell phone. Holloman picked up on the first ring.

"Ben! Lars Severin here."

"Lars Ssss—oh, right. How are things going?" Holloman stood up, pointing a remote control at his television. Severin saw the word *mute* appear in a corner of the screen.

"Just got back from China, actually."

"Did you? I hope the long flight was worthwhile."

"I have to tell you, you're doing well so far."

"Pardon?"

"The pause while you pretended to have to take a moment to remember where you'd heard my name before. The feigned ignorance about my trip to China. Smooth and convincing. It's all in the timing and delivery, just like in comedy. You know, they're always looking to hire good role players for the interrogation course at the Federal Law Enforcement Training Center down in Georgia. You should apply if they ever let you out of prison. 'Course they probably won't."

A longer pause. "Mr. Severin, I'm not—"

"It's okay. It's okay. Just jerking your chain a little bit. Can't help myself. Remember, I'm not a cop. As I'm sure you've divined by now, I'm a defrocked alcoholic burnout looking to make ends meet. My interest in this whole affair is purely financial. So why don't we help each other?"

"Help?"

"First off, I haven't been instructed to take my evidence to the police. But I haven't been told not to either. I figure that's my big stick. My leverage in our little negotiation here."

"Mr. Sev—"

"Hold on now. Hear me out. Kristin Powell's family promised to pay me $50,000 for what I've learned. That's a nice sum for three weeks work. But it isn't enough to get me out of the low-rent district in Seattle. That city has gotten so damned expensive. Anyway, my point is that I can be talked out of giving the information to them. You follow?" Silence. "No? Well, well. Let's try a different tack. How long have you been out of law school and in private practice? Are you still up on your criminal law?"

Silence.

"Correct me if I'm wrong, Ben, but I think we're looking at two counts each under U.S. Code Title 18, sections 1114 and 1119(b)—first-degree murder of a federal officer, and first degree murder of a U.S. national while outside the United States. Not sure what code section would apply to your murder of the Chinese van driver, Fang Xu. And I'm crap when it comes to math. Still, under that pesky mandatory minimums thing, I'm pretty sure that comes to at least four mandatory life sentences. That's a long time, Ben. A hell of a long time. Not in geological terms, of course. But it'd be the rest of your life. Unless they give you the death penalty, which is a possibility on any one of the four counts. Then again, they might just let the Chinese extradite you for killing one of their citizens. That would be a nice gesture that might win our government some goodwill points—some political capital they could use in their next agreement negotiation. That's how it works, right? Then the Chinese could harvest your organs, or whatever it is they do over there with murderers."

"Mr. Severin . . . ." He stopped.

"I know. It's a tight spot, isn't it? You're probably finding it a little harder to breathe. Feeling that weird tingle in your legs, like you need to sit down. So now we come to that proverbial question: What is your life and freedom worth? What are my broken arm and concussion worth? What is Wallace's ruined hair worth? I've put a lot of thought into this, Ben. I'm not greedy. I was raised Lutheran. I think $200,000 is entirely fair and reasonable. Two hundred thousand would make me very happy. And for you, this whole mess goes away."

More silence.

"You're close to saying yes, aren't you? But you have your doubts. You might be thinking to yourself, hey, this guy is full of shit. Does he really know anything? What are the chances? Did he actually find the three bodies I buried under the compost heap back on that lonely country road a few kilometers northeast of Yinzhen? Did he actually recover some of the Winchester Super X .32 ACP bullets from the skulls of my victims, and that one brass shell casing I couldn't find? Did he then get hold of a slug from the Fairfax County gun range where I got my nonresident concealed carry permit last year? Did he then have an old police lab buddy compare the bullets' striations, land and groove impressions, and other rifling characteristics? And did it turn out the bullets were fired by the same gun? And did the interpreter, Yu Lin, and the other Fang—Fang Hou—see that I was alone in the van when I passed them as they sat in their car on the shoulder, waiting for me on that fateful night? So many questions, right? And so much at stake." Severin took a breath, letting Holloman chew on what he'd just heard. "So, what does your gut tell you, Ben?"

Severin could hear Holloman breathing through his nose on the other end of the line. "Mr. Severin, what you're trying to do is called extortion. That's a felony. A *real* felony. Not some trumped up bull like what you're pushing on me."

"I'm not going to argue with you, Ben. I know you're good for the cash, though you probably won't be able to liquidate assets until banking hours tomorrow. But as I said, I'm a reasonable man. So here's the deal. At 4 p.m. tomorrow, you'll meet me at the front door of the Smithsonian National Air and Space Museum, bearing in mind that there will be lots of people and probably a handful of police officers there. You'll bring the money in a paper grocery bag. In fact, why don't you go ahead and double-bag it. You'll hand it off to me as though you're giving an old friend—a bachelor friend who can't cook—leftover pot roast that your nonexistent wife made a little extra of. If you don't do that, Ben, then tomorrow evening I'll give a copy of everything I have to the D.C. Bar Association, the D.C. Police, the State Department, the FBI, Kristin Powell's family, and the Chinese Embassy. See you tomorrow."

Severin hung up. Then he and Zhang watched as Holloman continued to hold the phone to his ear for several moments, looking perplexed. Finally, he set the phone down on a coffee table and sat back down on the couch.

"He sat back down!" Zhang said in disbelief. "Damn. He isn't the killer, is he?"

"I can still see the word 'mute' on the TV screen."

"Huh?"

"The sound on the TV is still off. Keep watching."

A few seconds later, Holloman sprang to his feet and disappeared down his hallway. And barely five minutes after that, his front door opened and he emerged wearing a heavy overcoat and toting a roller board suitcase. When he got to the sidewalk, he gave the western direction of his street a long stare. Then the eastern direction. There were no pedestrians. He gave each car a thorough look. Severin wasn't worried, knowing Holloman would never be able to see them through their tinted windshield and in the deep shadow of the chestnut tree at this distance. Then Holloman took off down the sidewalk at a fast pace, disappearing around the corner as he turned south on 30th Street.

"What should we do?" Zhang asked.

"I'm going to follow him on foot. You stay with the car. I'll call you. Then you keep me on speaker phone and follow in the car, but always out of sight. I'll tell you when it's safe to turn each corner."

Severin hopped out of the car and took off after Holloman, dialing Zhang as he did so. He kept a discreet distance, using parked vehicles and trees for cover, following Holloman down the block. Holloman looked over his shoulder about every five seconds.

"He's turning east onto N Street," Severin said.

"M?"

"N, as in Nincompoop. You can turn onto 30th now."

"That's a big 10-4, good buddy."

"Stay close. We need to be ready in case this numb nut hops a cab."

Severin followed Holloman east on N Street, south on 29th, east on Olive, and south on 28th, realizing as he did so that Holloman was, like someone in a spy movie, probably taking a zig-zagging route in an attempt to either pick up on or ditch any tails—probably also the reason he didn't just hail a cab close to home. Continuing his odd route through Georgetown, he made his way across Rock Creek and onto Pennsylvania Avenue, finally turning south once more, this time onto 24th.

"He might be making for the Foggy Bottom metro station. If he is, I'll probably lose my cell signal when I follow him in. If you lose me, just park close by and wait."

"Copy that."

As Severin predicted, Holloman crossed the street and disappeared down the tunnel entrance to the Foggy Bottom Metro station. Severin waited on a group of five young men wearing backpacks—probably students at nearby George Washington University—and then followed them onto the escalator, using the gathered cluster of them for concealment. Emerging onto the platform, he caught sight of Holloman standing at the far end, looking back toward the entrance. He looked tense. Afraid. His jaw was clenched. He was taking furtive looks at each of the people around him. Severin ducked behind a raised advertising structure, waited, and watched. A Blue Line train came roaring into the station, the breeze from its wake blasting Severin as it passed. Severin made ready to jump aboard. But Holloman didn't get on. He was waiting for either an Orange or Silver Line train in the direction of Vienna or Reston, Virginia. When an Orange Line train finally arrived seven minutes later, Holloman boarded the last car. Severin hopped aboard four cars away and took a seat right by the door. The doors slid shut, and the train zipped away, into the deep tunnel under the Potomac River and into Virginia. They headed west, stopping at numerous stations in Arlington. As soon as the tracks emerged from underground, Severin called Zhang and told him to race out to Dulles Airport and then more-or-less patrol the western half of the main terminal ticketing area, walking back and forth, watching for Holloman. When Severin got there, if he lost site of Holloman, then he'd do the same in the eastern half.

At each metro station stop, Severin stuck his head out of the open doors to watch for Holloman getting off the train. It wasn't until they reached the West Falls Church station that he finally got off. Exiting the station, he hopped in a cab. Severin followed suit. "You see that green cab that's pulling out?" he asked his obese driver. "Well, I've always wanted to say this. Follow that car." Holloman's cab made its way onto Virginia State Route 267—the Dulles Access Road—and sped west, with Severin's cab in pursuit.

Just over 20 minutes later, Severin watched as Holloman's cab pulled to the curb at the main terminal of Dulles Airport. As he followed Holloman into the ticketing area, he phoned Zhang, learning he was still five minutes away. Holloman went straight to a ticketing agent via an airline's preferred frequent-flier queue and began a conversation that lasted several minutes. Severin lurked close by, doing his best to stay concealed behind other people who stood in line. Holloman finally handed over a credit card and passport. The ticketing agent then printed out and stuck a baggage tag to the handle of Holloman's suitcase as Holloman put away his passport, credit card, and wallet. And in the brief moment that the suitcase sat exposed, waiting to be put on the luggage conveyor belt, Severin took the opportunity to make a quick, close pass—briefly tempted to give Holloman a wedgie as he walked behind him—and spied the three-letter code for the final destination airport printed on the luggage tag: KSA.

As Severin walked away, he punched the code into the search engine on his smart-phone. KSA was the code for Kosrea International Airport, in the Federated States of Micronesia.

"Don't park. Just pick me up on the departures curb," he told Zhang on the phone a minute later.

"Shouldn't we try to stop him?"

"To do what with? You going to make a citizen's arrest, Gomer Pyle?"

"We aren't getting on the flight with him? We aren't even calling the cops?"

"Would they arrest him based on his response to our faux blackmail scheme, or would they arrest us instead? No, we have everything we need. Thorvaldsson will be satisfied."

"So it's Miller Time."

"You drink Miller?"

"No."

*****

As Severin sat down in the car next to Zhang, he took a deep breath as though he'd just crossed the finish line of a footrace. "Well," he said. "Our adventure wasn't entirely unoriginal now, was it?"

"It had its original moments. Speaking of which, what are you going to call your memoir about all of this?"

"How about *Sorghum Wars*?"

"Too much like *Star Wars*."

"*Raiders of the Lost Sorghum*?"

"Better."

"But if I go to all the trouble of writing a manuscript, will it sell?" Severin asked.

"Definitely. The story really captures the zeitgeist."

"What's a zeitgeist? An abominable snow beast from a Nazi children's story?"

"The defining spirit of our times, sir. Think about it. Xenophobia. Sinophobia. Globalizationophobia. Biggovernmentconspiracyophobia."

"That's a lot of phobias."

"Phobias sell. The Big Six publishing houses will be all over it. It'll be a best seller."

"I'm sure."

THIRTY-EIGHT

"The tag on his suitcase bore the code for Kosrae International Airport, in Micronesia—a nation of small and very remote tropical islands just north of the Equator in the Western Pacific," Severin said as he sat in a massive leather chair back in the great room of Orin Thorvaldsson's house on Lopez Island, sipping another double Pappy Van Winkle bourbon. There was no roaring fire this time. The fireplace was dark and cold, as was the room.

"Micronesia?"

"No extradition treaty."

"Ah."

Thorvaldsson sat scanning a single sheet of paper Severin had handed to him. A summary page for his report.

"Given that he ran for it after I bluffed him, and considering all of the other evidence, I believe we can safely conclude that Holloman killed your niece in Shandong Province, China. I'm sure you'll want to recover her remains. There are contact numbers at the bottom of the page for the appropriate officials at both the U.S. State Department and the Embassy of China in D.C."

Quite suddenly, Thorvaldsson seemed to shrink before Severin's eyes. He didn't look like the confident, powerful, and possibly ruthless international trade magnate he had seemed at their last meeting. Now he looked mortal. Almost weak. And sad. "Thank you," he muttered.

Severin was tempted to ask him whether he'd indeed been using his beloved niece as a pawn to find out what his competition was up to, or to ensure their downfall via the application of high tariffs at the hands of the Commerce Department. But it would have served no useful purpose. And Severin figured he already knew the heartbreaking answer.

*****

Scant minutes after Severin left Thorvaldsson's estate on Lopez Island, Thorvaldsson retreated to a corner of his basement where he had an enclosed, two-position shooting range set up in a long, narrow room of cinderblock walls. There, he put on ear and eye protection, then opened a locker and took out four preloaded weapons. A Sig Sauer .45 pistol, a Remington 870 shotgun loaded with buckshot, a Belgian FN FAL battle rifle, and an H&K MP5 submachine gun—Kristin's old favorite. He spent the next few minutes firing each at a paper human silhouette target downrange until the target was nothing more than a wide ring of paper surrounded by confetti.

After putting the guns away, Thorvaldsson crossed to the opposite corner of his basement where the foundation abutted solid bedrock. There, he punched the keys of a 10-digit electronic cypher lock and opened a heavy metal door to a 6-by-10 strong room. To a casual observer, it would have appeared to contain nothing more than a table, desk lamp, chair, and antiquated laptop computer. But it also contained a concealed coupling wire connecting the laptop to the base of a large antenna embedded in concrete in the corner of the room—an antenna that protruded up through the floors of the house to an array disguised as a tin chimney on the roof.

Thorvaldsson stepped in, switched on the desk lamp, and secured the door behind him before sitting down and powering up the computer. Situated, he reflected with some amazement on the fact that that alcoholic washout, Lars Severin, had come through for him, despite having started with little more than the pitiful State Department report and the Seattle address for the importer Sun Ocean Trading. Thorvaldsson had expected him to do little more than serve as bait that might bring more information to the surface.

Hiring Severin had been a bit of a desperate move, given the risk that the man would blunder, get caught by Xiu's people, and be compelled to reveal that he was working for Thorvaldsson. But then again, it would have made little difference in the big picture. By now Xiu was well aware of the fact that Thorvaldsson and the rest of the trade cartel were out to get him, furious that he'd betrayed the cartel by disregarding their handshake import price-setting agreement and was now undercutting them with the help of that weasel attorney, Holloman. And if Severin had gotten himself arrested by the Chinese authorities, he wouldn't have known enough to cause Thorvaldsson any trouble where it really mattered.

With regard to that, Thorvaldsson was also somewhat surprised that, at least as far as he knew, nobody along the way had connected enough dots to suspect that he was a facilitator of espionage. For in truth, in addition to being an international trade magnate, he assisted in the placement and oversight of intelligence agents in the Far East for the Defense Clandestine Service arm of the U.S. Defense Intelligence Agency. And though it hardly mattered now, it brought Thorvaldsson a modicum of technical satisfaction and sense of absolution to know that nobody had exposed his niece or Bill Keen as the DIA spies that they were. Nobody had pierced their long-term cover as clean-handed Department of Commerce investigators whose work took them to China several times each year for the ostensible purpose of conducting antidumping investigations. What happened to them had nothing to do with the primary reason Thorvaldsson arranged to have them sent to Qingdao. And they probably hadn't suffered.

The one thing Thorvaldsson still couldn't wrap his head around was the fact that, despite all Kristin's achievements, experience, and training, she had been, at heart, a fragile and emotionally needy little girl. One who's self-esteem was so low that she could be lured into marriage by the self-serving attentions and strokes of a creep like Wesley Powell. Thorvaldsson knew that her childhood, under the roof of two hyper-overachieving type-A parents, hadn't been all hugs and pats on the back. But had it been utterly devoid of unconditional love? Had it really been so difficult for her to overcome? Was the hole it left in her heart really that big? And how could she—a worldly, accomplished, and intelligent young woman—have believed a man like Wesley could fill it? He would never understand.

Taking a deep breath, Thorvaldsson leaned forward and typed out a brief, three-paragraph report, paraphrasing a portion of Severin's own report, confirming that his niece and her colleague had not been arrested or liquidated by the Chinese Ministry of State Security. That their cover as Department of Commerce investigators, and their mission to obtain high-resolution side view photographs of the Chinese Type 096 ballistic missile submarine, were never blown. That is, there was no exposure—no apparent risk of fallout from an intelligence operations perspective.

Additionally, Thorvaldsson thought without adding it to his report, no one—on either the Chinese or U.S. side of things—figured out that Kristin had also been positioned to gather information on how the double-crossing Mr. Xiu had been getting away with fraud that harmed the competitive positions of one of Thorvaldsson's own subsidiary import firms. Indeed, the second secret component of Kristin's mission was never known to anyone other than her and Thorvaldsson. Instead, Kristin and Bill had been murdered by an American attorney whose fraud they'd discovered in the course of their overt cover work as Commerce investigators. A soulless D.C. lawyer who must have taken them by surprise, shooting them from behind before they could react.

When Thorvaldsson finished, his eyes wet with tears, he clicked a button that automatically encrypted the message and sent it off in a flash radio transmission to the Jim Creek Naval Radio Station, 30 miles to the southeast.

From there, the message would be instantaneously relayed by an extremely powerful VLF antenna, clear across the continent to a cubicle manned by a beached U.S. Navy commander in the Western Pacific Naval Operations section of Defense Intelligence Agency Headquarters in Washington, D.C. A week later, the classified file containing the records of the operation—with all of its names, stories, and lessons—would be closed, never to be opened again.

THIRTY-NINE

Having cashed his check from Thorvaldsson, the first thing Severin spent money on was a visit to a cardiologist, who—after testing his heart eight ways from Sunday and assuring Severin that it was just fine—referred him to a good psychiatrist at Swedish Hospital. To Severin's mild irritation, the head-shrinker confirmed know-it-all Wallace Zhang's diagnosis of panic attacks and prescribed an antidepressant that was supposed to also be very effective in treating anxiety. Two months of medication later, Severin's panic attacks and heart palpitations had all but stopped. He figured, begrudgingly, that he probably owed Zhang a beer or two for pushing him to get help.

Feeling much better about life in general, he dusted off his resume and applied for internal investigations positions with Boeing and Microsoft. They were full-time positions with good benefits. In the meantime, he was working as a line cook at the Spaghetti Factory in Downtown Seattle—and, to his mild surprise, enjoying it. He even tried to restart things with Janet—the woman who'd dumped him just before he took the Thorvaldsson job. They went on a handful of dates over the course of a month, with Severin half pleading to her that he deserved another chance. That he'd had an epiphany or two about himself in the preceding weeks. That he was cutting back on his drinking. That he was changing his ways. But then one day he got stone drunk while watching a Seahawks game and forgot that he'd promised to drive her to the airport to catch a redeye flight to Atlanta. After that, she cut the cord for good.

*****

It wasn't until nearly a year later that Severin, who had moved into a nicer apartment with a view of Seattle's Elliot Bay, learned of the final chapter of his unconventional vigilante investigation. Logging on to his email service always required that he pass through a tremendously annoying web page of clickbait quote-unquote news headlines that rarely involved more than the basest of gossip or sensational nonsense. Which reality TV star was pregnant with which washed-up country music star's baby. Which teenagers murdered their parents for the inheritance, and so that they could play Nintendo without someone nagging them about doing their homework. Which NFL superstar, high on cocaine, was arrested for driving his SUV 115 miles an hour down Hollywood Boulevard. But that day, as Severin sat in his kitchen chair with a steaming cup of decaf, about to click the mailbox icon that would take him away from the crap "news" page, one headline grabbed his attention. It said: "You Won't Believe What These D.C. Lawyers Got in the Mail."

Something told Severin he should click on the link, so he did. An article opened. It described how each of the five partners in the international trade practice group of the prestigious law firm of McElroy, Steen & Duff had received, via express mail originating in Micronesia, a small box containing a human finger. According to the FBI, the prints of the fingers matched those of a set that had previously been submitted to law enforcement when another of the firm's attorneys—one Benjamin Holloman, Esquire—had applied for a nonresident concealed carry handgun permit in Fairfax County, Virginia the previous year. According to his coworkers, Holloman had mysteriously disappeared without a trace 11 months earlier. A preliminary analysis of the tissue revealed that all but one of the fingers had been severed while Holloman was still alive—indicating that he may have been tortured. Indeed, given their varying levels of decay, it seemed the fingers had been severed over the course of several days. Stranger still, each box also held two small passport-sized photographs—one each of two U.S. Department of Commerce investigators who were murdered while on assignment in China last year, and whose remains had only recently been repatriated. An investigation into Holloman's disappearance had as yet yielded no viable leads.

Severin sat back in his kitchen chair and looked out his window, down onto Elliot Bay, where two bulk carrier cargo ships sat at anchor waiting their turn to dock at the massive Pier 86 grain terminal. There could be a number of people who wanted to see Holloman dead. Perhaps Xiu and his international trade fraudster goons, worried that Holloman might betray them to the U.S. government to save his own skin (Severin already knew that Xiu had a habit of at least threatening to sever people's fingers). Or maybe a current or former law practice colleague whom Holloman had stabbed in the back along the way in order to elevate his own career trajectory.

But there was only one person out there who knew Holloman had flown to Micronesia. Only one who would have bothered to send photographs of the Commerce investigators. Probably only one who would have been vengeful enough to ensure that the last days of Holloman's life were abounding with horror and terrible pain.

Severin closed the article and sat back in his chair, thinking that what goes around comes around. Then he went to the kitchen, put two ice cubes in a tumbler, and poured himself a giant bourbon.

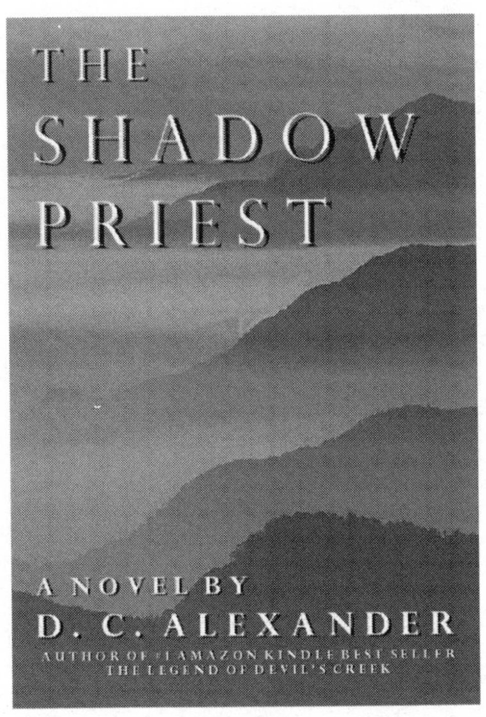
THE
SHADOW
PRIEST
A NOVEL BY
D. C. ALEXANDER
AUTHOR OF #1 AMAZON KINDLE BEST SELLER
THE LEGEND OF DEVIL'S CREEK

NOTE TO READERS

If you enjoyed this book, **PLEASE** tell your family, friends, and acquaintances about it. It is *not* the product of a massive New York corporate publishing house, with advertising and distribution departments publicizing and supporting its release. It is a product of independent publishing and is supported by a marketing budget of exactly jack squat. If the author has any hope of quitting his day job and writing full-time, he is going to need your assistance in promoting his book via word of mouth. In fact, the author would be utterly grateful for your help. Thank you.

ABOUT THE AUTHOR

D.C. Alexander is a former federal agent. He was born and raised in the Seattle area, and now lives in Louisville, Kentucky. He is also a former judge for the International Thriller Writers annual Best Thriller competition. He welcomes and appreciates your feedback. You can email him directly at:

authordcalexander@gmail.com

39903510R00157

Made in the USA
Middletown, DE
28 January 2017